FLASHMAN
AND THE MOUNTAIN
OF LIGHT

by the same author

FLASHMAN AND THE MOUNTAIN OF LIGHT

From The Flashman Papers 1845-46
Edited and Arranged by

GEORGE MacDONALD FRASER

Alfred A. Knopf   New York   1991

THIS IS A BORZOI BOOK
PUBLISHED BY ALFRED A. KNOPF, INC.

Copyright © 1990 by George MacDonald Fraser

Published in the United States by Alfred A. Knopf, Inc., New York. Distributed by
Random House, Inc., New York.
Originally published in Great Britain by Collins Harvill, London, in 1990.
Maps by Ken Lewis

Library of Congress Cataloging-in-Publication Data

Fraser, George MacDonald.
Flashman and the mountain of light: from the Flashman papers,
1945–46 / edited and arranged by George MacDonald Fraser.
p. cm.
ISBN 0–679–40071–0
I. Title.
PR6056.R287F65 1991
823'.914—dc20   90–45453
CIP

Manufactured in the United States of America
First American Edition

For Kath, as always,
and with salaams to
Shadman Khan and Sardul Singh,
wherever they are.

Explanatory Note

The life and conduct of Sir Harry Flashman, VC, were so irregular and eccentric that it is not surprising that he was also erratic in compiling his memoirs, that picturesque catalogue of misadventure, scandal, and military history which came to light, wrapped in oilskin packets, in a Midlands saleroom more than twenty years ago, and has since been published in a series of volumes, this being the ninth. Beginning, characteristically, with his expulsion from Rugby in 1839 for drunkenness (and thus identifying himself, to the astonishment of literary historians, with the cowardly bully of *Tom Brown's Schooldays*), the old Victorian hero continued his chronicle at random, moving back and forth in time as the humour took him, until the end of his eighth packet found him, again the worse for drink, being shanghaied from a Singapore billiard-room after the China War of 1860. Along the way he had ranged from the First Afghan War of 1842 to the Sioux campaign of 1876 (with a brief excursion, as yet unpublished, to a brawl in Baker Street as far ahead as 1894, when he was in his seventy-second year); it goes without saying that many gaps in his story remain to be filled, but with the publication of the present volume, which reverts to his early manhood, the first half of his life is almost complete; only an intriguing gap in the early 1850s remains, and a few odd months here and there.

Thus far, it is not an improving tale, and this latest chapter is consistent in its depiction of an immoral and unscrupulous rascal whose only commendable quality (terms like "virtue" and "saving grace" are not to be applied to one who gloried in having neither) was his gift of accurate observation; it was this, and the new and often unexpected light which it enabled him to cast on great events and famous figures of his time, that excited the interest of historians, and led to comparison of his memoirs with the Boswell Papers. Be that as it may, it was a talent fully if nervously employed in the almost forgotten imperial campaign described in this volume – "the shortest, bloodiest . . . and strangest, I think, of my whole life." Indeed it was strange, not least in its origins, and Flashman's account is a remarkable case-history of how a war can come about, and the freaks and perfidies and intrigues of its making and waging. It is also the story of a fabulous jewel, and of an extraordinary quartet – an Indian queen, a slave-girl, and two mercenary adventurers – who would be dismissed as too outlandish for fiction (although Kipling seems to have made use of one of them) if their careers were not easily verifiable from contemporary sources.

This, as with previous packets of Flashman's papers entrusted to me by their owner, Mr Paget Morrison, has been my chief concern – to satisfy myself that Flashman's narrative tallies with historic fact, so far as it can be tested. Beyond that I have only corrected occasional lapses in spelling, and supplied the usual footnotes, appendices and glossary.

G.M.F.

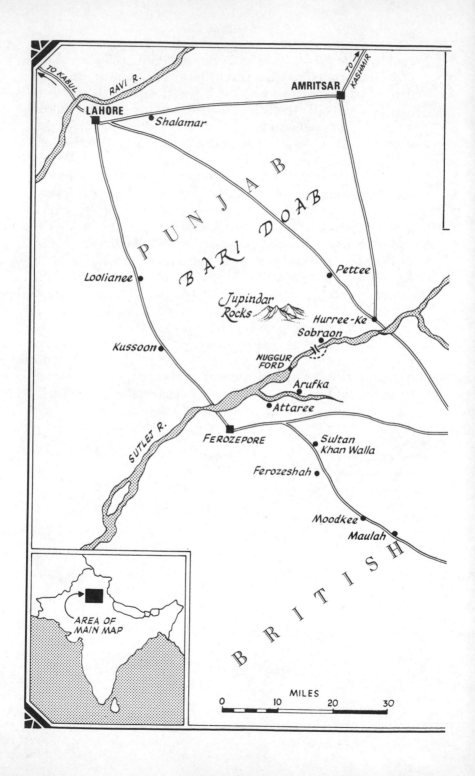

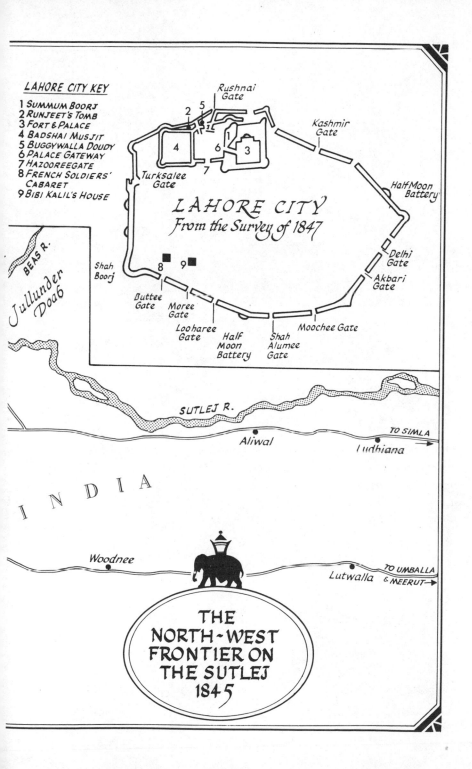

LAHORE CITY KEY

1 SUMMUM BOORJ
2 RUNJEET'S TOMB
3 FORT & PALACE
4 BADSHAI MUSJIT
5 BUGGYWALLA DOUDY
6 PALACE GATEWAY
7 HAZOOREEGATE
8 FRENCH SOLDIERS'
  CABARET
9 BIBI KALIL'S HOUSE

Rushnai Gate

Kashmir Gate

Half Moon Battery

Delhi Gate

Akbari Gate

Turksalee Gate

LAHORE CITY
From the Survey of 1847

Shah Boorj

Buttee Gate

Moree Gate

Looharee Gate

Half Moon Battery

Shah Alumee Gate

Moochee Gate

BEAS R.

Jullunder Doab

SUTLEJ R.

TO SIMLA

Aliwal

Ludhiana

I N D I A

Woodnee

Lutwalla

TO UMBALLA & MEERUT

THE
NORTH-WEST
FRONTIER ON
THE SUTLEJ
1845

"*Now*, my dear Sir Harry, I must tell you," says her majesty, with that stubborn little duck of her head that always made Palmerston think she was going to butt him in the guts, "I am *quite* determined to learn *Hindoostanee*."

This at the age of sixty-seven, mark you. I almost asked her what the devil for, at her time of life, but fortunately my idiot wife got in first, clapping her hands and exclaiming that it was a most splendid idea, since nothing so Improved the Mind and Broadened the Outlook as acquaintance with a Foreign Tongue, is that not so, my love? (Elspeth, I may tell you, speaks only English – well, Scotch, if you like – and enough nursery French to get her through Customs and bullyrag waiters, but anything the Queen said, however wild, always sent her into transports of approval.) I seconded loyally, of course, saying it was a capital notion, ma'am, bound to come in handy, but I must have looked doubtful, for our sovereign lady refilled my teacup pretty offhand, leaving out the brandy, and said severely that Dr *Johnson* had learned *Dutch* at the age of *seventy*.

"And I have an excellent *ear*," says she. "Why, I still recollect precisely those Indian words you spoke, at my dearest one's request, so many long years ago." She sighed, and sipped, and then to my dismay trotted them out. "*Hamare ghali ana, achha din*. Lord Wellington said it was a Hindoo greeting, I recall."

Well, it's what the Bengali whores used to cry to attract customers, so she wasn't far wrong. They'd been the only words I could think of, God help me, on that memorable day in '42 when the Old Duke had taken me to the Palace after my Afghan heroics; I'd stood trembling and half-witted

11

before royalty, and when Albert asked me to say something in Hindi, out they popped. Luckily, Wellington had had the wit not to translate. The Queen had been a pretty slip of a girl then, smiling timidly up as she pinned on the medal I didn't deserve; now she was a stout little old body, faded and grey, fussing over the teacups at Windsor and punishing the meringues. Her smile was still there, though; aye, cavalry whiskers, even white ones, still fetched little Vicky.

"It is such a *cheerful* language," says she. "I am sure it must have many *jokes*, does it not, Sir Harry?"

I could think of a few, but thought it best to give her the old harmless one that begins: "*Doh admi joh nashe men the, rail ghari men safar kar raha ta –*"

"But what does it *mean*, Sir Harry?"

"Well, ma'am, it means that two fellows were travelling by train, you see, and they were, I regret to say, intoxicated –"

"Why, Harry!" cries Elspeth, acting shocked, but the Queen just took another tot of whisky in her tea and bade me continue. So I told her that one chap said, where are we, and t'other chap replied, Wednesday, and the first chap said, Heavens, this is where I get out. Needless to say, it convulsed them – and while they recovered and passed the gingerbread, I asked myself for the twentieth time why we were here, just Elspeth and me and the Great White Mother, taking tea together.

You see, while I was used enough, in those later years, to being bidden to Balmoral each autumn to squire her about on drives, and fetch her shawl, and endure her prattle and those damned pipers of an evening, a summons to Windsor in the spring was something new, and when it included "dear Lady Flashman, our fair Rowena" – the Queen and she both pretended a passion for Scott – I couldn't think what was up. Elspeth, when she'd recovered from her ecstasy at being "commanded to court," as she put it, was sure I was to be offered a peerage in the Jubilee Honours (there's no limit to the woman's mad optimism); I damped her by observing that the Queen didn't keep coronets in the closet to hand out to visitors; it was done official, and any-

12

way even Salisbury wasn't so far gone as to ennoble *me*; I wasn't worth bribing. Elspeth said I was a horrid cynic, and if the Queen *herself* required our attendance it must be something grand, and whatever was she going to wear?

Well, the grandeur turned out to be Buffalo Bill's Wild West Show[1] – I concluded that I'd been dragged in because I'd been out yonder myself, and was considered an authority on all that was wild and woolly – and we sat in vile discomfort at Earl's Court among a great gang of Court toadies, while Cody pranced on a white horse, waving his hat and sporting a suit of patent buckskins that would have laid 'em helpless with laughter along the Yellowstone. There was enough paint and feathers to outfit the whole Sioux Nation, the braves whooped and ki-yikked and brandished their hatchets, the roughriders curvetted, a stagecoach of terrified virgins was ambushed, the great man arrived in the nick of time blazing away until you couldn't see for smoke, and the Queen said it was most curious and *interesting*, and what did the strange designs of the war paint *signify*, my dear Sir Harry?

God knows what I told her; the fact is, while everyone else was cheering the spectacle, I was reflecting that only eleven years earlier I'd been running like hell from the real thing at Little Bighorn, and losing my top hair into the bargain – a point which I mentioned to Cody later, after he'd been presented. He cried, yes, by thunder, that was one war-party he'd missed, and didn't he envy me the trip, though? Lying old humbug. That's by the way; I realised, when the Queen bore Elspeth and me back to Windsor, and bade us to tea *à trois* next day, that our presence at the show had been incidental, and the real reason for our invitation was something else altogether. A trifling matter, as it turned out, but it inspired this memoir, so there you are.

She wanted our opinion, she said, on a matter of the *first* importance – and if you think it odd that she should confide in the likes of us, the retired imperial roughneck of heroic record but dubious repute, and the Glasgow merchant's daughter . . . well, you don't know our late lamented Queen Empress. Oh, she was a stickler and a tartar, no error, the

13

highest, mightiest monarch that ever was, and didn't she know it, just – but if you were a friend, well, that was a different palaver. Elspeth and I were well out of Court, and barely half-way into Society, even, but we'd known her since long ago, you see – well, she'd always fancied me (what woman didn't?), and Elspeth, aside from being such an artless, happy beauty that even her own sex couldn't help liking her, had the priceless gift of being able to make the Queen laugh. They'd taken to each other as young women, and now, on the rare occasions they met *tête-à-tête*, they blethered like the grandmothers they were – why, on that very day (when I was safely out of earshot) she told Elspeth that there were some who wanted her to mark her Golden Jubilee by abdicating in favour of her ghastly son, Bertie the Bounder, "but I shall do *no such thing*, my dear! I intend to outlive him, if I can, for the man is not *fit* to reign, as none knows better than your own dear husband, who had the *thankless* task of instructing him." True, I'd pimped for him occasional, but 'twas wasted effort; he'd have been just as great a cad and whoremaster without my tuition.

However, it was about the Jubilee she wanted our advice, "and yours especially, Sir Harry, for you *alone* have the necessary knowledge." I couldn't figure that; for one thing, she'd been getting advice and to spare for months on how best to celebrate her fiftieth year on the throne. The whole Empire was in a Jubilee frenzy, with loyal addresses and fêtes and junketings and school holidays and water-trough inaugurations and every sort of extravagance on the rates; the shops were packed with Jubilee mugs and plates and trumpery blazoned with Union Jacks and pictures of her majesty looking damned glum; there were Jubilee songs on the halls, and Jubilee marches for parades, and even Jubilee musical bustles that played "God Save the Queen" when the wearer sat down – I tried to get Elspeth to buy one, but she said it was disrespectful, and besides people might think it was *her*.

The Queen, of course, had her nose into everything, to make sure the celebrations were dignified and *useful* – only she could approve the illuminations for Cape Town, the

14

chocolate boxes for Eskimo children, the plans for Jubilee parks and gardens and halls and bird-baths from Dublin to Dunedin, the special Jubilee robes (it's God's truth) for Buddhist monks in Burma, and the extra helpings of duff for lepers in Singapore: if the world didn't remember 1887, and the imperial grandmother from whom all blessings flowed, it wouldn't be her fault. And after years in purdah, she had taken to gallivanting on the grand scale, to Jubilee dinners and assemblies and soirées and dedications – dammit, she'd even visited Liverpool. But what had tickled her most, it seemed, was being photographed in full fig as Empress of India; it had given her quite an Indian fever, and she was determined that the Jubilee should have a fine flavour of curry – hence the resolve to learn Hindi. "But what *else*, Sir Harry, would best mark our *signal* regard for our Indian subjects, do you think?"

Baksheesh, booze, and bints was the answer to that, but I chewed on a muffin, looking grave, and said, why not engage some Indian attendants, ma'am, that'd go down well. It would also infuriate the lordly placemen and toad-eaters who surrounded her, if I knew anything. After some thought, she nodded and said that was a *wise* and *fitting* suggestion – in the event, it was anything but, for the Hindi-wallah she fixed on as her special pet turned out to be not the high-caste gent he pretended, but the son of a pugglc-wal-loper in Agra jail; if that wasn't enough, he spread her secret Indian papers all over the bazaars, and drove the Viceroy out of his half-wits. Aye, old Flashy's got the touch.[2]

At the time, though, she was all for it – and then she got down to cases in earnest. "For *now*, Sir Harry, I have *two* questions for you. *Most* important questions, so please to attend." She adjusted her spectacles and rummaged in a flat case at her elbow, breathing heavy and finally unearthing a yellowish scrap of paper.

"There, I have it. Colonel Mackeson's letter . . ." She peered at it with gooseberry eyes. ". . . dated the ninth of February, 1852 . . . now where is . . . ah, yes! The Colonel writes, in part: 'On this head, it will be best to consult those officers in the Company service *who have seen it*, and especi-

15

ally Lieutenant *Flashman* ...' " She shot me a look, no doubt to make sure I recognised the name " '. . . who is said to have been the *first* to see it, and can doubtless say *precisely* how it was then worn.' " She laid the letter down, nodding. "You see, I keep all letters most carefully *arranged*. One cannot tell when they may be *essential*."

I made nothing of this. Where the deuce had I been in '52, and what on earth was "it" on whose wearing I was apparently an authority? The Queen smiled at my mystification. "It may be somewhat changed," says she, "but I am sure you will remember it."

She took a small leather box from the case, set it down among the tea things, and with the air of a conjurer producing a rabbit, raised the lid. Elspeth gave a little gasp, I looked – and my heart gave a lurch.

It ain't to be described, you must see it close to . . . that glittering pyramid of light, broad as a crown piece, alive with an icy fire that seems to shine from its very heart. It's a matchless, evil thing, and shouldn't be a diamond at all, but a ruby, red as the blood of the thousands who've died for it. But it wasn't that, or its terrible beauty, that had shaken me . . . it was the memory, all unexpected. Aye, I'd seen it before.

"The Mountain of Light," says the Queen complacently. "That is what the nabobs called it, did they not, Sir Harry?"

"Indeed, ma'am," says I, a mite hoarse. "Koh-i-Noor."

"A little smaller than you remember it, I fancy. It was recut under the directions of my dear Albert and the Duke of Wellington," she explained to Elspeth, "but it is still the *largest*, most *precious* gem in all the world. Taken in our wars against the Sikh people, you know, more than forty years ago. But was Colonel Mackeson correct, Sir Harry? Did you see it then in its *native* setting, and could you describe it?"

By God, I could . . . but not to you, old girl, and certainly not to the wife of my bosom, twittering breathlessly as the Queen lifted the gleaming stone to the light in her stumpy fingers. "Native setting" was right: I could see it now as I saw it first, blazing in its bed of tawny naked flesh – in the

16

delectable navel of that gorgeous trollop Maharani Jeendan, its dazzling rays shaming the thousands of lesser gems that sleeved her from thigh to ankle and from wrist to shoulder . . . that had been her entire costume, as she staggered drunkenly among the cushions, laughing wildly at the amorous pawings of her dancing-boys, draining her gold cup and flinging it aside, giggling as she undulated voluptuously towards me, slapping her bare hips to the tom-toms, while I, heroically foxed but full of good intentions, tried to crawl to her across a floor that seemed to be littered with Kashmiri houris and their partners in jollity . . . "Come and take it, my Englishman! Ai-ee, if old Runjeet could see it now, eh? Would he leap from his funeral pyre, think you?" Dropping to her knees, belly quivering, the great diamond flashing blindingly. "Will you not take it? Shall Lal have it, then? Or Jawaheer? Take it, *gora sahib*, my English *bahadur!*" The loose red mouth and drugged, kohl-stained eyes mocking me through a swirling haze of booze and perfume . . .

"Why, Harry, you look quite upset! Whatever is the matter?" It was Elspeth, all concern, and the Queen clucked sympathetically and said I was *distrée*, and she was to blame, "for I am sure, my dear, that the sudden sight of the stone has recalled to him those dreadful battles with the Sikhs, and the loss of, oh, so many of our *gallant fellows*. Am I not right?" She patted my hand kindly, and I wiped my fevered brow and confessed it had given me a start, and stirred painful recollections . . . old comrades, you know, stern encounters, trying times, bad business all round. But yes, I remembered the diamond; among the Crown Jewels at the Court of Lahore, it had been . . .

"Much prized, and worn with *pride* and *reverence*, I am sure."

"Oh, absolutely, ma'am! Passed about, too, from time to time."

The Queen looked shocked. "Not from *hand* to *hand*?"

From navel to navel, in fact, the game being to pass it round, male to female, without using your hands, and anyone caught waxing his belly-button was disqualified and reported to Tattersalls . . . I hastened to assure her that only

17

the royal family and their, ah, closest intimates had ever touched it, and she said she was *glad* to hear it.

"You shall write me an *exact* description of how it was set and displayed," says she. "Of course, I have worn it myself in *various* settings, for while it is said to be unlucky, I am not superstitious, and besides, they say it brings ill fortune only to *men*. And while it was presented by Lord Dalhousie to me *personally*, I regard it as belonging to *all* the women of the Empire." Aye, thinks I absently, your majesty wears it on Monday and the scrubwoman has it on Tuesday.

"That brings me to my *second* question, and you, Sir Harry, knowing India so well, must *advise* me. Would it be proper, do you think, to have it set in the *State* Crown, for the great Jubilee service in the Abbey? Would it please our Indian subjects? Might it give the *least* offence to anyone – the princes, for example? Consider that, if you please, and give me your opinion presently." She regarded me as though I were the Delphic oracle, and I had to clear my mind of memories to pay heed to what she was saying.

So that, after all the preamble, was her question of "first importance" – of all the nonsense! As though one nigger in a million would recognise the stone, or knew it existed, even. And those who did would be fat crawling rajas ready to fawn and applaud if she proposed painting the Taj Mahal red white and blue with her damned diamond on top. Still, she was showing more delicacy of feeling than I'd have given her credit for; well, I could set her mind at rest . . . if I wanted to. On reflection, I wasn't sure about that. It was true, as she'd said, that Koh-i-Noor had been bad medicine only for men, from Aladdin to Shah Jehan, Nadir, old Runjeet, and that poor pimp Jawaheer – I could hear his death-screams yet, and shudder. But it hadn't done Jeendan much good, either, and she was as female as they come . . . "Take it, Englishman" – gad, talk about your Jubilee parties . . . No, I wouldn't want it to be unlucky for our Vicky.

Don't misunderstand; I ain't superstitious either. But I've learned to be leery of the savage gods, and I'll admit that the sight of that infernal gewgaw winking among the teacups had taken me flat aback . . . forty years and more . . . I could hear the tramp of the Khalsa again, rank on bearded rank pouring out through the Moochee Gate: "*Wah Guru-ji*! To Delhi! To London!" . . . the thunder of guns and the hiss of rockets as the Dragoons came slashing through the smoke . . . old Paddy Gough in his white "fighting coat", twisting his moustaches – "Oi nivver wuz bate, an' Oi nivver will be bate!" . . . a lean Pathan face under a tartan turban – "You know what they call this beauty? The Man Who Would Be King!" . . . an Arabian Nights princess flaunting herself before her army like a nautch-dancer, mocking them . . . and defying them, half-naked and raging, sword in hand . . . coals glowing hideously beneath a gridiron . . . lovers hand in hand in an enchanted garden under a Punjab moon . . . a great river choked with bodies from bank to bank . . . a little boy in cloth of gold, the great diamond held aloft, blood running through his tiny fingers . . . "Koh-i-Noor! Koh-i-Noor! . . ."

The Queen and Elspeth were deep in talk over a great book of photographs of crowns and diadems and circlets, "for I know my *weakness* about jewellery, you see, and how it can lead me astray, but your taste, dear Rowena, is quite *faultless* . . . Now, if it were set so, among the fleurs-de-lys . . ."

I could see I wasn't going to get a word in edgeways for hours, so I slid out for a smoke. And to remember.

I'd vowed never to go near India again after the Afghan fiasco of '42, and might easily have kept my word but for Elspeth's loose conduct. In those salad days, you see, she had to be forever flirting with anything in britches – not that I blame her, for she was a rare beauty, and I was often away, or ploughing with other heifers. But she shook her bouncers once too often, and at the wrong man: that foul nigger pirate Solomon who kidnapped her the year I took five for 12 against All-England, and a hell of a chase I had to win her back.* I'll set it down some day, provided the recounting don't scare me into the grave; it's a ghastly tale, about Brooke and the head-hunting Borneo rovers, and how I only saved my skin (and Elspeth's) by stallioning the mad black queen of Madagascar into a stupor. Quaint, isn't it? The end of it was that we were rescued by the Anglo-French expedition that bombarded Tamitave in '45, and we were all set for old England again, but the officious snirp who governed Mauritius takes one look at me and cries: "'Pon my soul, it's Flashy, the Bayard of Afghanistan! How fortunate, just when it's all hands to the pumps in the Punjab! You're the very man; off you go and settle the Sikhs, and we'll look after your missus." Or words to that effect.

I said I'd swim in blood first. I hadn't retired on half pay just to be pitched into another war. But he was one of your wrath-of-God tyrants who won't be gainsaid, and quoted Queen's Regulations, and bullied me about Duty and Honour – and I was young then, and fagged out with tupping Ranavalona, and easily cowed. (I still am, beneath the blus-

*See *Flashman's Lady*.

20

ter, as you may know from my memoirs, as fine a catalogue of honours won through knavery, cowardice, taking cover, and squealing for mercy as you'll ever strike.) If I'd known what lay ahead I'd have seen him damned first – those words'll be on my tombstone, so help me – but I didn't, and it would have shot my hard-earned Afghan laurels all to pieces if I'd shirked, so I bowed to his instruction to proceed to India with all speed and report to the C-in-C, rot him. I consoled myself that there might be advantages to stopping abroad a while longer: I'd no news from home, you see, and it was possible that Mrs Leo Lade's noble protector and that greasy bookie Tighe might still have their bruisers on the look-out for me – it's damnable, the pickle a little harmless wenching and welching can land you in.[3]

So I bade Elspeth an exhausting farewell, and she clung to me on the dockside at Port Louis, bedewing my linen and casting sidelong glances at the moustachioed Frogs who were waiting to carry her home on their warship – hollo, thinks I, we'll be calling the first one Marcel at this rate, and was about to speak to her sternly when she lifted those glorious blue eyes and gulped: "I was never so happy as in the forest, just you and me. Come safe back, my bonny jo, or my heart will break." And I felt such a pang, as she kissed me, and wanted to keep her by me forever, and to hell with India – and I watched her ship out of sight, long after the golden-haired figure waving from the rail had grown too small to see. God knows what she got up to with the Frogs, mind you.

I had hopes of a nice leisurely passage, to Calcutta for choice, so that whatever mischief there was with the Sikhs might be settled long before I got near the frontier, but the Cape mail-sloop arrived next day, and I was bowled up to Bombay in no time. And there, by the most hellish ill-luck, before I'd got the ghee-smell in my nostrils or even thought about finding a woman, I ran slap into old General Sale, whom I hadn't seen since Afghanistan, and who was the last man I wanted to meet just then.

In case you don't know my journal of the Afghan disaster,* I must tell you that I was one of that inglorious army which came out in '42 a dam' sight faster than it went in – what was left of it. I was one of the few survivors, and by glorious misunderstanding was hailed as the hero of the hour: it was mistakenly believed that I'd fought the bloodiest last-ditch action since Hastings – when in fact I'd been blubbering under a blanket – and when I came to in dock at Jallalabad, who should be at my bedside, misty with admiration, but the garrison commander, Fighting Bob Sale. He it was who had first trumpeted my supposed heroism to the world – so you may picture his emotion when here I was tooling up three years later, apparently thirsting for another slap at the paynim.

"This is the finest thing!" cries he, beaming. "Why, we'd thought you lost to us – restin' on your laurels, what? I should ha' known better! Sit down, sit down, my dear boy! *Kya-hai, matey*! Couldn't keep away, you young dog! Wait till George Broadfoot sees you – oh, aye, he's on the leash up yonder, and all the old crowd! Why, 'twill be like old times – except you'll find Gough's no Elphy Bey,[4] what?" He clapped me on the shoulder, fit to burst at the prospect of bloodshed, and added in a whisper they could have heard in Benares: "Kabul be damned – there'll be no retreat from Lahore! Your health, Flashman."

It was sickening, but I looked keen, and managed a groan of dismay when he admitted that the war hadn't started yet, and might not at all if Hardinge, the new Governor-General, had his way. Right, thinks I, count me as one of the Hardinge Ring, but of course I begged Bob to tell me how the land lay, feigning great eagerness – in planning a campaign, you see, you must know where the safe billets are likely to be. So he did, and in setting it down I shall add much information which I came by later, so that you may see exactly how things were in the summer of '45, and understand all that followed.

A word first, though. You'll have heard it said that the British Empire was acquired in a fit of absence of mind – one

*See *Flashman*.

of those smart Oscarish squibs that sounds well but is thoroughly fat-headed. *Presence* of mind, if you like – and countless other things, such as greed and Christianity, decency and villainy, policy and lunacy, deep design and blind chance, pride and trade, blunder and curiosity, passion, ignorance, chivalry and expediency, honest pursuit of right, and determination to keep the bloody Frogs out. And often as not, such things came tumbling together, and when the dust had settled, there we were, and who else was going to set things straight and feed the folk and guard the gate and dig the drains – oh, aye, and take the profit, by all means.

That's what study and eye-witness have taught me, leastways, and perhaps I can prove it by describing what happened to me in '45, in the bloodiest, shortest war ever fought in India, and the strangest, I think, of my whole life. You'll find it contains all the Imperial ingredients I've listed – stay, though, for "Frogs" read "Muslims", and if you like, "Russians" – and a few others you may not believe. When I'm done, you may not be much clearer on how the map of the world came to be one-fifth pink, but at least you should realise that it ain't something to be summed up in an epigram. Absence of mind, my arse. We *always* knew what we were doing; we just didn't always know how it would pan out.

First of all, you must do as Sale bade me, and look at the map. In '45 John Company held Bengal and the Carnatic and the east coast, more or less, and was lord of the land up to the Sutlej, the frontier beyond which lay the Five Rivers country of the Sikhs, the Punjab.[5] But things weren't settled then as they are now; we were still shoring up our borders, and that north-west frontier was the weak point, as it still is. That way invasion had always come, from Afghanistan, the vanguard of a Mohammedan tide, countless millions strong, stretching back as far as the Mediterranean. And Russia. We'd tried to sit down in Afghanistan, as you know, and got a bloody nose, and while that had been avenged since, we weren't venturing that way again. So it remained a perpetual threat to India and ourselves – and all that lay between was the Punjab, and the Sikhs.

23

You know something of them: tall, splendid fellows with uncut hair and beards, proud and exclusive as Jews, and well disliked, as clannish, easily-recognised folk often are – the Muslims loathed them, the Hindoos distrusted them, and even today T. Atkins, while admiring them as stout fighters, would rather be brigaded with anyone else – excepting their cavalry, which you'd be glad of anywhere. For my money they were the most advanced people in India – well, they were only a sixth of the Punjab's population, but they ruled the place, so there you are.

We'd made a treaty with these strong, clever, treacherous, civilised savages, respecting their independence north of the Sutlej while we ruled south of it. It was good business for both parties: they remained free and friends with John Company, and we had a tough, stable buffer between us and the wild tribes beyond the Khyber – let the Sikhs guard the passes, while we went about our business in India without the expense and trouble of having to deal with the Afghans ourselves. That's worth bearing in mind when you hear talk of our "aggressive forward policy" in India: it simply wasn't common sense for us to take over the Punjab – not while it was strong and united.

Which it was, until '39, when the Sikh maharaja, old Runjeet Singh, died of drink and debauchery (they say he couldn't tell male from female at the end, but they're like that, you know). He'd been a great man, and a holy terror, who'd held the Punjab solid as a rock, but when he went, the struggle for power over the next six years made the Borgia intrigues look like a vicarage soirée. His only legitimate son, Kuruk, an opium-guzzling degenerate, was quickly poisoned by *his* son, who lasted long enough to attend Papa's funeral, where a building collapsed on him, to no one's surprise. Second wicket down was Shere Singh, Runjeet's bastard and a lecher of such enthusiasm that I've heard they had to pry him off a wench to seat him on the throne. He had a fine long reign of two years, surviving mutiny, civil war, and a plot by Chaund Cour, Kuruk's widow, before they finally did for him (and his entire harem, the wasteful swine). Chaund Cour later expired in her bath, under a great stone dropped by her own slave-girls, whose hands and tongues were then removed, to prevent idle gossip, and when various other friends and relations had been taken off sudden-like, and the whole Punjab was close to anarchy, the way was suddenly clear for a most unlikely maharaja, the infant Dalip Singh, who was still on the throne, and in good health, in the summer of '45.

It was claimed he was the child of old Runjeet and a dancing-girl named Jeendan whom he'd married shortly before his death. There were those who doubted the paternity, though, since this Jeendan was notorious for entertaining the lads of the village four at a time, and old Runjeet had been pretty far gone when he married her; on the other hand, it was pointed out that she was a practised professional whose charms would have roused a stone idol, so old Runjeet might have done the deed before rolling over and going to God.

So now she was Queen Mother and joint regent with her drunken brother Jawaheer Singh, whose great party trick was to dress as a female and dance with the nautch-girls – by all accounts it was one continuous orgy at the Court of Lahore, with Jeendan galloping every man in sight, her lords and ladies all piling in, no one sober for days on end, treasure being spent like the wave of the sea, and the whole polity sliding downhill to luxurious ruin. I must say, it sounded quite jolly to me, bar the normal murders and tortures, and the furious plotting which apparently occupied everyone's sober moments.

And looming like a genie over all this delightful corruption was the Khalsa – the Sikh army. Runjeet had built it, hiring first-class European mercenaries who had turned it into a truly formidable machine, drilled, disciplined, modern, 80,000 strong – the finest army in India, barring the Company's (we hoped). While Runjeet lived, all had been well, but since his death the Khalsa had realised its power, and wasn't prepared to be cat's paw to the succession of rascals, degenerates, and drunkards who'd tumbled on and off the throne; it had defied its officers, and governed itself by soldiers' committees, called *panches*, joining in the civil

25

strife and bloodshed when it suited, slaughtering, looting, and raping in disciplined fashion, and supporting whichever maharaja took its fancy. One thing was constant about the Khalsa: it hated the British, and was forever demanding to be led against us south of the Sutlej.

Jeendan and Jawaheer controlled it as their predecessors had done, with huge bribes of pay and privileges, but with lakhs being squandered on their depravities, even the fabulous wealth of the Punjab was beginning to run dry – and what then? For years we'd been watching our northern buffer dissolve in a welter of blood and decay, in which we were treaty-bound not to intervene; now the crisis was come. How long could Jawaheer and Jeendan keep the Khalsa in hand? Could they prevent it (did they even want to?) taking a slap at us with the loot of all India as the prize? If the Khalsa did invade, would our own native troops stand true, and if they didn't . . . well, no one, except a few canny folk like Broadfoot, cared to think about *that*, or contemplate the kind of thing that half-happened twelve years later, in the Mutiny.

So that's how things stood in August '45,[6] but my alarms, as usual, were entirely personal. Meeting Sale had scuppered my hopes of lying low for a spell: he would see to it that I had a place on Gough's staff, says he, beaming paternally while I frisked in feigned enthusiasm with my bowels dissolving, for I knew that being old Paddy's galloper would be a one-way trip to perdition if the bugles blew in earnest. He was Commander-in-Chief, was Gough, an ancient Irish squireen who'd fought in more battles than any man living and was forever looking for more; loved by the troops (as such lunatics always are), and much sympathised with just then, when he was sweating to secure the frontier against the coming storm, and calling down Celtic curses on the head of that sensible chap Hardinge in Calcutta, who was forever cautioning him not to provoke the Sikhs, and countermanding his troop movements.[7]

But I had no way out; Sale was off now post-haste to resume his duties as Quartermaster-General on the frontier, with poor Flashy in tow, wondering how I could catch

26

measles or break a leg. Mind you, as we rode north I was much reassured by the assembly of men and material along the Grand Trunk Road: from Meerut up it was aswarm with British regiments, Native Infantry, dragoons, lancers, Company cavalry, and guns by the park – the Khalsa'll never tackle this crowd, thinks I; they'd be mad. Which of course they were. But I didn't know the Sikhs then, or the incredible shifts and intrigues that can make an army march to suicide.

Gough wasn't at headquarters in Umballa, which we reached early in September; he'd gone up to Simla for a breather, and since Sale's wife was living there we pushed straight on, to my delight. I'd heard of it as a great place for high jinks and good living, and, I foolishly supposed, safety.

It was a glorious spot then,[8] before Kipling's vulgarians and yahoos had arrived, a little jewel of a hill station ringed in by snow-clad peaks and pine forests, with air that you could almost drink, and lovely green valleys like the Scotch border country – one of 'em was absolutely called Annandale, where you could picnic and *fête* to heart's content. Emily Eden had made it *the* resort in the '30s, and already there were fine houses on the hillsides, and stone bungalows with log fires where you could draw the curtains and think you were back in England; they were building the church's foundations then, on the ridges above the Bazaar, and laying out the cricket ground; even the fruits and flowers were like home – we had strawberries and cream, I remember, that first afternoon at Lady Sale's house.

Dear dreadful Florentia. If you've read my Afghan story, you know her, a raw-boned old heroine who'd ridden with the army all through that nightmare retreat over the passes from Kabul, when a force of 14,000 was whittled almost to nothing by the Dourani snipers and Khyber knives. She hadn't shut up the whole way, damning the administration and bullying her bearers: Colin Mackenzie said it was a near thing which was more fearsome – a Ghazi leaping from the rocks yelling murder, or Lady Sale's red nose emerging from a tent demanding to know why the water was not *thoroughly* boiling. She hadn't changed, bar the rheumatics from which she could get relief only by cocking a foot up on the table – damned unnerving it was, to have her boot beside your cup, and a great lean shank in red flannel among the muffins.[9]

"Flashman keeps staring at my ankle, Sale!" cries she. "They are all alike, these young men. Don't make owl eyes at me, sir – I remember your pursuit of Mrs Parker at Kabul! You thought I had not noticed? Ha! I and the whole cantonment! I shall watch you in Simla, let me tell you." This between a harangue about Hardinge's incompetence and a blistering rebuke to her *khansamah** for leaving the salt out of the coffee. You'll gather I was a favourite of hers, and after tea she had me reviving Afghan memories by rendering "Drink, puppy, drink" in my sturdy baritone while she thumped the ivories, my performance being marred by a sudden falsetto when I remembered that I'd last sung that jolly ditty in Queen Ranavalona's boudoir, with her black majesty beating time in a most unconventional way.

That reminded me that Simla was famous for its diversions, and since the Sales were giving dinner that night to Gough and some cabbage-eating princeling who was making the Indian tour, I was able to cry off, Florentia dropping a hint that I should be home before the milk. I tooled down the hill to the dirt road that has since become the famous Mall, taking the air among the fashionable strollers, admiring the sunset, the giant rhododendrons, and Simla's two prime attractions – hundreds of playful monkeys and scores of playful women. Unattached, the women were, their menfolk being hard at it down-country, and the pickings were choice: civilian misses, saucy infantry wives, cavalry mares, and bouncing grass widows. I ran my eye over 'em, and fastened on a fortyish Juno with a merry eye and full nether lip who gave me a thoughtful smile before turning in to the hotel, where by the strangest chance I presently encountered her in a secluded corner of the tea verandah. We conversed politely, about the weather and the latest French novels (she found *The Wandering Jew* affecting, as I recall, while I stood

*Butler.

28

up for the *Musketeers*),[10] and she ate a dainty water-ice and started to claw at my thigh under the table.

I like a woman who knows her mind; the question was, where? and I couldn't think of anywhere cosier than the room I'd been allotted at the back of Sale's mansion – Indian servants have eyes in their buttocks, of course, but the walls were solid, not chick, and with dusk coming down we could slide in by the french windows unseen. Her good name had plainly died in the late '20s, for she said it was a capital lark, and presently we were slipping through the bushes of Sale's garden, keeping clear of the dinner guests' *jampan** bearers, who were squatting by the front verandah. We paused for a lustful grapple among the deodars before mounting the steps to the side verandah – and dammit, there was a light in my room, and the sound of a bearer hawking and shuffling within. I stood nonplussed while my charmer (a Mrs Madison, I think) munched on my ear and tore at my buttons, and at that moment some interesting Oriental came round the corner of the house, expectorating hugely, and without thinking I whisked her through the door next to mine, closing it softly.

It proved to be the billiard-room – dark, empty and smelling of clergymen, and since my little flirt now had my pants round my ankles and was trying to plumb my depths, I decided it would have to do. The diners would be beating their plates for hours yet, and Gough hadn't the look of a pool-shark, somehow, but caution and delicacy forbade our galloping on the open floor, and since there were little curtains between the legs of the table . . .

There ain't as much deck clearance under a billiard table as you might suppose, but after a cramped and feverish partial disrobing we settled down to play fifty up. And Mrs Madison proved to be a most expert tease, tittering mischievously and spinning things out, so that we must have been everywhere from beneath the baulk to the top cushion and back before I had her trapped by the middle pockets and was able to give of my best. And after she had subsided with

*A kind of sedan chair.

tremulous whimpers, and I had got my breath back, it seemed quite cosy, don't you know, and we whispered and played in the stuffy dark, myself drowsy and she giggling at what a frolic it was, and I was beginning to consider a return fixture when Sale decided he'd like a game of billiards.

I thought I was sent for. The door crashed open, light shone through the curtains, bearers came scurrying in to remove the cover and light the table candles, heavy footsteps sounded, men's voices laughing and talking, and old Bob crying: "This way, Sir Hugh . . . your highness. Now, what shall it be? A round game or sides, hey?"

Their legs were vague shadows beyond the curtains as I bundled Mrs Madison to the centre – and the abandoned trot was positively shaking with laughter! I hissed soundlessly in her ear, and we lay half-clad and quivering, she with mirth and I with fright, while the talk and laughter and clatter of cues sounded horrid close overhead. Of all the damned fixes! But there was nothing for it but to lie doggo, praying we didn't sneeze or have the conniptions.

I've had similar experiences since – under a sofa on which Lord Cardigan was paying court to his second wife, beneath a dago president's four-poster (that's how I won the San Serafino Order of Purity and Truth), and one shocking time in Russia when discovery meant certain death. But the odd thing is, quaking as you are, you find yourself eavesdropping for dear life; I lay with one ear between Mrs Madison's paps, and the other taking it all in – and it's worth recounting, for it was frontier gossip from our head men, and will help you understand what followed.

In no time I knew who was in the room: Gough, and Sale, and a pimpish affected lisp which could belong only to the German princeling, the pulpit growl of old Gravedigger Havelock (who'd ha' thought that he'd frequent poolrooms?), and the high, arrogant Scotch burr that announced the presence of my old Afghan chum George Broadfoot, now exalted as Agent for the North-west Frontier.[11] He was in full complaint, as usual:

". . . and Calcutta rebukes me for taking a high hand with the Maharani and her drunken durbar! I must not provoke them, says Hardinge. Provoke, indeed – while they run raids on us, and ignore my letters, and seduce our sepoys! Half the brothel bints in Ludhiana are Sikh agents, offering our *jawans** double pay to desert to the Khalsa."

"Double for infantry, six-fold for *sowars*,"† says Sale. "Temptin', what?[12] Spot or plain, prince?"

"Spot, if you please. But do many of your native soldiers desert, then?"

"Och, a few." This was Gough, in his pig-sty brogue. "Mind you, if ever the Khalsa invaded, God knows how many might jump on what they thought was the winnin' nag. Or refuse to fight agin' fellow-Injuns."

The pills clicked, and the prince says: "But the British will always be the winning side. Why, all India holds your army invincible." There was a long pause, then Broadfoot says:

"Not since Afghanistan. We went in like lions and came out like sheep – and India took note. Who knows what might follow a Sikh invasion? Mutiny? It's possible. A general revolt –"

"Oh, come!" cries the prince. "A Sikh invasion would be promptly repelled, surely! Is that not so, Sir Hugh?"

More pill-clicking, and then Gough says: "Put it this way, sorr. If John Sepoy turned tail – which I don't believe, mind – I'd be left wi' our British regiments alone agin' one hunnert t'ousand of the best fightin' fellows in India – European trained, mark'ee, wi' modern arms . . . How many do I get for a cannon, will ye tell me? Two? Mother o' God, is it worth it? Well, here goes." Click. "Damnation, me eyes is failin'. As I was sayin', your highness – I wouldn't have to make too many mistakes, now, would I?"

"But if there is such danger – why do you not march into the Punjab now, and nip it in the bud?"

Another long silence, then Broadfoot: "Breach of treaty if we did – and conquest isn't popular in England, since Sind.[13] No doubt it'll come to that in the end – and Hardinge knows it, for all he says British India's big enough already.

*Native infantrymen.
†Cavalry troopers.

31

But the Sikhs must strike first, you see, and Sir Hugh's right – that's our moment of peril, when they're south of the Sutlej in force, and our own sepoys may join 'em. If *we* struck first, treaty or not, and tackled the Khalsa *in* the Punjab, our stock would rise with the sepoys, they wouldn't waver, and we'd win hands down. We'd have to stay, in a territory London don't want – but India would be safe from Muslim invasion forever. A nice, circular problem, is it not?"

The Prince says thoughtfully: "Sir Henry Hardinge has a dilemma, it seems."

"That's why he waits," says Sale, "in the faint hope that the present Lahore government will restore stability."

"Meanwhile reproving me and hindering Sir Hugh, in case we 'provoke' Lahore," says Broadfoot. " 'Armed observation' – that's to be our ticket."

Mrs Madison gave a gentle snore, and I whipped my hand over her mouth, pinching her nostrils.

"What's that?" says a voice overhead. "Did you hear it?"

There was silence, while I trembled on the verge of heart failure, and then Sale says:

"Those dam' *geckoes*.* Your shot, Sir Hugh."

If that wasn't enough, Mrs Madison, now awake, put her lips to my ear: "When will they leave off? I am *ever* so cold." I made silent frantic motions, and she thrust her tongue in my ear, so that I missed the next exchange. But I'd heard enough to be sure of one thing – however pacific Hardinge's intentions, war was an odds-on certainty. I don't mean that Broadfoot was ready to start it himself, but he'd jump at the chance if the Sikhs gave him one – and so no doubt would most of our Army folk; it's a soldier's business, after all. And by the sound of it the Khalsa were ready to oblige – and when they did, I'd be in the middle, galloper to a general who led not only from the front but from the middle of the enemy's blasted army, given the chance. But the prince was talking again, and I strained my ears, trying

*House lizards.

32

to ignore Mrs Madison, who was burrowing underneath me, for warmth, presumably.

"But may Sir Henry not be right? Surely there is some Sikh noble capable of restoring order and tranquillity – this Maharani, for example . . . Chunda? Jinda?"

"Jeendan," says Broadfoot. "She's a hoor." They had to translate for the prince, who perked up at once.

"Indeed? One hears astonishing stories. They say she is of incomparable beauty, and . . . ah . . . insatiable appetite . . .?"

"Ye've heard of Messalina?" says Broadfoot. "Well, this lady has been known to discard six lovers in a single night."

Mrs Madison whispered: "I don't believe it," and neither did the prince, evidently, for he cries:

"Oh, scandalous rumours always multiply facts! Six in one night, indeed! How can you be sure of that?"

"Eye-witnesses," says Broadfoot curtly, and you could almost hear the prince blinking as his imagination went to work.

Someone else's was also taking flight: Mrs Madison, possibly inspired by all this disgraceful gossip, was becoming attentive again, the reckless bitch, and try as I would to still her, she teased so insistently that I was sure they must hear, and Havelock's coffin face would pop under the curtain at any moment. So what could I do, except hold my breath and comply as quietly as possible – it's an eerie business, I can tell you, in dead silence and palpitating with fear of discovery, and yet it's quite soothing, in a way. I lost all track of their talk, and by the time we were done, and I was near choking with my shirt stuffed into my mouth, they were putting up their cues and retiring, thank God. And then:

"A moment, Broadfoot." It was Gough, his voice down. "D'ye think his highness might talk, at all?"

There could only be the two of them in the room. "As the geese muck," says Broadfoot. "Everywhere. It'll be news to nobody, though. Half the folk in this damned country are spies, and the other half are their agents, on commission. I know how many ears I've got, and Lahore has twice as many, ye can be sure."

33

"Like enough," says Gough. "Ah, well – 'twill all be over by Christmas, devil a doubt. Now, then – what's this Sale tells me about young Flashman?"

How they didn't hear the sudden convulsion beneath the table, God knows, for I damned near put my head through the slates.

"I must have him, sir. I've lost Leech, and Cust will have to take his place. There isn't another political in sight – and I worked with Flashman in Afghanistan. He's young, but he did well among the Gilzais, he speaks Urdu, Pushtu, and Punjabi –"

"Hold yer horses." says Gough. "Sale's promised him the staff, an' the boy deserves it, none more. Forbye, he's a fightin' soldier, not a clerk. If he's to win his way, he'll do it as he did at Jallalabad, among hot shot an' cold steel –"

"With respect, Sir Hugh!" snaps Broadfoot, and I could imagine the red beard bristling. "A political is not a clerk. Gathering and sifting intelligence –"

"Don't tell me, Major Broadfoot! I was fightin', *an'* gatherin' intelligence, while your *grand*father hadn't got the twinkle in his eye yet. It's a war we're talkin' about – an' a war needs warriors, so now!" God help the poor old soul, he was talking about me.

"I am thinking of the good of the service, sir –"

"An' I'm not, damn yer Scotch impiddence? Och, what the hell, ye're makin' me all hot for nothin'. Now, see here, George, I'm a fair man, I hope, an' this is what I'll do. Flashman is on the staff – an' you'll not say a word to him, *mallum*?* But . . . the whole army knows ye've lost Leech, an' there's need for another political. If Flashman takes it into his head to *apply* for that vacancy – an' havin' *been* a political he may be mad enough for anythin' – then I'll not stand in his way. But under no compulsion, mind that. Is that fair, now?"

"No, sir," says George. "What young officer would exchange the staff for the political service?"

"Any number – loafers, an' Hyde Park hoosars – no dis-

*Understand?

34

respect to your own people, or to young Flashman. He'll do his duty as he sees it. Well, George, that's me last word to you. Now, let's pay our respects to Lady Sale . . ."

If I'd had the energy, I'd have given Mrs Madison another run, out of pure thanksgiving.

"I suppose ye know nothing at all," says Broadfoot, "about the law of inheritance and widows' rights?"

"Not a dam' thing, George," says I cheerily. "Mind you, I can quote you the guv'nor on poaching and trespass – and I know a husband can't get his hands on his wife's gelt if her father won't let him." Elspeth's parent, the loathly Morrison, had taught me that much. Rotten with rhino he was, too, the little reptile.

"Haud yer tongue," says Broadfoot. "There's for your education, then." And he pushed a couple of mouldering tomes across the table; on top was a pamphlet: *Inheritance Act, 1833.* That was my reintroduction to the political service.

You see, what I'd heard under Sale's pool-table had been the strains of salvation, and I'll tell you why. As a rule, I'd run a mile from political work – skulking about in nigger clobber, living on millet and sheep guts, lousy as the tinker's dog, scared stiff you'll start whistling "Waltzing Matilda" in a mosque, and finishing with your head on a pole, like Burnes and McNaghten. I'd been through all that – but now there was going to be a pukka *war*, you see, and in my ignorance I supposed that the politicals would retire to their offices while the staff gallopers ran errands in the cannon's mouth. Afghanistan had been one of those godless exceptions where no one's safe, but the Sikh campaign, I imagined, would be on sound lines. More fool me.[14]

So, having thanked the Fates that had guided me to roger Mrs Madison under the green baize, and taken soundings to satisfy myself that Leech and Cust had been peaceably employed, I'd lost no time in running into Broadfoot,

36

accidental-like. Great hail-fellowings on both sides, although I was quite shocked at the change in him: the hearty Scotch giant, all red beard and thick spectacles, was quite fallen away – liver curling at the edges, he explained, which was why he'd moved his office to Simla, where the quacks could get a clear run at him. He'd taken a tumble riding, too, and went with a stick, gasping when he stirred.

I commiserated, and told him my own troubles, damning the luck that had landed me on Gough's staff ("poodle-faking, George, depend upon it, and finding the old goat's hat at parties"), and harking back to the brave days when he and I had dodged Afridis on the Gandamack Road, having endless fun. (Jesus, the things I've said.) He was a downy bird, George, and I could see him marvelling at this coincidence, but he probably concluded that Gough had dropped me a hint after all, for he offered me an Assistant's berth on the spot.

So now we were in the chummery of Crags, his bungalow on Mount Jacko, with me looking glum at the law books and reflecting that this was the price of safety, and Broadfoot telling me testily that I had better absorb their contents, and sharp about it. That was another change: he was a sight sterner than he'd been, and it wasn't just his illness. He'd been a wild, agin-the-government fellow in Afghanistan, but authority had put him on his dignity, and he rode a pretty high horse as Agent – once, for a lark, I called him "major", and he didn't even blink; ah, well, thinks I, there's none so prim as a Scotsman up in the world. In fairness, he didn't blink at "George", either, and was easy enough with me, in between the snaps and barks.

"Next item," says he. "Did many folk see ye in Umballa?"

"Shouldn't think so. What's it matter? I don't owe money –"

"The fewer natives who know that Iflassman the soldier is on hand, the better," says he. "Ye haven't worn uniform since ye landed? Good. Tomorrow, ye'll shave off your moustache and whiskers – do it yourself, no *nappy-wallah** –

*Barber.

37

and I'll cut your hair myself into something decently civilian
– give ye a touch of pomade, perhaps –"

The sun had got him, not a doubt. "Hold on, George! I'll
need a dam' good reason –"

"I'm telling ye, and that's reason enough!" snarls he;
liver in rough order, I could see. Then he managed a sour
grin. "This isn't the kind of political *bandobast** ye're used
to; ye'll not be playing Badoo the Badmash this time."
Well, that was something. "No, you're a proper wee civilian
henceforth, in a tussore suit, high collar and tall hat, riding
in a *jampan* with a *chota-wallah*† to carry your green bag. As
befits a man of the law, well versed in widows' titles." He
studied me sardonically for a long moment, doubtless enjoying my bewilderment. "I think ye'd better have a look at
your brief," says he, and rose stiffly, cursing his leg.

He led me into the little hall, through a small door, and
down a short flight of steps into a cellar where one of his
Pathan Sappers (he'd had a gang of them in Afghanistan,
fearsome villains who'd cut your throat or mend your watch
with equal skill) was squatting under a lamp, glowering at
three huge jars, all of five feet high, which took up most of
the tiny cell. Two of them were secured with silk cords and
great red seals.

Broadfoot leaned on the wall to ease his leg, and signed to
the Pathan, who removed the lid from the unsealed jar,
holding the lamp to shine on its contents. I looked, and was
sufficiently impressed.

"What's up, George?" says I. "Don't you trust the
banks?"

The jar was packed to the brim with gold, a mass of coin
glinting under the light. Broadfoot gestured, and I picked up
a handful, cold and heavy, clinking as it trickled back into
the jar.

"I am the bank," says Broadfoot. "There's £140,000
here, in mohurs, ingots, and fashioned gold. Its disposal . . .
may well depend on you. *Tik hai*‡, Mahmud." He limped

*Organisation, business.
†Little fellow.
‡All right.

38

aloft again, while I followed in silence, wondering what the devil I was in for this time – not that it looked perilous, thank heaven. Broadfoot settled gratefully in his chair.

"That treasure," says he, " is the legacy of Raja Soochet Singh, a Punjabi prince who died two years ago, leading sixty followers against an army of twenty thousand." He wagged his red head. "Aye, they're game lads up yonder. Well, now, like most Punjabi nobles in these troubled times, he had put his wealth in the only safe place – in the care of the hated British. Infidels we may be, but we keep honest books, and they know it. There's a cool twenty million sterling of Punjab money south of the Sutlej this minute.

"For two years past the Court of Lahore – which means the regents, Jawaheer Singh and his slut of a sister – have been demanding the return of Soochet's legacy, on the ground that he was a forfeited rebel. Our line, more or less, has been that 'rebel' is an unsatisfactory term, since naebody kens who the Punjab government is from one day to the next, and that the money should go to Soochet's heirs – his widow, or his brother, Raja Goolab Singh. We've taken counsel's opinion," says he, straight-faced, "but the position is complicated by the fact that the widow was last heard of fleeing for her life from a beleaguered fort, while Goolab, who had designs on the Punjab throne at one time, has lately proclaimed himself King of Kashmir, and is sitting behind a rock up Jumoo way, with fifty thousand hillmen at his back. However, we have sure information that both he and the widow are of opinion that the money is fine where it is, for the time being."

He paused, and "Isn't it?" was on the tip of my tongue, for I didn't care for this above half; talk of besieged forts and hillmen unsettles me, and I had horrid visions of Flashy sneaking through the passes with a portmanteau, bearing statements of compound interest to these two eccentric legatees, both of whom were probably dam' dangerous to know.

"A further complication," says Broadfoot, "is that Jawaheer Singh is threatening to make this legacy a cause of war. As you know, peace is in the balance; those three jars down

39

there might tip the scale. Naturally, Sir Henry Hardinge wishes negotiations about the legacy to be reopened at Lahore – not with a view to settlement, of course, but to temporise." He looked at me over his spectacles. "We're not ready yet."

To settle – or to go to war? Having eavesdropped on Broadfoot's opinions, I could guess which. Just as I could see, with sudden horrible clarity, who the negotiator was going to be, in that Court of *bhang**-sodden savages where they murdered each other regular, after supper. But that apart, the thing made no sense at all.

"You want *me* to go to Lahore – but I ain't a lawyer, dammit! Why, I've only been in a court twice in my life!" Drunk and resisting arrest, and being apprehended on premises known to be a disorderly house, five quid each time, not that it mattered.

"They don't ken that," says Broadfoot.

"Don't they, though? George, I ain't puffing myself, but I'm not unknown over there! Man alive, when we had a garrison in Lahore, in '42, I was being trumpeted all over the shop! Why, you said yourself the fewer who knew Iflassman was back, the better! They know I'm a soldier, don't they – Bloody Lance, and all that rot?"

"So they may," says he blandly. "But who's to say ye haven't been eating your dinner in Middle Temple Hall these three years past? If Hardinge sends ye, accredited and under seal, they're not going to doubt ye. Ye can pick up the jargon, and as much law as ye'll need, from those." He indicated the books.

"But where's the point? A real lawyer can spin the thing out ten times better than I can! Calcutta's full of 'em –"

"But they can't speak Punjabi. They can't be my eyes and ears in Lahore Fort. They can't take the pulse in that viper's nest of intrigue. They're not politicals trained by Sekundar Burnes. And if the grip comes" – he tapped his desk triumphantly – "they can't turn themselves into a Khye-Keen or Barukzai *jezzailchi* and slip back over the Sutlej."

*Indian hemp.

So I was to be a spy – in that den of devilment! I sat appalled, stammering out the first objection that came to mind.

"And a fat chance I'll have of doing that, with my face shaved!" He waved it aside.

"Ye cannot go to Lahore with soldier written all over ye. Forbye, it'll never come to disguise, or anything desperate. You'll be a British diplomat, the Governor-General's envoy, and immune."

So was McNaghten, I wanted to holler, so was Burnes, so were Connolly and Stoddart and Uncle Tom Cobleigh, it's on their bloody tombstones. And then he unveiled the full horror of the thing.

"That immunity will enable you to remain in Lahore *after* the war has begun . . . supposing it does. And that is when your real work will begin."

And I'd exchanged a staff billet for this. The prospect was fit to make me puke – but I daren't say so, not to Broadfoot. Somehow I contained my emotion, assumed a ruptured frown, and said surely a diplomat would be expelled, or confined at least.

"Not for a moment." Oh, he had it all pat, blast him. "From the day you arrive in Lahore – and thereafter, whatever befalls – ye'll be the most courted man in the Punjab. It's this way: there's a war party, and a peace party, and the Khalsa, and the *panch* committees that control it, and a faction that wants us to *take* the Punjab, and a faction that wants us driven from India altogether, and some that hop from one side to t'other, and cabals and cliques that don't ken what they want because they're too drunk and debauched to think." He leaned forward, all eager red whiskers, his eyes huge behind the bottle lenses. "But they all want to be on the right side at the finish, and most have wit enough to see that that will be *our* side. Oh, they'll shift and swither and plot, and ye'll be approached (discreetly) with more hints and ploys and assurances of good will than ye can count. From enemies who'll be friends tomorrow – and vice versa. All of which ye'll transmit secretly to me." He sat back, well pleased with himself, while I kept a

41

straight face with my bowels in my boots. "That's the marrow of the business. Now, for your more particular information . . ."

He brought out a sheaf of those slim buff packets that I remembered from Burnes's office at Kabul. I knew what they held: maps, names, places, reports and summaries, laws and customs, biographies and artists' sketches, heights and distances, history, geography, even weights and measures – all that years of intelligence and espionage had gathered about the Punjab, to be digested and returned. "When ye've studied these, and the law books, we'll talk at more length," says he, and asked if I had any observations.

I could have made a few, but what was the use? I was sunk – through my own folly, as usual. If I hadn't thumped that randy baggage Madison, I'd never have overheard Gough and rushed rejoicing into this hellish political stew . . . it didn't bear thinking of. All I could do was show willing, for my precious credit's sake, so I asked him who the friends and enemies in Lahore were likely to be.

"If I knew that, ye wouldn't be going. Oh, I ken who our professed sympathisers and ill-willers are at the moment – but where they'll stand next week . . .? Take Goolab Singh, Soochet's fugitive heir – he's sworn that if the Khalsa marches, he'll stand by us . . . well, perhaps he will, in the hope that we'll confirm him in Kashmir. But if the Khalsa were to give us a wee set-back – where would Goolab and his hillmen be then, eh? Loyal . . . or thinking about the loot of Delhi?"

I could see where Flashy would be – stranded in Lahore among the raging heathen. I knew better than to ask him what other politicals and trusted agents would be on hand, so I went round about. "How shall I report to you – through the *vakil*?"*

"No such thing – he's a native, and not a sure one. He can take any letters ye may write about the Soochet legacy, but anything secret will be in cypher notes, which you'll leave in

*An agent, in this case Broadfoot's official representative in Lahore, through whom everyday business was openly transacted, and diplomatic messages exchanged.

Second Thessalonians on the bedside table in your quarters –"

"Second where?"

He looked at me as though I'd farted. "In your Bible, man!" You could see him wondering if my bedside reading wasn't more likely to be Tom and Jerry. "The cypher, and coding instructions, are in the packets. Your messages will be . . . collected, never fear."

So there *was* a trusted messenger at the Court – and the fact that I wasn't to be told *who* was another thought to chill my blood: what you don't know you can't tell if inquisitive folk approach you with hot irons . . . "What if I need to get word to you quickly? I mean, if the Khalsa march, all of a sudden –"

"I'll ken that before you do. What you must discover then is *why* they've marched. Who set them on, and for what purpose? If it's war . . . what's behind it, and how came it to begin? *That's* what I must know." He hunched forward again, intent. "Ye see, Flashy . . . to know precisely why your enemy is making war, what he hopes to gain and fears to lose . . . is to be half-way to winning. Mind that."

Looking back, I can say it made good sense, though I was in no state to appreciate it then. But I nodded dutifully, with that grim attentive mien which I've learned to wear while scheming frantically how to slide out from under.

"This Soochet legacy, then – it's all gammon?"

"By no means. It's your excuse for being in Lahore, to be sure – as their subtler folk will suspect – but it's still a genuine cause[15] which ye'll argue with their officials. Perhaps even in full durbar with the regents, if they're sober. In which case, keep your wits about you. Jawaheer's a frightened degenerate weakling, and Maharani Jeendan seems set on destroying herself by vicious indulgence . . ." He paused, fingering his beard, while I perked up a trifle, like Prince Whatsisname. He went on, frowning:

"I'm not sure about her, though. She had rare spirit and ability once, or she'd never have climbed from the stews to the throne. Aye, courage, too – d'ye know how she once quelled a mob of her mutinous soldiery, and them bent on slaughter?"

43

I said I'd no notion, and waited breathless.

"She *danced*. Aye, put on veils and castanets and danced them daft, and they went home like sheep." Broadfoot shook his head in admiration, no doubt wishing he'd been there. "Practising her trade – she danced in the Amritsar brothels as a child, before she caught Runjeet's fancy." He gave a grimace of distaste. "Aye, and what she learned there has obsessed her ever since, until her mind's unhinged with it, I think."

"Dancing?" says I, and he shot me a doubtful look – he was a proper Christian, you see, and knew nothing about me beyond my supposed heroics.

"Debauchery, with men." He gave a Presbyterian sniff, hesitating, no doubt, to sully my boyish mind. "She has an incurable lust – what the medicos call nymphomania. It's driven her to unspeakable excesses . . . not only with every man of rank in Lahore, but slaves and sweepers, too. Her present favourite is Lal Singh, a powerful general – although I hear she abandoned him briefly of late for a stable lad who robbed her of ten lakhs of jewels."

I was so shocked I couldn't think what to say, except easy come, easy go.

"I doubt if the stable lad thought so. He's in a cage over the Looharree Gate this minute, minus his nose, lips, ears . . . et cetera, they tell me. That," says Broadfoot, "is why I say I'm not sure about her. Debauched or not, the lady is still formidable."

And I'd been looking forward no end to meeting her, too; Flashy's ideal of womanhood, she'd sounded like – until this, the last grisly detail in the whole hideous business. That night, in my room at Crags, after I'd pored through Broadfoot's packets, flung the law-books in a corner, paced up and down racking my brains for a way out, and found none, I felt so low altogether that I decided to complete my misery by shaving my whiskers – that's how reduced I was. When I'd done, and stared at my naked chops in the glass, remembering how Elspeth had adored my face-furniture and sworn they were what had first won her girlish heart, I could have wept. "Beardie-beardie," she used to murmur fondly, and that sent me into a maudlin reverie about that first splendid tumble in the bushes by the Clyde, and equally glorious romps in the Madagascar forest . . . from which my mind naturally strayed to frenzied gallops with Queen Ranavalona, who hadn't cared for whiskers at all – leastways, she always used to try to wrench mine out by the roots in moments of ecstasy.

Well, some women don't like 'em. I reflected idly that the Maharani Jeendan, who evidently counted all time lost when she wasn't being bulled by Sikhs, must be partial to beards . . . then again, she might welcome a change. By George, that would ease the diplomatic burden; no place like bed for state secrets . . . useful patroness, too, in troubled times. Mind you, if she wore out six strong men in a night, Lahore bazaar had better be well stocked with stout and oysters . . .

Mere musing, as I say – but something similar may have been troubling the mind of Major Broadfoot, G., for while I was still admiring my commanding profile in the glass, in he tooled, looking middling uneasy, I thought. He apologised for intruding, and then sat down, prodding the rug with his stick and pondering. Finally:

"Flashy . . . how old are ye?" I told him, twenty-three.

He grunted. "Ye're married, though?" Wondering, I said I'd been wed five years, and he frowned and shook his head.

"Even so . . . dear me, you're young for this Lahore business!" Hope sprang at once, then he went on: "What I mean is, it's the deuce of a responsibility I'm putting on you. The price of fame, I suppose – Kabul, Mogala, Piper's Fort . . . man, it's a brave tale, and you just a bit laddie, as my grandam would have said. But this thing," says he seriously, ". . . perhaps an older head . . . a man of the world . . . aye, if there was anyone else . . ."

I know when not to snatch at a cue, I can tell you. I waited till I saw him about to continue, and then got in first, slow and thoughtful:

"George . . . I know I'm dead green, in some ways, and it's true enough, I'm more at home with a sabre than a cypher, what? I'd never forgive myself, if I . . . well, if I failed you of all people, old fellow. Through inexperience, I

45

mean. So . . . if you want to send an older hand . . . well
. . .'' Manly, you see, putting service before self, hiding my
disappointment. All it got me was a handclasp and a noble
gleam of his glasses.

"Flashy, ye're a trump. But the fact is, there's no one in
your parish for this work. Oh, it's not just the Punjabi, or
that you've shown a stout front and a cool head – aye, and
resource beyond your years. I think you'll succeed in this
because ye have a gift with . . . with folk, that makes them
take to you." He gave a little uneasy laugh, not meeting my
eye. "It's what troubles me, in a way. Men respect you;
women . . . admire you . . . and . . ."

He broke off, taking another prod at the carpet, and I'd
have laid gold to groceries his thoughts were what mine had
been before he came in. I've wondered since what he'd have
done if I'd said: "Very good, George, we both suspect that
this horny bitch will corrupt my youthful innocence, but if I
pleasure her groggy enough, why, I may turn her mind
inside out, which is what you're after. And how d'ye want
me to steer her then, George, supposing I can? What would
suit Calcutta?"

Being Broadfoot, he'd probably have knocked me down.
He was honest that far; if he'd been the hypocrite that most
folk are, he'd not have come up to see me at all. But he had
the conscience of his time, you see, Bible-reared and shun-
ning sin, and the thought that my success in Lahore might
depend on fornication set him a fine ethical problem. He
couldn't solve it – I doubt if Dr Arnold and Cardinal New-
man could, either. ("I say, your eminence, what price
Flashy's salvation if he breaks the seventh commandment
for his country's sake?" "That depends, doctor, on whether
the randy young pig enjoyed it.") Of course, if it had been
slaughter, not adultery, that was necessary, none of my
pious generation would even have blinked – soldier's duty,
you see.

I may tell you that, in Broadfoot's shoes, with so much at
stake, I'd have told my young emissary: "Roger's the answer," and wished him good hunting – but then, I'm a
scoundrel.

46

But I mustn't carp at old George, for his tortured conscience saved my skin, in the end. I'm sure it made him feel that, for some twisted reason, he owed me something. So he bent his duty, just a little, by giving me a lifeline, in case things went amiss. It wasn't much, but it might have imperilled another of his people, so as an amend I reckon it pretty high.

After he'd finished havering, and not saying what couldn't be said, he turned to go, still looking uneasy. Then he stopped, hesitated, and came out with it.

"See here," says he, "I should not be saying this, but if the grip *does* come – which I don't believe it will, mind – and ye find yourself in mortal danger, there's a thing you can do." He glowered at me, mauling his whiskers. "As a last resort only, *mallum*? Ye'll think it strange, but it's a word – a password, if ye like. Utter it anywhere within the bounds of Lahore Fort – dropped into conversation, or shouted from the housetops if need be – and the odds are there'll be those who'll pass it, and a friend will come to you. Ye follow? Well, the word is 'Wisconsin'."

He was as deadly serious as I'd ever seen him. " 'Wisconsin'," I repeated, and he nodded.

"Never breathe it unless ye have to. It's the name of a river in North America."

It might have been the name of a privy in Penzance for all the good it seemed likely to be. Well, I was wrong there.

I've set out on my country's service more times than I can count, always reluctantly, and often as not in a state of alarm; but at least I've usually known what I was meant to be doing, and why. The Punjab business was different. As I wended my sweltering, dust-driven way to Ferozepore on the frontier, the whole thing seemed more unlikely by the mile. I was going to a country in uproar, whose mutinous army might invade us at any moment. I was to present a legal case at a court of profligate, murderous intriguers on whom, war or no war, I was also to spy – both being tasks for which I was untrained, whatever Broadfoot might say. I had been assured that the work was entirely safe – and told almost in the same breath that when all hell broke loose I had only to holler "Wisconsin!" and a genie or Broadfoot's grandmother or the Household Brigade would emerge from a bottle and see me right. Just so. Well, I didn't believe a word of it.

You see, tyro though I was, I knew the political service and the kind of larks it could get up to, like not telling a fellow until it was too late. Two fearsome possibilities had occurred to my distrustful mind: either I was a decoy to distract the enemy from other agents, or I was being placed in the deep field to receive secret instructions when war started. In either case I foresaw fatal consequences, and to make matters worse, I had dark misgivings about the native assistant Broadfoot had assigned to me – you remember, the "*chota-wallah*" who was to carry my green bag.

His name was Jassa, and he wasn't *chota*. I had envisaged the usual fat babu or skinny clerk, but Jassa was a pock-marked, barrel-chested villain, complete with hairy *posh-*

48

teen,* skull-cap, and Khyber knife – just the man you'd choose, as a rule, to see you through rough country, but I was leery of this one from the start. For one thing, he pretended to be a Baloochi dervish, and wasn't – I put him down for Afghan *chi-chi*,† for he was grey-eyed, had no greater a gap between his first and second toes than I did, and possessed something rare among Europeans at that time, let alone natives – a vaccination mark. I spotted it at Ferozepore when he was washing at the tank, but didn't let on; he was from Broadfoot's stable, after all, and plainly knew his business, which was to act as orderly, guide, shield-on-shoulder, and general adviser on country matters. Still, I didn't trust him above half.

Ferozepore was the last outpost of British India then, a beastly hole not much better than a village, beyond which lay the broad brown flood of the Sutlej – and then the hot plain of the Punjab. We had just built a barracks for our three battalions, one British and two Native Infantry, who garrisoned the place, God help them, for it was hotter than hell's pavement; you boiled when it rained, and baked when it didn't. In my civilian role, I didn't call on Littler, who commanded, but put up with Peter Nicolson, Broadfoot's local Assistant. He was suffering for his country, that one, dried out and hollow-cheeked with the worst job in India – nurscmaiding the frontier, finding shelter for the endless stream of refugees from the Punjab, sniffing out the trouble-makers sent to seduce our sepoys and disaffect the *zamindars*,‡ chasing raiding parties, disarming *badmashes*,¶ ruling a district, and keeping the Queen's peace – all this, mind you, without provoking a hostile power which was spoiling for trouble.

"It can't last," says he cheerfully – and I wondered how long he could, with that impossible task and the mercury at 107. "They're just waitin' for an excuse, an' if I don't give 'em one – why, they'll roll over the river as soon as the cold

*Coat.
†Half-caste.
‡Land-holders.
¶Ruffians.

49

weather comes, horse, foot an' guns, you'll see. We ought to
go in an' smash 'em now, while they're in two minds an'
gettin' over the cholera – five thousand of the Khalsa have
died in Lahore, but it's past its worst."

He was seeing me down to the ferry at daybreak; when I
mentioned the great assembly of our troops I'd seen above
Meerut he laughed and pointed back to the cantonment,
where the 62nd were drilling, the red and buff figures like
dolls in the heat haze.

"Never mind what's on the Grand Trunk," says he.
"That's what's *here*, my boy – seven thousand men, one-
third British, an' only light guns. Up there," he pointed
north, "is the Khalsa – *one hundred* thousand of the finest
native army in Asia, with heavy guns. They're two days'
march away. Our nearest reinforcements are Gilbert's ten
thousand at Umballa, a week's march away, and Wheeler's
five thousand at Ludhiana – only five days' march. Strong on
mathematics, are you?"

I'd heard vague talk in Simla, as you know, about our
weakness on the frontier, but it's different when you're on
the spot, and hear the figures. "But why –?" I was beginning, and Nicolson chuckled and shook his head.

"– doesn't Gough reinforce now?" he mimicked me.
"Because it would provoke Lahore – my goodness, it
provokes Lahore if one of our sepoys walks north to
the latrines! I hear they're goin' to demand that we withdraw even the troops we have up here now – perhaps
that'll start the war, even if your Soochet legacy doesn't."
He knew about that, and had twitted me about how I'd
be languishing at the feet of "the fair sultana" while
honest soldiers like him were chasing infiltrators along the
river.

"Mind you, she may be out of office by the time you get
there. There's talk that Prince Peshora – he's another of old
Runjeet's by-blows – is goin' to have a try for the throne;
they say he has most of the Khalsa on his side. What price a
palace revolution, what? Why, if I were you, I'd apply for
the job!"

There was a great crowd of refugees camped about the

50

ghat* on the water's edge, and at the sight of Nicolson they set up a howl and swarmed round him, women mostly and fly-blown *chicos*† clamouring with hands stretched up. His orderlies pushed them back to let us through. "A few hundred more mouths to feed," sighs Nicolson, "an' they ain't even *ours*. Easy there, *havildar*!‡ Oh, *chubbarao*,¶ you noisy heathen – Papa'll bring your bread and milk in a moment! God knows how we're goin' to house 'em, though – I've screwed as much canvas out of stores as the Q.M. will bear, I think."

The ferry itself was a huge barge crewed by native boatmen, but with a light gun in the bows, manned by two sepoys. "That's another provocation," says Nicolson. "We've sixty of these tubs on the river, an' the Sikhs suspect we mean to use 'em as a bridge for invasion. You never know, one o' these days . . . Ah, see yonder!" He shaded his eyes, pointing with his crop across the swollen river; the mist was hanging on the far shore, but through it I could see a party of horsemen waiting, arms gleaming in the sun.

"There's your escort, my boy! The *vakil* sent word they was coming to see you into Lahore in style. Nothin' too good for an envoy with the scent of cash about him, eh? Well, good luck to you!" As we pushed off he waved and shouted: "It'll all come out right, you'll see!"

I don't know why I remember those words, or the sight of him with that great mob of niggers chattering about him while his orderlies cuffed and pushed them up to the camp where they'd be fed and looked after; he was for all the world like a prepostor marshalling the fags, laughing and swearing by turns, with a *chico* perched on his shoulder – I'd not have touched the verminous imp for a pension. He was a kindly, cheery ass, working twenty hours a day, minding his frontier. Four months later he got his reward: a bullet. I wonder if anyone else remembers him?

The last time I'd crossed the Sutlej had been four years

*River-landing.
†Children.
‡Sergeant.
¶Shut up!

51

earlier, where there was a British army ahead, and we had posts all the way to Kabul. Now there were no friends before me, and no one to turn to except the Khyberie thug Jassa and our gaggle of bearers – they were there chiefly because Broadfoot had said I should enter Lahore in a *jampan*, to impress the Sikhs with my consequence. Thanks, George, but I felt damned unimportant as I surveyed my waiting escort (or captors?), and Jassa did nothing to raise my spirits.

"*Gorracharra*," grunts he, and spat. "Irregular cavalry – it is an insult to thee, *husoor*.* These should have been men of the palace, pukka cavalry. They seek to put shame on us, the Hindoo swine!"

I told him pretty sharp to mind his manners, but I saw what he meant. They were typical native irregulars, splendid cavalry undoubtedly, but dressed and armed any old how, with lances, bows, *tulwars*,† and ancient firearms, some in mail coats and helmets, others bare-legged, and all grinning most familiarly. Not what you'd call a guard of honour – yet that's what they were, as I learned when their officer, a handsome young Sikh in a splendid rigout of yellow silk, addressed me by name – and by fame.

"Sardul Singh, at your service, Flashman *bahadur*,"‡ cries he, teeth flashing through his beard. "I was by the Turksalee Gate when you came down from Jallalabad, and all men came to see the Afghan Kush." So much for Broadfoot's notion that shaving my whiskers would help me to pass unnoticed – mind you, it was famous to hear myself described as "the slayer of Afghans", if quite undeserved. "When we heard you were coming with the book and not the sword – may it be an omen of peace for our peoples – I sought command of your escort – and these are volunteers." He indicated his motley squadron. "Men of the Sirkar¶ in their time. A fitter escort for Bloody Lance than Khalsa cavalry."

*Sir, lord.
†Sikh swords.
‡Champion.
¶British government.

Well, this was altogether grand, so I thanked him, raised my civilian kepi to his grinning bandits, saying *"Salaam, bhai,"** which pleased them no end. I took the first chance to remind Jassa how wrong he'd been, but the curmudgeon only grunted: "The Sikh speaks, the cobra spits – who grows fat on the difference?" There's no pleasing some folk.

Between the Sutlej and Lahore lie fifty of the hottest, flattest, scrubbiest miles on earth, and I supposed we'd cover them in a long day's ride, but Sardul said we should lie overnight at a *serai*† a few miles from the city: there was something he wanted me to see. So we did, and after supper he took me through a copse to the loveliest place I ever saw in India – there, all unexpected after the heat and dust of the plain, was a great garden, with little palaces and pavilions among the trees, all hung with coloured lanterns in the warm dusk; streams meandered among the lawns and flower-beds, the air was fragrant with night-blooms, soft music sounded from some hidden place, and everywhere couples were strolling hand in hand or deep in lovers' talk under the boughs. The Chinese Summer Palace, where I walked years later, was altogether grander, I suppose, but there was a magic about that Indian garden that I can't describe – you could call it perfect peace, with its gentle airs rustling the leaves and the lights winking in the twilight; it was the kind of spot where Scheherazade might have told her unending stories; even its name sounds like a caress: Shalamar.[16]

But this wasn't the sight that Sardul wanted me to see – *that* was something unimaginably different, and we viewed it next morning. We left the *serai* at dawn, but instead of riding towards Lahore, which was in full view in the distance, we went a couple of miles out of our way towards the great plain of Maian Mir where, Sardul assured me mysteriously, the true wonder of the Punjab would be shown to me; knowing the Oriental mind, I could guess it was something designed to strike awe in the visiting foreigner – well, it did all of that. We heard it long before we saw it, the flat crash of artillery

*"Greetings, brothers."
†Inn, rest-house.

at first, and then a great confused rumble of sound which resolved itself into the squealing of elephants, the high bray of trumpets, the rhythm of drums and martial music, and the thunder of a thousand hooves making the ground tremble beneath us. I knew what it was before we rode out of the trees and halted on a *bund** to view it in breathtaking panorama: the pride of the Punjab and the dread of peaceful India: the famous Khalsa.

Now, I've taken note of a few heathen armies in my time. The Heavenly Host of Tai'ping was bigger, the black tide of Cetewayo's legions sweeping into Little Hand was surely more terrifying, and there's a special place in my nightmares for that vast forest of tipis, five miles wide, that I looked down on from the bluffs over Little Bighorn – but for pure military might I've seen nothing outside Europe (and dam' little inside) to match that great disciplined array of men and beasts and metal on Maian Mir. As far as you could see, among the endless lines of tents and waving standards, the broad *maidan*† was alive with foot battalions at drill, horse regiments at field exercise, and guns at practice – and they were all uniformed and in perfect order, that was the shocking thing. Black, brown, and yellow armies in those days, you see, might be as brave as any, but they didn't have centuries of drill and tactical movement drummed into 'em, not even the Zulus, or Ranavalona's Hova guardsmen. That was the thing about the Khalsa: it was Aldershot in turbans. It was an army.[17]

That's worth bearing in mind when you hear some smart alec holding forth about our imperial wars being one-sided massacres of poor club-waving heathen mown down by Gatlings. Oh, it happened, at Ulundi and Washita and Omdurman – but more often than not the Snider and Martini and Brown Bess were facing odds of ten to one against in country where shrapnel and rapid fire don't count for much; your savage with his blowpipe or bow or *jezzail*‡ behind a rock has a deuce of an advantage: it's his rock, you

*Embankment.
†Plain.
‡Afghan musket.

54

see. Anyway, our detractors never mention armies like the Khalsa, every bit as well-armed and equipped as we were. So how did we hold India? You'll see presently.

That morning on Maian Mir the confidence I'd felt, viewing our forces on the Grand Trunk, vanished like Punjabi mist. I thought of Littler's puny seven thousand isolated at Ferozepore, our other troops scattered, waiting to be eaten piecemeal – by this juggernaut, a hundred thousand strong. A score of vivid images stay in my mind: a regiment of Sikh lancers *wheeling* at the charge in perfect dressing, the glittering points falling and rising as one; a battalion of Jat infantry with moustaches like buffalo horns, white figures with black crossbelts, moving like clockwork as they performed "at the halt on the left form companies"; Dogra light infantry advancing in skirmishing order, the blue turbans suddenly closing in immaculate line, the bayonet points ripping into the sandbags to a savage yell of "Khalsa-ji!"; heavy guns being dragged through swirling dust by trumpeting elephant teams while the gunners trimmed their fuses, the cases being thrust home, the deafening roar of the salvo – and damme! if those shells didn't burst a mile away in perfect unison, all above ground. Even the sight of the light guns cutting their curtain targets to shreds with grape wasn't as sickening as the precision of the heavy batteries. They were as good as Royal Artillery – aye, and with bigger shot.

They made all their own material, too, from Brown Bess to howitzers, in the Lahore foundry, from our regulation patterns. Only one fault could I find with their gunners and infantry: their drill was perfect, but slow. Their cavalry . . . well, it was fit to ride over Napoleon.

Sardul took good care to let me see all this, *pour encourager les feringhees*. We tiffened with some of their senior men, all courteous to a fault, and not a word about the likelihood that our armies would be at each other's throats by Christmas – the Sikhs are damned good form, you know. There wasn't a European mercenary in sight, by the way; having built an army, they'd retired for the best of reasons: disgust at the state of the country, and reluctance to find themselves fighting John Company.

I saw another side to the Khalsa when we set out for Lahore after noon, Flashy now riding in state in his *jampan*, white topper and fly-whisk at the high port, with Jassa kicking the bearers' arses to give tone to our progress. We were swaying along in fine style past the headquarters tents when we became aware of a crowd of soldiery gathered before the main pavilion, listening to some *upper rojer** on a dais. Sardul reined in to listen, and when I asked Jassa what this might be he growled and spat. "The *panchayats!* If old Runjeet had seen the day, he'd have cut his beard!"

So these were the Khalsa's notorious military committees, of whom we'd heard so much. You see, while their field discipline was perfect, Khalsa policy was determined by the *panches*, where Jack Jawan was as good as his master, and all went by democratic vote – no way to run an army, I agreed with Jassa; small wonder they hadn't crossed the Sutlej yet. They were an astonishing mixture: bare-legged sepoys, officers in red silk, fierce-eyed Akalis[18] in peaked blue turbans and gold beard-nets, a portly old *rissaldar-major†* with white whiskers a foot wide, irregular *sowars* in lobster-tail helmets, Dogra musketeers in green, Pathans with long camel guns – there seemed to be every rank, caste, and race crowding round the speaker, a splendid Sikh, six and a half feet tall in cloth of silver, bellowing to make himself heard.

"All that we heard from Attock is true! Young Peshora is dead, and Kashmiri Singh with him, taken in sleep, after the hunting, by Chuttur Singh and Futteh Khan –"

"Tell us what we don't know!" bawls a heckler, and the big fellow raised his arms to still the yells of agreement.

"You don't know the manner of it – the shame and black treachery! Imam Shah was in Attock Fort – let him tell you."

A burly bargee in a mail jacket, with a bandolier of ivory-hilted knives round his hips, jumps on the dais, and they fell silent.

*Leading light.
†Cavalry sergeant-major.

56

"It was foully done!" croaks he. "Peshora Singh knew it was his time, for they had him in irons, and bore him before the jackal, Chuttur Singh. Peshora looked him in the eye, and called for a sword. 'Let me die like a soldier,' says he, but Chuttur would not look on him, but wagged his head and made soft excuses. Again the young hawk cried for a sword. 'You are thousands, I am alone – there can be but one end, so let it be straight!' Chuttur sighed, and whined, and turned away, waving his hands. 'Straight, coward!' cries Peshora, but they bore him away. All this I saw. They took him to the Kolboorj dungeon, and choked him like a thief with his chains, and cast him in the river. This I did not see. I was told. God wither my tongue if I lie."

Peshora Singh had been the form horse in the throne stakes, according to Nicolson. Well, that's politics for you. I wondered if this would mean a change of government, for Peshora had been the Khalsa's idol, and while his death seemed to be old news, the manner of it seemed to put them in a great taking. They were all yelling at once, and the tall Sikh had to bellow again.

"We have sent the *parwana** to the palace. You all approved it! What is there to do but wait?"

"Wait – while the snake Jawaheer butchers other true men?" bawls a voice. "*He*'s Peshora's murderer, for all he skulks in the Kwabagh† yonder! Let us visit him now, and give him a sleep indeed!"

This got a rousing hand, but others shouted that Jawaheer was the hope of the side, and innocent of Peshora's death.

"Who bribed thee to say that?" roars the *rissaldar-major*, all fire and whiskers. "Did Jawaheer buy thee with a gold chain, *boroowa*?‡ Or perchance Mai Jeendan danced for thee, fornicating strumpet that she is!" Cries of "Shame!", "*Shabash!*"¶ and the Punjabi equivalent of "Mr Chairman!", some pointing out that the Maharani had promised them fifteen rupees a month to march against the

*Summons.
†Sleeping Palace.
‡Pimp.
¶Bravo!

57

bastardised British pigs (the spectator in the *jampan* drew his curtain tactfully at this point) and Jawaheer was just the chap to lead them. Another suggested that Jawaheer wanted war only to draw the Khalsa's fury from his own head, and that the Maharani was an abominable whore of questionable parentage who had lately had a Brahmin's nose sliced off when he rebuked her depravities, so there. A beardless youth, frothing with loyalty, offered to eat the innards of anyone who impugned the honour of that saintly woman, and the meeting seemed likely to dissolve in riot when a gorgeously-robed old general, hawk-faced and commanding, mounted the dais and let them have it straight from the shoulder.

"Silence! Are ye soldiers or fish-wives? Ye have heard Pirthee Singh – the *parwana* has been sent, summoning Jawaheer to come out to us on the sixth of Assin, to answer for Peshora's death or show himself guiltless. There is no more to be said, but this . . ." He paused, and you could have heard a pin drop as his cold eye ranged over them. "We are the Khalsa, the Pure, and our allegiance is to none but our Maharaja, Dalip Singh, may God protect his innocence! Our swords and lives are his alone!" Thunderous cheers, the old *rissaldar-major* spouting tears of loyalty. "As to marching against the British . . . that is for the *panchayats* to decide another day. But if we do, then I, General Maka Khan" – he slapped his breast – "shall march because the Khalsa wills it, and not for the wiles of a naked *cunchunee** or the whim of a drunken dancing-boy!"

With that summary of the regents' characters the day's business concluded, and I was relieved, as Sardul led us past the dispersing soldiery, to note that any glances in my direction were curious rather than hostile; indeed, one or two saluted, and you may be sure I responded civilly. This heartened me, for it suggested that Broadfoot was right, and whatever upheavals in government took place – dramatic ones, by the sound of it – the stranger Flashy would be respected within their gates, their opinion of his country notwithstanding.

*Dancing-girl.

We approached Lahore roundabout, skirting the main town, which is a filthy maze of crooked streets and alleys, to the northern side, where the Fort and palace building dominate the city. Lahore's an impressive place, or was then, more than a mile across and girdled by towering thirty-foot walls which overlooked a deep moat and massive earthworks – since gone, I believe. In those days you were struck by the number and grandeur of its gates, and by the extent of the Fort and palace on their eminence, with the great half-octagon tower, the Summum Boorj, thrusting up like a giant finger close to the northern ramparts.

It loomed above us as we entered by the Rushnai, or Bright Gate, past the swarms of dust-covered workmen labouring on old Runjeet's mausoleum, and into the Court Garden. To the right a tremendous flight of steps led up to Badshai Musjit, the great triple mosque said to be the biggest on earth – mind you, the Samarkandians say the same of *their* mosque – and to the left was the inner gate up to the Fort, a bewildering place full of contradictions, for it contains not only the Sleeping Palace but a foundry and arsenal close by, the splendid Pearl Mosque which is used as a treasury, and over one of the gates a figure of the Virgin Mary, which they say Shah Jehan put up to keep the Portugee traders happy. But there was something stranger still: I'd just bidden farewell to Sardul's escort and my *jampan*, and was being conducted on foot by a yellow-clad officer of the Palace Guard, when I noticed an extraordinary figure lounging in an embrasure above the gate, swigging from an enormous tankard and barking orders at a party of Guardsmen drilling with the light guns on the wall. He was a real Pathan mercenary, with iron moustaches and a nose like a hatchet – but he was dressed from top to toe, *puggaree*,* robe, and *pyjamys*, in the red tartan of the 79th Highlanders! Well, I've seen a Madagascar nigger in a Black Watch kilt, but this beat all. Stranger still, he carried a great metal collar in one hand, and each time before he drank he would clamp it round his throat, almost as though he expected the liquor

*Turban.

59

to leak out through his Adam's apple.

I turned to remark on this to Jassa – and dammit, he'd vanished. Nowhere to be seen. I stared about, and demanded of the officer where he had got to, but he hadn't seen him at all, so in the end I found myself being led onward alone, with all my former alarms rushing back at the gallop.

You may wonder why, just because my orderly had gone astray. Aye, but he'd done it at the very moment of entering the lion's den, so to speak, and the whole mission was mysterious and chancy enough to begin with, and I'm God's own original funk, so there. And I smelled mischief here, in this maze of courts and passages, with high walls looming about me. I didn't even care for the splendid apartments to which I was conducted. They were on an upper storey of the Sleeping Palace, two lofty, spacious rooms joined by a broad Moorish arch, with mosaic tiles and Persian murals, a little marble balcony overlooking a secluded fountain court, silks on the bed, silent bearers to stow my kit, two pretty little maids who shimmied in and out, bringing water and towels and tea (I didn't even think of slapping a rump, which tells you how jumpy I was), and a cooling breeze provided by an ancient *punkah-wallah* in the passage, when the old bugger was awake, which was seldom. For some reason, the very luxury of the place struck me as sinister, as though designed to lull my fears. At least there were two doors, one from either chamber – I do like to know there's a line of retreat.

I washed and changed, still fretting about Jassa's absence, and was about to lie down to calm my nerves when my eye lit on a book on the bedside table – and I sat up with a start. For it was a Bible, placed by an unknown hand – in case I'd forgotten my own, of course.

Broadfoot, thinks I, you're an uneasy man to work for, but by God you know your business. It reminded me that I wasn't quite cut off; I found I was muttering "Wisconsin", then humming it shakily to the tune of "My bonnie is over the ocean", and on the spur of the moment I dug out my cypher key – *Crotchet Castle*, the edition of 1831, if you're interested – and began to write Broadfoot a note of all that I'd heard on Maian Mir. And I had just completed it, and

60

inserted it carefully at Second Thessalonians, and was glumly pondering a verse that read "Pray without ceasing", and thinking a fat lot of good that'll do, when the door slammed open, there was a blood-curdling shriek, a mad dwarf flourishing a gleaming sabre leaped into the archway, and I rolled off the bed with a yell of terror, scrabbling for the pepperbox in my open valise, floundering round to cover the arch, my finger snatching at the trigger ring . . .

In the archway stood a tiny boy, not above seven years old, one hand clutching his little sabre, the other pressed to his teeth, eyes shining with delight. My wavering pistol fell away, and the little monster fairly crowed with glee, clapping his hands.

"Mangla! Mangla, come and see! Come on, woman – it is he, the Afghan killer! He has a great gun, Mangla! He was going to shoot me! Oh, *shabash, shabash!*"

"I'll give you *shabash*, you little son-of-a-bitch!" I roared, and was going for him when a woman came flying into the archway, scooping him up in her arms, and I stopped dead. For one thing, she was a regular plum – and for another the imp was glaring at me in indignation and piping:

"No! No! You may shoot me – but don't dare strike me! I am a maharaja!"

I've met royalty unexpected a number of times – face to face with my twin, Carl Güstaf, in the Jotunberg dungeon, quaking in my rags before the black basilisk Ranavalona, speechless as Lakshmibai regarded me gravely from her swing, stark naked and trussed in the presence of the future Empress of China – and had eyes only for the principal, but in the case of Dalip Singh, Lord of the Punjab, my attention was all for his protectress. She was a little spanker, this Mangla – your true Kashmiri beauty, cream-skinned and perfect of feature, tall and shapely as Hebe, eyes wide at me as she clasped him to her bosom, the lucky lad. He didn't know when he was well off, though, for he slapped her face and yelled:

"Set me down, woman! Who bade thee interfere? Let me go!"

I'd have walloped the tyke, but after another searching glance at me she set him down and stepped back, adjusting her veil with a little coquettish toss of her head – even with my panic still subsiding I thought, aha! here's another who fancies Flash at short notice. The ungrateful infant gave her a push for luck, straightened his shoulders, and made me a jerky bow, hand over heart, royal as bedamned in his little aigretted turban and gold coat.

"I am Dalip Singh. You are Flashman *bahadur*, the famous soldier. Let me see your gun!"

I resisted an impulse to tan his backside, and bowed in turn. "Forgive me, maharaj'. I would not have drawn it in your presence, but you took me unawares."

"No, I didn't!" cries he, grinning. "You move as the cobra strikes, too quickly to see! Oh, it was fine, and you must be the bravest soldier in the world – now, your gun!"

"Maharaj', you forget yourself!" Mangla's voice was sharp, and not at all humble. "You have not given proper welcome to the English lord sahib – and it is unmannerly to burst in on him, instead of receiving him in durbar.* What will he think of us?" Meaning, what does he think of me, to judge from another glance of those fine gazelle eyes. I gave her my gallant leer, and hastened to toady her overlord.

"His majesty honours me. But will you not sit, maharaj', and your lady also?"

"Lady?" He stared and laughed. "Why, she's a slave! Aren't you, Mangla?"

"Your mother's slave, maharaj'," says she coldly. "Not yours."

"Then go and wait on my mother!" cries the pup, not meeting her eye. "I wish to speak with Flashman *bahadur*."

You could see her itching to upend him, but after a moment she gave him a deep *salaam* and me a last appraisal, up and down, which I returned, admiring her graceful carriage as she swayed out, while the little pest tried to disarm me. I told him firmly that a soldier never gives his weapon to anyone, but that I'd hold it for him to see, if he showed me his sword in the same way. So he did, and then stared at my pepperbox,[19] mouth open.

"When I am a man," says he, "I shall be a soldier of the Sirkar, and have such a gun."

I asked, why the British Army and not the Khalsa, and he shook his head. "The Khalsa are mutinous dogs. Besides, the British are the best soldiers in the world, Zeenan Khan says."

"Who's Zeenan Khan?"

"One of my grooms. He was flank-man-first-squadron-fifth-Bengal-Cavalry-General-Sale-Sahib-in-Afghanistan." Rattled out as Zeenan must have taught him. He pointed at me. "He saw you at Jallalabad Fort, and told me how you slew the Muslims. He has only one arm, and no *pinshun*."

Now that's a pension we'll see paid, with arrears, thinks I:

*"Durbar", as Flashman employs it, means variously an audience of royalty, the durbar room in which audience is given, and the Punjab government (e.g. "Lahore durbar").

63

an ex-*sowar* of Bengal Cavalry who has a king's ear is worth a few chips a month. I asked if I could meet Zeenan Khan.

"If you like, but he talks a lot, and always the same story of the Ghazi he killed at Teizin. Did you kill many Ghazis? Tell me about them!"

So I lied for a few minutes, and the bloodthirsty little brute revelled in every decapitation, eyes fixed on me, his small face cupped in his hands. Then he sighed and said his Uncle Jawaheer must be mad.

"He wants to *fight* the British. Bhai Ram says he's a fool – that an ant can't fight an elephant. But my uncle says we must, or you will steal my country from me."

"Your uncle is mistaken," says diplomatic Flashy. "If that were true, would I be here in peace? No – I'd have a sword!"

"You have a gun," he pointed out gravely.

"That's a gift," says I, inspired, "which I'll present to a friend of mine, when I leave Lahore."

"You have friends in Lahore?" says he, frowning.

"I have now," says I, winking at him, and after a moment his jaw dropped, and he squealed with glee. Gad, wasn't I doing my country's work, though?

"I shall have it! That gun? Oh! Oh!" He hugged himself, capering. "And will you teach me your war-cry? You know, the great shout you gave just now, when I ran in with my sword?" The small face puckered as he tried to say it: "Wee . . . ska . . . see . . .?"

I was baffled – and then it dawned: Wisconsin. Gad, my instinct for self-preservation must be working well, for me to squeal that without realising it. "Oh, that was nothing, maharaj'. Tell you what, though – I'll teach you to shoot."

"You will? With that gun?" He sighed ecstatically. "Then I shall be able to shoot Lal Singh!"

I remembered the name – a general, the Maharani's lover.

"Who's Lal Singh, maharaj'?"

He shrugged. "Oh, one of my mother's bed-men." Seven years old, mark you. "He hates me, I can't tell why. All her other bed-men like me, and give me sweets and toys." He shook his head in perplexity, hopping on one leg, no doubt

64

to assist thought. "I wonder why she has so many bed-men? Ever so many –"

"Cold feet, I dare say . . . look, younker – maharaj', I mean – hadn't you better be running along? Mangla will be –"

"Mangla has bed-men, too," insists this fount of scandal. "But Uncle Jawaheer is her favourite. Do you know what Lady Eneela says they do?" He left off hopping, and took a deep breath. "Lady Eneela says they –"

Fortunately, before my delicacy could receive its death blow, Mangla suddenly reappeared, quite composed considering she'd plainly had her ear at the keyhole, and informed his garrulous majesty peremptorily that his mother commanded him to the durbar room. He pouted and kicked his heels, but finally submitted, exchanged salaams, and allowed her to shoo him into the passage. To my surprise, she didn't follow, but closed the door and faced me, mighty cool – she didn't look at all like a slave-girl, and she didn't talk like one.

"His majesty speaks as children do," says she. "You will not mind him. Especially what he says of his uncle, Wazir Jawaheer Singh."

No "sahib", or downcast eyes, or humble tone, you notice. I took her in, from the dainty Persian slippers and tight silk trousers to the well-filled bodice and the calm lovely face framed by the flimsy head veil, and moved up for a closer view.

"I care nothing about your Wazir, little Mangla," smiles I. "But if our small tyrant speaks true . . . I envy him."

"Jawaheer is not a man to be envied," says she, watching me with those insolent gazelle eyes, and a drift of her perfume reached me – heady stuff, these slave-girls use. I reached out and drew a glossy black tress from beneath the veil, and she didn't blink; I stroked her cheek with it, and she smiled, a provocative parting of the lips. "Besides, envy is the last deadly sin I'd expect from Flashman *bahadur*."

"But you can guess the first, can't you?" says I, and gathered her smoothly in by tit and buttock, not omitting a chaste salute on the lips, to which the coy little creature

65

responded by slipping her hand down between us, taking hold, and thrusting her tongue halfway down my throat – at which point that infernal brat Dalip began hacking at the door, clamouring for attention.

"To hell with him!" growls I, thoroughly engrossed, and for a moment she teased with hand and tongue before pulling her trembling softness away, panting bright-eyed.

"Yes, I know the first," she murmurs, taking a last fond stroke, "but this is not the time –"

"Ain't it, by God? Never mind the pup – he'll go away, he'll get tired –"

"It is not that." She pushed her hands against my chest, pouting and shaking her head. "My mistress would never forgive me."

"Your mistress? What the blazes – ?"

"Oh, you will see." She disengaged my hands, with a pretty little grimace as that whining whelp kicked and yammered at the panels. "Be patient, Flashman *bahadur* – remember, the servant may sup last, but she sups longest." Her tongue flickered at my lips again, and then she had slipped out, closing the door to the accompaniment of shrill childish reproaches, leaving me most randily frustrated – but in better trim than I'd been for days. There's nothing like a brisk overhaul of a sporty female, with the certainty of a treat in store, for putting one in temper. And it goes to show – whiskers ain't everything.

I wasn't allowed to spend long in lustful contemplation, though, for who should loaf in now but the bold Jassa, looking fit for treason, and no whit put out when I damned his eyes and demanded where he'd been. "About the *husoor*'s business," was all the answer I got, while he took a wary prowl through the two rooms, prodding a hanging here and tapping a panel there, and remarking that these Hindoo swine did themselves uncommon well. Then he motioned me out on to the little balcony, took a glance up and down, and says softly: "Thou has seen the little raja, then – and his mother's pimp?"

"What the devil d'ye mean?"

"Speak low, *husoor*. The woman Mangla – Mai Jeendan's

66

spy and partner in all mischief. A slave – that stands by her mistress's purdah in durbar, and speaks for her. Aye, and makes policy on her own account, and is grown the richest woman in Lahore. Think on that, *husoor*. She is Jawaheer's whore – and betrayer, like enough. Not a doubt but she was sent to scout thee . . . for whatever purposes." He grinned his evil, pock-marked grin, and cut me off before I could speak.

"*Husoor*, we are together in this business, thou and I. If I am blunt, take it not amiss, but harken. They will come at thee all ways, these folk. If some have sleek limbs and plump breasts, why then . . . take thy pleasure, if thou'rt so minded," says this generous ruffian, "but remember always what they are. Now . . . I shall be here and there awhile. Others will come presently to woo thee – not so well favoured as Mangla, alas!"

Well, damn his impudence – and thank God for him. And he was right. For the next hour Flashy's apartments were like London Bridge Station in Canterbury week. First arrival was a tall, stately, ancient grandee, splendidly attired and straight from a Persian print. He came alone, coldly begging my pardon for his intrusion, and keeping an ear cocked; damned uneasy he seemed. His name was Dewan Dinanath, familiar to me from Broadfoot's packets, where he was listed as an influential Court adviser, inclined to the peace party, but a weathercock. His business was simple: did the Sirkar intend to return the Soochet fortune to the Court of Lahore? I said that would not be known until I'd reported to Calcutta, where the decision would be taken, and he eyed me with bleak disapproval.

"I have enjoyed Major Broadfoot's confidence in the past," sniffs he. "You may have equal confidence in me." Both of which were damned lies. "This treasure is vast, and its return might be a precedent for other Punjab monies at present in the . . . ah, care of the British authorities. In the hands of our government, these funds would have a stabilising effect." They'd help Jawaheer and Jeendan to keep the Khalsa happy, he meant. "A word in season to me, of Hardinge sahib's intentions . . ."

67

"I'm sorry, sir," says I. "I'm only an advocate."

"A young advocate," snaps he, "should study concili-
ation as well as law. It is to go to Goolab, is it?"

"Or Soochet Singh's widow. Or the Maharaja's government. Unless it is retained by Calcutta, for the time being.
That's all I can tell you, sir, I'm afraid."

He didn't like me, I could see, and might well have told
me so, but a sound caught his ear, and he was through into
my bedchamber like an elderly whippet. I heard the door
close as my next unexpected guests arrived: two other grave
seniors, Fakir Azizudeen, a tough, shrewd-looking
heavyweight, and Bhai Ram Singh, portly, jovial, and
bespectacled – staunch men of the peace party, according to
the packets. Bhai Ram was the one who thought Jawaheer a
fool, according to little Dalip.

He opened the ball, with genial compliments about my
Afghan service. "But now you come to us in another capacity . . . as an advocate. Still of the Army, but in Major
Broadfoot's service." He twinkled at me, stroking his white
beard. Well, he probably knew the colour of George's
drawers, too. I explained that I'd been studying law at
home – .

"At the Inns of Court, perhaps?"

"No, sir – firm in Chancery Lane. I hope to read for the
Bar some day."

"Excellent," purrs Bhai Ram, beaming. "I have a little
law, myself." I'll lay you do, thinks I, bracing myself. Sure
enough, out came the legal straight left. "I have been asking
myself what difficulty might arise, if in this Soochet business,
it should prove that the widow had a coparcener." He
smiled at me inquiringly, and I looked baffled, and asked
how that could possibly affect matters.

"I do not know," says he blandly. "That is why I ask
you."

"Well, sir," says I, puzzled, "the answer is that it don't
apply, you see. If the lady were Soochet's *descendant*, and
had a sister – a female in the same degree, that is – then
they'd take together. As coparceners. But she's his *widow*,
so the question doesn't arise." So put that in your pipe and

smoke it, old Cheeryble; I hadn't sat up in Simla with towel round my head for nothing.

He regarded me ruefully, and sighed, with a shrug to Fakir Azizudeen, who promptly exploded. "So he is a lawyer, then! Did you expect Broadfoot to send a farmer? As if this legacy matters! We know it does not, and so does he!" This with a gesture at me. He leaned forward. "Why are you here, sahib? Is it to take up time, with this legal folly? To whet the hopes of that drunken fool Jawaheer –"

"Gently, gently," Bhai Ram reproved him.

"Gently – on the brink of war? When the Five Rivers are like to run red?" He swung angrily on me. "Let us talk like sane men, in God's name! What is in the mind of the *Malki lat*?* Does he wait to be given an excuse for bringing his bayonets across the Sutlej? If so, can he doubt it will be given him? Then why does he not come *now* – and settle it at a blow? Forget your legacy, sahib, and tell us that!"

He was an angry one this, and the first straight speaker I'd met in the Punjab. I could have fobbed him as I had Dinanath, but there was no point. "Hardinge sahib hopes for peace in the Punjab," says I. He glared at me.

"Then tell him he hopes in vain!" snarls he. "Those madmen at Maian Mir will see to it! Convince him of that, sahib, and your journey will not have been wasted!" And on that he stalked out, by way of the bedroom.[20] Bhai Ram sighed and shook his head.

"An honest man, but impetuous. Forgive his rudeness, Flashman sahib – and my own impertinence." He chuckled. "Coparceners! Hee-hee! I will not embarrass you by straining your recollection of Bracton and Blackstone on inheritance." He heaved himself up, and set a chubby hand on my arm. "But I will say this. Whatever your purpose here – oh, the legacy, of course! – do what you can for us." He regarded me gravely. "It will be a British Punjab in the end – that is certain. Let us try to achieve it with as little pain as may be." He smiled wanly. "It will bring order, but little

*Lit. "Lord of the land", i.e. Sir Henry Hardinge.

69

profit for the Company. I am ungenerous enough to wonder if that is why Lord Hardinge seems so reluctant."

He tooled off through the bedroom, but paused at the door.

"Forgive me – but this Pathan orderly of yours . . . you have known him long?"

Startled, I said, not long, but that he was a picked man.

He nodded. "Just so . . . would it be forward of me to offer the additional services of two men of my own?" He regarded me benevolently over his specs. "A needless precaution, no doubt . . . but your safety is important. They would be discreet, of course."

You may judge that this put the wind up me like a full gale – if this wily old stick thought I was in danger, that was enough for me. I was sure he meant me no harm; Broadfoot had marked him A3. So, affecting nonchalance, I said I'd be most obliged, while assuring him I felt as safe in Lahore as I would in Calcutta or London or Wisconsin, even, ha-ha. He gave me a puzzled look, said he would see to it, and left me in a rare sweat of anxiety, which was interrupted by my final visitor.

He was a fat and unctuous villain with oily eyes, one Tej Singh, who waddled in with a couple of flunkeys, greeting me effusively as a fellow-soldier – he sported an enormous jewelled sabre over a military coat crusted with bullion, his insignia as a Khalsa general. He was full of my Afghan exploits, and insisted on presenting me with a superb silk robe – not quite a dress of honour, he explained fawning, but rather more practical in the sultry heat. He was such a toad, I wondered if the robe was poisoned, but after he'd Heeped his way out, assuring me of his undying friendship and homage, I decided he was just dropping dash where he thought it might do good. A fine garment it was, too; I peeled down and donned it, enjoying its silky coolness while I reflected on the affairs of the day.

Broadfoot and Jassa had been right: I was receiving attention from all kinds of people. What struck me was their impatience – I wasn't even here yet, officially, and wouldn't be until I'd been presented in durbar, but they'd come flock-

70

ing like sparrows to crumbs. Most of their motives were plain enough; they saw through the legacy sham, and recognised me as Broadfoot's ear trumpet. But it was reassuring that they thought me worth cultivating – Tej Singh, a Khalsa big-wig, especially; if that damned old Bhai Ram hadn't shown such concern for my safety, I'd have been cheery altogether. Well, I had more news for Broadfoot, for what it was worth; at this rate, Second Thessalonians was going to take some traffic. I ambled through to the bedside table, picked up the Bible – and dropped it in surprise.

The note I'd placed in it a bare two hours earlier was gone. And since I'd never left the room, Broadfoot's mysterious messenger must be one of those who had called on me.

Jassa was my first thought, instantly dismissed – George would have told me, in his case. Dinanath and Fakir Azizudeen had each passed alone through my bedroom . . . but they seemed most unlikely. Tej Singh hadn't been out of sight, but I couldn't swear to his flunkeys – or the two little maids. Little Dalip was impossible, Bhai Ram hadn't been near my bedside, nor had Mangla, worse luck . . . could she have sneaked in unobserved while I was with Dalip, beyond the arch? I sifted the whole thing while I ate a solitary supper, hoping it was Mangla, and wondering if she'd be back presently . . . it was going to be a lonely night, and I cursed the Indian protocol that kept me in purdah, so to speak, until I was summoned to durbar, probably next day.

It was dark outside now, but the maids (working tandem to avoid molestation, no doubt) had lit the lamps, and the moths were fluttering at the mosquito curtain as I settled down with *Crotchet Castle*, enjoying for the hundredth time the passage where old Folliott becomes agitated in the presence of bare-arsed statues of Venus . . . which set me thinking of Mangla again, and I was idly wondering which of the ninety-seven positions taught me by Fetnab would suit her best, when I became aware that the *punkah* had stopped.

The old bastard's caulked out again, thinks I, and hol-

71

lered, without result, so I rolled up, seized my crop, and strode forth to give him an enjoyable leathering. But his mat was empty, and so was the passage, stretching away to the far stairs, with only a couple of lamps shining faint in the gloom. I called for Jassa; nothing but a hollow echo. I stood a moment; it was damned quiet, not a sound anywhere, and for the first time my silk robe felt chill against my skin.

I went inside again, and listened, but apart from the faint pitter of the moths at the screen, no sound at all. To be sure, the Kwabagh was a big place, and I'd no notion where I was within it, but you'd have expected some noise . . . distant voices, or music. I went through the screen on to the little balcony, and looked over the marble balustrade; it was a long drop, four storeys at least, to the enclosed court, high enough to make my crotch contract; I could just hear the faint tinkle of the fountain, and make out the white pavement in the gloom, but the walls enclosing the court were black; not a light anywhere.

I found I was shivering, and it wasn't the night air. My skin was crawling with a sudden dread in that lonely, sinister darkness, and I was just about to turn hurriedly back into my room when I saw something that brought the hair bristling up on my neck.

Far down in the court, on the pale marble by the fountain, there was a shadow where none had been before. I stared, thrilling with horror as I realised it was a man, in black robes, his upturned face hidden in a dark hood. He was looking up at my balcony, and then he stepped back into the shadows, and the court was empty.

I was inside and streaking across the room in an instant – and if you say I start at shadows, I'll agree with you, pointing out only that behind every shadow there's substance, and in this case it wasn't out for an evening stroll. I yanked open the door, preparing to speed down the passage in search of cheer and comfort – and my foot wasn't over the threshold before I froze in my tracks. At the far end of the passage, beyond the last light, dark figures were advancing, and I caught the gleam of steel among them.

I skipped back, slamming the door, looking wildly about

72

for a bolt-hole which I knew didn't exist. There wasn't time to get my pepperbox; they'd be at the door in a second – there was nothing for it but to slip through the screen to the balcony, shuddering back against the balustrade even as I heard the door flung open and men bursting in. In unthinking panic I swung over the side of the balustrade, close to the wall, clutching its pillars from the outside, cowering low with my toes scrabbling for a hold and that appalling drop beneath me, while heavy footsteps and harsh voices rang out from my room.

It was futile, of course. They'd be ravening out on the balcony in a moment, see me through the pillars – I could hear the yell of triumph, feel the agony of steel slicing through my fingers, sending me hurtling to hideous death. I crouched lower, gibbering like an ape, trying to peer under the balcony – God, there was a massive stone bracket supporting it, only inches away! I thrust a foot through it, slipped, and for a ghastly instant was hanging at full stretch before I got one leg crooked over the bracket, made a frantic grab, and found myself clinging to it like a bloody sloth, upside down beneath the balcony, with my fine silk robe billowing beneath me.

I've no head for heights, did I tell you? That yawning black void was dragging my mind down, willing me to let go, even as I clung for dear life with locked ankles and sweating fingers – I must drag myself up and over the bracket somehow, but even as I braced myself a voice sang out just overhead, and the toe of a boot appeared between the pillars only a yard above my upturned face. Thank God the balcony rail was a broad projecting slab which hid me from view as he shouted down – and only then did I remember blasted Romeo below, who must have been watching my frantic acrobatics . . .

"Ai, Nurla Bey – what of the *feringhee*?" cries the voice above – a rasping croak in Pushtu, and I could hear my muscles creaking with the awful strain as I waited to be announced.

"He came out a moment since, Gurdana Khan," came the answer – Jesus, it sounded a mile down. "Then he went back within."

He hadn't seen me? Pondering it later – which you ain't inclined to do while hanging supine under a balcony of murderers – I concluded that he must have been looking elsewhere or relieving himself when I made my leap for glory, and my robe being dark green, he couldn't make me out in the deep shadow beneath the balcony. I embraced the bracket, blubbering silently, while Gurdana Khan swore by the Seven Lakes of Hell that I wasn't in the room, so where the devil was I?

"Perchance he has the gift of invisibility," calls up the wag in the court. "The English are great chemists." Gurdana damned his eyes, and for no sane reason I found myself thinking that this was the kind of crisis in which, Broadfoot had said, I might drop the magic word "Wisconsin" into the conversation. I didn't care to interrupt, though, just then, while Gurdana stamped in fury and addressed his followers.

"Find him! Search every nook, every corner in the palace! Stay, though – he may have gone to the durbar room!"

"What – into the very presence of Jawaheer?" scoffs another.

"His best refuge, fool! Even thou wouldst not cut his throat in open durbar. Away, and search! Nurla, thou dirt – back to the gate!"

For a split second, as he shouted down, his sleeve came into view – and even in the poor light there was no mistaking that pattern. It was the tartan of the 79th, and Gurdana Khan was the Pathan officer I'd seen that afternoon – dear God, the Palace Guard were after me!

How I held on for those last muscle-cracking moments, with fiery cramps searing my arms, I can't fathom, much less how I manged to struggle up astride of the bracket. But I did, and sat gasping and shaking in the freezing dark. They were gone, and I must steel myself to reach out and up for a hold on the balcony pillars, and somehow find the strength to drag myself to safety. I knew it was death to try, but equally certain death to remain, so I drew myself into a crouch, feet on the bracket like some damned cathedral gargoyle, leaned out, and reached slowly up with one trembling hand, too terrified to make the snatch which had to be made . . .

A hideous face shot over the balustrade, glaring down at me, I squealed in terror, my foot slipped, I clawed wildly at thin air as I began to fall – and a hand like a vice clamped on my wrist, almost wrenching my arm from its socket. For two bowel-chilling seconds I swung free, wailing, then another hand seized my forearm, and I was dragged up and over the balustrade, collapsing in a quaking heap on the balcony, with Jassa's ugly face peering into mine.

I'm not certain what line our conversation took, once I'd heaved up my supper, because I was in that state of blind funk and shock where talk don't matter, and I made it worse – once I'd recovered the strength to crawl indoors – by emptying my pint flask of brandy in about three great gulps, while Jassa asked damfool questions.

That brandy was a mistake. Sober, I'd have begun to reason straight, and let him talk some sense into me, but I sank the lot, and the short result was that, in the immortal words of Thomas Hughes, Flashy became beastly drunk. And when I'm foxed, and shuddering scared into the bargain . . . well, I ain't responsible. The odd thing is, I keep all my faculties except common sense; I see and hear clearly, and remember, too – and I know I had only one thought in mind, seared there by that tartan villain who was bent on murdering me: "The durbar room – his best refuge!" If there's one thing I respect, drunk or sober, it's a professional opinion, and if my *hunters* thought I'd be safe there then by God not Jassa or fifty like him were going to keep me from it. He must have tried to calm me, for I fancy I took him by the throat, to make my intentions clear, but all I'm sure of is that I went blundering off along the passage, and then along another, and down a long spiral staircase that grew lighter as I descended, with the sound of music coming closer, and then I was in a broad carpeted gallery, where various interesting Orientals glanced at me curiously, and I was looking out at a huge chandelier gleaming with a thousand candles, and below it a broad circular floor on which two men and a woman were dancing, three brilliant

75

figures whirling to and fro. There were spectators down there, too, in curtained booths round the walls, all in extravagant costumes – aha, thinks I, this is the spot, and a fancy dress party in progress, too; capital, I'll go as a chap in a green silk robe with bare feet. It's a terrible thing, drink.

"Flashman *bahadur*! Why, have you received the *parwana*, then?"

I turned, and there was Mangla walking towards me along the gallery, wearing a smile of astonishment and very little besides. Plainly it was fancy dress, and she'd come as a dancer from some select brothel (which wasn't far out, in fact). She wore a long black sash low on her hips, knotted so that it hung to her ankles before and behind, leaving her legs bare; her fine upper works were displayed in a bodice of transparent gauze, her hair hung in a black tail to her waist, she tinkled with bangles, and there were silver castanets on her fingers. A cheering sight, I can tell you, at any time, but even more so when you've been hanging out of windows to avoid the broker's men.

"No *parwana*, I'm afraid," says I. "Here, I say, that's a fetching rig! Well, now . . . is that the durbar room down yonder?"

"Why, yes – you wish to meet their highnessses?" She came closer, eyeing me curiously. "Is all well with you, *bahadur*? Why, you are shaking! Are you ill?"

"Not a bit of it!" says I. "Took a turn in the night air . . . chilly, eh?" Some drunken instinct told me to keep mum about my balcony adventure, at least until I met higher authority. She said I needed something to warm me, and a lackey serving the folk in the gallery put a beaker in my hand. What with brandy and funk I was parched as a camel's oxter, so I drank it straight off, and another – dry red wine, with a curious effervescent tang to it. D'you know, it settled me wonderfully; a few more of these, thinks I, and they can bring the nigger in. I took another swig, and Mangla laid a hand on my arm, smiling roguishly.

"That is your third cup, *bahadur*. Have a care. It is . . . strangely potent, and the night has only begun. Rest a moment."

I didn't mind. With the liquor taking hold I felt safe among the lights and music, with this delectable houri to hand. I slipped an arm round her waist as we looked down on the dancers; the guests reclining in the booths around the floor were clapping to the music and throwing silver; others were drinking and eating and dallying – it looked a thoroughly jolly party, with most of the women as briefly attired as Mangla. One black charmer, naked to the waist, was supporting a shouting reveller as he weaved his way across the floor; there was excited laughter and shrill voices, and one or two of the booths had their curtains discreetly closed . . . and not a Pathan in sight.

"Their highnesses are merry," says Mangla. "One of them, at least." A man's voice was shouting angrily below, but the music and celebration continued uninterrupted. "Never fear, you will find a welcome – come and join our entertainment."

Capital, thinks I, we'll entertain each other in one of those curtained nooks, so I let her lead me down a curved stair giving on to an open space at one side of the floor, where there were buffets piled high with delicacies and drink. The angry man's voice greeted us as we descended, and then he was in view beside the tables: a tall, well-made fellow, handsome in the pretty Indian way, with a curly beard and moustache, a huge jewelled turban on his head and only baggy silk pantaloons on the rest of him. He was staggering tight, with a goblet in one hand and the other round the neck of the black beauty who'd been helping him across the floor. Before him stood Dinanath and Azizudeen, grim and furious as he railed at them, stuttering drunkenly.

"Tell 'em to go to the devil! Do they think the Wazir is some *mujbee** who'll run to their bidding! Let 'em come to me – aye, and humbly! Khalsa scum! Sons of pigs and owls! Do they think they rule here?"

"They know it," snaps Azizudeen. "Persist in this folly and they'll prove it."

"Treason!" bawls the other, and flung the goblet at him.

*Sweeper.

77

It missed by yards, and he'd have tumbled over if the black wench hadn't caught him. He clung tipsily to her, flecks of spittle on his beard, crying that he was the Wazir, they wouldn't dare –

"And what's to stop them?" demands Azizudeen. "Your Palace Guard – whom the Khalsa have promised to blow from guns if you escape? Try it, my prince, and you'll find your Guards have become your jailers!"

"Liar!" yammers the other, and then from raging and cursing he burst into tears, bleating about how well he'd paid them, half a lakh to a single general, and they'd stand by him while the British ate the Khalsa alive. "Oh, aye – the British are marching on us even now!" cries he. "Don't the fools know that?"

"They know you say so – but that it is not true," puts in Dinanath sternly. "My prince, this is foolish. You know you must go out to the Khalsa tomorrow, to answer for Peshora's death . . . if you speak them fair, all may be well . . ." He stepped closer, speaking low and earnest, while the fellow mowed and wept – and then, damme if he didn't lose interest and start nuzzling and fondling his black popsy. First things first seemed to be his motto, and he pawed with such ardour that they tumbled down and sprawled in a drunken embrace at the stair foot, while Dinanath and Azizudeen stood speechless. The drunkard raised his face from between her boobies once, blubbering at Dinanath that he daren't go out to the Khalsa, they'd do him a mischief, and then went back to the matter in hand, trying to climb on top of her with his great turban all awry.

Mangla and I were standing only a few steps above them, and I was thinking, well, you don't often see this at Windsor – the astonishing thing was that no one else in the durbar room was paying the least heed; while the drunkard alternately mauled his wench and whimpered and snarled at the two counsellors, the dance was reaching its climax, the band piping away in fine style, the spectators applauding. I glanced at Mangla, and she shrugged.

"Raja Jawaheer Singh, Wazir," says she, indicating the turbaned sportsman. "Do you wish to be presented?"

Now he was struggling to his feet again, calling for drink, and the black girl held the cup while he gulped and slobbered. Azizudeen turned on his heel in disgust, and Dinanath followed him towards one of the booths. Jawaheer pushed the cup away, staggered, and clutched at a table for support, calling for them to come back, and that was when his eye fell on us. He goggled stupidly, and started forward.

"Mangla!" cries he. "Mangla, you bitch! Who's that?"

"It is the English envoy, Flashman sahib," says she coolly.

He gaped at me, blinking, and then a crafty look came into his eyes, and he loosed a great shout of laughter, yelling that he'd been right – the British had come, as he'd said they would.

"See, Dinanath! Look, Azizudeen! The British are here!" He swung round, stumbling, weaving towards them in a sort of crazy dance, crowing with high-pitched laughter. "A liar, am I? See – their spy is here!" Dinanath and Azizudeen had turned in the entrance of one of the booths, and as Jawaheer capered and fell down, and Mangla brought me to the foot of the staircase, I saw Dinanath white with fury – shame and loss of face before a foreigner, you see. The dancing and music had stopped, folk were craning to look, and flunkeys were running to help Jawaheer, but he lashed out at them, staggering round to point unsteadily at me.

"British spy! Filth! Your Company bandits will come to plunder us, will they? Brigands, *wilayati,** vermin!" He glared from me to Dinanath. "Ai-ee, the British will come – they will have *cause* to come!" shrieks he, pointing at me, and then they'd hustled him off, still yelling and laughing, Mangla clapped her hands, the music began again, and folk turned away, whispering behind their hands, just as they do at home when Uncle Percy's had one of his bad turns during evensong.

I dare say I should have been embarrassed, but with a couple of quarts of mixed brandy and puggle inside me, I

*Foreigner.

79

didn't mind one little bit. Jawaheer was plainly all that rumour said of him, but I had deeper concerns: I was suddenly thirsty again, and beginning to feel so monstrous randy that if Lady Sale had happened by she'd have had to look damned lively, rheumatics and all. Doubtless the curious liquor Mangla had plied me with was responsible for both conditions; very well, she could take the consequences . . . there she was, the luscious little teaser, by the booth where Azizudeen and Dinanath had been a moment since. I lurched towards her, gloating, but even as I hove to beside her a woman spoke from beyond the open curtains.

"Is this your Englishman? Let me look at him."

I turned in surprise – not only at the words, but at the slurred, appraising arrogance of the tone. Mangla stepped back, and with a little gesture of presentation, said: "Flashman sahib, *kunwari*,"* and that title told me I was in the presence of the notorious Maharani Jeendan, Indian Venus, modern Messalina, and uncrowned queen of the Punjab.

Here and there in my memoirs I've remarked on the attraction of the female sex, and how it's seldom a matter of beauty alone. There are breathtakers like Elspeth and Lola and Yehonala whom you can't wait to chivvy into the shrubbery; equally classic creatures (Angie Burdett-Coutts, for example, or the Empress of Austria) who are as exciting as cold soup but appeal to the baser aesthetic senses; and plain Janes who could start a riot in a monastery. In each case, Aphrodite or the governess, the magic is different, you see; there is always some unique charm or singular attraction, and it can be hard to define. In Mai Jeendan, though, it stood out a mile: she was simply the lewdest-looking strumpet I ever saw in my life.

Mind you, when a young woman with the proportions of an erotic Indian statue is found reclining half-naked and three parts drunk, while a stalwart wrestler rubs her down with oil, it's easy to leap to conclusions. But you could have covered this one with sackcloth in the front row of the

Kunwar=the son of a maharaja, and *kunwari* is presumably the female honorific.

80

church choir, and they'd still have ridden her out of town on a rail. You've heard of voluptuaries whose vices are stamped on their faces – mine, for example, but I'm over eighty. She was in her twenties, and lust was in every line of her face: the once perfect beauty turned fleshy, the lovely curves of lip and nostril thickened by booze and pleasure into the painted mask of a depraved angel – gad, she was attractive. She looked like those sensual pictures of Jezebel and Delilah which religious artists paint with such loving enthusiasm; Arnold could have got enough sermons out of her to last the half. Her eyes were large and wanton and slightly protruding, with a vacant, sated expression which may have been due to drink or the recent attentions of the wrestler – a bit shaky, he looked to me – but as I made my bow they widened in what was either drunken interest or yearning lechery – the same thing, really, with her.

Considering the size of her endowments, she was quite small, light coffee in colour, and fine-boned under her smooth fat – a *tung bibi*, as they say; a "tight lady". Like Mangla, she was decked out as a dancer, with a crimson silk loin-cloth and flimsy bodice, but instead of bangles her legs and arms were sheathed in gauze sewn with tiny gems, and her dark red hair was contained in a jewelled net.

To see her then, you'd never have guessed that when she wasn't guzzling drink and men, Mai Jeendan was another woman altogether; Broadfoot was wrong in thinking debauchery had dulled her wits. She was shrewd and resolute and ruthless when the need arose; she was also an accomplished actress and mimic, talents developed when she'd been the leading jester in old Runjeet's obscene private entertainments.

Just now, though, she was too languid with drink to do more than struggle up on one elbow, pushing her masseur away to view me better, slowly up and down – it reminded me of being on the slave-block in Madagascar, when no one bought me, rot them. This time, so far as one could judge from the lady's tipsy muttering as she lolled back on her cushions, fluttering a plump hand at me, the market was more buoyant.

81

"You were right, Mangla . . . he's big!" She gave a drunken chuckle, adding an indelicate remark which I won't translate. "Well, must make him comfortable . . . have him take off his robe . . . come sit down here, beside me. You, get out . . ." This to the wrestler, who salaamed himself off in haste. "You too, Mangla . . . draw the curtains . . . want to talk with big Englishman."

And not about the Soochet legacy, from the way she patted the cushions and smiled at me over the rim of her glass. Well, I'd heard she was game, but this was informality with a vengeance. I was all for it, mind you, even if she was as drunk as Taffy's sow and spilling most of the drink down her front – if any ass tells you that there's nothing so disgusting as a beauty in her cups, I can only say she looks a sight more interesting than a sober schoolmarm. I was wondering if I should offer to help her out of her wet things when Mangla got in before me, calling for a cloth, so I hung back, polite-like, and found myself being addressed most affably by a tall young grandee with a flashing smile who made me a pretty little speech, welcoming me to the Court of Lahore, and trusting that I would have a pleasant stay.

His name was Lal Singh, and I still give him top marks for style. After all, he was Jeendan's principal lover, and here was his mistress cussing like Sowerberry Hagan and having her *déshabillé* mopped in the presence of a stranger whom she'd been about to drag into the woodshed; it didn't unsettle him a bit as he congratulated me on my Afghan exploits and drew me into conversation with Tej Singh, my fat little warrior of the afternoon, who bobbed up grinning at his elbow to tell me how well I suited the robe he'd given me. By this time I was beginning to feel a trifle confused myself, having in short order survived an assassination plot – what a long time ago it seemed – been filled with strong waters and (I suspected) aphrodisiac, trotted up and down by a half-naked slave girl, verbally assailed in public by the Wazir of the Punjab, and indecently ogled by his drunken fleshtrap of a sister. Now I was discussing, more or less coherently, the merits of the latest Congreve rockets with two knowledgeable military men, while a yard away the

82

Queen Regent was being dried off by her attendants and protesting tipsily, and at my back a vigorous ballet was being danced by a score of young chaps in turbans and baggy trousers, with the orchestra going full steam.

I was new to Lahore, of course, and not *au fait* with their easygoing ways. I didn't know, for example, that recently, when Lal Singh and Jawaheer had quarrelled publicly, the Maharani had composed things by presenting each of them with a naked houri and telling them to restore their tempers by doing honour to her gifts then and there. Which, by all accounts, they had done. I mention that in case you think my own account is at all exaggerated.

"We must have a longer talk presently," says Lal Singh, taking me by the arm. "You see the deplorable condition of affairs here. It cannot continue – as I am sure Hardinge sahib is aware. He and I have had some correspondence – through your esteemed chief, Major Broadfoot." He flashed me another of his smiles, all beard and teeth. "They are both very practical and expert men. Tell me, you have their confidence – what price do you suppose they would consider fair . . . for the Punjab?"

Well, I was drunk, and he knew it, which was why he asked the impossible, treasonable question, in the hope that my reaction would tell him something. Even fuddled, I knew that Lal Singh was a clever, probably desperate man, and that the best answer to the unanswerable is to put a question of your own. So I said, "Why, does someone want to sell it?" At which he gave me a long smile, while little Tej held his breath; then Lal Singh clapped me on the shoulder.

"We shall have our long talk by day," says he. "The night is for pleasure. Would you care for some opium? No? Kashmiri opium is the finest obtainable – like Kashmiri women. I would offer you one, or even two, of them, but I fear my lady Jeendan's displeasure. You have aroused some expectation in that quarter, Mr Flashman, as I'm sure you noticed." His smile was as easy and open as though he were telling me she'd be bidding me to tea presently. "May I suggest a fortifying draught?" He beckoned a matey, and I

83

was presented with another beaker of Mangla's Finest Old Inspirator, which I sipped with caution. "I see you treat it with greater respect than does that impossible sot, our Wazir. Look yonder, *bahadur* . . . and have pity on us."

For now Jawaheer was to the fore again, reeling noisily in front of Jeendan's booth, with his black tart trying vainly to hold him upright; he was delivering a great tirade against Dinanath, and Jeendan must have sobered somewhat under Mangla's ministrations, for she told him pretty plain, with barely a hiccough, to pull himself together and drink no more.

"Be a man," says she, and indicated his wench. "With her . . . practise for acting like a man among men. Go on . . . take her to bed. Make yourself brave!"

"And tomorrow?" cries he, flopping down on his knees before her. He was having another of his blubbering fits, wailing and rocking to and fro.

"Tomorrow," says she, with drunken deliberation, "you'll go out to Khalsa –"

"I cannot!" squeals he. "They'll tear me to pieces!"

"You'll go, little brother. And speak to them. Make your peace with 'em . . . all will be right . . ."

"You'll come with me?" he pleaded. "You and the child?"

"Be assured . . . we'll all come. Lal and Tej . . . Mangla here." Her sleepy gaze travelled to me. "Big Englishman, too . . . he'll tell the *Malki lat* and *Jangi lat** how the troops acclaimed their Wazir. Cheered him!" She flourished her cup, spilling liquor again. "So they'll know . . . a man rules in Lahore!"

He stared about vacantly, and his face was that of a frightened ape, all streaked with tears. I doubt if he saw me, for he leaned closer to her, whispering hoarsely: "And then – we'll march on the British? Take them unawares –"

"As God wills," smiles she, and looked at me again – and for an instant she didn't seem drunk at all. She stroked his face, speaking gently, as to a fractious infant.

*"Lord of War", i.e. Gough.

84

"But first . . . the Khalsa. You must take them gifts . . . promises of pay . . ."

"But . . . but . . . how can I pay? Where can I –"

"There is treasure in Delhi, remember," says she, and glanced at me a third time. "Promise them that."

"Perhaps . . . if I gave them *this*?" He fumbled in his belt and brought out a little case on a chain. "I shall wear it tomorrow –"

"Why not? But I must wear it tonight." She snatched it from him, laughing, and held it beyond his reach. "Nay, nay – wait! It is for the dance! Would you like that, little brother-who-wishes-he-weren't-a-brother? Mmh?" She slipped her free hand round his neck, kissing him on the lips. "Tomorrow is tomorrow . . . this is tonight, so we'll take our pleasure, eh?"

She nodded to Mangla, who clapped her hands. The music died away, the dancers skipped off the floor, and there was a general withdrawal by the guests. Jawaheer flopped down beside Jeendan on the cushions, leaning his head against her.

"So government is conducted." Lal Singh spoke in my ear. "Would Hardinge sahib approve, think you? Until tomorrow then, Flashman sahib."

Tej Singh gave another of his greasy chuckles and nudged me. "Remember the saying: 'Below the Sutlej there are brothers and sisters; beyond it, only rivals.' " He went off with Lal Singh.

I didn't know what the devil he meant – nor, in my growing inebriation, did I care. All these gassing intruders were keeping me from the company of that splendid painted trollop who was now wasting her talents in soothing her whining oaf of a brother yonder, cradling him against that superb bosom and pouring drink into him and herself. I was itching to be at her, and even when Mangla came to lead me to the neighbouring booth, I wasn't distracted: I guess my tastes are coarse, and I'd developed a craving for the mistress that wasn't to be satisfied by the maid – who kept the curtains open, anyway, and had a matey standing by to keep me liquored through the entertainment which now began. As I

85

said, most of the courtiers seemed to have gone, leaving the Maharani and her chosen intimates to riot with the performers.

The first of these was a troupe of Kashmiri girls, spanking little creatures in scanty silver armour, with bows and toy swords, who cavorted in a parody of military drill which would have scandalised the General Staff and terrified their horses. This was something from Runjeet's day, Mangla told me: the girls were his female bodyguard, with whom the old lecher had been wont to battle through the night.

Then there was a serious interlude by Indian wrestlers, who are the best on earth outside Cumberland, muscular young bucks who fought like greased lightning, all science and sinew – none of your crude Turkish grunting or the unspeakable Japanese vulgarity. Jeendan, I noticed, roused from her lethargy during these bouts, rising unsteadily to her feet to applaud the falls, and summoning the victors to drink from her cup while she stroked and petted them. Meanwhile their place was taken by female wrestlers, strapping wenches who fought naked (another of old Runjeet's fancies), with the male wrestlers and Kashmiri girls kneeling round the floor, egging them on, and then wrestling with each other, to the inevitable conclusion, while the band played appropriate music. They were all over the floor in no time, seriously impeding a troupe of dancing girls and boys who had come on to frolic in a measure which proved to be a considerable advance on the polka.

Now, you may not credit this, but I'm not much of a hand at orgies. I ain't what you'd call a prude, but I do hold that an Englishman's brothel is his castle, where he should behave according – as many flash-tails as he likes, but none of these troop fornications that the Orientals indulge in. It's not the indecency I mind, but the company of a lot of boozy brutes hallooing and kicking up the deuce of a row when I want to concentrate and give of my best. A regular bacchanalia is something to see, right enough, but I'm with the discriminating Frog who said that one is interesting, but only a cad would make a habit of it.

Still, evil associations corrupt good manners, especially

86

when you're horny as Turvey's bull and full of love-puggle; Mangla'll have to do, thinks I, if I ain't too foxed to carry her out of this bedlam, and I was just looking about for her when there was a great drunken cheer from the floor, and Jeendan came swaying out of her booth, helped by a couple of her dancing-boys. She pushed them away, took a couple of shaky steps, and began to writhe like a Turkish wedding dancer, flaunting her hips and rotating her plump little bottom, flirting the tails of her crimson loin-cloth, giving little squeals of laughter as she turned, stamping, then clapping her hands above her head while the others took up the rhythm and the tom-toms throbbed and the cymbals clashed.

That was my first glimpse of Koh-i-Noor, gleaming in her navel like a live thing as she fluttered her belly in and out – but it didn't hold my attention long, for as she danced she screamed over her shoulder, and one of the dancing-boys leaped in behind her, sliding his hands up her body, unclasping her bodice and letting it fall, fondling her as she danced back into him and slowly turned herself until they were face to face. They writhed against each other while the onlookers shrieked with delight and the music beat ever faster, and then he retreated from her slowly, sweat pouring down his body – and burn me if the stone wasn't in his navel now! How the devil they did it, I can't think; Swedish exercises, perhaps. The boy yelled and pirouetted in triumph, and Jeendan staggered into the arms of one of the wrestlers, giggling while he pawed and kissed her. One of the Kashmiri bints flung herself at the boy, clasping him round the waist and wriggling against him; damned if I could see any better this time, but she came away with the stone in turn, undulating to let the onlookers see it, and then subsiding under another youth, the pair of them heaving to wake the dead – but either he was less expert or something else caught their interest, for the diamond slipped out from between them and rolled across the floor, to cat-calls and groans of disappointment.

I was watching all this through a haze of booze and disbelief, taking another refreshing swig, and thinking, wait till I get back to Belgravia and teach 'em the new dance step,

87

and when I looked again there was Jeendan, struggling and laughing wildly in the arms of another dancing-boy, and the great stone was back on her belly again – hollo, thinks I, someone's been handling in the scrimmage. She seized the boy's wine-cup, drained it and tossed it over her shoulder, and then began to dance towards me, the tawny hourglass body agleam as though it had been oiled, her limbs shimmering in their sheaths of gems. Now she was slapping her bare flanks to the tom-tom beat, drawing her fingers tantalisingly up her jewelled thighs and across her body, lifting the fat round breasts and laughing at me out of that painted harlot's face.

"Will you have it, Englishman? Or shall I keep it for Lal – or Jawaheer? Come, take it, *gora sahib*, my English *bahadur*!"

You mayn't credit it, but I was recalling a line by some poet or other – Elizabethan, I think – who must have witnessed a similar performance, for he wrote of "her brave vibrations each way free."[21] Couldn't have put it better myself, thinks I, as I made a heroic lurch for her and fell on all fours, but the sweet thoughtful girl sank down before me, arms raised from her sides, making her muscles quiver from her fingertips up her arms and beyond, shuddering her bounties at me, and I seized them with a cry of thanksgiving. She squealed, either in delight or to signify "Foul!", whipped her loincloth off and round my neck, and drew my face towards her open mouth.

"Take it, Englishman!" she gasps, and then she had my robe open, thrusting her belly against mine and kissing me as though I were beefsteak and she'd been fasting for a week. And I don't know who the considerate chap was who drew the curtains to, but suddenly we were alone, and somehow I was on my feet with her clinging to me, her legs clasped round my hips, moaning as I settled her in place and began the slow march, up and down, keeping time to the tom-toms, and I fear I broke the rules, for I removed the jewel manually before it did me a mischief. I doubt if she noticed; didn't mention it, anyway.

Well, I can't think when I've enjoyed a dance so much,

unless it was when we set to partners again, an hour or so later, I imagine. I seem to remember we drank considerable in between, and prosed in an incoherent way – most of it escapes me, but I recall distinctly that she said she purposed to send little Dalip to an English public school when he was older, and I said capital, look what it had done for me, but the devil with going up to Oxford, just a nest of bookworms and bestial, and how the deuce did she do that navel exercise with the diamond? So she tried to teach me, giggling through incredible contortions which culminated in her plunging and squirming astride of me as though I were Running Reins with only a furlong to go – and in the middle of it she screamed a summons and two of her Kashmiri girls popped in and urged her on by whipping her with canes – intrusive, I thought, but it was her home ground, after all.

She went to sleep directly we'd passed the post, sprawled on top of me, and the Kashmiris left off lashing her and snickered to each other. I sent them packing, and having heaved her off was composing myself to slumber likewise, when I heard them chattering beyond the curtain, and presently they peeped in again, giggling. Their mistress would wake presently, they said, and it was their duty to see that I was clean, bright, slightly oiled, and ready for service. "Walk-er!" says I, but they insisted, respectfully covering her with a shawl before renewing their pestering of me, telling me I must be bathed and combed and perfumed and made presentable, or there'd be the devil to pay. I saw I'd get no peace, so I lumbered up, cursing, and warning them that their mistress would be out of luck, for I was ruined beyond redemption.

"Wait until we have bathed you," giggles one of the houris. "You will make her scream for mercy."

I doubted that, but told them to lead on, and they conducted me, one holding me up on either side, for I was still well foxed. Beyond the curtains the durbar room was empty now, and the great chandelier was out, with only a few candles on the walls making little pools of light in the gloom. They led me under the staircase, along a dim-lit passage, and down a short flight of stairs to a great stone and marble chamber like a Turkish bath-house; it was in deep shadow about its walls and high ceiling, but in the centre, surrounded by tall slender pillars, was a tiled area with a sunken bath in which water was steaming. There was a brazier close by, and towels piled to hand, while all about stood flagons of oils and soaps and shampoos; altogether it was as luxurious a wallow as you could wish. I asked if this was where the Maharani bathed.

"Not this maharani," says one. "This was the bath of the Lady Chaund Cour, peace be upon her."

"It is altogether finer than our mistress's," says the other, sidling up to me, "and is reserved for those whom she delights to honour." She took a playful tease at me, and her companion drew off my robe, squeaking with admiration. "*Bahadur*, indeed! Oh, fortunate Mai Jeendan!"

She'll be fortunate to get any good out of me after a bath with you two, thinks I, admiring them boozily as they laid by their little bows and arrows and toy swords, and stripped off their silver skirts and breastplates. Lovely little nymphs they were, and there was much playing and giggling as we stepped down into the bath. It was about three feet deep by seven square, half-filled with warm scented water into which I subsided drowsily, letting it lap over my exhausted frame while one of the Kashmiris cradled my head and gently sponged my face and hair, and the other went to work on my feet and then on to my ankles and calves. You're on the right lines, thinks I, and closed my eyes, reflecting on what a delightful time of it Haroun al-Raschid must have had, and wondering if he'd ever become bored and yearned for the life of a jolly waggoner or productive farm labour in the open air. You wouldn't catch Flashy prowling the streets of Baghdad in disguise, looking for adventure, not while there was soap and water at home . . .

The lower wench was soaping my knees now, and I opened my eyes, contemplating the ceiling far above, all coloured Persian designs, with a picture in the centre, of a cove with a stiff neck sitting under an awning and lording it over a platoon of bearded wallahs crouched in supplication. That's your sort, thinks I, whoever you are, some Sikh

90

nabob ... and that reminded me of the names I'd memorised so painfully from Broadfoot's packets: Heera Singh and Dehan Singh and Soochet Singh and Buggerlugs Singh and Chaund Cour and . . . Chaund Cour? Where had I heard that name recently . . .? Why, only a few moments since, from the houris; this was her bathroom – and suddenly a tiny maggot that had been wandering aimlessly through my mind snapped to attention, even as I heard swirling of water and realised that the girl had stopped soaping my knees and was swinging herself nimbly out of the bath ... Chaund Cour's bath ... *Chaund Cour who'd been smashed to pieces while bathing!*

If the wench washing my hair had moved less sharply I'd have been a goner, but when her mate jumped out she dropped my head like a hot brick, and I went under and came out spluttering – to see her in the act of heaving herself out on the tiles, and from the tail of my eye I saw the huge coloured picture in the ceiling overhead start to quiver, with a dreadful scraping sound. For an instant I was frozen, sprawled in the water, and it can only have been instinct that galvanised my flaccid muscles, so that I thrust myself out of the water, turning and clutching for the edge of the bath, my hand closing on the girl's ankle. That hold saved me from toppling back, and gave me a purchase to hurl myself out on to the tiles, while she was catapulted back into the water, her scream of terror lost in a deafening grinding thunder like an avalanche, followed by an almighty crash that seemed to shake the whole building and made the tiles start from their settings beneath my face. I rolled away with a yell of terror, sprawling on the wet tiles and staring back in disbelief.

Where the bath had been there was a flat expanse of rough stone, filling the cavity like a huge plug flush with the surrounding tiles. From that monstrous square of rock great rusty chains snaked up, clanking to and fro, into a gaping hole in the patterned ceiling. Foam was gushing up in a curtain from the narrow fissures between the fallen slab and the sides of the bath, washing over me in a wave, and even as I stared in horror it continued to ooze out, pink at first and then a hideous crimson. Beyond the bath the second Kashmiri was cowering against a pillar, her mouth wide in scream after scream. She turned and ran, water flying from her bare body, and then stopped dead, her shrieks changing to a terrified wail.

Three men were standing just clear of the shadows on that side, drawn scimitars in their hands. They wore only loose grey *pyjamy* trousers and great wide hoods so deep that their faces were invisible; the girl shrank away from them, blubbering and covering her face; she slipped and fell on the wet tiles and tried to scramble away while they stood like grey statues, and then one stepped forward, lightly hefting his sword, she bounded to her feet, screeching as she turned to run, but before she'd gone a step his point was through her back; it came out like a ghastly silver needle between her breasts, and she pitched forward lifeless on the stone block. Then they were flitting towards me in dead silence, expert assassins of whom two skirted wide to take me in flank while the third came straight for me, his blood-smeared blade out before him. I turned to run, slipped, and came down headlong.

Cowardice has its uses. I'd be long dead without it, for it's driven me to try, in blind panic, ploys which no thinking man would even attempt. A brave man would have scrambled up to run or fling himself at the nearest enemy bare-handed; only Flashy, landing arse over tip on one of the little piles of gear discarded by the Kashmiri girls, would have grabbed at her pathetic tinsel bow, snatched a dart from its quiver, fumbled it gibbering on to the string and let fly at the leading thug as he came leaping over the girl's corpse at me, swinging up his scimitar. It was only a fragile toy, but it was tight-strung, and that small shaft must have been sharp as a chisel, for it sank to the flights in his midriff and he twisted howling in mid-air, his scimitar clashing on the tiles before me. I grabbed it, knowing I was done for, with one of the flank men driving at me, but I managed to turn his thrust and hurl myself sideways, expecting to feel his mate's point searing into my back. There was a yell and clash of steel behind me as I landed on my shoulder and rolled over and up, slashing blindly and bawling like an idiot for help.

Wasted breath, for it had arrived. The other flank man was desperately trying to parry the sweep of a Khyber knife in the hand of a tall robed newcomer – which with a scimitar is rather like opposing a pea-shooter to a rifle. One slash and the scimitar blade was a shattered stump, another and the thug was down with a cloven skull – and the man whose thrust I'd parried leaped back and was off like a hare, dodging for the shadows. The robed apparition turned from his victim without undue haste, took one long stride and brought over his sword-arm like a fast bowler, letting the Khyber knife go; it turned once in the air and drove into the fugitive's back, he hurtled against a pillar, clinging to it with that dreadful cleaver imbedded in his body, and slid slowly to the floor. Twenty seconds earlier I'd been having my knees washed.

The robed man strode past me, recovered his knife, and cursed as blood splashed his coat – and only then did I realise it was a crimson garment in the tartan of the 79th. He stalked back, hunkering down to wash his blade in the water lapping over the tiles, and surveyed the shambles where the bath had been, the great rock that filled it, and the dangling chains.

"Well, I'll be a son of a bitch," says he. "So that's how they did for old lady Chaund Cour. No wonder we never saw the body – guess she didn't look like much with *that* on top of her." He stood up and barked at me. "Well, sir? You aim to stand around bollock-naked and take your death of cold? Or would you prefer to make tracks before the coroner gets here?"

The words were English. The accent was pure American.

Since I've seen a Welshman in a top hat leading a Zulu impi, and have myself ridden in an Apache war party in paint and breech-clout, I dare say I shouldn't have been surprised to find that Gurdana Khan, the complete Khyberie hillman, could talk the lingo of Brother Jonathan – there were some damned odd fellows about in the earlies, I can tell you. But the circumstances were unusual, you'll allow, and I probably gaped for several seconds before scrambling into my robe. Then reaction seized me, and I vomited, while he stood glowering like a Nonconformist at the three hooded bodies, and the naked white corpse of the poor little Kashmiri slut with the bloody water lapping round her. I say poor slut – she'd done her damnedest to have me squashed flatter than a fluke. The man I'd shot was writhing about, wailing in agony.

"Let him linger," growls Gurdana Khan. "Mistreatment of women is something I cannot endure! Come away."

He strode off to a staircase hidden in the shadows on the other side of the bath-house, ushering me impatiently ahead of him. We ascended, and he chivvied me along miles of turning passages, ignoring my incoherent questions, then across a lofty hall, through a guardroom where black-robed irregulars lounged, and at last into a spacious, comfortable room for all the world like a bachelor's den at home, with prints and trophies on the walls, book cases, and fine leather easy chairs. I was shivering with chill and shock and bewilderment; he sat me down, threw a shawl over my legs, and poured out two stiff pegs – malt whisky, if you please. He laid by his Khyber knife and pulled off his *puggaree* – he *was* a Pathan, though, with that close-cropped skull, hawk face, and grizzled beard, for all he grunted "*Slàinte*" as he

94

lifted his tumbler, first clamping his neck in that strange iron collar I'd seen in the afternoon – dear God, was it only twelve hours ago? Having drunk, he stood scowling down at me like a headmaster at an erring fag.

"Now see here, Mr Flashman – where the devil were you this evening? We combed the palace, even looked under your bed, godammit! Well, sir?"

I made no sense of this – all I knew was that someone was trying to murder me, but plainly it wasn't this cross-grained fellow . . . so I'd risked horrible death hanging out of windows while he and his gang had been looking for me to *protect* me, by the sound of it! I removed the glass from my chattering teeth.

"I . . . I was out. But . . . who on earth are you?"

"Alexander Campbell Gardner!" snaps he. "Formerly artillery instructor to the Khalsa, presently guard commander to the Maharaja, and recently at your service – and think yourself lucky!"

"But you're an American!"

"That I am." He fixed me with an eye like a gimlet. "From the territory of Wisconsin."

I must have been a picture of idiocy, for he clapped that iron object to his neck again, gulped whisky, and rasped:

"Well, sir? You passed that word, as Broadfoot instructed you should, in an emergency. *When*, you ask? Dammit, to the little Maharaja, and again to old Ram Singh! It reached me – no matter how – and I came directly to help you, and not a hair of you in sight! Next I hear, you're with the Maharani, playing the Devil and Jenny Golightly! Was that intelligent conduct, sir, when you knew Jawaheer Singh was out to cut your throat?" He emptied his glass, clashed his iron clamp on the table, and glared. "How the dooce did you know he was after you, anyway?"

This tirade had me all adrift. "I didn't know any such thing! Mr Gardner, I'm at a loss –"

"Colonel Gardner! Then why the blue blazes did you sound the alarm? Hollering Wisconsin to everyone you met, concern it!"

"Did I? I may have said it inadvertently –"

95

"Inadvertently? Upon my soul, Mr Flashman!"

"But I don't understand . . . it's all mad! Why should Jawaheer want to kill me? He don't even know me – barely met the fellow, and he was tight as Dick's hatband!" An appalling thought struck me. "Why, they weren't his people – they were the Maharani's! Her slave-girls! They lured me to that bloody bathroom – they knew what was to happen! She must have ordered them –"

"How dare you, sir!" So help me, it's what he said, with his whiskers crackling. "To suggest that she would . . . What, after the . . . the kindness she had shown you? A fine thing that would be! I tell you those Kashmiris were bribed and coerced by Jawaheer and by Jawaheer alone – those were his villains down there, sent to silence the girls once you'd been disposed of! D'you think I don't know 'em? The Maharani, indeed!" He was in a fine indignation, right enough. "I'm not saying," he went on, "that she's the sort of young woman I'd take home to meet mother . . . but you mind this, sir!" He rounded on me. "With all her weaknesses – of which you've taken full advantage – Mai Jeendan is a charming and gracious lady and the best hope this god-abandoned territory has seen since Runjeet Singh! You'll remember that, by thunder, if you and I are to remain friends!"

I wasn't alone in my enthusiasm for the lady, it seemed, although I guessed his was of a more spiritual variety. But I was as much in the dark as ever.

"Very well, you say it was Jawaheer – why the devil should he want to murder me?"

"Because he wants a war with the British! That's why! And the surest way to start one is to have a British emissary kiboshed right here in Lahore! Why, man, Gough would be over the Sutlej with fifty thousand bayonets before you could say Jack Robinson – John Company and the Khalsa would be at grips . . . *that's* what Jawaheer wants, don't you see?"

I didn't, and said so. "If he wants a war – why doesn't he just order the Khalsa to march on India? They're spoiling for a fight with us, ain't they?"

"Sure they are – but not with Jawaheer leading them! They've never had any use for him, so the only way he can get 'em to fight is if the British strike first. But dammit, you won't oblige him, however much he provokes you along the border – and Jawaheer has gotten desperate. He's bankrupt, the Khalsa hates and distrusts him and is ready to skin him alive for Peshora's death, they hold him prisoner in his own palace, his balls are in the mangle!" He took a deep breath. "Don't you know anything, Mr Flashman? Jawaheer *needs* a war, *now*, to keep the Khalsa occupied and save his own skin. That's why he tried to put you out with the bath water tonight, confound it, don't you see?"

Well, put that way, it made sense. Everyone seemed to want a bloody war except Hardinge and yours truly – but I could see why Jawaheer's need was more urgent than most. I'd heard the Khalsa's opinion of him that afternoon, and seen the almighty funk he was in. That's what he'd meant, by God, when he'd pointed at me and yelled that the British would have *cause* to come – the evil, vicious bastard! He'd been lying in wait for my arrival . . . and suddenly a dreadful, incredible suspicion rushed in on me.

"My God! Did Broadfoot *know* that Jawaheer would try to kill me? Did he send me here to –"

He gave a barking laugh. "Say, you have a high opinion of your betters, don't you? First Mai Jeendan, now Major Broadfoot! No, sir – that is not his style! Why, if he had foreseen such a thing . . ." He broke off, frowning, then shook his head. "No, Jawaheer hatched his plot in the last few hours, I reckon – your arrival must have seemed to him a heaven-sent opportunity. He'd have taken it, too, if I hadn't been on your tail from the moment you arrived in the durbar room." He blew out his cheeks in disbelief. "I still can't get over that damned bath! You won't linger among the soap-suds again, I reckon."

That was enough to bring me to my feet, reaching for his decanter without even a by-your-leave. God, what a tarantula's nest Broadfoot had plunged me into! I still couldn't put it straight in my mind, numb with the whirlwind of the last few hours. Had I fallen asleep over *Crotchet Castle* and

97

dreamed it all – my balcony acrobatics, Mangla and Jawa-heer and the dazzling spectacle of the durbar room, the drunken ecstatic coupling with Jeendan, the horror of the descending stone, the furious bloody scramble in which five lives were snuffed out in a bare minute, this incredible tartan Nemesis with his Khyber knife and Yankee twang,[22] eyeing me bleakly as I punished his malt? Belatedly, I mumbled my thanks, adding that Broadfoot was lucky to have such an agent in Lahore. He snapped my head off.

"I'm not his confounded agent! I'm his friend – and so far as my duty to the Maharaja allows, I'm sympathetic to British interest. Broadfoot knows I'll help, which is why he gave you my watchword." He restrained himself with diffi-culty. "Inadvertently, by jiminy! But that's all, Mr Flash-man. You and I will now go our separate ways, you won't address or even recognise me henceforth except as Gurdana Khan –"

"Henceforth? But I'll be going back – man alive, I can't stay here now, with Jawaheer –"

"The devil you can't! It's your duty, isn't it? Just because the war isn't going to start tomorrow doesn't mean it won't happen eventually. Oh, it will – and that's when Broadfoot needs you here." For someone who wasn't Broadfoot's man, he seemed to know a deal about my duty. "Besides, after tonight you're in clear water. That bath-house will tell its own story: everyone will know Jawaheer tried to rub you out – and why. But no one will breathe a word about it – including yourself." Seeing me about to protest, he cut in: "Not a word! It would cause a scandal that might start Jawaheer's war for him – so mum, Mr Flashman. And don't fret yourself – now that you're under Mai Jeendan's protec-tion, the worst Jawaheer'll dare give you is a black look."

I'd heard this kind of assurance before. "Why the blazes should she protect me?"

"Now, don't come the delicate with me, sir!" He stabbed a lean finger at me, Uncle Sam with a Kandahar haircut. "You know right well why, and so does every tattle-tale in this blasted royal bordello! Oh, sure, she has her political reasons, too. Well, just keep your mouth shut and be thank-

98

ful." He nodded grimly. "And now, if you're recovered, we'll return you to your quarters. And don't say Wisconsin again unless you mean it. *Jemadar, idderao!*"*

An under-officer appeared like magic, and Gardner told him I was to have a couple of discreet shadows henceforth. He asked if anyone had been seeking me, and the *jemadar* said only my orderly.

Gardner frowned. "Who's he – one of Broadfoot's Pathans? I didn't see him arrive with you."

I explained that Jassa had a habit of vanishing when most needed, and that he wasn't a Pathan – or the dervish he claimed to be.

"A dervish?" He stared. "What does he look like?"

I described Jassa, down to the vaccination mark, and he swore in astonishment and took a turn round the room.

"I'll be . . . no, it couldn't be! I haven't heard of him for years – and even he wouldn't have the hard neck . . . You're sure he's a Broadfoot man? And no beard, eh? Well, we'll see! *Jemadar*, find the orderly, tell him the *husoor* wants him, double quick – and if he asks, say I'm out at Maian Mir. You sit down, Mr Flashman . . . I suspect this may interest you."

After the events of the night, I doubted if Lahore could hold any further surprises – but d'you know, what followed was perhaps the most astonishing encounter between two men that ever I saw – and I was at Appomattox, remember, and saw Bismarck and Gully face to face with the mauleys, and held the shotgun when Hickok confronted Wesley Hardin. But what took place in Gardner's room laid over any of them.

We waited in silence until the *jemadar* knocked, and Jassa slid in, shifty as always. The moment his eye fell on the grim tartan figure he started as though he'd trod on hot coals, but then he recovered and looked inquiringly to me while Gardner viewed him almost in admiration.

"Not bad, Josiah," says he. "You may have the guiltiest conscience east of Suez, but by God you've sure got the

*"Lieutenant, come here!"

99

brazenest forehead to go with it. I'd never ha' known you, clean-shaven." His voice hardened to a bark. "Now then – what's the game? Speak up, *jildi!*"

"None o' your goddam' business!" snaps Jassa. "I'm a political agent in British service – ask him if you don't believe me! And that puts me outside your touch, Alick Gardner! So now!"

Said in Pushtu, I'd have held it a good answer – reckless, from what I'd seen of Gardner, but about what you'd expect from a Khyberie tough. But it was said in English – with an accent even more American than Gardner's own! I couldn't credit my ears – *one* bloody Yankee promenading about in Afghan fig was bad enough – but two? And the second one my own orderly, courtesy of Broadfoot . . . if I sat open-mouthed, d'you wonder? Gardner exploded.

"British political, my eye! Why, you crooked Quaker, you, if you're working for Broadfoot it must mean he doesn't know who you are! And he doesn't, I'll bet! No, because you're before his time, Josiah – you skipped out of Kabul before the British arrived, and wise you were! Sekundar Burnes knew you, though – for the double-dealing rascal you are! Pollock knows you, too – he ran you out of Burma, didn't he? Damn me if there's a town between Rangoon and Basra that you haven't left a shirt in! So, let's have it – what's your lay this time?"

"I don't answer to you," says Jassa. "Mr Flashman, if you care for this, I don't. You know I'm Major Broadfoot's agent –"

"Hold your tongue or I'll have it out!" roars Gardner. "Outside my touch, are you? We'll see! You know this man as Jassa," says he to me. "Well, let me perform the honours by presenting Dr Josiah Harlan of Philadelphia, former packet-rat, impostor, coiner, spy, traitor, revolutionary, and expert in every rascality he can think of – and can't he think, just? No common blackguard, mind you – Prince of Ghor once, weren't you, Josiah, and unfrocked governor of Gujerat, to say nothing of being a pretender (it's the truth, Flashman) to the throne of Afghanistan, no less! You know what they call this beauty up in the high hills? The Man Who

100

Would Be King!" He came forward, thumbs in his belt, and stuck his jaw in Jassa's face. "Well, you have one minute to tell me what you would be in Lahore, doctor! And don't say you're an orderly, pure and simple, because you've never been either!"

Jassa didn't move a muscle of his ugly, pock-marked face, but turned to me with a little inclination of his head. "Leaving aside the insults, part of what he says is true. I was Prince of Ghor – but Colonel Gardner's memory is at fault. He hasn't told you that Lord Amherst personally appointed me surgeon to His Britannic Majesty's forces in the Burmese campaign –"

"*Assistant* surgeon, stealing spirits in an artillery field hospital!" scoffs Gardner.

"– or that I held high military command and the governorship of three districts under his late majesty, Raja Runjeet Singh –"

"Who kicked you out for counterfeiting, you damned scamp! Go ahead, tell him how you were ambassador to Dost Mohammed, and tried to start a revolution in Afghanistan, and sold him out more times than he could count! Tell him how you suborned Muhammed Khan to betray Peshawar to the Sikhs! Tell him how you lined your pockets on the Kunduz expedition, and cheated Reffi Bey, and had the gall to plant the Stars and Stripes on the Indian Caucasus, damn your impudence!" He paused for breath while Jassa stood cool as a trout. "But why waste time? Tell him how you passed yourself off on Broadfoot. I'd enjoy hearing that, myself!"

Jassa gave him an inquiring look, as though to make sure he was done, and addressed me. "Mr Flashman, I owe you an explanation, but not an apology. Why should I have told you what your own chief didn't? Broadfoot enlisted me more than a year ago; how much of my history he knows, I can't say – and I don't care. He knows his business and he trusts me, or I wouldn't be here. If you doubt me now, write to him, telling him what you've heard tonight . . . like everyone who's mixed in diplomacy in these parts, I'm used to having my reputation blown upon –"

101

"So hard that it's scattered all over the bloody Himalayas!" snarls Gardner. "If you're so all-fired trustworthy . . . where were you tonight when Jawaheer tried to kill Flashman?"

He was clever, Gardner. Knowing his man as he did, the question must have been in his mind from the first, but he'd held it back to take Jassa off guard. He succeeded; Jassa gaped, stared from Gardner to me and back, and gasped hoarsely: "What the hell d'you mean?"

Gardner told him in a few fierce sentences, watching him lynx-eyed, and Jassa was a sight to see. The bounce had quite gone out of him, and all he could do was rub his face and mutter "Jesus!" before turning helplessly to me.

"I . . . I don't know . . . I must have been asleep, sir! After I pulled you on to the balcony, and you went off to the durbar room . . . well, I reckoned you were there for the night . . ." He avoided my eye. "I . . . I went to bed, woke up an hour ago, saw you hadn't returned, asked around for you, but no one had seen you . . . then the *jemadar* came for me just now. That's the truth." He rubbed his face again, and caught Gardner's eye. "Christ, you don't think –"

"No, I don't!" growls Gardner, and shook his head at me. "Whatever else you are – and that's plenty – you're not a murderer. And if you were, you'd be in the tall timber this minute. No, Josiah," says he with grim satisfaction, "you're just a lousy bodyguard – and I suggest Mr Flashman reports that to Major Broadfoot, too. And until he gets a reply, you can cool your heels in a cell, doctor –"

"The hell I can!" cries Jassa, and turns to me. "Mr Flashman . . . I don't know what to say, sir! I've failed you, I know that – and I'm sorry for it. If Major Broadfoot sees fit to recall me . . . well, so be it. But it's not *his* business, sir!" He pointed at Gardner. "As far as he's concerned, I'm under British protection, and entitled to immunity. And with respect, sir – in spite of my failure tonight . . . I'm still at your service. You mustn't disown me, sir."

Well, I'd had a long day, and night. The shock of discovering that my Afghan orderly was an American medical man[23] (and no doubt as big a villain as Gardner said) was

102

quite small beer after all the rest. No more of a shock than Gardner himself, really. One thing was sure: Jassa, or Josiah, was Broadfoot's man, and he was right, I couldn't disown him on Gardner's suspicions. I said so, and much to my surprise, Gardner didn't shout me down, although he gave me a long hard stare.

"After what I've told you about him? Well, sir, it's on your own head. It's possible you won't rue the day, but I doubt it." He turned to Jassa. "As for you, Josiah . . . I don't know what brings you back to the Punjab in another of your disguises. I know it wasn't Jawaheer, or anything as simple as British political work . . . no, it's some dirty little frolic of your own, isn't it? Well, you forget it, doctor – because if you don't, immunity or not, I'll send you back to Broadfoot by tying you over a gun and blowing you clear to Simla. You can count on that Good-night, Mr Flashman."

The *jemadar* led us back to my quarters through a maze of corridors that was no more confused than my mind; I was dog-tired and still mortally shaken, and had neither the wit nor the will to question my newly-revealed Afghan-American orderly, who kept up a muttered stream of apology and justification the whole way. He'd never have forgiven himself if any harm had come to me, and I must write to Broadfoot instanter to establish his bona fides; he wouldn't rest until Gardner's calumnies had been disproved.

"Alick means no harm – we've known each other for years, but truth is, you see, he's jealous, us both being American and all, and he hasn't risen any too high, while I've been prince and ambassador, as he said – course, fate hasn't been too kind lately, which is why I took any honourable employment that came . . . God, I've no words of excuse or apology, sir, for my lapse tonight . . . what must you think, what will Broadfoot think? Say, though, I'd like him to understand about my losing my governorship – it wasn't coining, no sir! I dabble in chemistry, see, and there was this experiment that went wrong . . ."

He was still chuntering when we reached my door, where I was reassured to see two stalwart constables, presumably sent by Bhai Ram Singh. Jassa – with that ugly frontier dial and dress I could think of him by no other name – swore he'd be on hand too, from this moment, closer than a brother, why, he'd bed down right here in the passage . . .

I closed my door, head swimming with fatigue, and rested a moment in blessed solitude and quiet before walking unsteadily through the arch to the bedchamber, where two lights burned dimly either side of the pillow – and stopped, the hairs rising on my neck. There was someone in the bed, and a drift of perfume on the air, and before I could move or cry out, a woman whispered out of the gloom.

"Mai Jeendan must have eaten her fill," says Mangla. "It is almost dawn."

I stepped closer, staring. She was lying naked beneath a flimsy veil of black gauze spread over her like a sheet – they've nothing to learn about erotic display in the Punjab, I can tell you. I looked down at her, swaying, and it shows how fagged out I was, for I asked, like a damfool:

"What are you doing here?"

"Do you not remember?" murmurs she, and I saw her teeth gleam as she smiled up from the pillow, her black hair spread across it like a fan. "After the mistress has supped, it is the maid's turn."

"Oh, my God," says I. "I ain't hungry."

"Are you not?" whispers she. "Then I must whet your appetite." And she sat up, slow and languid, stretching that transparent veil tight against her body, pouting at me. "Will you taste, *husoor*?"

For a moment I was tempted. Altogether used up, fit only for the knacker's yard, I wanted sleep as I wanted salvation. But as I contemplated that magnificent substance stirring beneath the gauze, I thought: to thine own self be true, and put temptation aside.

"Right you are, my dear," says I. "Got any more of that jolly drink, have you?"

She laughed softly and reached out for the cup beside the bed.

If you've read *Robinson Crusoe* you may recall a passage where he weighs up his plight on the desert island like a book-keeper, evil on one side, good on t'other. Dispiriting stuff, mainly, in which he croaks about solitude, but concludes that things might be worse, and God will see him through, with luck. Optimism run mad, if you ask me, but then I've never been shipwrecked, much, and philosophy in the face of tribulation ain't my line. But I did use his system on waking that second day in Lahore, because so much had happened in such short space that I needed to set my mind straight. Thus:

EVIL	GOOD
I am cut off in a savage land which will be at war with my own country presently.	I enjoy diplomatic immunity, for what it's worth, and am in good health, but ruined.
An attempt has been made to assassinate me. These buggers would sooner murder people than eat their dinners.	It failed, and I am under the protection of the queen bee, who rides like a rabbit. Also, Gardner will look out for me.
My orderly turns out to be the greatest villain since Dick Turpin, and is an American to boot.	Broadfoot chose him, and since I see no reason why he should be hostile to me, I shall watch him like a hawk.
Damn Broadfoot for landing me in this stew, when I could have been safe at home rogering Elspeth.	Rations and quarters are A1, and Mangla sober is a capital mount, though she don't compare to Jeendan drunk.
If I were a praying man, the Almighty would hear from me in no uncertain terms, and much good it would do me.	Being a pagan (attached C of E) with no divine resources, I shall tread uncommon wary and keep my pepperbox handy.

That was my accounting, cast up in the drowsy hour after Mangla slipped away like a lovely ghost at daybreak, and it could have been worse. My first task must be to make a searching examination of the bold Jassa, or Josiah, before sending off a cypher about him to Broadfoot. So I had him in while I shaved, watching that crafty hill figurehead in my mirror, and listening to the plausible Yankee patter that came out of it. Oddly enough, after the character Gardner had given him, I felt inclined to take him at face value. You see, I'm a knave myself, and know that we wrong 'uns ain't *always* bent on mischief; it seemed to me that Jassa, the professional soldier of fortune, was quite likely just marking time in Broadfoot's employ, as he'd claimed, until something better turned up. The queerest fish swim into the political mill, with not too many questions asked, and I felt I could accept if not trust him. Like Gardner, I was sure he'd had no hand in the plot against my life – if he'd wanted me dead he could have let me drop from the balcony instead of saving me.

It was comforting, too, to have one of my own kind alongside me – and one who knew the Punjab and its politics inside out. "Though how you hoped to pass unrecognised, I don't see," says I. "If you were so high under Runjeet, half the country must know you, surely?"

"That was six years ago, behind a full set o' beard an' whiskers," says he. "Clean-shaven, I reckoned to get by – 'cept with Alick, but I planned to keep out o' his way. But it don't matter," he added coolly, "there are no reward notices out for Joe Harlan, here or anywhere else."

He was such a patent rascal that I took to him – and even now I won't say I was wrong. He had a fine political nose, too, and had been using it about the Fort that morning.

"Jawaheer seems to be in luck. The whole palace knows he tried to get you, and the talk was that the Maharani would have him arrested. But she had him to her boudoir first thing today, all smiles, embraced him, and drank toasts to his reconciliation to the Khalsa, her maids say. It seems Dinanath and Azizudeen have made his peace for him; they were out talking to the *panches* at dawn, and Jawaheer's

106

appearance this afternoon will be a formality. He and the whole royal family will review the troops – and you'll be invited, no doubt so that you can pass word to Broadfoot that all's well with the Lahore durbar." He grinned. "Yes, sir, you'll have quite a packet of news for Simla. How d'you send out your cyphers – through Mangla?"

"As you said yourself, doctor, why should I tell you what Broadfoot didn't? Are you really a doctor, by the way?"

"No diploma," says he frankly, "but I studied surgery back in Pennsylvania. Yep . . . I'll bet it's Mangla; that little puss is in everyone's pocket, so why not John Company's? A word of advice, though: cover her all you've a mind to, but don't trust her – or Mai Jeendan." And before I could damn his impudence he took himself off to change, as he put it, into his mess kit.

That meant his best robes, for our durbar appearance at noon, with Flashy in full fig of frock coat and go-to-meeting roof, making my official bow to little Dalip enthroned in state; you'd not have recognised the lively imp of yesterday in the regal little figure all in silver, nodding his aigretted turban most condescendingly when I was presented by Lal Singh, who was second minister. Jawaheer was nowhere in sight, but Dinanath, old Bhai Ram Singh, and Azizudeen were present, solemn as priests. It was eerie, knowing that they were all well aware that their Wazir had tried to murder me a few hours earlier, and that I'd rioted with their Maharani in this very chamber. There wasn't so much as a flicker on the handsome, bearded faces; damned good form, the Sikhs.

Behind Dalip's throne hung a fine lace curtain, the purdah of his mother, the Maharani – it being the custom of quality Indian ladies to seclude themselves, when they ain't belly-dancing at orgies, that is. By the curtain stood Mangla, unveiled but most modestly dressed, and formal as though we'd never laid eyes on each other. Her duty was to relay conversation to and from her mistress behind the screen, and she did it most properly, welcoming me to Lahore, inviting blessings on my work, and finally, as Jassa had forecast, bidding me to attend his majesty when he reviewed the Khalsa that afternoon.

107

"You shall ride on an elephant!" squeaks the said majesty, lapsing from kingly dignity for a moment, and then stiffening before the reproving glances of his court. I said gravely that I'd be honoured beyond measure, he shot me a shy little smile, and then I backed from the presence, turning and resuming my tile only when I reached the rug in the doorway, as form demanded. To my surprise, Lal Singh came after me, taking my arm, all smiles, and insisting on giving me a conducted tour of the arsenal and foundry, which were close by the Sleeping Palace. Since I'd spent half the night sporting with his lady love, I found this affability disconcerting, until he took me flat aback by speaking of her with alarming frankness.

"Mai Jeendan had hoped to come out from purdah to greet you after the durbar," confides he. "Alas, she is a little drunk from toasting her abominable brother, in a vain effort to put some courage into him. You can have no notion what a poltroon he is! The thought of facing the Khalsa quite unmans him, even now when all is settled. But she will certainly send for you afterwards; she has important messages for the envoy of the Sirkar."

I said I was at her majesty's service, and he smiled.

"So I have heard." Seeing me stare, he laughed aloud. "My dear friend, you look at me as though I were a rival! Believe me, with Mai Jeendan there is no such thing! She is no one's mistress but her own. Let us fortunate fellows thank God for it. Now, you shall give me your opinion of our Punjabi muskets – are they not a match for Brown Bess?"

At the time, I was all suspicion; only later did I realise that Lal Singh meant every word he said – and Mai Jeendan was the least of what he wanted to tell me that day. When we'd examined the small arms, stocked in impressive numbers, and the forges, and the casting of a great white-hot nine-pounder gun, and the rain of lead hitting the steaming vats in the shot tower, and I'd agreed that the Khalsa's armoury compared well with our own, he took me by the arm as we walked, most confidential.

"You are right," says he, "but arms are not everything.

On the day, victory and defeat rest with the generals. If ever the Khalsa took the field, it might well be under my leadership, and Tej Singh's." He sighed, smiling, and shook his head. "Sometimes I wonder how we should acquit ourselves against . . . oh, against such a seasoned campaigner as your Sir Hugh Gough. What would you think, Flashman sahib?"

Wondering, I said that Gough wasn't the most scientific soldier since Boney, but he was probably the toughest. Lal Singh nodded, stroking his beard, and then laughed merrily. "Well, we must hope it is never put to the test, eh? Now, we set out for Maian Mir in an hour – may I offer you some refreshment?"

They're so devious, these folk, you never know what they're up to. Was he hinting that if it came to war, he was ready to fight a cross? Or trying a bamboozle? Or just gassing? Whatever his purpose, he must know that nothing he said could make Gough drop his guard. It was all most interesting, and gave me food for thought until the horns sounded to signal the departure of the royal progress to Maian Mir.

The procession was drawn up outside the Bright Gate, and when I saw it I thought: that's India. It was Arabian Nights come to life: two battalions of the Palace Guard in their red and yellow silks, and in their midst half a dozen elephants, gorgeously caparisoned in blue and gold saddlecloths that swept the ground, jewelled harness on their heads, their tusks and even the mahouts' goads tipped with gold. The howdahs were little coloured palaces topped with minarets and silk canopies which stirred as the great beasts swayed and bellowed, the keepers quieting them as they waited for their royal freight. Horsemen in steel casques that shone like silver in the sunlight rode up and down the elephant line, their sabres drawn; they converged like clockwork to form a lane from the gate for porters who came bearing enormous panniers brimming with coin, preceded by chamberlains who supervised the strapping of the panniers to the howdahs of the third and second elephants. When some of the coins fell in a tinkling shower to the dust, there was a great "Oo-h!" from the crowd assembled to see the show; two or three of the horsemen leaned from their saddles, scooping up the rupees and hurling them over the heads of the rigid guardsmen to the mob, who yelled and scuffled for them – for a country that was supposed to be short of blunt, there seemed to be no lack of *pice** to fling to the beggars.

Two of the chamberlains mounted the third elephant, and now came a little knot of courtiers, led by Lal Singh, all brave in green and gold; they mounted into the fifth howdah, and a chamberlain who'd been shepherding Jassa and me indicated that we should mount the ladder on the fourth beast. We climbed up and as I seated myself the muted grumble of the crowd took on a new note – I knew exactly why: they were asking each other, who's the foreigner, then, who takes precedence over the royal courtiers? He must be an infidel of note, doubtless the English Queen's son, or a Jewish moneylender from Karachi; well, give the unbelieving swine a cheer. I doffed my tile, looking out over that astonishing scene: ahead, the great mammoths with their swaying howdahs, and either side the horsemen, the yellow Guards, and beyond a vast sea of brown faces; the walls flanking the Bright Gate were black with spectators, as were the buildings behind, with the great column of the Summum Boorj towering over all. The baying of the crowd rose again, and now there was a disturbance below my elephant, the yellow line of Guardsmen breaking to let in a wild figure who capered and waved to me: he was a burly Ghazi of a fellow, bandoliered and bearded to the eyebrows, yelling in Pushtu:

"Ai-ee, Bloody Lance! It is I, Shadman Khan! Remember me? *Salaam*, soldier, heep-heep-heep-hoorah!"

Well, I didn't remember him, but plainly he was someone from the old days, so I lifted my lid again, calling: "Salaam, Shadman Khan!" and he shouted with delight and yelled, in English: "Stand fast, foortee-foorth!" – and in an instant I was looking down on the bloody snow over Gandamack, with the remnants of the 44th being cut down by the

*Coppers.

110

tribesmen swarming over their position . . . and I wondered which side he'd been on then. (I've since remembered that there was a Shadman Khan among those ruffians who held me in Gul Shah's dungeon, and yet another among the band who saved me from the Thugs at Jhansi in '57 and stole our horses on the way to Cawnpore. I wonder if they were all the same man. It has no bearing on my present tale, anyway; it was just an incident at the Bright Gate. But I think it was the same man; everybody changed sides in the old days.)

Now there was a sudden hush, broken by the strains of sweet music, and out from the Bright Gate came a native band, followed by a tiny figure in cloth of gold, mounted on a white pony; a thunderous *salaam* rolled out from the waiting crowd: "Maharaj'! Maharaj'!" as little Dalip was lifted from his saddle by a richly-clad courtier whom I recognised with a shock as Jawaheer Singh. He seemed sober enough now, and I've never seen a man grin so eagerly as he perched Dalip on his shoulder and gestured to the crowd, inviting their acclaim. They roared willingly enough, but I detected an undertone of groans which I imagine were meant for Jawaheer himself. He mounted with Dalip to the first elephant, and then out from the gate stalks Gardner, staring grimly right and left, and followed by a party of his black robes, guarding a *palki** beside which Mangla walked unveiled. It stopped, and she drew the curtains and handed out the Maharani Jeendan: she was all in shimmering white, and although she wore a gauzy purdah veil I believe I'd have recognised that hourglass figure anywhere. She'd got over her drunk, by the looks of it, for she walked steadily to the second elephant, and Gardner handed her up to an absolute bellow of cheering – there's no doubt about it, all the world loves Nell Gwynn. Mangla mounted beside her, and then Gardner stepped back and surveyed the procession, your good bodyguard alert for trouble. His eye passed over me and lingered for a moment on Jassa; then he had given the signal, the band struck up a march, the elephant lurched and bellowed beneath us, and off we swayed with a great creak-

*Litter, usually curtained.

111

ing of harness and jingling of outriders, while the mob roared again and the dust swirled up from the tramp of the Guardsmen.

We skirted under the high city walls, thronged with folk who threw blossoms and shouted blessings on the little Maharaja; they were swarming like bees on the ramparts of the Kashmir Gate, and then as we rounded the angle of the wall beneath the huge Half-moon Battery there came from far ahead the report of cannon – a continuous rumble of firing, one gun after another (a hundred and eighty, I'm told, though I didn't count 'em). The elephants squealed in alarm, and the howdahs bucked from side to side so hard that we had to cling on to prevent being pitched out, with the mahouts flat on their beasts' heads, steadying them with goad and voice. As we came under the Delhi Gate the firing ceased, to be replaced by a distant measured tread, thousands of marching men, and I craned out to look as the procession swung away from the city, and saw an astonishing sight.

Coming towards us, all in immaculate line, were four battalions of the Khalsa, a solid wall of infantry half a mile from wing to wing, the dust rising before them in a low cloud, their drummers and standard bearers to the fore. I didn't know it then, but they were absolutely marching on Lahore to bring Jawaheer out by force, having lost patience after waiting for him all day; you could almost read the purpose in the grim inexorable approach of that disciplined host, the green jackets of Sikh infantry and the blue turbans of the Dogras on the left, the scarlet coats and shakos of regular foot on the right.

Our procession slowed and half-halted, but with the howdahs of Jeendan and the chamberlains in front I couldn't see what was happening with Jawaheer – I could hear him, though, shouting shrilly, and the armoured horsemen converged on his elephant, while the yellow Guardsmen tramped stolidly on. Our procession forged ahead towards the centre of the Khalsa line, and just as it seemed as though we must collide the advancing host split into two, wheeling into columns which advanced down either side of

112

us – and I've never seen anything to match it for drill, not even on Horse Guards. I watched them striding by beyond our yellow Guardsmen, and wondered for a moment if they meant to pass us altogether, but a burly *rissaldar-major* came tearing out on the flank, reining in midway down the procession, rose in his stirrups, and at the exact moment bawled in a voice you could have heard in Delhi: "Battalions – abou-tah!"

There was the tremendous one-two-three-four crash as they marked time and turned – and then they were marching with us, a solid mass of two thousand infantry on either flank, shakos and red coats to the right, blue and green turbans to the left. Well, thinks I, whether Jawaheer takes it for a prisoner's escort or a guard of honour, he can't complain that they haven't received him in style. I could hear him, crying "Shabash!" in compliment, and on the elephant ahead of us the chamberlains were on their feet, scooping up rupees in little hand-shovels, and hurling them over the yellow Guardsmen at the Khalsa battalions. They glittered in the air like silver rain, falling among the marching Sikhs – and not a man wavered in his step or even glanced aside. The chamberlains shovelled away for dear life, emptying the panniers and spraying the dust with their rupees, screaming to the troops that this was the gift of their loving monarch and his Wazir, Raja Jawaheer Singh, God bless him, but for all the heed the Khalsa paid it might as well have been bird-droppings, and behind me I heard Jassa mutter: "Save your dollars, boys, they ain't buying you a thing."

Another roar from the *rissaldar-major* and the escorting battalions crashed to a halt, stock-still in the swirling dust. Our procession lumbered on, wheeling left as we emerged from between those grim ranks, and as our beast turned to follow the leaders, there all of a sudden on our right flank was the whole Khalsa, drawn up in review, horse, foot, and guns, squadron upon squadron, battalion upon battalion, as far as the eye could see.

I'd seen it before, and been impressed; what I felt now was awe. Then it had been at exercise; now it was dead still, at attention, eighty thousand men and not a movement

113

except for the gentle stirring of the standards before the battalions, the flutter of pennons on the lances at rest, and the occasional tossing of a horse's mane. And it's strange: the tramp of our Guardsmen and the groaning of the elephants' harness must have been loud enough to wake the dead, but all I remember now is the silence as we passed slowly before that tremendous army.

There was a sudden shrill voice from the second elephant, and damme if Jeendan and Mangla weren't flinging out baksheesh, too, as the chamberlains had done, and calling out to the soldiers to accept their bounty, to remember their oaths to the Maharaja, and to stand true to their salt for the honour of the Khalsa. Still not a man moved, and as the women's voices died away I felt a chill in spite of the heat of the westering sun, and then someone shouted a command to halt, and the elephants lumbered to a standstill.

There was a little cluster of tents ahead, beside the leading beast, and a group of senior officers before it. Akalis were moving down the line, shouting to the mahouts to dismount, and as our elephant sank to its knees I felt nothing but relief – you're uncomfortably conspicuous in a howdah, I can tell you, especially with eighty thousand bearded graven images glaring blindly at you from point-blank range. There was a clatter of hooves, and there was Gardner by the second elephant, ordering servants who helped Jeendan and Mangla down and led them towards one of the pavilions, where hand-maidens were waiting to receive them – pretty butterfly figures in silks and gauzes altogether out of place before that great martial host in leather and serge and steel. Gardner caught my eye and jerked his head, and without waiting for a ladder I dropped to the ground with as much dignity as I could, clutching my topper in place. Jassa followed, and I saw that Lal Singh and the courtiers had also descended. I walked towards Gardner's horse, and noticed that only Jawaheer's elephant was still standing; he was sitting in the howdah, clutching little Dalip to him and complaining shrilly to the Akalis who were angrily ordering his mahout to make the elephant kneel.

Another order was shouted, and now the yellow Guardsmen began to march away, the armoured horsemen cantering ahead of them. At this Jawaheer was on his feet, demanding to know where his escort was going, shouting to his mahout not to take the elephant down; he was in a great passion, and as his head turned I caught the gleam of the great diamond in his turban aigrette – Good Lord, that's Jeendan's belly-button, thinks I, how it does get about . . . and now Gardner was leaning down from his saddle and addressing me rapidly in English:

"Go and help the Maharaja down – go on, man, quickly! It'll please the troops – make a fine impression! Get him, Flashman!"

It all happened in split seconds. There I was, aware only that Jawaheer was in a fine taking about the reception he was receiving, that Gardner was making what sounded like an excellent diplomatic suggestion – kindly old John Bull giving the heathen princeling a piggy-back before his powers assembled, and all that – but even as he spoke I saw that an Akali had scrambled up into the howdah and seemed to be trying to pull Dalip away; Jawaheer screamed, the Akali hit him in the face, Jawaheer dropped the child and cowered away, there was a zeep! of drawn steel at my back – and I started round to find half a dozen Sikhs almost on top of me, *tulwars* drawn and yelling blue murder.

I didn't wait to advise Gardner to help the Maharaja down himself. I was past his horse like a stung whippet – and ran slap into the elephant's arse, fell back with a yell of terror into the path of the charging Sikhs, made a dive to get under the elephant's trailing saddle-cloth, stumbled and became entangled, struggled free – and something hit me an almighty blow across the shoulders, driving me to my knees. I clutched wildly behind me, and found myself with little Dalip in my arms, fallen from aloft, and a mob of raging madmen hurling me aside to get at the elephant.

There was a choking scream from overhead, and there was Jawaheer sprawling over the side of the howdah, arms outstretched, with a spear shaft buried in his chest, blood spewing from his mouth and showering down on me. The attackers were swarming into the howdah, slashing at him;

115

suddenly his face was a bloody mask, his turban slipped from his head, a great length of blood-sodden silk snaking down at me. Gardner's horse reared above me, men were yelling and women shrieking, I could hear the hideous sound of the *tulwars* cutting into Jawaheer's body, and still he was screaming and blood was everywhere, in my eyes and mouth, on the gold coat of little Dalip in my arms – I tried to throw him away, but the young blighter had me fast round the neck and wouldn't leave go. Someone seized me by the arm – Jassa, a pistol in his free hand. Gardner urged his horse between us and the slaughter, knocking Jassa's pistol from his grasp and shouting to him to get us away, and I blundered towards the tents with that confounded infant hanging from my neck – and not a sound out of him, either.

The turban cloth had draped itself across my face, and as I dragged the disgusting thing clear and sank to my knees, Dalip still clung to me with one hand, and in the other, dripping with his uncle's gore, was the great diamond that had fallen from Jawaheer's aigrette. How the brat had got hold of it, God knows, but there it was, almost filling his small hand, and he stared at me with great round eyes and piped: "Koh-i-Noor! Koh-i-Noor!" Then he was whisked away from me, and as I came to my feet I saw he was clasped in his mother's arms beside the tent, bloodying her veil and white sari.

"Oh, my Christ!" groans Jassa, and I looked past him and saw Jawaheer, crimson from head to foot, slide over the side of the howdah and fall headlong in the dust with his life flooding out of him – and still those fiends hacked and stabbed at his corpse, while some even emptied their muskets and pistols into it, until the air was thick with the reek of black powder smoke.

It was Gardner who hustled us to one of the smaller tents while his black robes surrounded Jeendan, Dalip, and the screeching women, shepherding them to the main pavilion. He cast a quick glance at the mob struggling about Jawaheer's corpse, and then twitched our tent curtain shut. He was breathing hard, but cool as you please.

"Well, how d'ye like that for a drumhead court-martial,

116

Mr Flashman?" He laughed softly. "Khalsa justice – the damned fools!"

I was a-tremble at the shocking, sudden butchery of it. "You knew that was going to happen?"

"No, sir," says he calmly, "but nothing in this country surprises me. By the holy, you're a sight! Josiah, get some water and clean him up! You're not wounded? Good—now, lie low and be quiet, both of you! It's over and done, see? The damned fools – listen to 'em, celebrating their own funerals! Now, don't you budge till I come back!"

He strode out, leaving us to collect our breath and our wits – and if you wonder what my thoughts were as Jassa. sponged the blood from my face and hands, I'll tell you. Relief, and some satisfaction that Jawaheer was receipted and filed, and that I'd come away with nothing worse than a ruined frock coat. Not that they'd been out to get me, but when you walk away from a scrimmage of that sort, you're bound to put it down on Crusoe's good side, in block capitals.

Jassa and I shared my flask, and for about half an hour we sat listening to the babble of shouting and laughter and *feux de joie* of the murderers' celebration, and the lamentations from the neighbouring tent, while I digested this latest of Lahore's horrors and wondered what might come of it.

I suppose I'd seen the signs the previous day, in the rage of the Khalsa *panches*, and Jawaheer's own terrors last night – but this morning the talk had been that all was well . . . aye, designed, no doubt, to bring him out to the Khalsa in false hope, to a doom already fixed. Had his peacemakers, Azizudeen and Dinanath, known what would happen? Had his sister? Had Jawaheer himself known, even, but been powerless to avert it? And now that the Khalsa had shown its teeth . . . would it march over the Sutlej? Would Hardinge, hearing of yet another bloody coup, decide to intervene? Or would he still wait? After all, it was nothing new in this horrible country.

I didn't know, then, that Jawaheer's murder was a turning-point. To the Khalsa, it was just another demonstration of their own might, another death sentence on a leader who

117

displeased them. They didn't realise they'd handed power to the most ruthless ruler the Punjab had seen since Runjeet Singh . . . she was in the next tent, having hysterics so strident and prolonged that the noisy mob outside finally gave over celebrating and looting the gear from the royal procession; the shouting and laughter died away, and now there was the sound of her voice alone, sobbing and screaming by turns – and then it was no longer in her tent, but outside, and Gardner slipped back through our curtain, beckoning me to join him at the entrance. I went, and peered out.

It was full dark now, but the space before the tents was lit bright as day by torches in the hands of a vast semi-circle of Khalsa soldiery, thousands strong, staring in silence at the spot where Jawaheer's body still lay on the blood-soaked earth. The elephants and the regiments had gone; all that remained was that great ring of bearded, silent faces (and one of 'em was wearing my tall hat, damn his impudence!), the huddled corpse, and kneeling over it, wailing and beating the earth in an ecstasy of grief, the small white-clad figure of the Maharani. Close by, their hands on their hilts and their eyes on the Khalsa, a group of Gardner's black robes stood guard.

She flung herself across the body, embracing it, calling to it, and then knelt upright again, keening wildly, and began to rock to and fro, tearing at her clothing like a mad thing until she was bare to the waist, her unbound hair flying from side to side. Before that dreadful uncontrolled passion the watchers recoiled a step; some turned away or hid their faces in their hands, and one or two even started towards her but were pulled back by their mates. Then she was on her feet, facing them, shaking her little fists and screaming her hatred.

"Scum! Vermin! Lice! Butchers! Coward sons of dishonoured mothers! A hundred thousand of you against one – you gallant champions of the Punjab, you wondrous heroes of the Khalsa, you noseless bastard offspring of owls and swine who boast of your triumphs against the Afghans and the prowess you'll show against the British! You, who

118

would run in terror from one English camp sweeper and a Kabuli whore! Oh, you have the courage of a pack of pidogs, to set on a poor soul unarmed – aiee, my brother, my brother, my Jawaheer, my prince!" From raging she was sobbing again, rocking from side to side, trailing her long hair across the body, then stooping to cradle the horrid thing against her breast while she wailed on a tremulous high note that slowly died away. They watched her, some grim, some impassive, but most shocked and dismayed at the violence of her grief.

Then she laid down the body, picked up a fallen *tulwar* from beside it, rose to her feet, and began slowly to pace to and fro before them, her head turned to watch their faces. It was a sight to shiver your spine: that small, graceful figure, her white sari in rags about her hips, her bare arms and breasts painted with her brother's blood, the naked sword in her hand. She looked like some avenging Fury from legend as she threw back her hair with a toss of her head and her glare travelled along that silent circle of faces. A stirring sight, if you know what I mean – there's a picture I once saw that could have been drawn from her: Clytemnestra after Agamemnon's death, cold steel and brazen boobies and bedamned to you. Suddenly she stopped by the body, facing them, and her voice was hard and clear and cold as ice as she passed her free hand slowly over her breasts and throat and face.

"For every drop of this blood, you will give a million. You, the Khalsa, the pure ones. Pure as pig dung, brave as mice, honoured as the panders of the bazaar, fit only for –" I shan't tell you what they were fit for, but it sounded all the more obscene for being spoken without a trace of anger. And they shrank from it – oh, there were angry scowls and clenched fists here and there, but the mass of them could only stare like rabbits before a snake. I've seen women, royal mostly, who could cow strong men: Ranavalona with her basilisk stare, or Irma (my second wife, you know, the Grand Duchess) with her imperious blue eye; Lakshmibai of Jhansi could have frozen the Khalsa in its tracks with a lift of her pretty chin. Each in her own way – Jeendan did it by

119

shocking 'em out of their senses, flaunting her body while she lashed them quietly with the language of the gutter. At last one of them could take no more of it – an old white-bearded Sikh flung down his torch and cries:

"No! No! It was no murder – it was the will of God!"

Some murmured in support of him, others cried him down, and she waited until they were silent again.

"The will of God. Is that your excuse . . . you will blaspheme, and hide behind God's will? Then hear mine – the will of your Maharani, mother of your king!" She paused, looking from one side to the other of the silent crowd. "You will give me the murderers, so that they may pay. You will give them to me, or by that God with whose will you make so free, I shall throw the snake in your bosom!"

She struck the *tulwar* into the earth on the last word, turned her back on them and walked quickly towards the tents – Clytemnestra as ever was. With this difference, that where Mrs Agamemnon had committed one murder, she was contemplating a hundred thousand. As she passed into her tent the light from within fell full on her face, and there wasn't a trace of grief or anger. She was smiling.[24]

If there was one thing worse than Jawaheer's murder it was his funeral, when his wives and slavegirls were roasted alive along with his corpse, according to custom. Like much beastliness in the world, *suttee* is inspired by religion, which means there's no sense or reason to it – I've yet to meet an Indian who could tell me why it's done, even, except that it's a hallowed ritual, like posting a sentry to mind the Duke of Wellington's horse fifty years after the old fellow had kicked the bucket. That, at least, was honest incompetence; if you want my opinion of widow-burning, the main reason for it is that it provides the sort of show the mob revels in, especially if the victims are young and personable, as they were in Jawaheer's case. I wouldn't have missed it myself, for it's a fascinating horror – and I noticed, in my years in India, that the breast-beating Christians who denounced it were always first at the ringside.

No, my objection to it is on practical, not moral grounds, it's a shameful waste of good womanhood, and all the worse because the stupid bitches are all for it. They've been brought up to believe it's meet and right to be broiled along with the head of the house, you see – why, Alick Gardner told me of one funeral in Lahore where some poor little lass of nine was excused burning as being too young, and the silly chit threw herself off a high building. They burned her corpse anyway. That's what comes of religion and keeping women in ignorance. The most educated (and devout) Indian female I ever knew, Rani Lakshmibai, thought *suttee* beneath contempt; when I asked her why, as a widow, she hadn't hopped on the old man's pyre herself, she looked at me in disbelief and asked: "Do you think I'm a fool?"

She wasn't, but her Punjabi sisters knew no better.

121

Jawaheer's body was brought, in several pieces, to the city on the day after his death, and the procession to the ground of cremation took place under a red evening sky, before an enormous throng, with little Dalip and Jeendan and most of the nobility prostrating themselves before the *suttees* – two wives, stately handsome girls, and three Kashmiri slaves, the prettiest wenches ever you saw, all in their best finery with jewelled studs in their ears and noses and gold embroidery on their silk trousers. I ain't a soft man, but it would have broken your heart to see those five little beauties, who were made for fun and love and laughter, walking to the pyre like guardsmen, heads up and not a blink of fear, serenely scattering money to the crowd, according to custom – and you wouldn't credit it, those unutterable bastards of Sikh soldiers who were meant to be guarding 'em, absolutely tore the money from their hands, and yelled taunts and insults at them when they tried to protest. Even when they got to the pyre, those swine were tearing their jewels and ornaments from them, and when the fire was lit one villain reached through the smoke and tore the gold fringe from one of the slaves' trousers – and these, according to their religion, were meant to be sacred women.

There were groans from the crowd, but no one dared do anything against the all-powerful military – and then an astounding thing happened. One of the wives stood up among the flames, and began to curse them. I can see her still, a tall lovely girl all in white and gold, blood on her face where her nose-stud had been ripped away, one hand gripping her head-veil beneath her chin, the other raised as she damned 'em root and branch, foretelling that the race of Sikhs would be overthrown within the year, their women widowed, and their land conquered and laid waste – and *suttees*, you know, are supposed to have the gift of prophecy. One of the spoilers jumped on the pyre and swung his musket butt at her, and she fell back into the fire where the four others were sitting calmly as the flames rose and crackled about them. None of them made a sound.[25]

I saw all this from the wall, the black smoke billowing up to mingle with the low clouds under the crimson dusk, and

122

came away in such a boiling rage as I never felt on behalf of anyone except myself. Aye, thinks I, let there be a war (but keep me out of it) so that we can stamp these foul woman-butchers flat, and put an end to their abominations. I guess I'm like Alick Gardner: I can't abide wanton cruelty to good-looking women. Not by other folk, anyway.

That brave lass's malediction filled the crowd with superstitious awe, but it had an even more important effect – it put the fear of God into the Khalsa, and that shaped their fate at a critical time. For after Jawaheer's death they were in a great state of uncertainty and division, with the hot-heads clamouring for an immediate war against us, and the more loyal element, who'd been dismayed by Jeendan's harangue at Maian Mir, insisting that nothing could be done until they'd made their peace with her, the regent of their lawful king. The trouble was, making peace meant surrendering those who'd plotted the murder of Jawaheer, and they were a powerful clique. So the debate raged among them, and meanwhile Jeendan played her hand to admiration, refusing even to acknowledge the Khalsa's existence, going daily to weep at Jawaheer's tomb, heavily veiled and bowed with grief, and winning the admiration of all for her piety; the rumour ran that she'd even sworn off drink and fornication – a portent that reduced the Khalsa to a state of stricken wonder by all accounts.

In the end they gave in, and in response to their appeals for audience she summoned them not to durbar but to the yard under the Summum Boorj, receiving them in cold silence while she sat veiled and swathed in her mourning weeds, and Dinanath announced her terms. These sounded impressively severe – total submission to her will, and instant delivery of the murderers – but were in fact part of an elaborate farce stage-managed by Mangla. She and Lal Singh and a few other courtiers had been taken prisoner by the Khalsa at the time of the murder, but released soon after, since when they'd been politicking furiously with Dinanath and the *panches*, arranging a compromise.

It amounted to this: the Khalsa grovelled to Jeendan, gave up a few token prisoners, and promised to deliver Pirthee

123

Singh and the other leading plotters (who had already decamped to the hills, by previous arrangement) as soon as they were caught. In the meantime, would she please forgive her loyal Khalsa, since they were showing willing, and consider making war on the damned British in the near future? For their part, they swore undying loyalty to her as Queen Regent and Mother of All Sikhs. To this she replied through Dinanath that while it was hardly good enough, she was graciously pleased to accept their submission, and hand back the token prisoners as a liberal gesture. (Sensation and loyal cheers.) They must now give her a little time to complete her mourning and recover from the grievous shock of her brother's death; thereafter she would receive them in full durbar to discuss such questions as making war and appointing a new Wazir.

It was the kind of face-saving settlement that's arranged daily at Westminster and in parish councils, and no one's fooled except the public – and not all of them, either.

You may ask, where was Flashy during all these stirring events? To which the answer is that, having mastered an impulse to steal a horse and ride like hell for the Sutlej, I was well in the background, doing what I'd ostensibly come to Lahore for – namely, negotiate about the Soochet legacy. This entailed sitting in a pleasant, airy chamber for several hours a day, listening to interminable submissions from venerable government officials who cited precedents from Punjabi and British law, the Bible, the Koran, *The Times*, and the *Bombay Gazette*. They were the most tireless old bores you ever struck, red herring worshippers to a man, asking nothing from me beyond an occasional nod and an instruction to my babu to make a note of that point. That kept 'em happy, and was good for another hour's prose – none of which advanced the cause one iota, but since the Punjabi taxpayers were stumping up their salaries, and I was content to sit under the *punkah* sipping brandy and soda, all was for the best in the best of all possible civil services. We could have been there yet – my God, they probably are.

I was busy enough in my spare time, though, chiefly writing cypher reports for Broadfoot and committing them to

Second Thessalonians, from which they vanished with mysterious speed. I still couldn't figure who the postman (or postmistress) was, but it was a most efficient service to Simla and back; within a week of my writing off about Jassa a note turned up in my Bible saying, among other things: "Number 2 A2," which meant that, notwithstanding his colourful past, my orderly was trustworthy to the second degree, which meant only a step below Broadfoot and his Assistants, including myself. I didn't tell Jassa this, but contrived a quick word with Gardner to give him the glad tidings. He grunted: "Broadfoot must be sicker than I thought," and passed on, the surly brute.

For the rest, Broadfoot's communication amounted to little more than "Carry on, Flash." The official news from British India, through the *vakil*, was that Calcutta deplored the untimely death of Wazir Jawaheer and trusted that his successor would have better luck – that was the sense of it, along with a pious hope that the Punjab would now settle down to a period of tranquillity under Maharaja Dalip, the only ruler whom the British power was prepared to recognise. The message was clear: murder each other as often as you please, but any attempt to depose Dalip and we shall be among you, horse, foot and guns.

So there it was, status quo, the question of the hour being, would Jeendan, for her own and Dalip's safety, give way before the Khalsa's demand for war, and turn 'em loose over the Sutlej? I couldn't for the life of me see why she should, in spite of her half-promise to them; she seemed to be able to deal with them as her brother had failed to do, dividing and ruling and keeping them guessing; if she could hold the rein on them while she tightened her grip on the government of the country, I couldn't see how war would be in her interest.

Time would tell; a more pressing matter began to vex me as the first week lengthened into the second. Lal Singh had assured me that Jeendan was anxious to know me better, politically and personally, but devil a sign of it had there been for almost a fortnight, and I was champing at the bit. As the horrors of those first two days receded, the pleasures

125

became more vivid, and I was plagued by fond memories of that painted little trollop writhing against me in the durbar room, and strutting wantonly before her troops at Maian Mir. Quite fetching, those recollections were, and bred a passion which I knew from experience could be satisfied by the lady herself and no other. I'm a faithful soul, you see, in my fashion, and when a new bundle takes my fancy more than ordinary, as about a score have done over the years, I become quite devoted for a spell. Oh, I'd done the polite by Mangla (and repeated the treatment when she called clandestine three nights later) but that was journeyman work which did nothing to quench my romantic lust to put Jeendan over the jumps again, and the sooner the better.

I can't account for these occasional infatuations, but then neither can the poets – uncommon randy, those versifiers. In my own case, though, I have to own that I've been particularly susceptible to crowned heads – empresses and queens and grand duchesses and so forth, of whom I've encountered more than a few. I dare say the trappings and luxury had something to do with it, and the knowledge that the treasury would pick up any bills that were going, but that ain't the whole story, I'm sure. If I were a German philosopher, I'd no doubt reflect on Superman's subjection of the Ultimate Embodiment of the Female, but since I ain't I can only conclude that I'm a galloping snob. At all events, there's a special satisfaction to rattling royalty, I can tell you, and when they have Jeendan's training and inclinations it only adds to the fun.

Like most busy royal women, she had the habit of mixing sport with politics, and contrived our next encounter so that it dealt with both, on the day of her emergence from mourning for her eagerly-awaited durbar with the Khalsa *panches*. I'd tiffened in my quarters, and was preparing for an afternoon's drowse with the Soochet-wallahs when Mangla arrived unannounced; at first I supposed she'd looked in for another quarter-staff bout, but she explained that I was summoned to royal audience, and must follow quietly and ask no questions. Nothing loth, I let her conduct me, and had quite a let-down when she ushered me into a nursery where little

126

Dalip, attended by a couple of nurses, was wreaking carnage with his toy soldiers. He jumped up, beaming, at the sight of me, and then stopped short to compose himself before advancing, bowing solemnly, and holding out his hand.

"I have to thank you, Flashman *bahadur*," says he, "for your care of me . . . that . . . that afternoon . . ." Suddenly he began to weep, head lowered, and then stamped and dashed his tears away angrily. "I have to thank you for your care of me . . ." he began, gulping, and looked at Mangla.

". . . and for the great service . . .," she prompted him.

". . . and for the great service you rendered to me and my country!" He choked it out pretty well, head up and lip trembling. "We are forever in your debt. *Salaam, bahadur.*"

I shook his hand and said I was happy to be of service, and he nodded gravely, glanced sidelong at the women, and murmured: "I was so frightened."

"Well, you didn't look it, maharaj'," says I – which was the honest truth. "I was frightened, too."

"Not you?" cries he, shocked. "You are a soldier!"

"The soldier who is never frightened is only half a soldier," says I. "And d'ye know who told me that? The greatest soldier in the world. His name's Wellington; you'll hear about him some day."

He shook his head in wonder at this, and deciding butter wouldn't hurt I asked if I might be shown his toys. He squeaked with delight, but Mangla said it must be another time, as I had important affairs to attend to. He kicked over his castle and pouted, but as I was salaaming my way out he did the strangest thing, running to me and hugging me round the neck before trotting back to his nurses with a little wave of farewell. Mangla gave me an odd look as she closed the door behind us, and asked if I had children of my own; I said I hadn't.

"I think you have now," says she.

I'd supposed that was the end of the audience, but now she conducted me through that labyrinth of palace passages until I was quite lost, and from her haste and the stealthy way she paused at corners for a look-see, I thought, aha,

127

we're bound for some secret nook where she means to have her wicked will of me. Watching her neat little bottom bobbing along in front of me, I didn't mind a bit – tho' I'd rather it had been Jeendan – and when she ushered me into a pretty boudoir, all hung in rose silk and containing a large divan, I lost no time in seizing her opportunities; she clung for a moment, and then slipped away, cautioning me to wait. She drew the curtain from a small alcove, pressed a spring, and a panel slid noiselessly back to reveal a narrow stairway leading down. Sounds of distant voices came from somewhere below. Having had experience of their architecture, I hesitated, but she drew me towards it with a finger to her lips.

"We must make no sound," she breathed. "The Maharani is holding durbar."

"Capital," says I, kneading her stern with both hands. "Let's have a durbar ourselves, shall we?"

"Not now!" whispers she, trying to wriggle free. "Ah, no! It is by her command . . . you are to watch and listen . . . no, please! . . . they must not hear us . . . follow me close . . . and make no noise . . ." Well, she was at a splendid disadvantage, so I held her fast and played with her for a moment or two, until she began to tremble and bite her lip, moaning softly for me to leave off or we'd be overheard, and when I had her nicely on the boil and fit to dislocate herself – why, I let her go, reminding her that we must be quiet as mice. I'll learn 'em to lure me into boudoirs on false pretences. She gulped her breath back, gave me a look that would have splintered glass, and led the way cautiously down.

It was a dim, steep spiral, thickly carpeted against sound, and as we descended the murmur of voices grew ever louder; it sounded like a meeting before the chairman brings 'em to order. At the stair foot was a small landing, and in the wall ahead an aperture like a horizontal arrow-slit, very narrow on our side but widening to the far side of the wall so that it gave a full view of the room beyond.

We were looking down on the durbar room, at a point directly above the purdah curtain which enclosed one end of

128

it. To the right, in the body of the room before the empty throne and dais, was a great, jostling throng of men, hundreds strong – the *panches* of the Khalsa, much as I'd seen them that first day at Maian Mir, soldiers of every rank and regiment, from officers in brocaded coats and aigretted turbans to barefoot *jawans*; even in our eyrie we could feel the heat and impatience of the close-packed throng as they pushed and craned and muttered to each other. Half a dozen of their spokesmen stood to the fore: Maka Khan, the imposing old general who'd harangued them at Maian Mir; the burly Imam Shah, who'd described Peshora's death; my *rissaldar-major* of the heroic whiskers, and a couple of tall young Sikhs whom I didn't recognise. Maka Khan was holding forth in a loud, irritated way; I suppose you feel a bit of an ass, addressing two hundred square feet of embroidery.

To our left, hidden from their view by the great curtain, and paying no heed at all to Maka Khan's oratory, the Queen Regent and Mother of All Sikhs was making up for her recent enforced abstinence from drink and frivolity. For two weeks she'd been appearing in public sober, grief-stricken, and swathed in mourning apparel; now she was enjoying a leisurely toilet, lounging goblet in hand against a table loaded with cosmetics and fripperies, while her maids fluttered silently about her, putting the finishing touches to an appearance plainly calculated to enthrall her audience when she emerged. Watching her drain her cup and have it refilled, I wondered if she'd be sober enough; if she wasn't, the Khalsa would miss a rare treat.

From mourning she had gone to the other extreme, and was decked out in a dancing-girl's costume which, in any civilised society, would have led to her arrest for breach of the peace. Not that it was unduly scanty: her red silk trousers, fringed with silver lace, covered her from hip to ankle, and her gold weskit was modestly opaque, but since both garments had evidently been designed for a well-grown dwarf I could only wonder how she'd been squeezed into them without bursting the seams. For the rest she wore a head veil secured by a silver circlet above her brows, and a profusion of rings and wrist-bangles; the lovely, sullen face

129

was touched with rouge and kohl, and one of her maids was painting her lips with vermilion while another held a mirror and two more were gilding her finger and toe nails.

They were all intent as artists at a canvas, Jeendan pouting critically at the mirror and directing the maid to touch up the corner of her mouth; then they all stood back to admire the result before making another titivation – and beyond the purdah her army coughed and shuffled and waited and Maka Khan ploughed on.

"Three divisions have declared for Goolab Singh as Wazir," cries he. "Court's, Avitabile's, and the Povinda. They wish the durbar to summon him from Kashmir with all speed."

Jeendan continued to study her mouth in the mirror, opening and closing her lips; satisfied, she drank again, and without looking aside gestured to her chief maid, who called out: "What say the other divisions of the Khalsa?"

Maka Khan hesitated. "They are undecided . . ."

"Not about Goolab Singh!" shouts the *rissaldar-major*. "We'll have no rebel as Wazir, and the devil with Court's and the Povinda!" There was a roar of agreement, and Maka Khan tried to make himself heard. Jeendan took another pull at her goblet before whispering to the chief maid, who called: "There is no majority, then, for Goolab Singh?"

A great bellow of "No!" and "Raja Goolab!" with the leaders trying to quiet them; one of the young Sikh spokesmen shouted that his division would accept whoever the Maharani chose, which was greeted with cheering and a few groans, to the amusement of Jeendan and the delight of the maids, who were now holding up three long pier-glasses so that she might survey herself from all sides. She turned and posed, emptied her cup, pulled her trouser waist lower on her stomach, winked at her chief maid, then raised a finger as Maka Khan shouted hoarsely:

"We can do nothing until the *kunwari* speaks her mind! Will she have Goolab Singh or no?"

There was a hush at that, and Jeendan whispered to the chief maid, who stifled a fit of the giggles and called back:

130

"The Maharani is only a woman, and can't make up her mind. How is she to choose, when the great Khalsa cannot?"

That sent them into noisy confusion, and the maids into stitches. One of them was bringing something from the table on a little velvet cushion, and to my astonishment I saw it was the great Koh-i-Noor stone which I'd last seen streaked with blood in Dalip's hand. Jeendan took it, smiling a question at her maids, and the wicked sluts all nodded eagerly and clustered round as the Khalsa fumed and bickered beyond the curtain and one of the young Sikhs shouted:

"We have asked her to choose! Some say she favours Lal Singh!" A chorus of groans. "Let her come out to us and speak her mind!"

"It is not seemly that her majesty should come out!" cries the chief maid. "She is not prepared!" This while her majesty, with the diamond now in place, was flexing her stomach to make it twinkle, and her maids hugged themselves, giggling, and egged her on. "It is shameful to ask her to break her purdah in durbar. Where is your respect for her, to whom you swore obedience?"

At this there was a greater uproar than ever, some crying that her wish was their command and she should stay where she was, others that they'd seen her before and no harm done. The older men scowled and shook their heads, but the youngsters fairly bayed for her to come out, one bold spirit even demanding that she dance for them as she had done in the past; someone started up a song about a Kashmiri girl who fluttered her trouser fringes and shook the world thereby, and then from the back of the room they began to chant "Jeendan! Jeendan!" The conservatives swore in protest at this indecent levity, and a big lean Akali with eyes like coals and hair hanging to his waist burst out of the front rank yelling that they were a pack of whore-mongers and loose-livers who had been seduced by her wiles, and that the Children of God the Immortal (meaning his own set of fanatics) would stand no more of it.

"Aye, let her come out!" bawls he. "Let her come humbly, as befits a woman, and let her forswear her scandalous

131

life that is a byword in the land, and appoint a Wazir of our approving – such a one as will lead us to glory against the foreigners, Afghan and English alike . . ."

The rest was lost in pandemonium, some howling him down, others taking up his cry for war, Maka Khan and the spokesmen helpless before the storm of noise. The Akali, frothing at the mouth, leaped on to the front of the dais, raving at them that they were fools if they gave obedience to a woman, and a loose woman at that; let her take a suitable husband and leave men's affairs to men, as was fitting and decent – and behind the purdah Jeendan nodded to her chief maid, draped a silver scarf over one arm, took a last look at her reflection, and walked quickly and fairly steadily round the end of the curtain.

Speaking professionally, I'd say she wasn't more than half-soused, but drunk or sober, she knew her business. She didn't sidle or saunter or play any courtesan tricks, but walked a few paces and stopped, looking at the Akali. There had been a startled gasp from the mob at her appearance – well, dammit, she might as well have been stark naked, painted scarlet from the hips down and gilded across her top hamper. There was dead silence – and then the Akali stepped down from the dais like an automaton, and without another glance she continued to the throne, seated herself without haste, arranged her scarf just so on the arm-rest to cushion her elbow, leaned back comfortably with a finger to her cheek, and surveyed the gathering with a cool little smile.

"Here are many questions to be considered at once." Her voice was slightly slurred, but carried clearly enough. "Which will you take first, general?" She spoke past the Akali, who was glaring from side to side in uncertainty, and Maka Khan, looking as though he wished she'd stayed out of sight, drew himself up and bowed.

"It is said, *kunwari*, that you would make Lal Singh Wazir. Some hold that he is no fit man –"

"But others have bound themselves to accept my choice," she reminded him. "Very well, it is Lal Singh."

This brought the Akali to life again, an arm flung out

132

in denunciation. "Your bed-man!" he bawled. "Your paramour! Your male whore!"

There was a yell of rage at this, and some started forward to fall on him, but she checked them with a raised finger and answered the Akali directly, in the same calm voice.

"You would prefer a Wazir who has *not* been my bed-man? Then you can't have Goolab Singh, for one. But if you wish to nominate yourself, Akali, I'll vouch for you."

There was a moment's stunned hush, followed by scandalised gasps – and then a huge bellow of laughter echoing through the great room. Insults and obscene jests were showered on the Akali, who stood mouthing and shaking his fists, the rowdies at the back began to stamp and cheer, Maka Khan and the seniors stood like men poleaxed, and then as the tumult grew the old soldier roused himself and thrust past the Akali to the foot of the dais. In spite of the din, every word reached us through that cunningly-designed spy-hole.

"*Kunwari*, this is not seemly! It is to shame . . . to shame the durbar! I beg you to withdraw . . . it can wait till another day . . ."

"You didn't bid that thing withdraw, when he brayed his spite against me," says she, indicating the Akali, and as it was seen that she was speaking, the noise died on the instant. "What are you afraid of – the truth that everyone knows? Why, Maka Khan, what an old hypocrite you are!" She was laughing at him. "Your soldiers are not children. Are you?" She raised her voice, and of course the mob roared "No!" with a vengeance, applauding her.

"So let him have his say." She flirted a hand at the Akali. "Then I shall have mine."

Maka Khan was staring in dismay, but with the others shouting at him to give way, he could only fall back, and she turned her painted smile on the Akali. "You rebuke me for my lovers – my male whores, you call them. Very well . . ." She looked beyond him, and the thick heavy voice was raised again. "Let every man who has never visited a brothel step forward!"

I was lost in admiration. The most beardless innocent

133

there wasn't going to confess his unworldliness to his mates – and certainly not with that mocking Jezebel watching. Even Tom Brown would have hesitated before stepping forth for the honour of the old School-house. The Akali, who hadn't the advantage of Arnold's Christian instruction, was simply too dumbfounded to stir. She timed it well, though, looking him up and down in affected wonder before he'd collected his wits, and drawling:

"There he stands, rooted as the Hindoo Kush! Well, at least he is honest, this wayward Child of God the Immortal. But not, I think, in a position to rebuke my frailty."

That was the moment when she put them in her pocket. If the laughter had been loud before, now it was thunderous – even Maka Khan's lips twitched, and the *rissaldar-major* fairly stamped with delight and joined in the chorus of abuse at the Akali. All he could do was rage at her, calling her shameless and wanton, and drawing attention to her appearance, which he likened to that of a harlot plying for hire – he was a braver man than I'd have been, with those fine eyes regarding him impassively out of that cruel mask of a face. I remembered the story of the Brahmin whose nose had been sliced off because he'd rebuked her conduct; looking at her, I didn't doubt it.

The Akalis are a privileged sect, to be sure, and no doubt he counted on that. "Get you gone!" he bawled. "You are not decent! It offends the eye to look at you!"

"Then turn your eyes away ... while you still have them," says she, and as he fell back a pace, silenced, she rose, keeping a firm grip of the throne to steady herself, and stood straight, posing to let them have a good view. "In my private place, I dress as you see me, to please myself. I would not have come out, but you called me. If the sight of me displeases you, say so, and I shall retire."

That had them roaring for her to stay, absolutely, which was just as well, for without the throne to cling to I believe she'd have measured her length on the floor. She swayed dangerously, but managed to resume her seat with dignity, and as some of the younger men startled to hustle the Akali away, she stopped them.

"A moment. You spoke of a suitable husband for me . . . have you one in mind?"

The Akali was game. He flung off the hands pulling at him and growled: "Since you cannot do without a man, choose one – only let him be a *sirdar*,* or a wise man, or a Child of God the Immortal!"

"An Akali?" She stared in affected astonishment, then clapped her hands. "You are making me a proposal! Oh, but I am confused . . . it is not fitting, in open durbar, to a poor widow woman!" She turned her head bashfully aside, and of course the mob crowed with delight. "Ah, but no, Akali . . . I cannot deliver my innocence to one who admits openly that he frequents brothels and chases the barber's little girls. Why, I should never know where you were! But I thank you for your gallantry." She gave him a little ironic bow, and her smile would have chilled Medusa. "So, you may keep your sheep's eyes . . . this time."

He was glad to escape into the jeering crowd, and having entertained them by playing the flirt, the fool, and the tyrant in short order, she waited till they were attentive again, and gave them her Speech from the Throne, taking care not to stutter.

"Some of you call for Goolab Singh as Wazir. Well, I'll not have him, and I'll tell you why. Oh, I could laugh him out of your esteem by saying that if he is as good a statesman as he was a lover, you'd be better with Balloo the Clown." The young ones cheered and guffawed, while the older men scowled and looked aside. "But it would not be true. Goolab is a good soldier, strong, brave, and cunning – too cunning, for he corresponds with the British. I can show you letters if you wish, but it is well known. Is that the man you want – a traitor who'll sell you to the *Malki lat* in return for the lordship of Kashmir? Is that the man to lead you over the Sutlej?"

That touched the chord they all wanted to hear, and they roared "*Khalsa-ji!*" and "*Wa Guru-ji ko Futteh!*", clamouring to know when they'd be ordered to march.

*Chief.

135

"All in good time," she assured them. "Let me finish with Goolab. I have told you why he is not the man for you. Now I'll tell you why he is not the man for me. He is ambitious. Make him Wazir, make him commander of the Khalsa, and he'll not rest until he has thrust me aside and mounted to my son's throne. Well, let me tell you, I enjoy my power too much ever to let that happen." She was sitting back at ease, confident, smiling a little as she surveyed them. "It will never happen with Lal Singh, because I hold him here . . ." She lifted one small hand, palm upwards, and closed it into a fist. "He is not present today, by my order, but you may tell him what I say, if you wish . . . and if you think it wise. You see, I am honest with you. I choose Lal Singh because I will have my way, and at my bidding he will lead you . . ." She paused for effect, sitting erect now, head high, ". . . wherever it pleases me to send you!"

That meant only one thing to them, and there was bedlam again, with the whole assembly roaring "*Khalsa-ji!*" and "Jeendan!" as they crowded forward to the edge of the dais, bearing the spokesmen in front of them, shaking the roof with their cheers and applause – and I thought, bigod, I'm seeing something new. A woman as brazen as she looks, with the courage to proclaim absolutely what she is, and what she thinks, bragging her lust of pleasure and power and ambition, and let 'em make of it what they will. No excuses or politician's fair words, but simple, arrogant admission: I'm a selfish, immoral bitch out to serve my own ends, and I don't care who knows it – and because I say it plain, you'll worship me for it.

And they did. Mind you, if she hadn't promised them war, it might have been another story, but she had, and she'd done it in style. She knew men, you see, and was well aware that for every one who shrank from her in disgust and anger and even hatred at the shame she put on them, there were ten to acclaim and admire and tell each other what a hell of a girl she was, and lust after her – that was her secret. Strong, clever women use their sex on men in a hundred ways; Jeendan used hers to appeal to the dark side of their natures, and bring out the worst in them. Which, of course, is what

136

you must do with an army, once you've gauged its temper. She knew the Khalsa's temper to an inch, and how to shock it, flirt with it, frighten it, make love to it, and dominate it, all to one end: by the time she'd done with 'em, you see . . . they trusted her.

I saw it happen, and if you want confirmation, you'll find it in Broadfoot's reports, and Nicolson's, and all the others which tell of Lahore in '45. You won't find them approving her, mind you – except Gardner, for whom she could do no wrong – but you'll get a true picture of an extraordinary woman.[26]

Order was restored at last, and their distrust of Lal Singh was forgotten in the assurance that *she* would be leading them; there was only one question that mattered, and Maka Khan voiced it.

"When, *kunwari*? When shall we march on India?"

"When you are ready," says she. "After the *Dasahra*."*

There were groans of dismay, and shouts that they were ready now, which she silenced with questions of her own.

"You are ready? How many rounds a man has the Povinda division? What remounts are there for the *gorracharra*? How much forage for the artillery teams? You don't know? I'll tell you: ten rounds, no remounts, forage for five days." Alick Gardner's been priming you, thinks I. It silenced them, though, and she went on:

"You won't go far beyond the Sutlej on that, much less beat the Sirkar's army. We must have time, and money – and you have eaten the Treasury bare, my hungry Khalsa." She smiled to soften the rebuke. "So for a season you must disperse the divisions about the country, and live on what you can get – nay, it will be good practice against the day when you come to Delhi and the fat lands to the south!"

That cheered them up – she was telling them to loot their own countryside, you'll notice, which they'd been doing for six years. Meanwhile, she and their new Wazir would see to it that arms and stores were ready in abundance for the

*The ten-day festival in October after which the Sikhs were accustomed to set out on expeditions.

great day. Only a few of the older hands expressed doubts.

"But if we disperse, *kunwari*, we leave the country open to attack," says the burly Imam Shah. "The British can make a *chapao** and be in Lahore while we are scattered!"

"The British will not move," says she confidently. "Rather, when they see the great Khalsa disperse, they will thank God and stand down, as they always do. Is it not so, Maka Khan?"

The old boy looked doubtful. "Indeed, *kunwari* – yet they are not fools. They have their spies among us. There is one at your court now . . ." He hesitated, not meeting her eye. ". . . this Iflassman of the Sirkar's Army, who hides behind a fool's errand when all the world knows he is the right hand of the Black-coated Infidel.† What if he should learn what passes here today? What if there is a traitor among us to inform him?"

"Among the Khalsa?" She was scornful. "You do your comrades little honour, general. As to this Englishman . . . he learns what I wish him to learn, no more and no less. It will not disturb his masters."

She had a way with a drawled line, and the lewd brutes went into ribald guffaws – it's damnable, the way gossip gets about. But it was eerie to hear her talk as though I were miles away, when she knew I was listening to every word. Well, no doubt I'd discover eventually what she was about – I glanced at Mangla, who smiled mysteriously and motioned me to silence, so I must sit and speculate as that remarkable durbar drew to a close with renewed cheers of loyal acclaim and enthusiastic promises of what they'd do to John Company when the time came. Thereafter they all trooped out in high good humour, with a last rouse for the small red and gold figure left in solitary state on her throne, toying with her silver scarf.

Mangla led me aloft again to the rose-pink boudoir, leaving the sliding panel ajar, and busied herself pouring wine into a beaker that must have held near a quart – anticipating

*Sudden attack.
†The Afghan nickname for George Broadfoot.

138

her mistress's needs, you see. Sure enough, a stumbling step and muttered curse on the stair heralded the appearance of the Mother of All Sikhs, looking obscenely beautiful and gasping for refreshment; she drained the cup without even sitting down, gave a sigh that shuddered her delightfully from head to foot, and subsided gratefully on the divan.

"Fill it again . . . another moment and I should have died! Oh, how they stank!" She drank greedily. "Was it well done, Mangla?"

"Well indeed, *kunwari*. They are yours, every man."

"Aye, for the moment. My tongue didn't trip? You're sure? My feet did, though . . ." She giggled and sipped. "I know, I drink too much – but could I have faced them sober? D'you think they noticed?"

"They noticed what you meant them to notice," says Mangla dryly.

"Baggage! It's true enough, though . . . Men!" She gave her husky laugh, raised a shimmering leg and admired its shapeliness complacently. "Even that beast of an Akali couldn't stare hard enough . . . heaven help some wench tonight when he vents his piety on her. Wasn't he a godsend, though? I should be grateful to him. I wonder if he . . ." She chuckled, drank again, and seemed to see me for the first time. "Did our tall visitor hear it all?"

"Every word, *kunwari*."

"And he was properly attentive? Good." She eyed me over the rim of her cup, set it aside, and stretched luxuriously like a cat, watching me to gauge the effect of all that goodness trying to burst out of the tight silk; no modest violet she. My expression must have pleased her, for she laughed again. "Good. Then we'll have much to talk about, when I've washed away the memory of those sweaty warriors of mine. You look warm, too, my Englishman . . . show him where to bathe, Mangla – and keep your hands off him, d'you hear?"

"Why, *kunwari*!"

"'Why *kunwari*' indeed! Here, unbutton my waist." She laughed and hiccoughed, glancing over her shoulder as Mangla unfastened her at the back. "She's a lecherous slut,

139

our Mangla. Aren't you, my dear? Lonely, too, now that Jawaheer's gone – not that she ever cared two *pice* for him." She gave me her Delilah smile. "Did you enjoy her, Englishman? She enjoyed you. Well, let me tell you, she is thirty-one, the old trollop – five years my senior and twice as old in sin, so beware of her."

She reached for her cup again, knocked it over, splashed wine across her midriff, cursed fluently, and pulled the diamond from her navel. "Here, Mangla, take this. He doesn't like it, and he'll never learn the trick." She rose, none too steadily, and waved Mangla impatiently away. "Go on, woman – show him where to bathe, and set out the oil, and then take yourself off! And don't forget to tell Rai and the Python to be within call, in case I need them."

I wondered, as I had a hasty wash-down in a tiny chamber off the boudoir, if I'd ever met such a blatant strumpet in my life – well, Ranavalona, of course, but you don't expect coy flirtation from a female ape. Montez hadn't been one to stand on ceremony either, crying "On guard!" and brandishing her hairbrush, and Mrs Leo Lade could rip the britches off you with a sidelong glance, but neither had paraded their dark desires as openly as this tipsy little houri. Still, one must conform to the etiquette of the country, so I dried myself with feverish speed and strode forth as nature intended, eager to ambush her as she emerged from her bathroom – and she was there ahead of me.

She was half-reclining on a broad silken quilt on the floor, clad in her head-veil and bangles – and I'd been looking forward to easing her out of those pants, too. She was fortifying herself with her wine cup, as usual, and it struck me that unless I went to work without delay she'd be too foxed to perform. But she could still speak and see, at least, for she surveyed me with glassy-eyed approval, licked her lips, and says:

"You're impatient, I see. . . . No, wait, let me look at you . . . Mm-m . . . Now, come here and lie down beside me . . . and wait. I said we should talk, remember. There are things you must know, so that you can speak my mind to Broadfoot sahib and the *Malki lat*." Another sip of puggle and a

140

drunken chuckle. "As you English say, business before pleasure."

I was boiling to contradict her by demonstration, but as I've observed, queens are different – and this one had told Mangla to have "Rai and the Python" standing by; they didn't sound like lady's maids, exactly. Also, if she had something for Hardinge, I must hear it. So I stretched out, nearly bursting at the prospect of the abundances thrusting at me within easy reach, and the wicked slut bobbed them with one hand while she poured tipple into herself with the other. Then she put down the cup, scooped her hand into a deep porcelain bowl of oil at her side, and kneeling forward above me, let it trickle on to my manly breast; then she began to rub it in ever so gently with her finger-tips, all over my torso, murmuring to me to lie still, while I gritted my teeth and clawed at the quilt, and tried to remember what an ablative absolute was – I had to humour her, you see, but with that painted harlot's face breathing warm booze at me, and those superb poonts quivering overhead with every teasing movement, and her fingers caressing . . . well, it was distracting, you know. To make things worse, she talked in that husky whisper, and I must try to pay attention.

Jeendan: This is what killed Runjeet Singh, did you know? It took a full bowl of oil . . . and then he died . . . smiling . . .

Flashy (a trifle hoarse): You don't say! Any last words, were there?

J: It was my duty to apply the oil while we discussed the business of the state. It relieved the tedium of affairs, he used to say, and reminded him that life is not all policy.

F (musing): No wonder the country went to rack and ruin . . . Ah, steady on! Oh, lor'! State business, eh? Well, well . . .

J: You find it . . . stimulating? It is a Persian custom, you know. Brides and grooms employ it on their wedding night, to dispel their shyness and enhance their enjoyment of each other.

F (through clenched teeth): It's a fact, you can always learn something new. Oh, Holy Moses! I say, don't you care

141

for a spot of oil yourself . . . after your bath, I mean . . .
mustn't catch COLD! I'd be glad to –

J: Presently . . . not yet. What splendid muscles you have,
my Englishman.

F: Exercise and clean living – oh, God! See here, *kunwari*,
I think that'll do me nicely, don't you know –

J: I can judge better than you. Now, be still, and listen.
You heard all that passed at my durbar? So . . . you can
assure Broadfoot sahib that all is well, that my brother's
death is forgotten, and that I hold the Khalsa in the hollow
of my hand . . . like this . . . no, no, be still – I was only
teasing! Tell him also that I entertain the friendliest feelings
towards the Sirkar, and there is nothing to fear. You
understand?

F (whimpering): Absolutely. Speaking of friendly feelings –

J: A little more oil, I think . . . But you must warn him to
withdraw no regiments from the Sutlej, is that clear? They
must remain at full strength . . . like you, my mighty English
elephant . . . There now, I have teased you long enough.
You must be rewarded for your patience. (Leaves off and
kneels back, reaching for drink.)

F: Not before time –

J (fending him off): No, no – it is your turn to take the oil!
Not too much, and begin at my finger-tips, so . . . very gently
. . . smooth it into my hands . . . good . . . now the wrists . . .
You will inform Broadfoot sahib that the Khalsa will be
dispersed until after the *Dasahra*, when I shall instruct the
astrologers to choose a day for opening the war . . . now my
elbows. But no day will be propitious for many weeks. I shall
see to that . . . now slowly up to the shoulders . . . softly, a
little more oil . . . Yes, I shall know how to postpone and
delay . . . so the Sirkar will have ample time to prepare for
whatever may come . . . The shoulders, I said! Oh, well, you
have been patient, so why not? More oil, on both hands . . .
more . . . ah, delicious! But gently, there is more news for
Broadfoot sahib –

F (oiling furiously): Bugger Broadfoot!

J: Patience, beloved, you go too fast. Pleasure hasted is

142

pleasure wasted, remember . . . Tell him Lal Singh and Tej Singh will command the Khalsa – are you listening? Lal and Tej – don't forget their names . . . There, now, all is told – so lie down again, elephant, and await your mahout's pleasure . . . so-o . . . oh, gods! Ah-h-h . . .! Wait, lie still – and observe this time-glass, which tells the quarter-hour . . . its sands must run out before yours, do you hear? So, now, slowly . . . you remember the names? Lal and Tej . . . Lal and Tej . . . Lal and . . .

Young chaps, who fancy themselves masterful, won't credit it, but these driving madames who insist on calling the tune can give you twice the sport of any submissive slave, if you handle them right. If they want to play the princess lording it over the poor peasant, let 'em; it puts them on their mettle, and saves you no end of hard work. I've known any number of the imperious bitches, and the secret is to let them set the pace, hold back until they've shot their bolt, and then give 'em more than they bargained for.

Knowing Jeendan's distempered appetite, I'd thought to be hard put to stay the course, but now that I was sober, which I hadn't been at our first encounter, it was as easy as falling off a log – which is what she did, if you follow me, after a mere five minutes, wailing with satisfaction. Well, I wasn't having that, so I picked her up and bulled her round the room until she hollered uncle. *Then* I let her have the minute between rounds, while I oiled her lovingly, and set about her again – turning the time-glass in the middle of it, and drawing her attention to the fact, although what with drink and ecstasy I doubt if she could even see it. She was whimpering to be let alone, so I finished the business leisurely as could be, and damned if she didn't faint – either that or it was the booze.

After a while she came to, calling weakly for a drink, so I fed her a few sips while I debated whether to give her a thrashing or sing her a lullaby – you must keep 'em guessing, you know. The first seemed inadvisable, so far from home, so I carried her to and fro humming "Rockabye, baby", and so help me she absolutely went to sleep, nestling against me. I laid her on the divan, thinking this'll give us time to restore our energies, and went into the wash-room to rid myself of the oil – I've known randy women have some odd tastes: birches, spurs, hair-brushes, peacock feathers, baths, hand-cuffs, God knows what, but Jeendan's the only grease-monkey I can recall.

I was scrubbing away, whistling "Drink, puppy, drink", when I heard a hand-bell tinkle in the boudoir. You'll have to wait a while, my dear, thinks I, but then I heard voices and realised she had summoned Mangla, and was giving instructions in a dreamy, exhausted whisper.

"You may dismiss Rai and the Python," murmurs she. "I shall have no need of them today . . . perhaps not tomor-row . . ."

I should think not, indeed. So I sang "Rule, Britannia".

If you consult the papers of Sir Henry Hardinge and Major Broadfoot for October, 1845 (not that I recommend them as light reading), you'll find three significant entries early in the month: Mai Jeendan's court moved to Amritsar, Hardinge left Calcutta for the Sutlej frontier, and Broadfoot had a medical examination and went on a tour of his agencies. In short, the three principals in the Punjab crisis took a breather – which meant no war that autumn. Good news for everyone except the dispersed Khalsa, moping in their outlying stations and spoiling for a fight.

My own immediate relief was physical. Jeendan's departure came in the nick of time for me, for one more amorous joust with her would have doubled me up forever. I've seldom known the like: you'd have thought, after the wild passage I've just described, that she'd have rested content for a spell, but no such thing. A couple of hours' sleep, a pint of spirits, and drum up the town bull again, was her style, and I doubt if I saw daylight for three days, as near as I could judge, for you tend to lose count of time, you know. We may well have set a record, but I didn't keep tally (some Yankee would be sure to claim best, anyway). All I'm sure of is that my weight went down below twelve and a half stone, and that ain't healthy for a chap my size. I was the one who needed medical inspection, I can tell you, never mind Broadfoot.

And on the fourth morning, when I was a mere husk of a man, wondering if there was a monastery handy, what d'you think she did? Absolutely had a chap in to paint my portrait. At first, when he dragged his easel and colours into the boudoir, and started waving his brush, I thought it was

145

another of her depraved fancies, and she was going to have him sketch us performing at the gallop; the devil with this, thinks I, if I'm to be hung at the next Punjab Royal Academy it'll be with my britches on and my hair brushed. But it proved to be a pukka sitting, Flashy fully clad in romantic native garb like Lord Byron, looking noble with a hookah to hand and a bowl of fruit in the foreground, while Jeendan lounged at the artist's elbow, prompting, and Mangla made helpful remarks. Between the two of them he was in a fine sweat, but did a capital likeness of me in no time – it's in a Calcutta gallery now, I believe, entitled *Company Officer in Seekh Costume*, or something of the sort. Ruined Stag at Bay, more like.

"So that I shall remember my English *bahadur*," says Jeendan, smiling slantendicular, when I asked her why she wanted it. I took it as a compliment – and wondered if it was a dismissal, too, for it was in the same breath that she announced she was taking little Dalip to Amritsar, which is the Sikhs' holy city, for the *Dasahra*, and wouldn't return for some weeks. I feigned dismay, concealing the fact that she'd reduced me to a state where I didn't care if I never saw a woman again.

My first act, when I'd staggered back to my quarters, was to scribble a report of her durbar and subsequent conversation with me, and commit it to Second Thessalonians. That report was what convinced Hardinge and Broadfoot that they had time in hand: no war before winter. I was right enough in that; fortunately I didn't give them my further opinion, which was that there probably wouldn't be a war even then.

You see, I was convinced that Jeendan didn't want one. If she had, and believed the Khalsa could beat us and make her Queen of all Hindoostan, she'd have turned 'em loose over the Sutlej by now. By hocussing them into delay she'd spoiled their best chance, which would have been to invade while the hot weather lasted, and our white troops were at their feeblest; by the cold months, our sick would be on their feet again, dry weather and low rivers would assist our transport and defensive movement, and the freezing nights, while

146

unpleasant for us, would plague the Khalsa abominably. She was also double-dealing 'em by warning us to stay on guard, and promising ample notice if they did break loose in spite of her.

Now there, you'll say, is a clever lass who knows how to keep in with both sides – and will cross either of 'em if it suits her. But already she'd ensured that, if war did come, the odds were in our favour – and there was no profit to *her* in getting beat.

All that aside, I didn't believe war was in her nature. Oh, I knew she was a shrewd politician, when she roused herself, and no doubt as cruel and ruthless as any other Indian ruler – but I just had to think of that plump, pleasure-sodden face drowsing on the pillow, too languid for anything but drink and debauchery, and the notion of her scheming, let alone directing, a war was quite out of court. Lord love us, she was seldom sober enough to plot anything beyond the next erotic experiment. No, if you'd seen her as I did, slothful with booze and romping, you'd have allowed that Broadfoot was right, and that here was a born harlot killing herself with kindness, a fine spirit too far gone to undertake any great matter.

So I thought – well, I misjudged her, especially in her capacity for hatred. I misjudged the Khalsa, too. Mind you, I don't blame myself too much; there seems to have been a conspiracy to keep Flashy in the dark just then – Jeendan, Mangla, Gardner, Jassa, and even the Sikh generals had me in mind as they pursued their sinister ends, but I'd no way of knowing that.

Indeed, I was feeling pretty easy on the October morning when the court departed for Amritsar, and I turned out to doff my tile as the procession wound out of the Kashmir Gate. Little Dalip was to the fore on his state elephant, acknowledging the cheers of the mob as cool as you like, but twinkling and waving gaily at sight of me. Lal Singh, brave as a peacock and riding with a proprietary air beside Jeendan's *palki*, didn't twinkle exactly; when she nodded and smiled in response to my salute he gave me a stuffed smirk as much as to say, back to the pavilion, infidel, it's my

147

innings now. You're welcome, thinks I; plenty of Chinese ginger and rhinoceros powder and you may survive. Mangla, in the litter following, was the only one who seemed to be sorry to be leaving me behind, waving and glancing back until the crowd swallowed her up.

The great train of beasts and servants and guards and musicians was still going by as Jassa and I turned away and rode round to the Rushnai Gate. Have a jolly *Dasahra* at Amritsar, all of you, thinks I, and by the time you get back Gough will have the frontier reinforced, and Hardinge will be on hand to talk sense to you face to face; among you all you can keep the Khalsa in order, everything can be peacefully settled, and I can go home. I said as much to Jassa, and he gave one of his Yankee-Pathan grunts.

"You reckon? Well, if I was you, lieutenant, I'd not say that till I was riding the gridiron again."*

"Why not – have you heard something?"

"Just the *barra choop*," says he, grinning all over his ugly mug.

"What the devil's that?"

"You don't know – an old Khyber hand like you? *Barra choop* – the silent time before the tempest." He cocked his head. "Yes, sir, I can hear it, all right."

"Oh, to blazes with your croaking! Heavens, man, the Khalsa's scattered all over the place, and by the time they're mustered again Gough will have fifty thousand bayonets at the river –"

"If he does, it'll be a red rag to a Punjabi bull," says this confounded pessimist. "Then they'll be *sure* he means to invade. Besides, your lady friend's promised the Khalsa a war come November – they're going to be mighty sore if they don't get it."

"They'll be a dam' sight sorer if they do!"

"You know that – but maybe they don't." He turned in the saddle to look back at the long procession filing along the dusty Amritsar road, shading his eyes, and when he spoke again it was in Pushtu. "See, *husoor*, we have in the Punjab

*Aboard an East Indiaman. The reference is to the Company's flag.

148

the two great ingredients of mischief: an army loose about the land, and a woman's tongue unbridled in the house." He spat. "Together, who knows what they may do?"

I told him pretty sharp to keep his proverbs to himself; if there's one thing I bar it's croakers disturbing my peace of mind, especially when they're leery coves who know their business. Mind you, I began to wonder if he did, for now, after the terrors and transports of my first weeks in Lahore, there came a long spell in which nothing happened at all. We prosed daily about the Soochet legacy, and damned dull it was. The Inheritance Act of 1833 ain't a patch on the *Police Gazette*, and after weeks of listening to the drivel of a garlic-breathing dotard in steel spectacles on the precise meaning of "universum jus" and "seisin" I was bored to the point where I almost wrote to Elspeth. *Barra choop*, indeed.

But if there was no sign of the tempest foretold by Jassa, there was no lack of rumour. As the *Dasahra* passed, and October lengthened into November, the bazaars were full of talk of British concentration on the river, and Dinanath, of all people, claimed publicly that the Company was preparing to annex Sikh estates on the south bank of the Sutlej; it was also reported that he had said that "the Maharani was willing for war to defend the national honour." Well, we'd heard that before; the latest definite word was that she'd moved from Amritsar to Shalamar, and was rioting the nights away with Lal. I was surprised that he was still staying the course; doubtless Rai and the Python were spelling him.

Then late in November things began to happen which caused me, reluctantly, to sit up straight. The Khalsa began to reassemble on Maian Mir, Lal was confirmed as Wazir and Tej as commander-in-chief, both made proclamations full of fire and fury, and the leading generals took their oaths on the Granth, pledging undying loyalty to young Dalip with their hands on the canopy of Runjeet's tomb. You may be sure I saw none of this; diplomatic immunity or not, I was keeping my head well below the parapet, but Jassa gave me eye-witness accounts, taking cheerful satisfaction at every new alarm, curse him.

"They're just waiting for the astrologers to name the

149

day," says he. "Even the order of march is cut and dried – Tej Singh to Ferozepore with 42,000 foot, while Lal crosses farther north with 20,000 *gorracharra*. Yes, sir, they're primed and ready to fire."

Not wanting to believe him, I pointed out that strategically the position was no worse than it had been two months earlier.

"Except that there isn't a rupee left in the Pearl Mosque, and nothing to pay 'em with. I tell you, they either march or explode. I just hope Gough's ready. What does Broadfoot say?"

That was the most disquieting thing of all – for two weeks I hadn't had a line from Simla. I'd been cyphering away until Second Thessalonians was dog-eared, without reply. I didn't tell Jassa that, but reminded him that the final word lay with Jeendan; she'd charmed the Khalsa into delay before, and she could do it again.

"I've got ten chips* says she can't," says he. "Once the astrologers say the word, it'd be more than her pretty little hide was worth to hold back. If those stars say 'Go,' she's bound to give 'em their heads – and God help Ferozepore!"

He lost his bet. "I shall instruct the astrologers," she had told me, and she must have done, for when the wise men took a *dekko* at the planets, they couldn't make head or tail of them. Finally, they admitted that the propitious day was obvious enough, but unfortunately it had been last week and they hadn't noticed, dammit. The *panches* weren't having that, and insisted that another date be found, and sharp about it; the astrologers conferred, and admitted that there was a pretty decent-looking day about a fortnight hence, so far as they could tell at this distance. That didn't suit either, and the soldiery were ready to string them up, at which the astrologers took fright and said tomorrow was the day, not a doubt of it; couldn't think how they'd missed it before. Their credit was pretty thin by this time, and although the *gorracharra* were ordered out of Lahore, Lal took them only a little way beyond Shalamar before hurrying back to the

*Rupees.

150

city and the arms of Jeendan, who was once more in residence at the Fort. Tej sent off the infantry by divisions, but stayed at home himself, and the march was petering out, Jassa reported.

I heaved a sigh of relief; plainly Jeendan was being as good as her word. Now that she was back, under the same roof, I considered and instantly dismissed the notion of trying to have a word with her; nothing could have been worse just then than talk spreading in the bazaar and the camp that she'd been colloguing with a British officer. So I sat down to compose a cypher to Broadfoot, describing the confusion caused by the astrologers, and how the Khalsa were marching round in rings without their two leading generals. "In all this (I concluded) I think we may discern a certain lady's fine Punjabi hand." Elegant letter-writers, we politicals were in those days – sometimes too elegant for our own good.

I sent it off by way of the Scriptures, and suggested to Jassa that he might canvass Gardner, who had returned with Jeendan, to find out the state of play, but my faithful orderly demurred, pointing out that he was the last man in whom Gardner would confide at any time, "and if the jealous son-of-a-bitch gets the idea that I'm nosing about right now, he's liable to do me harm. Oh, sure, he's Broadfoot's friend – but it's Dalip's salt he eats – and Mai Jeendan's. Don't forget that. If it comes to war, he can't be on our side."

I wasn't sure about that, but there was nothing to do but wait – for news of the Khalsa's intentions, and word from Broadfoot. Three days went by, and then a week, in which Lahore buzzed with rumours: the Khalsa were marching, the British were invading, Goolab Singh had declared first for one side then for the other, the Raja of Nabla had announced that he was the eleventh incarnation of Vishnu and was raising a holy war to sweep the foreigners out of India – all the usual twaddle, contradicted as soon as it was uttered, and I could do nothing but endure the Soochet legacy by day, and pace my balcony impatiently in the evening, watching the red dusk die into purple, star-filled night over the fountain court, and listen to the distant murmur of the great city, waiting, like me, for peace or war.

151

It was nervous work, and lonely, and then on the seventh night, when I had just climbed into bed, who should slip in, all unannounced, but Mangla. News at last, thinks I, and was demanding it as I turned up the lamp, but all the reply she made was to pout reproachfully, cast aside her robe, and hop into bed beside me.

"After six weeks I have not come to talk politics," says she, rubbing her bumpers across my face. "Ah, taste, *bahadur* – and then eat to your heart's content! Have you missed me?"

"Eh? Oh, damnably!" says I, taking a polite munch. "But hold on . . . what's the news? Have you a message from your mistress? What's she doing?"

"This – and this – and this," says she, teasing busily. "With Lal Singh. Rousing his manhood – but whether for an assault on herself or on the frontier, who knows? Are you jealous of him, then? Am I so poor a substitute?"

"No, dammit! Hold still, can't you? Look, woman, what's happening, for heaven's sake? One moment I hear the Khalsa's marching, the next that it's been recalled – is it peace or war? She swore she'd give warning – here, don't take 'em away! But I must know, don't you see, so that I can send word –"

"Does it matter?" murmurs the randy little vixen. "At this moment . . . does it truly matter?"

She was right, of course; there's a time for everything. So for the next hour or so she relieved the tedium of affairs and reminded me that life isn't all policy, as old Runjeet said before expiring blissfully. I was ready for it, too, for since my protracted bout with Jeendan I hadn't seen a skirt except my little maids, and they weren't worth turning to for.

Afterwards, though, when we lay beneath the *punkah*, drowsing and drinking, there wasn't a scrap of news to be got out of her. To all my questions she shrugged her pretty shoulders and said she didn't know – the Khalsa were still on the leash, but what was in Jeendan's mind no one could tell. I didn't believe it; she must have some word for me.

"Then she has not told me. Do you know," says Mangla, gnawing at my ear, "I think we talk too much of Jeendan –

152

and you have ceased to care for her, I know. All men do. She is too greedy of her pleasure. So she has no lovers – only bed-men. Even Lal Singh takes her only out of fear and ambition. Now I," says the saucy piece, teasing my lips with hers, "have true lovers, because I delight to give pleasure as well as to take it – especially with my English *bahadur*. Is it not so?"

D'you know, she was right again. I'd had enough of Punjabi royalty to last a lifetime, and she'd put her dainty finger on the reason: with Jeendan, it had been like making love to a steam road roller. But I still had to know what was in her devious Indian mind, and when Mangla continued to protest ignorance I got in a bate and swore that if she didn't talk sense I'd thrash it out of her – at which she clapped her hands and offered to get my belt.

So the night wore out, and a jolly time we had of it, with only one interruption, when Mangla complained of the cold draft from the fan. I bawled to the *punkah-wallah* to go easy, but with the door closed he didn't hear, so I turned out, cursing. It wasn't the usual ancient, but another idiot – they're all alike, fast asleep when you want a cool waft, and freezing you with a nor'easter in the small hours. I leathered the brute, and scampered back for some more Kashmiri culture; it was taxing work, and when I awoke it was full morning, Mangla had gone . . . and there was a cypher from Broadfoot waiting in Second Thessalonians.

So Jassa had been right – she *was* the secret courier after all. Well, the little puss . . . mixing business with pleasure, if you like. I'd wondered if it was she, you remember, on that first day, when she and others had had the opportunity to be at my bedside table. She was the perfect go-between, when you thought about it, able to come and go about the palace as she pleased . . . the slave-girl who was the richest woman in Lahore – easy for her to bribe and command other couriers, one of whom must have deputised while she was away in Amritsar. How the deuce had Broadfoot recruited her? My respect for my chief had always been high, but it doubled now, I can tell you.

Which was just as well, for if anything could have shaken

153

my faith it was the contents of that cypher. When I'd decoded it I sat staring at the paper for several minutes, and then construed it again, to be sure I had it right. No mistake, it was pukka, and the sweat prickled on my skin as I read it for the tenth time:

> Most urgent to Number One alone. On the first night after receipt, you will go in native dress to the French Soldiers' cabaret between the Shah Boorj and the Buttee Gate. Use the signals and wait for word from Bibi Kalil. Say nothing to your orderly.

Not even an "I remain" or "Believe me &c". That was all.

*   *   *

The trouble with the political service, you know, is that they can't tell truth from falsehood. Even members of Parliament *know* when they're lying, which is most of the time, but folk like Broadfoot simply ain't aware of their own prevarications. It's all for the good of the service, you see, so it must be true – and that makes it uncommon hard for straightforward rascals like me to know when we're being done browner than an ape's behind. Mind you, I'd feared the worst when he'd assured me: "It'll never come to disguise, or anything desperate." Oh, no, George, never that! Honestly, you'd be safer dealing with lawyers.

And now here it was, my worst fears realised. Flashy was being sent into the deep field – clean-shaven, too, and never a bolt-hole or friend-in-need to bless himself with. Come, you may say, what's the row – it's only a rendezvous in disguise, surely? Aye . . . and then? Who the blazes was this Bibi Kalil – the name might mean anything from a princess to a bawd – and what horror would she steer me to at Broadfoot's bidding? Well, I'd find out soon enough.

The disguise was the least of it. I had a *poshteen* in my valise, and had gathered a few odds and ends since coming to Lahore – Persian boots, *pyjamys* and sash for lounging on the hotter days, and the like. My own shirt would do, once I'd trampled it underfoot, and I improvised a *puggaree* from a couple of towels. Ordinarily I'd have borrowed Jassa's

154

gear, but he was to be kept in the dark – that was something about the cypher that struck me as middling odd: the last sentence was unnecessary, since the word "alone" at the beginning meant that the whole thing was secret to me. Presumably George was just "makin' siccar", as he would say.

Leaving the Fort was less simple. I'd strolled out once or twice of an evening, but never beyond the market at the Hazooree Gate on the inner wall, which was the better-class bazaar serving the quality homes which lay south of the Fort, before you came to the town proper. I daren't assume my disguise inside the palace, so I stuffed it into a handbag, all but the boots, which I put on under my unutterables.* Then it was a case of making sure that Jassa wasn't on hand, and slipping out to the gardens after dark. There were few folk about, and in no time I was behind a bush, staggering about with my foot tangled in my pants, damning Broadfoot and the mosquitoes. I wrapped the *puggaree* well forward over my head, dirtied my face, put the bag with my civilised duds into a cleft in the garden wall, prayed that I might return to claim them, and sallied forth.

Now, I've "gone native" more times than I can count, and it's all a matter of confidence. Your amateur gives himself away because he's sure everyone can see through his disguise, and behaves according. They can't, of course; for one thing, they ain't interested, and if you amble along doing no harm, you'll pass. I'll never forget sneaking out of Lucknow with T. H. Kavanaugh during the siege;† he was a great Irish murphy without sense or a word of Hindi, figged out like the worst kind of pantomime pasha with the lamp-black fairly runnning off his fat red cheeks, and cursing in Tipperary the whole way – and not a mutineer gave him a second look, hardly. Now, my beardless chops were my chief anxiety, but I'm dark enough, and an ugly scowl goes a long way.

I had my pepperbox, but I bought a belt and a Kashmiri short sword in the market for added security, and to test my appearance and elocution. I'm at my easiest as a Pathan

*Civilian trousers.
†See *Flashman in the Great Game*.

155

ruffler speaking Pushtu or, in this case, bad Punjabi, so I spat a good deal, growled from the back of my throat, and beat the booth-wallah down to half-price; he didn't even blink, so when I reached the alleys of the native town I stopped at a stall for a *chapatti* and a gossip, to get the feel of things and pick up any shave* that might be going. The lads of the village were full of the impending war, and how the *gorracharra* had crossed the river unopposed at the Harree ghat, and the British were abandoning Ludhiana – which wasn't true, as it happened.

"They have lost the spirit," says one know-all. "Afghanistan was the death of them."

"Afghanistan is everyone's death," says another. "Didn't my own uncle die at Jallalabad, peace be on him?"

"In the British war?"

"Nay, he was cook to a horse caravan, and a bazaar woman gave him a loathsome disease. He had ointments, from a *hakim*,† to no avail, for his nose fell off and he died, raving. My aunt blamed the ointments. Who knows, with an Afghan *hakim*?"

"That is how we should slay the British!" cackles an ancient. "Send the Maharani to infect them! Hee-hee, she must be rotten by now!"

I didn't care for that, and neither did a burly cove in a cavalry coat. "Be decent, pig! She is the mother of thy king, who will sit on the throne in London Fort when we of the Khalsa have eaten the Sirkar's army!"

"Hear him!" scoffs the old comedian. "The Khalsa will march on the ocean then, to reach London?"

"What ocean, fool? London lies only a few *cos*‡ beyond Meerut."

"Is it so far?" says I, playing the yokel. "Have you been there?"

"Myself, no," admitted the Khalsa bird. "But my *havildar* was there as a camel-driver. It is a poor place, by all accounts, not so great as Lahore."

*Rumour.
†Chemist.
‡Cos = one and a half miles.

156

"Nay, now," cries the one with the poxy uncle. "The houses in London are faced with gold, and even the public privies have doors of silver. This I was told."

"That was before the war with the Afghans," says the Khalsa's prize liar, whose style I was beginning to admire. "It beggared the British, and now they are in debt to the Jews; even Wellesley sahib, who broke Tipoo and the Maharattas aforetime, can get no credit, and the young queen and her waiting-women sell themselves on the streets. So my *havildar* tells; he had one of them."

"Does he have his nose still?" cries another, and there was great merriment.

"Aye, laugh!" cries the ancient. "But if London is grown poor, where is all this loot on which we are to grow fat when you heroes of the Pure have brought it home?"

"Now God give him wit! Where else but in Calcutta, in the Hebrews' strong-boxes. We shall march on thither when we have taken London and Glash-ka where they grow tobacco and make the iron boats."

About as well-informed, you see, as our own public were about India. I lingered a little longer, until I was thinking in Punjabi, and then, with that well-known hollow feeling in my innards, set off on my reluctant way.

The Shah Boorj is at the south-western corner of Lahore city, less than a mile away as the crow flies, but nearer two when you must pick your way through the winding ways of the old town. Foul ways they were, too, running with filth past hovels tenanted by ugly beggar folk who glared from doorways or scavenged among the refuse with the rats and pi-dogs; the air was so poisonous that I had to wrap my *puggaree* over my mouth, as though to strain the pestilential vapours as I picked my way past pools of rotting filth. A few fires among the dung-heaps provided the only light, and everywhere there were bright, wicked eyes, human and animal, that shrank away as I approached, lengthening my stride to get through that hellish place, but always I could imagine horrid shapes pressing behind me, and blundered on like the chap in the poem who daren't look back because he knows there's a hideous goblin on his heels.

Presently the going was better, between high tenements and warehouses, and only a few night-lurkers hurrying by. Near the south wall the streets were wider, with decent houses set back behind high walls; a couple of *palkis* went by, swaying between their bearers, and there was even a *chowkidar** patrolling with his lantern and staff. But I still felt damnably alone, with the squalid, hostile warren between me and home – that was how I now thought of the Fort which I'd approached with such alarm a couple of months ago. Very adaptable, we funks are.

The French Soldiers' cabaret was close to the Buttee Gate, and if the Frog mercenaries whose crude portraits adorned its walls could have seen it, they'd have sought redress at law. They squinted out of their frames on a great, noisy, reek-filled chamber – Ventura, Allard, Court, and even my old chum Avitabile, looking like the Italian bandit he was with his tasselled cap and spiky moustachioes. I'd settle for you alongside this minute, thinks I, as I surveyed the company: villainous two-rupee bravos, painted harpies who should have been perched in trees, a seedy flute-and-tom-tom band accompanying a couple of gyrating nautches whom you wouldn't have touched with a long pole, and Sikh brandy fit to corrode a bucket. I'll never say a word against Boodle's again, says I to myself; at least there you don't have to sit with your back to the wall.

I found a stool between two beauties who'd evidently been sleeping in a camel stable, bought a glass of arrack that I took care not to drink, growled curtly when addressed, and sat like a good little political, using the signals – thumb between the first two fingers and scratching my right armpit from time to time. Half the clientele were clawing themselves in the same way, with good reason, which was disconcerting, but I sat grimly on, wishing I'd gone into Holy Orders and ignoring the blandishments of sundry viragos of the sort you can have for fourpence with a mutton pie and a pint of beer thrown in, but better not, for the pie meat's sure to be off. They sulked or snarled at me, according to taste,

*Constable.

158

but the last one, a henna'd banshee with bad teeth, said I was choosy, wasn't I, and what had I expected in a place like this – Bibi Kalil?

There was so much noise that I doubted if anyone else had heard her, but I waited till she'd flounced off, and another ten minutes for luck. Then I rose and shouldered my way to the door, taking my time; sure enough, she was waiting in the shadow of the porch. Without a word she led on up the alley, and I followed close, my heart thumping and my hand on the pepperbox under my *poshteen* as I scanned the shadows ahead. We went by twisting ways until she stopped by a high wall with an open wicket. "Through the garden and round the house. Your friend is waiting," she whispered, and vanished into the dark.

I glanced about to mark lines of flight, and went cautiously in. A small bushy enclosure surrounded a tall well-kept house, and directly before me a steep outside stair led up to a little arched porch on the upper floor, with a dimly-lit doorway beyond. Round the angle of the house to my left light was spilling from a ground-floor room that I couldn't see – that was my way, then, but even as I set forward the light in the arch overhead shone brighter as the door beyond was fully opened, and a woman came out silently on to the little porch. She stood looking down into the garden, this way and that, but by then I was in the bushes, taking stock.

Peering up through the leaves I could see her clearly, and if this was Bibi Kalil I didn't mind a bit. She was tall, fine-featured as an Afghan, heavy of hip and bosom in her fringed trousers and jacket, a matronly welterweight and just my style. Then she moved back inside, and since my immediate business was round the corner on the ground floor (alas!), I heaved a sigh and turned that way . . . and stopped dead as I recalled a word that my guide had used.

"Friend"? That wasn't political talk. "Brother" or "sister" was usual . . . and whoever had instructed her would have told her the exact words to say. Back to my mind came that other queer phrase in Broadfoot's message: "Say nothing to your orderly . . ." That hadn't been quite pukka,

159

either. They were just two tiny things, but all of a sudden the dark seemed deeper and the night quieter. Coward's instinct, if you like, but if I'm still here and in good health, bar my creaky kidneys and a tendency to wind, it's because I shy at motes, never mind beams – and I don't walk straight in where I can scout first. So instead of going openly round the house as directed, I skulked round, behind the bushes, until I was past the angle and could squint through the foliage into that well-lit ground floor room with its open screens . . . and have a quiet apoplectic fit to myself, holding on to a branch for support.

There were half a dozen men in the room, armed and waiting, and they included, *inter alia,* General Maka Khan, his knife-toting sidekick Imam Shah, and that crazy Akali who'd denounced Jeendan at the durbar. Leading men of the Khalsa, sworn enemies of the Sirkar, waiting for old Flash to roll in . . . "friends", bigod! And I was meant to believe that Broadfoot had directed me to *them*?

Well, I didn't, not for an instant – which was the time it took me to realise that something was hellishly, horribly wrong . . . that this was a trap, and my head was all but in its jaws, and nothing for it but instant flight. You don't stop to reason how or why at times like that – you grit your teeth to keep 'em from chattering, and back away slowly through the bushes with your innards dissolving, taking care not to rustle the leaves, until you're close by the gate, when you think you hear furtive movement out in the alley, and start violently, treading on a stick that snaps with a report like a bloody howitzer, and you squeal and leap three feet – and if you're lucky an angel of mercy in fringed trousers reappears on the porch overhead, hissing: "Flashman sahib! This way, quickly!"

I was up that stair like a fox with an arseful of buckshot, tripping on the top step and falling headlong past the woman and slap into the arms of a burly old ruffian who was hobbling nimbly out of the inner doorway. I had a glimpse of huge white whiskers and glaring eyes under a black turban, but before I could exclaim I was in a bear's grip with a hand like a ham over my mouth.

160

*"Chub'rao! Khabadar!"** growls he. "A thousand hells –
get your great infidel foot off my toe! Don't you English
know what it is to have the gout, then?" And to the woman:
"Have they heard?"

She stood a moment on the porch, listening, and then slid
in, closing the door softly. "There are men in the alley, and
sounds from the garden room!" Her voice was deep and
husky, and in the dim light I could see her poonts bouncing
with agitation.

"Shaitan take them!" snarls he. "It's now or not at all,
then! Down, *chabeli*,† by the secret stair – look for Donkal
and the horses!" He was bundling me into the room.
"Haste, woman!"

"He won't be there yet!" whispers the woman. "With
their look-outs in the streets he must even wait!" She shot
me a swift look, moistening her full lips. "Besides, I fear the
dark. Do you go, while I wait here with him."

"God, she would flirt on the edge of the Pit!" fumes the
old buck. "Have ye no sense of fitness, with the house
crawling with foes and my foot like to burst? Away and look
out from the street window, I say! You can ravish him
another time!"

She glared but went, flitting across the shadowy chamber
to a low door in the far wall, while he stood gripping my
arm, the great white-whiskered head raised to listen, but the
only sounds were my heart hammering and his own gusty
breathing. He glanced at me, and spoke hoarse and low.

"Flashman the Afghan killer – aye, ye have the beastly
look! They are down there – rats of the Khalsa, lying in wait
for you –"

"I know – I saw them! How –"

"You were lured, with a false message. Subtle fellows,
these."

I stared, horror-stricken. "But that's impossible! It . . . it
can't be false! No one could –"

"Oho, so you're not here, and neither are they!" says
he, grinning savagely. "Wait till their flayers set about

*"Be quiet! Careful!".
†Sweetheart.

161

you, fool, and you'll change your mind! Are you armed?"

I showed him, and would you believe it, he fell into whispered admiration of my pepperbox? "It turns so? Six shots, you say? A marvel! With one of these, who needs rent collectors? By God, at need we can cut our way out, you with shot and I with steel! Fiend take the woman, where is she? Ogling some prowler, like as not! Ah, my poor foot – they say drink inflames it, but I believe it comes of kneeling at prayer! Alas, why did I rise from my bed this day?"

All this in muttered whispers in the gloom, and me beside myself with fear, not knowing what the devil was up, except that the hosts of Midian were after me, but that I seemed to have found two eccentric friends, thank God – and whoever they might be, they weren't common folk. You don't take careful note at such times, but even in the grip of funk I was aware that while the lady might have a wanton eye, she talked like a sultana; the tiny room was opulent as a palace, with dim lamps shining on silk and silver; and my gouty old sportsman could only be some tremendous swell. Command was in every line of the stout, powerful figure, bold curved nose, and bristling beard, and he was dressed like a fighting raja – a great ruby in his turban, silver studs on the quilted leather jack, black silk *pyjamys* tucked into high boots, and a jewel-hilted broadsword on his hip. Who on earth was he? Keeping my voice down, I asked him, and he chuckled and answered in his growling whisper, his eye on the door.

"You cannot guess? So much for fame! Ah, but you know me well, Flashman sahib – and that sweet hussy whose tardiness perils our safety. Aye, ye've been busy about our affairs these two months!" He grinned at my bewilderment. "Bibi Kalil is only her pet name – she is the widow of my brother, Soochet Singh, peace be on him. And I am Goolab Singh."

If I stared, it wasn't in disbelief. He fitted the description in Broadfoot's packets, even to the gout. But Goolab Singh, once pretender to the throne, the rebel who'd made himself king in Kashmir in defiance of the durbar, should have been "behind a rock up Jumoo way, with fifty thousand hillmen", as George had put it. He must be the most wanted man in Lahore this minute, for while there had been some in the

162

Khalsa who'd nominated him for Wazir, Jeendan had since exposed him as a British ally – which was fine by me just then, but didn't explain his presence here.

"Let that explain it," says he, as Bibi Kalil emerged from the low door. "This is her house, and the pretty widow has admirers –" he pointed downwards – "men high in the Khalsa *panches*. She makes them welcome, they talk freely, and I, lying close to Lahore in these days of trouble, hear it all from her. So when they hatch a plot to take you – why, here am I, gout and all, to prove my loyalty to the Sirkar by rescuing its servant –"

"What the hell do they want with me?"

"To talk with you – over a slow fire, I believe . . . well, little jujube, what of Donkal?"

"No sign of him – Goolab, there are men in the streets, and others in the garden!" Her voice shook, and her eyes were wide in alarm, but she wasn't one of your vapouring pieces. "I heard Imam Shah call for the wench who brought you," she adds to me.

"Aye, well, there's an end to waiting," says Goolab cheerfully. "She'll tell them you entered, they'll beat the bushes – then they'll bethink them of upstairs . . ." He cocked an ear as distant voices came from the garden below. "Maka Khan grows impatient. Have your revolving gun ready, Englishman!"

Bibi Kalil gave a little gasp, and pressed close to me, trembling, but I was in no case to enjoy it; she put an arm round me, and I clasped her instinctively – for reassurance, not lust, I can tell you. The questions that had been racing pell-mell through my mind – how I'd come to be trapped in this gilded hell-hole, how those Khalsa swine had known I was coming, why Goolab and this palpitating armful were on hand to aid me – mattered nothing beside those terrible words "slow fire", uttered almost idly by this crazy old bandit who, with fifty thousand hillmen at his call, had apparently brought only one who was farting about in the dark . . . and then my blood froze and I clutched the widow for support, as footsteps sounded on the outside stair.

She clung in return, Goolab's hand dropped to his hilt,

163

and we waited there still as death, until a sharp knock fell on the door. A moment's pause, and then a man's voice:

"Lady? Are you there? My lady?"

She turned those fine eyes on me, helplessly, and then Goolab stepped close, his lips at her ear. "Who is he? D'ye know him?"

Her reply was a faint perfumed breath. "Sefreen Singh. Aide to Maka Khan."

"An admirer?" The old devil was bright with mischief, even now, and it was a moment before she shrugged and whispered: "From a distance."

Another knock. "Lady?"

"Ask him what he wants," whispers Goolab.

I felt her tremble, but she did it well, calling out in a sleepy voice: "Who is it?"

"Sefreen Singh, my lady." A pause. "Are you . . . pardon me . . . are you alone?"

She waited and then called: "I'm asleep . . . what was that? Of course I'm alone . . ." Goolab grimaced over her head at me – he was *enjoying* this, rot him!

"A thousand pardons, lady." The voice was all apology. "I have orders to search. There is a *badmash* about. If you will please to open . . ."

"Well, he's not here," she was beginning, but Goolab was at her ear again:

"We must let him in! But first . . . beguile him." He winked. "If he is to enter with a weapon ready, let it not be a steel one."

She glared, but nodded, gave me a melting glance as she disengaged her right tit from my unwitting grasp, and called out impatiently. "Oh, very well . . . a moment . . ."

Goolab drew his sabre noiselessly, passed it to me, and took the short sword from my belt, pricking his thumb on the point. "He's mine. If I miss . . . take off his head." He limped swiftly to the latch side of the door, motioned me to stand behind it, and nodded to the widow. She set her hand on the bolt and spoke softly:

"Sefreen Singh . . . are *you* alone?" Honey wouldn't have melted.

164

"Why . . . why, yes, my lady!"

"You're sure?" She gave a little murmuring laugh. "In that case . . . if you promise to stay a while . . . you may come in . . ."

She slipped the bolt, opened the door, and turned away, glancing over her shoulder, and in steps Barnacle Bill, not believing his luck, to receive Goolab's updriven point beneath his bearded chin before he'd gone a step. One savage, expert thrust into the brain – he went down without a sound, Goolab breaking his fall, and when I turned from fumbling the door to with a shaking hand the old ruffian was wiping his blade on the dead man's shirt.

"Eighty-two," chuckles he, and Bibi Kalil gave a long, shuddering sigh between clenched teeth; her eyes were shining with excitement. Aye, well, that's India for you.

"Now, away!" snaps Goolab. "This buys us moments, no more! Do you show him the way down, *chabeli*! I'll bide here until you're at the street door –"

"Why?" cries the widow.

"Oh, to beguile my leisure!" snarls he. "In case others come knocking, you witless heifer! Can I keep up, with my foot afire? But I can hold a door – aye, or parley, perchance! They may think twice before putting steel into Goolab Singh!" He thrust us away. "Out with him, woman, so that he can sing the praise of this night's work to Hardinge sahib! Go! Never fear, I'll follow!"

But first she must embrace him, and he laughed and kissed her, saying that she was a good-sister to be proud of. Then she had me by the hand, and we were through the low door and down stone steps to a passage which ended in an iron grille. Beyond it the alley lay dark and deserted, but she shrank back, gasping that we must wait. Between the danger behind and the unknown perils out yonder, I was scared neutral, and in a moment Goolab came hobbling down, yelping at each step.

"I heard them on the outer stair! God's love, if this doesn't win me the White Queen's seal on Kashmir, there's no gratitude left! What, an empty street! Well, empty or not, we cannot wait! My sabre, Flashman – we stout bellies need

165

a full sweep! Now, harken – back to back if we must, but if it grows hot, each for himself!"

"I'll not leave you, my lord!" cries Bibi Kalil.

"You'll do as I bid, insolence! At all costs, he must win clear, or our labour's wasted! Now – one either side of me, and open the gate, softly . . ."

"But Donkal is not come!" wails the widow.

"Donkal be damned! We have five feet among us, but we'll lack three heads if we linger! Come on!"

We stumbled into the alley, the widow and I supporting his ponderous weight, and blundered ahead into the dark, myself in blind panic, Bibi Kalil whimpering softly, and the Lord of Kashmir gasping blasphemies and encouragement – all we needed was a bowl to put to sea in. From beyond the house we could hear voices raised, and the distant sound of hammering on a door, with someone calling for Sefreen Singh. We reached the alley end, and as Bibi Kalil sped ahead to scout, Goolab hung on my shoulder, panting.

"Aye, get up, Sefreen, and let them in!" croaks he. "All clear, sweetheart? Bless her plump limbs, when we come to Jumoo she'll have a new emerald each day, and singing girls to tell her stories – aye, and twenty stalwart lads as bodyguards – on, on, quickly! Oh, for five sound toes again!"

We stumbled round the corner and on into a little court where four ways met, and a torch guttered in a bracket overhead, casting weird shadows. Bibi Kalil sped to one of the openings – and screamed suddenly, darting back, Goolab stubbed his gouty foot and tumbled down, cursing, and as I hauled him up two men came bounding out of the alley and hurled themselves on us.

If they'd been out to kill, we'd have been done for, with me hauling at the stranded Goolab – but capture was what they were after. The first clutched for my sword-arm, and got my point in the shoulder for his pains. "*Shabash*, Afghan killer!" roars Goolab, still on his knees, and ran him through the body, but even as the fellow went down, his comrade threw himself on Goolab, choking off the triumphant yell of "Eighty-three!" and bearing him to earth. Bibi Kalil ran in, screaming and tearing at the attacker's face with her nails, while I danced about making shrill noises and looking for a chance to pink him – until it occurred to me that there were better uses for my time than this, and I turned tail up the nearest alley.

Well, Goolab had said each for himself, but I won't pretend that I've ever needed leave to bolt. I hadn't been given the precious gift of life to cast it away in back alleys, brawling on behalf of fat rajas and randy widows, and I was going like a startled fawn and rejoicing in my youth when I saw a glare of torchlight ahead of me, and realised with horror that round the next corner running feet were approaching. Serve you right, poltroon, says you, for leaving pals in the lurch, now you'll get your cocoa – but we practised absconders don't give up so easy, I can tell you. I came to a slithering halt, and as the powers of darkness came surging into view, full of spite and action, I was stock-still and pointing back to the little court, where Goolab and the widow could be seen apparently disembowelling the Second Robber, who wasn't taking it quietly.

"Here they are, brothers!" I shouted. "On, on, and take them! They're ours!"

I even started back towards the court, stumbling artistically to let them catch up – and if you think it was a desperate stratagem . . . well, it was, but it seldom fails, and it would have succeeded then if I'd had the wit to follow a yard or two farther as they raced past me. But I was too quick to turn again and flee; one of them must have seen me from the tail of his eye and realised that this vociferous *badmash* wasn't one of the gang, for he pulled up, yelling, and came after me. I held my lead round one corner and the next, saw a convenient opening and dodged through it, and crouched gasping in the shadows as the pursuit went tearing by. I leaned against the wall, eyes closed, utterly done with fear and exertion, getting my breath back, and only when I took a cautious peep out did it strike me that the scenery was familiar . . . the little wicket in the opening . . . I squealed aloud, wheeling round, and sure enough, there before me was the outside stairway up to the porch, and two fellows were carrying down the earthly remains of Sefreen Singh,

167

and from various parts of Bibi Kalil's garden about a dozen bearded faces were regarding me with astonishment. Among them, not ten feet away, arms akimbo and scowling like a teetotal magistrate, was General Maka Khan, and beside him, exclaiming with unholy delight, was the Akali fanatic.

I've said I don't give up easy, and it's with pride that I recall tumbling out into the alley and tottering away, calling for the police, but they were on me within five yards, bearing me bodily into the garden, while I announced my name and consequence at the top of my voice, until they stuffed a gag into my mouth. They dragged me round to the garden room and thrust me into a chair, two holding my arms and a third my hair; they were street rascals, but the others who crowded in were Khalsa to a man, some in uniform; apart from Maka and the Akali there were Sikh officers, a burly *naik**
of artillery with a hideously-pitted face, and Imam Shah, knives and all. He threw my blood-stained short sword on the table.

"Two dead in the street, lord general," says he. "And your aide, Sefreen. The others who were with this one have not yet been found –"

"Then stop the search," says Maka Khan. "We have what we want – and if one of the others is who I think he is . . . the less we see of him the better."

"And the widow?" cries the Akali. "That practising slut who has betrayed us?"

"Let them both go! They'll do us less harm alive than if we had their deaths to answer for." He pointed at me. "Remove the gag."

They did, and I choked down my fear and was beginning my diplomatic bluster, demanding release and safe-conduct and immunity and the rest, but I'd barely got the length of warning them of the consequences of assaulting an accredited envoy when Maka Khan snapped me off short.

"You are no envoy – and you've forgotten what it is to be a soldier!" barks he. "You are a murderer and a spy!"

"It's a lie! I didn't kill him, I swear! It was Goolab Singh!

*Corporal.

168

Damn you all, loose me this instant, you villains, or it'll be the worse for you! I'm an agent of Sir Henry Hardinge –"

"An agent of Black-coat Broadfoot!" blazes the Akali, shaking his fist. "You send out cyphers, betraying the secrets of our durbar! You put them in the Holy Book by your bed – blaspheming your own putrid faith! – whence your old *punkah-wallah* took them to a courier for Simla! Aye, until we found him out two weeks ago, and questioned him," gloats this maniac, "and learned enough to nail your guilt to your forehead! Aye, gape, spy! We *know!*"

No doubt I was gaping – in part, at the news that the mysterious messenger of Second Thessalonians was not Mangla, as I'd suspected, but that lean-shanked ancient who'd operated my fan so inefficiently . . . and who must have vanished without my noticing, to be replaced by the clown I'd leathered only last night. But they were bluffing; they could question the old buffoon until Hell froze – those cyphers were Greek to him, and to everyone else, save Broadfoot and me. I wasn't reasoning too clearly, you understand, but I saw the line I must take.

"General Maka Khan!" cries I, no doubt in indignant falsetto. "This is outrageous! I demand to be set free at once! To be sure I send coded messages to my chief – so does every ambassador, and you know it! But to suggest that they contain any . . . any secrets of the durbar, is . . . is, why, it's a damnable insult! They . . . they were my confidential opinions on the Soochet legacy, for Sir Henry and his advisers –"

"Including your opinion that the astrologers' failure to find a date for our march was caused by 'a lady's fine Punjabi hand'?" says he, sternly. "Yes, Mr Flashman, we have read that message, and every other that you've sent this ten days past, as well as those coming to you from Simla." So that was why George's correspondence had dried up . . .

"We have enough to hang you, spy!" shouts the Akali, spraying me with spittle. "But first we would know what else you've betrayed – and you'll tell us, you sneaking dog!"

I wasn't hearing aright . . . or they were lying. They might

169

have intercepted messages – but they couldn't have deciphered them, not in a century. Yet Maka had just quoted my own words to Broadfoot . . . and Goolab had spoken of a false message to entrap me. I hadn't had time to ponder that impossibility . . . no, it couldn't be so! The key to that cypher was based on random words in an English novel that they'd never heard of – and even if they had, it would be as useless to them as a safe to which they didn't know the combination.

"It's all false, I tell you!" I stammered. "General, I appeal to you! Those messages were innocent, on my honour!"

He gave me a long cold stare while I babbled, and then he called out, and in trooped the oddest trio – a bespectacled little weed of a *chi-chi* in a soiled European suit, and two jelly-fat babus who smirked uneasily among all these rough military men. The *chi-chi* carried a sheaf of papers which, at a sign from Maka Khan, were thrust before my eyes . . . and my heart missed a beat. For it was a manuscript, in English, copied exactly, line for line, space for space, and the top sheet bore the unbelievable words:

"*Crotchet Castle*. By Thomas Love Peacock".

And beneath the title, in a clerkly Indian hand, but again in English, were precise directions for using the book in the encoding of messages.

Reviewing my career in India, I'd say that of all the wonders I saw there, that was the greatest. I dare say one should be prepared for anything in a land where an illiterate peasant girl can give you the square root of a six-figure number at first glance, but when I reflect on the skill and speed of those copyists, and the analytical genius that penetrated that code . . . well, it can still rob me of breath. Not as entirely as it did at the time, though.

"Your *punkah-wallah* confessed how you wrote your cyphers with the aid of a book," sneers the Akali. "It was copied in your absence, and compared with the intercepted cyphers by these men, who are skilled in cryptography – an Indian invention, as Major Broadfoot should have borne in mind!"

"Oah, indeed! A veree simple cypher," chirps the *chi-chi*, while the babus beamed and nodded. "Quite elementaree, you know, page numbers, dates of Christian calendar, initial letters of arl-tarnate lines –"

"That will do," says Maka Khan, and dismissed them, but one of the babus couldn't resist a backward gleek at me. "Doctor Folliott and Mr McQuedy are jolly good fun!" squeaks he, and waddled out as fast as he could go.

I sat sick and trembling. No wonder they'd been able to fake a message to trap me – with one tiny error of style which I'd been fool enough to ignore. What the devil had I written in my cyphers, though . . . they'd spotted the allusion to Jeendan, but I hadn't named her . . . but what else had I said . . .?

"You see?" says Maka Khan. "What you have written of late, we know. What else have you learned, up at the Fort yonder?"

171

"Nothing, as God's my witness!" I bleated. "General, upon my honour, sir! I protest . . . your cryptographers are mistaken – or lying! Yes, that's it!" I hollered. "It's a beastly plot, to discredit me – to give you an excuse for war! Well, it won't serve, you scoundrels! What? Yes, it will, I mean – you'll learn fast enough –"

"Let's have him below!" snarls the Akali. "He'll babble as freely as his creature did!" There were growls of agreement from the others, and I fairly neighed in alarm.

"What d'you mean, damn you? I'm a British Officer, and if you lay a finger –" They clapped the gag over my mouth again, and I could only listen in horror while the Akali swore that time was pressing, so the sooner they set about me the better, and they argued to and fro until Maka Khan turned them all out of the room, except for my three guards and the pock-marked *naik* – his face gave me the shudders, but I took some comfort from the fact that Maka had taken matters on himself; damned uncivil he'd been, what with "spy" and "murderer", but he was a gentleman and a soldier, after all, and like calls to like, you know. Why, standing there tall and erect, glaring at me and twisting his grizzled moustache, he might have been any staff colonel at Horse Guards, bar the turban. Better still, he addressed me in English, so that the others should be none the wiser.

"You spoke of war," says he. "It has begun. Our advance guard is already across the Sutlej.[27] In a few days there will be a general engagement between the Khalsa and the Company army under Sir Hugh Gough. I tell you this so that you may understand your position – you are now beyond help from Simla."

So it had finally come, and I was a prisoner of war. Well, better here than there – at least I'd be out of harm's way.

"No, you are not a prisoner!" snaps Maka Khan. "You are a spy! Be quiet!" He took a turn about, and leaned down to stare grimly into my face. "We of the Khalsa know that our queen regent has turned traitor. We also suspect the loyalty of Lal Singh, our Wazir, and Tej Singh, our field commander. You have been Mai Jeendan's intimate – her lover. We know she has sent assurances through you to

172

Broadfoot – so much is plain from your recent cyphers. But what has she betrayed, in detail, of our plan of campaign – numbers, dispositions, lines of march, objectives, equipment?" He paused, his black eyes boring into mine. "Your one hope, Flashman, lies in full disclosure ... immediately."

"But I don't know anything, I tell you! Nothing! I've not heard a word of . . . of plans or objectives or any such thing! And I haven't even seen Mai Jeendan for weeks –"

"Her woman Mangla visited you last night!" His words came out like rapid fire. "You spent hours together – what did she tell you? How have you passed it to Simla? Through her? Or the man Harlan, who poses as your orderly? Or by some other means? We know you sent no cypher today –"

"As God's my judge, it ain't true! She told me nothing!"

"Then why did she visit you?"

"Why . . . why . . . because, well, we've grown friendly, don't you know? I mean . . . we talk, you see, and . . . Not a word of politics, I swear! We just . . . converse . . . and so forth . . ."

God, it sounded lame, as the truth often does, and it drove him into a rage. "Either you're a fool, or you think I am!" he rasped. "Very well, I'll waste no more time! Your *punkah-wallah* spoke under persuasion . . . in unspeakable pain, which I trust you will spare yourself. You have a choice: speak to me now, in this room . . . or to this fellow . . ." He indicated the pock-marked *naik*, who took a pace forward, scowling ". . . in the cellar below."

For a moment I didn't believe my ears. Oh, I'd been threatened with torture before, by savages like Gul Shah and those beastly Malagassies – but this was a man of honour, a general, an aristocrat! I wouldn't believe it, not from someone who might have been Cardigan's own brother, dammit –

"You don't mean it!" I yelped. "I don't believe you! It's a trick . . . a mean, cowardly trick! You wouldn't dare! But you're trying to frighten me, damn you . . ."

"Yes, I am." His voice and eyes were dead level. "But it is no empty threat. There is too much at stake. We are

173

beyond diplomatic niceties, or the laws of war. Very soon now, hundreds – perhaps thousands – of men will be dying in agony beyond the Sutlej, Indian and British alike. I cannot afford to spare you, when the fate of the war may depend on what you can tell me."

By God, he *did* mean it – and before that iron stare I broke down utterly, weeping and begging him to believe me.

"But I don't know a damned thing! For Christ's sake, it's the truth! Yes, yes, she's betraying you! She promised to warn us . . . and, yes! she's delayed, and made the astrologers bungle it –"

"You tell me what I know already!" cries he impatiently.

"But it's all *I* know, blast you! She never said a word of plans – oh, if she had I'd tell you! Please, sir, for pity's sake, don't let them torture me! I can't bear it – and it'd do no good, damn you, you cruel old bastard, because I've nothing to confess! Oh, God, if I had, I'd tell you, if I could –"

"I doubt it. Indeed, I am sure you would not," says he, and before those words and tone, suddenly so flat, almost weary, I left off blubbering to stare. He was standing ramrod straight, but not in disgust or contempt at my ravings – if anything, he looked regretful, with a touch of ruptured nobility, even. I couldn't fathom it until, to my horrified amazement, he went on, in the same quiet voice:

"You overplay the coward's part too far, Mr Flashman. You would have me believe you an abject, broken thing, dead to honour, a cur who would confess everything, betray everything, at a mere threat – and on whom, therefore, torture would be wasted." He shook his head. "Major Broadfoot does not employ such people – and your own reputation belies you. No, you will tell nothing . . . until pain robs you of your reason. You know your duty, as I know mine. It drives us both to shameful extremes – me, to barbarism for my country's sake; you, to this pretence of cowardice – a legitimate ruse in a political agent, but not convincing from the man who held Piper's Fort! I am sorry." His mouth worked for a moment, and I won't swear there wasn't a tear in his blasted eye. "I can give you an hour . . . before they begin. For God's sake, use it to see reason! Take him down!"

He turned away, like a strong suffering man who's had the last word. He hadn't, though. "Pretence!" I screamed, as they hauled me from the chair. "You bloody old halfwit, it's true! I'm not shamming, damn you, I swear it! I can't tell you anything! Oh, Jesus! Please, please, let me be! Mercy, you foul old kite! Can't you see I'm telling the truth!"

By that time they were dragging me through the garden to the back of the house, thrusting me through a low iron-shod door and down an immensely long flight of stone steps into the depths of a great cellar, a dank tomb of rough stone walls with only a small window high up on the far side. A choking acrid smell rose to meet us, and as the *naik* set a burning torch in a bracket by the stair foot, the source of that stench became horribly apparent.

"Are you weary, *Daghabazi Sahib*?"* cries he. "See, we have a fine bed for you to rest on!"

I looked, and almost swooned. In the centre of the earth floor lay a great rectangular tray in which charcoal glowed faintly under a coating of ash, and about three feet above it was a rusty iron grill like a bedstead – with manacles at head and foot. Watching my face, the *naik* cackled with laughter, and taking up a long poker, went forward and tapped open two little vents on either side of the tray. The charcoal near the vents glowed a little brighter.

"Gently blows the air," gloats he, "and slowly grows the heat." He laid a hand on the grill. "A little warm, only . . . but in an hour it will be warmer. *Daghabazi Sahib* will begin to feel it, then. He may even find his tongue." He tossed the poker aside. "Put him to bed!"

I can't describe the horror of it. I couldn't even scream as they ran me forward and flung me down on that diabolic gridiron, snapping the fetters on my wrists and ankles so that I was held supine, unable to do more than writhe on the rusty bars – and then the pock-marked fiend picked up a pair of bellows from the floor, grinning with savage delight.

"You will be in some discomfort when we return,

*Daghabazi=treachery.

175

Daghabazi Sahib! Then we shall open the vents a little more – your *punkah-wallah* cooked slowly, for many hours – did he not, Jan? Oh, he spoke long before he began to roast . . . that followed, though I think he had no more to tell." He leaned down to laugh in my face. "And if you find it tedious, we may hasten matters – thus!"

He thrust the bellows under the foot of the grill, pumping once, a sudden gust of heat struck my calves – and I found my tongue at last, in a shriek that tore my throat, again and again, as I struggled helplessly. They crowed with laughter, those devils, as I raved in terror and imagined agony, swearing I had nothing to tell, pleading for mercy, promising them anything – a fortune if they'd let me go, rupees and mohurs by the lakh, God knows what else. Then perhaps I swooned in earnest, for all I remember is the *naik*'s jeering voice from far off: "In an hour's time! Rest well, *Daghabazi Sahib*!" and the clang of the iron door.

There are, in case you didn't know it, five degrees of torture, as laid down by the Spanish Inquisition, and I was now suffering the fourth – the last before the bodily torment begins. How I kept my sanity is a mystery – I'm not sure but that I *did* go mad, for a spell, for I came out of my swoon babbling: "No, no, Dawson, I swear I didn't peach! 'twasn't me – it was Speedicut! He blabbed on you to her father – not me! I swear it – oh, please, please, Dawson, don't roast me!", and I could see the fat brute's great whiskered moon face leering into mine as he held me before the schoolroom fire, vowing to bake me till I blistered. I know now that that roasting at Rugby was worse, for real corporal anguish, than my ordeal at Lahore – but at least I'd known that Dawson must leave off at the last, whereas in Bibi Kalil's cellar, with the growing heat only beginning to make my back and legs tingle and run rivers of sweat, I knew that it would continue, hotter and ever hotter, to the unspeakable end. That's the horror of the fourth degree, as the Inquisitors knew – but while their heretics and religious idiots could always get off by telling the bloody Dagoes what they wanted to hear, I couldn't. *I didn't know.*

The mind's a strange mechanism. Chained to that

abominable grill, I began to *burn*, and strained to arch my body away from the bars, until I fainted again – and when I came to my senses, why, I was only uncomfortably warm for a moment – until I remembered where I was, and in an instant my clothes were catching fire, the flames were scorching my flesh, and I shrieked my way into oblivion once more. Yet it was only in my mind; my clothing was barely being singed – whereas Dawson burned my britches' arse out, the fat swine, and I couldn't sit for a week.

I can't tell how long it was before I realised that, while undoubtedly getting hotter and being half-suffocated by fumes, I had not yet burst into flames. The discovery steadied me enough to leave off my incoherent squealing and weeping, and rave to some purpose, bellowing my name, rank, and diplomatic status at the very top of my voice, in the faint hope that it might carry through that high window to the distant alleys around the house and attract the attention of a friendly passer-by – you know, some reckless adventurer or knight errant who'd think nothing of invading a house full of Khalsa thugs to rescue a perfect stranger who was browning nicely in the cellar.

Aye, laugh, but it saved me – and taught me the folly of stoic silence. If I'd been Dick Champion, biting the bullet and disdaining to cry out, I'd have been broiled to cinders; roaring my coward head off did the trick – but only just in time. For my hollering was starting to fade to a hoarse whimper, and the growing heat beating up from below was forcing me to toss and turn continuously, when I heard the noise. I couldn't place it at first . . . a distant scraping, too heavy for a rat, coming from overhead. I forced myself to lie still, labouring for breath . . . there it was again! Then it stopped, to be followed by a different sound, and for a dreadful moment I knew I *had* gone mad in that hellish dungeon . . . it wasn't possible, it could only be a tortured delusion, that in the darkness above me someone, very softly, was whistling "Drink, puppy, drink".

Suddenly I knew it was real. I was in my senses, writhing on that grill, gasping for air – but there it was again, faint but clear from outside the window, the little hunting song that

177

I've whistled all my life – "Harry's Pibroch", Elspeth calls it. Someone was using it to signal – I tried to moisten my parched lips with a tongue like leather, found I couldn't, and in desperation began to croak:

For he'll grow into a hound,
So we'll pass the bottle round,
And merrily we'll whoop and holloa![28]

Silence, except for my gasps and groans, then a scrambling rush, a thud, and through the suffocating mist a figure was looming over me, and a horrified face was peering into mine.

"Holy Jesus!" cries Jassa – and as the bolt rasped back in the door he fairly flung himself away, burrowing among the rubble in the shadows along the wall. The door swung open, and the *naik* appeared on the threshold. For a long, awful moment he stood looking down at me as I struggled and panted on the grill – in a frenzy of fear that he'd seen Jassa, that the fatal hour was up . . . and then he sang out:

"Is the bed to your liking, *Daghabazi Sahib*? What, not warm enough yet? Oh, patience . . . only a moment now!"

He guffawed at his own priceless wit, and went out, leaving the door ajar – and here was Jassa, muttering hideous oaths as he worked at my fetters. They were simple bolts, and in a moment he had them loose and I had lurched off that hellish gridiron and was lying face down on the filthy cool earth, panting and retching. Jassa knelt beside me, urging haste, and I forced myself up; my back and legs were smarting, but didn't feel as though they were badly burned, and with the *naik* plainly about to return at any moment I was in a fever to be away.

"Can you climb?" whispers Jassa, and I saw there was a camel rope dangling from the window fifteen feet above our heads. "I'll go first – if you can't make it, we'll haul you!" He seized the rope and walked up the wall like an acrobat, until he had his legs over the sill. "Up – quick!" he hissed, and I leaned on the wall a second to fetch my breath and my senses, rubbed my hands on the dirt, and laid hold on the rope.

I may not be brave, but I'm strong, and exhausted as I was

178

I climbed by my arms alone, hauling my dead weight hand over hand, bumping and scraping against the wall – no work for a weakling, but my mortal funk was such that I could have done it with Henry VIII on my back. Up I went, nearly sick with hope, and the sill wasn't a yard above me when I heard the door thrown back in the cell below.

I almost let go my hold in despair, but even as a yell sounded from the doorway, Jassa's hand was on my collar, and I heaved for my life. I got an elbow on the sill, looked down, and saw the *naik* bounding down the steps with his gang at his heels. Jassa was through the window, hauling at me, and I got a leg over the sill; from the tail of my eye I saw one of the ruffians below swinging back his hand, there was a flash of steel, and I winced away as a thrown knife struck sparks from the wall. Jassa's pistol banged deafeningly before my face, and I saw the *naik* stagger and fall. I yelled with joy, and then I was over the sill. "Drop!" shouts Jassa, and I fell about ten feet, landing with a jar that sent a stabbing pain through my left ankle. I took one step and went down, bleating, as Jassa dropped beside me and heaved me up again.

My heart went out to Goolab Singh and his gouty foot in that moment, as I thought: crocked, bigod, and only one leg to run with. Jassa had me by the shoulders; he let out a piercing whistle and suddenly there was a man on my other side, stooping beneath my arm. Between them they half-carried me, howling at every step; two shots sounded somewhere to my left, I saw pistol-flashes in the gloom, people were yelling, branches whipped my face as we blundered along, and then we were in an alley, a mounted man was alongside, and Jassa was heaving me almost bodily up behind. I clasped the rider round the waist, turning to look back, and there was Bibi Kalil's gate, and a cowled black figure was cutting with a sabre at someone within and then sprinting after us.

The alley seemed to be full of horsemen – in fact there were only four, including Jassa. Voices were yelling behind us, feet were pounding, a torch was flaring in the gateway – and then we were round the corner.

179

"Gently does the trick," says Jassa, at my elbow. "They ain't horsed. You doing well there, lieutenant? Right, *jemadar*, walk-march – trot!" He urged his beast ahead, and we swung in behind him.

However he came there, he was a complete hand, our Philadelphia sawbones. Left to myself I'd have been off full tilt, blundering heaven knows where and coming to grief like as not. Jassa knew just where he wanted to go, and what time he had in hand; we trotted round a corner into a little court which I recognised as the one in which Goolab and I had opened the batting, and lo! there were two more riders on post, and to my astonishment I recognised them, and my rescuers, as black robes of Alick Gardner's. Well, no doubt all would be made clear presently. They led the way up a long lane, and at the end Jassa reined in to look back – by George, there were torches entering the lane at a run, a bare fifty paces behind, and suddenly all my pain and fear and bewilderment vanished in overwhelming blind rage (as often happens when I've been terrified to death, and reckon I'm safe). By God, I'd make 'em pay, the vile, torturing scoundrels; there was a pistol in my rider's saddle holster, and I plucked it out, bellowing, while Jassa demanded to know what the devil I was about.

"I'm going to kill one of those murdering bastards!" I roared. "Lay hands on me, you poxy vermin, you! Broil me on a damned gridiron, will you? Take that, you sons-of-bitches!" I blazed away, and had the satisfaction of seeing the torches scatter, though none of them went down.

"Say, won't that larn 'em, though!" cries Jassa. "You feel better now, lieutenant? You're sure – don't want to go back and burn their barn down? Fine – *achha, jemadar, jildi jao!*"

Which we did, at a steady canter in the broader ways, and at a walk in the twisting alleys, and as we rode I learned from Jassa what had brought my saviours at the eleventh hour.

He, it seemed, had been keeping a closer eye on me for weeks than ever I knew. He had spotted me leaving the Fort, and trailed me, wondering, to the French Soldiers' canteen and Bibi Kalil's house. Skulking in the shadows,

180

he'd seen me received by the widow, and having a foul mind, supposed I was bedded for the night. Fortunately, he'd skulked farther, spied the Khalsa bigwigs downstairs, and realised that there was villainy afoot. Deciding that he could do nothing alone, he'd legged it for the Fort, and made straight for Gardner.

"I figured you were treed, and needed help in numbers. Alick was the only hope – he may not cotton to me, exactly, but when I told him how you were under the same roof as Maka Khan and the Akali, didn't he jump, just? Didn't come himself, though – bad policy for him to be seen crossing the Khalsa, don't you know? But he told off the *jemadar* and a detail, and we hit the leather. I scouted the house, but no sign of you. A couple of sentries perambulating in the garden, though, and then I heard you hollering from the back of the house. I took a quiet slant that way, and marked the window your noise seemed to be coming from – say, you're a right audible soldier, ain't you? After that, two of the *jemadar*'s fellows smoothed out the sentries, and took station while he and I slipped along to your window – and here you are. They're capable, Alick's boys, no error. But what took you into that bear's den – and what in Creation were they doing to you?"

I didn't tell him. The events of the night were still a hideous jumble in my mind, and reaction had me in its grip. I was shaking so hard I barely kept the saddle, I wanted to vomit, and my ankle was throbbing with pain. Once again, when all seemed well, Lahore had become a nightmare, with enemies all about – the only bright side was that there seemed no lack of worthy souls eager to pluck me out of the soup. God bless America, if you like – they'd turned up trumps again, at no small risk to themselves, for if the Khalsa got wind that Gardner was aiding enemies of the state, he'd be in queer street.

"Don't you fret about Alick!" snorts Jassa. "He's got more lives'n a cat, and more nuts on the fire than you can count. He's Dalip's man, and Jeendan's man, and best chums with Broadfoot, and he's Goolab Singh's agent in Lahore, and –"

181

Goolab Singh! That was another who took an uncommon interest in Flashy's welfare. I was beginning to feel like a fives pill being thrashed about in a four-hand fifteen-up, with my seams split and the twine showing. Well, to the devil with it, I'd had enough. I reined in and demanded of Jassa where we were going; I'd been half aware that we were threading our way through the alleys near the south wall, and once or twice we'd skirted under the wall itself; we'd passed the great Looharree Gate and the Halfmoon Battery and were abreast of the Shah Alumee, which meant we were holding east, and were no nearer the Fort than when we'd started. Not that I minded that.

"For I'm not going back there, I can tell you! Broadfoot can peddle his pack and be damned! This bloody place ain't safe –"

"That's what Gardner reckoned," says Jassa. "He thinks you should make tracks for British territory. You know the war's started? Yes, sir, the Khalsa's over the river at half a dozen places between Harree-ke-puttan and Ferozepore – eighty thousand horse, foot, and guns on a thirty-mile front. God knows where Gough is – halfway to Delhi with his tail between his legs if you believe the bazaar, but I doubt it."

Seven thousand at Ferozepore, I was thinking. Well, Littler was done for – Wheeler, too, with his pitiful five thousand at Ludhiana . . . unless Gough had managed to reinforce. I'd had no sure word for three weeks, but it didn't seem possible that he could have concentrated strongly enough to resist the overwhelming Sikh tide that was pouring over the Sutlej. I thought of the vast horde I'd seen on Maian Mir, the massed battalions of foot, the endless squadrons of horse, those superb guns . . . and of Gough frustrated at every turn by that ass Hardinge, our sepoys on the edge of desertion or mutiny, our piecemeal garrisons strung along the frontier and down the Meerut road. Now it had come, like a hammer-blow, and we'd been caught napping, as usual. Well, Gough had better have God on his side, for if he didn't . . . farewell, India.

Which mattered rather less to me than the fact that I was a fugitive with a game ankle in the heart of the enemy camp.

So much for Broadfoot's idiot notions – I'd be safe in Lahore during hostilities, indeed! A fat lot of protection Jeendan could give me now, with the Khalsa wise to her treachery; it would be a *tulwar*, not a diamond, that would be decorating her pretty navel shortly.

"Moochee Gate," says Jassa, and over the low hovels I saw the towers ahead and to our right. We were approaching a broad street leading down to the gate, and the mouth of the alley was crowded with bystanders, even at that time of night, all craning to see; a band of music was playing a spirited march, there was the steady tramp of feet, and down the avenue to the gate came three regiments of Khalsa infantry – stalwart musketeers in white with black cross-belts, their pieces at the shoulder, bayonets fixed; then Dogra light infantry in green, with white trousers, muskets at the trail; a battalion of spearmen in white flowing robes, their sashes bristling with pistols, their broad turbans wound round steel caps surmounted by green plumes. They swung along with a fierce purpose that made my heart sink, the flaring cressets on the wall glittering on that forest of steel as it passed under the arch, the girls showering them with petals as they passed, the *chicos* striding alongside, shrilling with delight – half Lahore seemed to have left its bed that night to see the troops march away to join their comrades on the river.

As each regiment approached the arch it gave a great cheer, and I thanked God for the shadows as I saw that they were saluting a little knot of mounted officers in gorgeous coats, with the rotund figure of Tej Singh at their head. He was wearing a *puggaree* as big as himself, and enough jewellery to start a shop; he shook a sheathed *tulwar* over his head in response to the troops' weapons brandished in unison as they chanted: "*Khalsa-ji! Wa Guru-ji ko Futteh!* To Delhi! To London! Victory!"

After them came cavalry, regular units, lancers in white and dragoons in red, jingling by, and finally a baggage train of camels, and Tej left off saluting, the band gave over, and people turned away to the booths and grog shops. Jassa told the *jemadar* to have the riders follow us singly, and then my

183

rider dismounted and Jassa began to lead my beast down towards the gate.

"Hold on," says I. "Where away?"

"That's your way home, wouldn't you say?" says he, and when I reminded him that I was all in, dry, famished, and one-legged, he grinned all over his ugly mug and said that would be attended to directly, I'd see. So I let him lead on under the great arch, past the spearmen standing guard in their mail coats and helms; my *puggaree*, like my sword and pepperbox, had gone during the evening's activities, but one of the riders had lent me a cloak with a hood, which I kept close about my face; no one gave us a second glance.

Beyond the gate were the usual shanties and hovels of the beggars, but farther out on the *maidan* a few camp fires were winking, and Jassa made for one beside a little grove of white poplars, where a small tent was pitched, with a couple of horses picketed close by. The first streak of dawn was lightening the sky to the east, silhouetting the camels and wagons on the southern road; the night air was dry and bitter cold, and I was shivering as we reached the fire. A man squatting on a rug beside it rose at our approach, and before I saw his face I recognised the long rangy figure of Gardner. He nodded curtly to me, and asked Jassa if there had been any trouble, or pursuit.

"Now, Alick, you know me!" cries that worthy, and Gardner growled that he did, and how many signatures had he forged along the way. The same genial Gurdana Khan, I could see – but just the sight of that fierce eye and jutting nose made me feel safe for the first time that night.

"What's wrong with your foot?" snaps he, as I climbed awkwardly down and leaned, wincing, on Jassa. I told him, and he swore.

"You have a singular gift for making the sparks fly upward! Let's have a look at it." He prodded, making me yelp. "Damnation! It'll take days to mend! Very well, *Doctor* Harlan, there's cold water in the *chatti* – let's see you exercise the medical skill that was the talk of Pennsylvania, I don't doubt! There's curry in the pan, and coffee on the fire."

He picketed the horse while I wolfed curry and *chapattis* and Jassa bound my ankle with a cold cloth; it was badly sprained and swollen like a football, but he had a soothing touch and made it feel easier. Gardner came back to squat cross-legged beyond the fire, drinking coffee with the aid of his iron neck-clamp and eyeing me sourly. He'd left off his bumbee tartan rig, no doubt to avoid notice, and wore a cowled black robe, with his Khyber knife across his knees: a damned discouraging sight all round, with questions to match.

"Now, Mr Flashman," growls he. "Explain yourself. What folly took you among the Khalsa – and at such a time, too? Well, sir – what were you doing in that house?"

I knew I would be relying on him for my passage home, so I told him – all of it, from the false message to Jassa's rescue, and he listened with a face like flint. The only interruption came from Jassa, when I mentioned my encounter with Goolab Singh.

"You don't say! The old Golden Hen! Now what would he be doing so far from Kashmir?" Gardner rounded on him.

"Minding his own dam' business! And you'll do likewise, Josiah, you hear me? Not a word about him! Yes . . . while I think on it, you'd best take yourself out of earshot."

"That's for Mr Flashman to say!" retorts Jassa.

"Mr Flashman agrees with me!" barks Gardner, fixing me with a cold eye, so I nodded, and Jassa loafed off in a pet. "He did well by you tonight," says Gardner, watching him go, "but I still wouldn't trust him across the street. Go on."

I finished my tale, and he observed with grim satisfaction that it had all fallen out for the best. I said I was glad he thought so, and pointed out that it wasn't his arse that had been toasted over a slow fire. He just grunted.

"Maka Khan'd never ha' gone through with it. He'd try to scare you, but torture isn't his style."

"The devil it ain't! Good God, man, I was half-broiled, I tell you! Those swine would have stopped at nothing! Why, they roasted my *punkah-wallah* to death –"

185

"So they told you. Even if they did, a no-account nigger's one thing, a white officer's another. Still, you were lucky . . . thanks to Josiah. Yes, and to Goolab Singh."

I asked him why he thought Goolab and the widow had taken such risks on my behalf, and he stared at me as though I were half-witted.

"He told you plain enough, I'd say! The more good turns he does the British, the better they'll like him. He's promised to stand by 'em in the war, but protecting you is worth a thousand words. He's counting on you to do him credit with Hardinge – and you do it, d'you hear? Goolab's an old fox, but he's a brave man and a strong ruler, and deserves to have your people confirm him as king in Kashmir when this war's over."

It seemed to me he was being optimistic in thinking we'd be in a position to confirm *anyone* in Kashmir when the Khalsa had done with us, but I didn't care to croak in front of a Yankee, so I said offhand: "You think we'll beat the Khalsa quite handily, then?"

"There'll be some damned long faces in Lahore Fort if you don't," says he bluntly, and before I could ask him to explain that bewildering remark, he added: "But you'll be able to watch the fight from the ringside yourself, before the week's out."

"I don't see that," says I. "I agree I can't stay in Lahore, but I'm in no case to ride for the frontier in a hurry, either – not with this confounded leg. I mean, even in disguise, you never know – I might have to cut and run, and I'd rather have two sound pins for that, what?" So you'd best find me a safe, comfortable spot to lie up in meanwhile, was what I was hinting, and waited for him to agree. He didn't.

"We can't wait for your leg to mend! This war is liable to be won and lost in a few days at most – which means you must be across the Sutlej without delay, even if you have to be carried!" He glared at me, whiskers bristling. "The fate of India may well depend on that, Mr Flashman!"

The sun couldn't have got him, not in December, and he wasn't tight. Tactfully I asked him how the fate of India came into it, since I had no vital intelligence to take with me,

186

and my addition to the forces of the Company, while no doubt welcome in its small way, could hardly be decisive.

"Forces of the Company my aunt's petticoat!" snarls he. "You're going in with the Khalsa!"

If life has taught me anything at all, it's how to keep my countenance in the presence of strong, authoritative men whose rightful place is in a padded cell. I've known a power of them, to my cost, and Alick Gardner's a minor figure in a list that includes the likes of Bismarck, Palmerston, Lincoln, Gordon, John Charity Spring, M.A., George Custer, and the White Raja, to say nothing of my beloved mentor, Dr Arnold, and my old guv'nor (who *did* end his days in a blue-devil factory, bless him). Many of them men of genius, no doubt, but all sharing the delusion that they could put any proposal, however lunatic, to young Flashy and make him like it. There's no arguing with such fellows, of course; all you can do, if you're lucky, is nod and say: "Well, sir, that's an interesting notion, to be sure – just before you tell me more about it, would you excuse me for a moment?" and once you're round the corner, make for the high ground. I've seldom had that chance, unfortunately, and there's nothing for it but to sit with an expression of attentive idiocy trying to figure a way out. Which is what I did with Gardner while he elaborated his monstrous suggestion.

"You're going with the Khalsa," says he, "to ensure its defeat. It's doomed and damned already, thanks to Mai Jeendan – but you can make it certain."

You see what I mean – the man was plainly *must,** doolali,* afflicted of Allah, too long in the hills altogether – but one doesn't like to say so, straight out, not to a chap who affects tartan pants and has a Khyber knife across his lap. So I

Must is the madness of the rogue elephant. Doolali=insane, from Deolali Camp, inland from Bombay, where generations of British soldiers (including the editor) were received in India, and supposedly were affected by sunstroke.

188

avoided the main point for a lesser but equally curious one.

"I don't quite follow, Gardner, old fellow," says I. "You say the Khalsa's doomed . . . and it's *Jeendan*'s doing? But . . . she never wanted this war, you know. She's been working to avoid it – hocussing the Khalsa, delaying 'em, holding 'em back. They know it, too – Maka Khan told me. And now they've broken loose, in spite of her –"

"In spite of . . . why, you jackass!" cries he, glaring like the Ancient Mariner. "She *started* it! Don't you understand – she's been planning this war for months! Why? To destroy the Khalsa, of course – to see it exterminated, root and branch! Sure, she held 'em back – until the cold weather, until she'd fixed it so they have the worst possible generals, until she'd bought time for Gough! But not to *avoid* war, no sir! Just to make sure that when she *did* send 'em in, the Khalsa would get whipped five ways to Sunday! Don't you know that?"

"Talk sense – why should she want to destroy her own army?"

"Because if she doesn't, it will sure as hell destroy *her* in the end!" He fetched a deep breath. "See here . . . you know the Khalsa's gotten too big for its britches, don't you? For six years it's been ruining the Punjab, defying government, doing as it dam' well pleases –"

"I know all that, but "

"Well, don't you see, the ruling clique – Jeendan and the nobles – have had their power and fortunes wiped out, their very existence threatened? So of course they want the Khalsa crushed – and the only force on earth that can do that is John Company! *That*'s why they've been trying to provoke a war – that's why Jawaheer wanted one! But they murdered him – and that's another score Mai Jeendan has to settle. You remember her that night at Maian Mir, don't you? She was sentencing the Khalsa then, Mr Flashman – now she's executing them!"

I remembered her screaming hate at the Khalsa over Jawaheer's body – but Gardner still wasn't making sense. "Dammit, if the Khalsa goes under, she'll go with it!" I protested. "She's their queen – and you say she's set

189

them on! Well, if they lose, she'll be finished, won't she?"

He sighed, shaking his head. "Son, it won't even take the dander out of her hair. When they *lose*, she's *won*. Consider . . . Britain doesn't want to *conquer* the Punjab – too much trouble. It just wants it nice and quiet, with no Khalsa running wild, and a stable Sikh government who'll do what Hardinge tells 'em. So . . . when the Khalsa's licked, your chiefs won't annex the Punjab – no, sir! They'll find it convenient to keep little Dalip on the throne, with Jeendan as regent – which means that she and the nobles will be riding high again, squeezing the fat out of the country just like old times – and with no Khalsa to worry about."

"Hold on! Are you saying that this war's a put-up job – that they *know*, in Simla, that Jeendan is hoping we'll destroy her army, for her own benefit? I won't have that! Why, it'd be collusion . . . conspiracy . . . aiding and abetting –"

"No such thing! Oh, they know in Simla what she's after – or they suspect, leastways. But what can they do about it? Give the Khalsa free passage to Delhi?" He snorted. "Hardinge's *got* to fight, whether he likes it or not! And while he may not welcome the war, there are plenty of 'forward policy' men like Broadfoot who do. But that doesn't mean they're in cahoots with Mai Jeendan – the way she's fixed things, they don't need to be!"

I sat silent, trying to take it in . . . and feeling no end of a fool. Evidently I had misjudged the lady. Oh, I'd guessed there was steel inside my drunken, avid little houri, but hardly of the temper that could slaughter scores of thousands of men just for her own political convenience and personal comfort. Mind you, what other reasons do statesmen and princes ever have for making war, when all the sham's been stripped away? Oh, and she had her sot of a brother to avenge, to be sure. But I wondered if her calculations were right; I could spot one almighty imponderable, and I voiced it to Gardner, whether it sounded like croaking or not.

"But suppose we don't beat the Khalsa? How can she be so sure we will? There's a hell of a lot of 'em, and we're

190

spread thin . . . Wait, though! Maka Khan was in a great sweat in case she'd betrayed their plans of campaign! Well, has she?"

Gardner shook his head. "She's done better than that. She's put the conduct of the war in the hands of Lal Singh, her Wazir and lover, and Tej Singh, her commander-in-chief who'd set fire to his own mother to keep warm." He nodded grimly. "They'll see to it that Gough doesn't have too much trouble."

Suddenly I remembered Lal Singh's words to me . . . "I wonder how we should acquit ourselves against such a seasoned campaigner as Sir Hugh Gough . . .?"

"My God," says I, with reverence. "You mean they're ready to . . . to fight a cross? To sell the pass? But . . . does Gough know? I mean, have they arranged with him –?"

"No, sir. That's your part. That's why you have to join the Khalsa." He leaned forward, the hawk face close to mine. "You're going to Lal Singh. By tomorrow he'll be lying before Ferozepore with twenty thousand *gorracharra.* He'll tell you his plans, and Tej Singh's – numbers, armaments, dispositions, intentions, all of it – and you'll carry them to Gough and Hardinge. And then . . . well, it should be an interesting little war . . . what's the matter?"

I'd been struggling for speech during this fearful recital, but when I found words it wasn't to protest, or argue, or scream, but to pose a profound military question:

"But . . . hell's bells! Look here . . . they can give away plans – arrange for a few regiments to go astray – lose a battle on purpose, I dare say . . . But, man alive, how do they betray an army of a hundred thousand men? I mean . . . how d'you sell *a whole war?*"

"It'll take management, no denying. As I said, an interesting little war." He tossed another billet on the fire, and rose. "When it's over, and you're back in Lahore with the British peace mission – you can tell me all about it."

*   *   *

My first thought, as I sat by the fire with my head in my

191

hands, was: this is Broadfoot's doing. He's planned the whole hideous thing, start to finish, and kept me in the dark till the last moment, the treacherous, crooked, conniving, Scotch . . . political! Well, I was doing him an injustice; for once, George was innocent. He might welcome the war, as Gardner had said, and have a shrewd notion that Jeendan was launching the Khalsa in the hope of seeing it wrecked, but neither he nor anyone else in Simla knew that the Sikhs' two leading commanders were under her orders to give the whole game away. Nor could he guess the base use that was being made of his prize agent, Lieutenant Flashman, late 11th Hussars, in this hour of crisis.

The notion that I should be the messenger of betrayal had been another inspiration of Jeendan's, according to Gardner. How long she'd had me in mind for the role of go-between, he didn't know; she'd confided it to him only the previous day, and he and Mangla would have brought me my marching orders that same night – if I hadn't been away gallivanting with the Khalsa and Goolab and the merry widow. Most inconsiderate of me, but all's ill that ends ill – here I was still, ankle crocked and guts fermenting with fright, meet to be hurled into the soup in furtherance of that degenerate royal doxy's intrigues, and no way to cry off that I could see.

I tried, you may be sure, pleading my ankle, and the impossibility of taking orders from any but my own chiefs, and the folly of venturing again among enemies who'd already toasted me to a turn – Gardner answered every objection with the blunt fact that someone had to take Lal's plans to Gough, and no one else had my qualifications. It was my duty, says he, and if you wonder that I bowed to his authority – well, take a squint at the portrait in his *Memoirs*; that should convince you.

I'm still not sure, by the way, exactly where his loyalties lay. To Dalip and Jeendan, certainly: what she ordered, he performed. But he played a staunch game on our behalf, too, and on Goolab Singh's. When I ventured to ask him where he stood, he looked down that beak of a nose and snapped: "On my own two feet!" So there.

192

He had Jeendan's infernal scheme all pat, and after I'd had a couple of hours' sleep and Jassa had rebound my swollen ankle, he lined it out to me; horrid risky it sounded. "You ride straight hence to Lal's camp beyond the Sutlej, with four of my men as escort, all of you disguised as *gorracharra*. Ganpat there will act as leader and spokesman; he's a safe man." This was his *jemadar*, a lean Punjabi with an Abanazar moustache; he and the half-dozen other riders had come out from the city by now, and were loafing round the fire, chewing betel and spitting, while Gardner bullied me privately.

"You'll arrive by night, presenting yourselves as messengers from the durbar; that'll see you into Lal's presence. He'll be expecting you; word of mouth goes to him today from Jeendan."

"Suppose Maka Khan or that bloody Akali turn up – they'll recognise me straight off –"

"They'll be nowhere near! They're infantrymen – Lal commands only cavalry and horse guns. Besides, no one's going to know you in *gorracharra* gear – and you won't be in their camp long enough to signify. A few hours at most – just long enough to learn what Lal and Tej mean to do."

"They'll take Ferozepore," says I. "That's plain. They're bound to put Littler out of the game before Gough can relieve him."

He gave an impatient snarl. "That's what they'd do if they wanted to *win* the goddam war! They don't! But their brigadiers and colonels *do*, so Lal and Tej are going to have to *look* as though they're trying like hell! Lal's going to have to think of some damned good reason for *not* storming Ferozepore, and since he's a duffer of a soldier as well as a yellow-belly, he's liable to go cross-eyed if his subordinates present him with a sound plan . . . Now what?"

"It won't do!" I bleated. "Maka Khan told me the Khalsa already suspect them of disloyalty. Well, heavens above, the moment Lal makes a move, or gives an order, even, that looks fishy . . . why, they'll see he's pissing on his own wicket!"

"Will they? Who's to say what's a fishy move, or why it's

193

being made? You were in Afghanistan – how many times did
Elphinstone do the sensible thing, tell me that? He was
always wrong, godammit!"

"Yes, but that was fat-headedness – not treachery!"

"Who knows the difference, confound it? You did what
you were told, and so will the Khalsa colonels! What do they
know, if they're told to march from A to B, or retire from C,
or open a candy store at D? They can't see the whole canvas,
only their own corner of it. Sure, they know Lal and Tej are
cowardly rascals who'd turn tail sooner than eat, but they're
still bound to obey." He gnawed his whiskers, growling. "I
said it'll take managing, by Lal and Tej – and by Gough,
once he's learned from you what they're about." He stabbed
me with a bony finger. "From *you* – that's the point! If Lal
sent a native agent, promising betrayal, Gough wouldn't
give him the time of day. But he knows you, and can trust
what you tell him!"

And much good it would do him, I thought, for however
Lal and Tej mismanaged the Khalsa, they couldn't alter its
numbers, or the zeal of its colonels, or the quality of its
soldiers, or the calibre of its guns. They might supply Gough
with full intelligence, but he was still going to have to engage
and break a disciplined army of a hundred thousand men,
with a Company force one-third the size and under-gunned.
I'd not have wagered two *pice* on his chances.

But then, you see, I didn't know him. For that matter, I
didn't know much about war: Afghanistan had been a rout,
not a campaign, and Borneo an apprenticeship in piracy. I'd
never seen a pukka battle, or the way a seasoned commander (even one as daft as Paddy Gough) can manage an army,
or the effect of centuries of training and discipline, or that
phenomenon which I still don't understand but which I've
watched too often to doubt: the British peasant looking
death in the face, and hitching his belt, and waiting.

My chief concern, of course, was the prospect of venturing
into the heart of the Khalsa and conspiring with a viper like
Lal Singh – with a game leg to prevent me lighting out at
speed if things went amiss, as they were bound to do. Even
sitting a mount hurt like sin, and to make matters worse,

Gardner said Jassa must stay behind. I couldn't demur: half the Punjab knew that crafty phiz, and that he was my orderly. But he'd pulled me clear twice now, and I'd feel naked without him.

"Broadfoot needs a foot on the ground here, anyway," says Gardner. "Never fear, dear Josiah will be safe under my wing – and under my eye. While the war lasts I'm to be governor of Lahore – which between ourselves is liable to consist of protecting Mai Jeendan when her disappointed soldiery come pouring back over the river. Yes, sir – we surely earn our wages." He surveyed me in my *gorracharra* outfit, of which the most important part was a steel cap, like a Roundhead's, with long cheek-pieces that helped conceal my face. "You'll do. Let your beard grow, and leave the talking to Ganpat. You'll make Kussoor this afternoon; lie up there and go down to the river *ghat* after dark and you should fetch up with Lal Singh around dawn tomorrow. I'll ride along with you a little ways."

We set off, the six of us, at about ten o'clock, riding parallel with the south road. It was heavy with traffic for the Khalsa – baggage and ration carts, ammunition wagons, even teams of guns, for we were riding with the rearguard of the army, a vast host spread across the dusty plain, moving slowly south and east. Ahead of us the *doab** would be alive with the main body as far as the Sutlej, beyond which Lal Singh was already investing Ferozepore and Tej Singh's infantry would be advancing . . . whither? We rode at a fast trot, which troubled my ankle, but Gardner insisted we must keep up the pace if I was to reach Lal in time.

"He's been over the Sutlej two days now. Gough must be moving, and Lal's going to have to take order pretty sharp, or his colonels will want to know why. I only hope," says Gardner grimly, "that the weak-kneed son-of-a-bitch doesn't run away – in which case we might just have the *gorracharra* under the command of someone who knows what the hell he's doing."

The more I thought of it, the madder the whole thing

*The name given to the tracts between the rivers of the Punjab.

sounded – but the maddest part of it was still to be revealed. We'd made our noon halt, and Gardner was turning back to Lahore, but first he rode a little way apart with me to make sure I had it all straight. We were on a little knoll about a furlong from the road, along which a battalion of Sikh infantry was marching, tall stalwarts all in olive green, with their colonel riding ahead, colours flying, drums beating, bugles sounding a rousing air. Gardner may have said something to prompt my question, but I don't recall; at any rate, I asked him:

"See here . . . I know the Khalsa's been spoiling for this – but if they know their own maharani has been conspiring with the enemy, and suspect their own commanders . . . well, even the rank and file must have a shrewd idea their rulers want to see 'em beat. So . . . why are they allowing themselves to be sent to war at all?"

He pondered this, and gave one of his rare wintry smiles. "They reckon they can whip John Company. Whoever may be crossing or betraying 'em, don't matter – they think they can be champions of England. In which case, they'll be the masters of Hindoostan, with an empire to plunder. Maybe Mai Jeendan has that possibility in mind, too, and figures she'll win, either way. Oh, she could charm away the suspicions of treason; most of 'em still worship her. Another reason they have for marching is that they believe you British will invade them sooner or later, so they might as well strike first."

He paused for a moment, frowning, and then said: "But that's not the half of it. They're going to war because they've taken their oaths to Dalip Singh Maharaja, and he's sent them out in his name – never mind who put the words in his mouth. So even if they knew they were doomed beyond a doubt . . . they'd go to the sacrifice." He turned to look at me. "You don't know the Sikhs, sir. I do. They'll fight their way to hell and back . . . for that little boy. And for their salt."

He sat gazing across the plain, where the marching battalion was disappearing into the heat haze, the sun twinkling on the bayonets, the sound of the bugles dying away. He

196

shaded his eyes, and it was as though he was talking to himself.

"And when the Khalsa's beat, and Jeendan and her noble crew are firm in the saddle again, and the Punjab's quiet under Britannia's benevolent eye, and little Dalip's getting his hide tanned at Eton College . . . why then" – he gestured towards the road – "then, sir, John Company will find he has a hundred thousand of the best recruits on earth, ready to fight for the White Queen. Because that's their trade. And it'll all have turned out best for everybody, I guess. Lot of good men will have died first, though. Sikh. Indian. British." He glanced at me, and nodded. "That's why Hardinge has held off all this time. He's probably the only man in India who thinks the price is too high. Now it's going to be paid."

He was a strange bird this – all bark and fury most of the time, then quiet and philosophical, which sorted most oddly with his Ghazi figurehead. He chucked the reins and wheeled his pony. "Good luck, soldier. Give my *salaams* to old Georgie Broadfoot."

I've never cared, much, for service with foreign forces. At best it's unfamiliar and uncomfortable, and the rations are liable to play havoc with your innards. The American Confederates weren't bad, I suppose, bar their habit of spitting on carpets, and the worst I can say of the Yankees is that they took soldiering seriously and seemed to be under the impression that they had invented it. But the Malagassy army, of which I was Sergeant-General, was simply disgusting; the Apaches stink and know dam' all about camp discipline; no one in the Foreign Legion speaks decent French, the boots don't fit, and the bayonet scabbard is a clanking piece of scrap. All round, the only aliens in whose military employ I could ever be called happy were the Sky-Blue Wolves of Khokand – and that was only because I was full of hashish administered by their general's mistress after I'd rogered her in his absence. As for the Khalsa, the one good thing about my service in its ranks (or perhaps I should say on its general staff) was that it was short and to the point.

I count it from the moment we set out south, the six of us in column of twos, *gorracharra* to the life in our oddments of mail and plate and eccentric weapons; Gardner had furnished me with two pistols and a sabre, and while I'd have swapped the lot for my old pepperbox, I consoled myself that with luck I'd never need to use them.

I was in two minds as we cantered down towards Loolianee. On the one hand, I was relieved to elation at leaving the horrors of Lahore behind me; when I thought of that hellish gridiron, and Chaund Cour's bath, and the ghastly fate of Jawaheer, even the knowledge that I was venturing into the heart of the Khalsa didn't seem so fearful.

198

A glance at the scowling unshaven thug reflected in Gardner's pocket mirror had told me that I needn't fear detection; I might have come straight from Peshawar Valley and no questions asked. And Lal Singh, being up to his arse in treason, would be sure to speed me on my way in quick time; in two days at most I'd be with my own people again – with fresh laurels, too, as the Man Who Brought the News that Saved the Army. If it did save it, that is.

That was t'other side of the coin, and as we rode into the thick of the invading army, all my old fears came flooding back. We kept clear of the road, which was choked with transport trains, but even on the *doab* we found ourselves riding through regiment after regiment marching in open order across the great sunbaked plain. Twice, as you know, I'd seen the Khalsa mustered, but it seemed that the half hadn't been shown unto me: now they covered the land to the horizon, men, wagons, horses, camels, and elephants, churning up the red dust into a great haze that hung overhead in the windless air, making noontide like dusk and filling the eyes and nostrils and lungs. When we came to Kussoor late in the afternoon, it was one great park of artillery, line upon line of massive guns, 32 and 48 pounders – and I thought of our pathetic 12 and 16 pounders and horse artillery, and wondered how much use Lal's betrayal would be. Well, whatever befell, I'd just have to play my game leg for all it was worth, and keep well clear of the action.

There's great debate, by the way, about how large the Khalsa was, and how long it took to cross the Sutlej, but the fact is that even the Sikhs don't know. I reckoned about a hundred thousand were on the move from Lahore to the river, and I know *now* that they'd been crossing in strength for days and already had fifty thousand on the south bank, while Gough and Hardinge were trying to scramble their dispersed thirty thousand together. But muster rolls don't win wars. Concentration does – not only getting there fustest with the mostest, as the chap said, but bringing 'em to bear *in the right place*. That's the secret – and if you run into Lars Porsena he'll be the first to tell you.[29]

At the time, I only knew what I could see – camp fires all

199

about us in a vast twinkling sea as we came down by night to the Ferozepore *ghat*. Even in the small hours they were swarming over the ferry in an endless tide; great burning bales had been set on high poles on either bank, glaring red on the three hundred yards of oily water, and men and guns and beasts and wagons were being poled across on anything that could float – barges and rafts and even rowing boats. There were whole regiments waiting in the dark to take their turn, and the *ghat* itself was Bedlam, but Ganpat thrust ahead, bawling that we were durbar couriers, and we were given passage in a fisher craft carrying a general and his staff. They ignored us poor *gorracharra*, and presently we came to the noisy confusion of the southern bank, and made our way by inquiry to the Wazir's headquarters.

Ferozepore itself lay a couple of miles or so from the river, with the Sikhs in between, and how far their camp extended up the south bank, God alone knows. They'd been crossing as far up as Hurree-ke, and I suppose they'd made a bridge-head of about thirty miles, but I ain't certain. As near as I've been able to figure, Lal's headquarters lay about two miles due north of Ferozepore, but it was still dark when we passed through the lines of tent-lanes, all ablaze with torches. Most of his force were *gorracharra*, like ourselves, and my memory is of fierce bearded faces and steel caps, beasts stamping in the dark, and the steady throb of drums that they kept up all night, doubtless to encourage Littler in his beleaguered outpost two miles away.

Lal's quarters were in a pavilion big enough to hold Astley's circus – it even had smaller tents within it to house him and his retinue of staff and servants and personal body-guard. These last were tall villains with long chainmail head-dresses and ribbons on their muskets; they barred our way until Ganpat announced our business, which caused a great scurry and consultation with chamberlains and butlers. Although it was still the last watch, and the great man was asleep, it was decided to wake him at once, so we didn't have to wait above an hour before being ushered into his sleeping pavilion, a silken sanctum decked out like a bordello, with Lal sitting up naked in bed while one wench

200

dressed his hair and combed his beard, another sprayed him with perfume, and a third plied him with drink and titbits.

I've never seen a man in such a funk in my life. At our previous meetings he'd been as cool, urbane, and commanding as a handsome young Sikh noble can be; now he was like a virgin with the vapours. He gave me one terrified glance and looked quickly away, his fingers tugging nervously at the bedclothes while the wenches completed his toilet, and when one of them dropped her comb he squealed like a spoiled child, slapped her, and drove them out with shrill curses. Ganpat followed them, and the moment he'd gone Lal was tumbling out of bed, hauling his robe about him and yammering at me in a hoarse whisper.

"Praise God you are here at last! I thought you would never come! What is to be done?" He was fairly quivering with fright. "I've been at my wits' end for two days – and Tej Singh is no help, the swine! He sits at Arufka, pretending he must supervise the assembly, and leaves me here alone! Everyone is looking to me for orders – what in God's name am I to say to them?"

"What have you said already?"

"Why, that we must wait! What else can I say, man? But we can't wait forever! They keep telling me that Ferozepore can be plucked like a ripe fruit, if I will but give the word! And how can I answer them? How can I justify delay? I don't know!" He seized me by the wrist, pleading. "You are a soldier – you can think of reasons! What shall I tell them?"

I hadn't reckoned on this. I'd always thought myself God's own original coward, but this fellow could have given me ten yards in the hundred, and won screaming. Well, Gardner had warned me of that, and also that Lal might have difficulty thinking of reasons for not attacking Ferozepore – but I hadn't expected to find him at such a complete nonplus as this. The man was on the edge of hysterics, and plainly the first thing to be done was to calm his panic (before it infected me, for one thing) and find out how the land lay. I began by pointing out that I was an invalid – I'd only been able to limp into his presence with the aid of a stick – and that my first need was food, drink, and a

201

doctor to look at my ankle. That took him aback – it always does, when you remind an Oriental of his manners – and his women were summoned to bring refreshments while a little *hakim* clucked over my swollen joint and said I must keep my bed for a week. What they thought, to see a hairy *gorracharra sowar* treated with such consideration by their Wazir, I don't know. Lal fretted up and down, and couldn't wait to drive them out again, and renew his appeals for guidance.

By that time I'd got my thoughts into some order, at least as far as his Ferozepore dilemma was concerned. There are always a hundred good reasons for doing nothing, and I'd hit on a couple – but first I must have information. I asked him how many men he had ready to march.

"At hand, twenty-two thousand cavalry – they are lying a bare mile from Ferozepore, with the enemy lines in full view, I tell you! And Littler Sahib has a bare seven thousand – only one British regiment, and the rest sepoys ready to desert to us! We know this from some who have already come over!" He gulped at his cup, his teeth chattering on the rim. "We could overrun him in an hour! Even a child can see that!"

"Have you sent messengers to him?"

"As if I would dare! Who could I trust? Already these Khalsa bastards look at me askance – let them suspect that I traffic with the enemy, and . . ." He rolled his eyes and flung his cup away in a passion. "And that drunken bitch in Lahore gives me no help, no orders! While she couples with her grooms, I wait to be butchered like Jawaheer –"

"Now, see here, Wazir!" says I roughly, for his whining was starting to give me the shakes. "You take hold, d'you hear? Your position ain't all that desperate –"

"You see a way out?" quavers he, clutching at me again. "Oh, my dear friend, I knew you would not fail me! Tell me, tell me, then – and let me embrace you!"

"You keep your bloody distance," says I. "What's Littler doing?"

"Fortifying his lines. Yesterday he came out with his whole garrison, and we thought he meant to attack us, and held our ground. But my colonels say it was a feint to gain

202

time, and that I must storm his trenches! Oh, God, what can I –"

"Hold on – he's entrenched, you say? Is he still digging? Capital – you can tell your colonels he's mining his defences!"

"But will they believe me?" He wrung his hands. "Suppose the deserters deny it?"

"Why should you trust deserting sepoys? How d'ye know Littler hasn't sent 'em to give you false reports of his strength, eh? To lure you into attacking him? Ferozepore's a ripe fruit, is it? Come, raja, you know the British – foxy bastards, every one of us! Deuced odd, ain't it, that we've left a weak garrison, cut off, just asking to be attacked, what?"

He stared wide-eyed. "Is this true?"

"I doubt it – but you don't know that," says I, warming to my work. "Anyway, it's a dam' good reason to give your colonels for not attacking headlong. Now then, what force has Tej Singh, and where?"

"Thirty thousand infantry, with heavy guns, behind us along the river." He shuddered. "Thank God I have only light artillery – with heavy pieces I should have no excuse for not blowing Littler's position to rubble!"

"Never mind Littler! What news of Gough?"

"Two days ago he was at Lutwalla, a hundred miles away! He will be here in two days – but word is that he has scarcely ten thousand men, only half of them British! If he comes on, we are sure to defeat him!" He was almost crying, wrenching off his beard net and trembling like a fever case. "What can I do to prevent it? Even if I give reasons for not taking Ferozepore, I cannot avoid battle with the *Jangi lat*! Help me, Flashman *bahadur*! Tell me what I must do!"

Well, this was a real facer, if you like. Gardner, for all his misgivings about Lal, had been sure that he and Tej would have some scheme for leading their army to destruction – that was what I was here for, dammit, to carry their plans to Gough! And it was plain as a pikestaff that they hadn't any. And Lal expected me, a junior officer, to plot his own defeat for him. And as I stared at that shivering, helpless clown, it

203

came to me with awful clarity that if I didn't, no one else would.

It ain't the kind of problem you meet every day. I doubt if it's ever been posed at Staff College . . . "Now then, Mr Flashman, you command an army fifty thousand strong, with heavy guns, well supplied, their lines of communication protected by an excellent river. Against you is a force of only ten thousand, with light guns, exhausted after a week's forced marching, short of food and fodder and damned near dying of thirst. Now then, sir, answer directly, no hedging – how do you *lose*, hey? Come, come, you've just given excellent reasons for not taking a town that's lying at your mercy! This should be child's play to a man with your God-given gift of catastrophe! Well, sir?"

Lal was gibbering at me, his eyes full of terrified entreaty – and I knew that if I wavered now it would be all up with him. He'd break, and his colonels would either hang or depose him, and put a decent soldier in his place – the very thing that Gardner had feared. And that would be the end of Gough's advancing force, and perhaps the war, and British India. And no doubt, of me. But if I could rally this spineless wreck, and think of some plan that would satisfy his colonels and at the same time bring the Khalsa to destruction . . . Aye, just so.

To gain time, I asked for a map, and he pawed among his gear and produced a splendid illuminated document with all the forts in red and the rivers in turquoise, and little bearded wallahs with *tulwars* chasing each other round the margin on elephants. I studied it, trying to think, and gripping my belt to keep my hand from trembling.

I've told you I didn't know much about war, in those days. Tactically, I was a novice who could bungle a section flanking movement with the worst of them – but strategy's another matter. At its simplest, it's mere common sense – and if the First Sikh War was anything, it was simple, thank God. Also, strategy seldom involves your own neck. So I conned the map, weighing the facts that Lal had given me, and applied the age-old laws that you learn in the school playground.

204

To *win*, the Khalsa need only take Ferozepore and wait for Gough to come and be slaughtered by overwhelming odds and big guns. To *lose*, they must be divided, and the weaker part sent to meet Gough with as little artillery as possible. If I could contrive that the first battle was on near level terms, or even odds of three to two against us, I'd have given Gough victory on a lordly dish. Daft he might be, but he could still out-manoeuvre any Sikh commander, and if they didn't have their big guns along, British cavalry and infantry would do the business. Gough believed in the bayonet: give him a chance to use it, and the Khalsa were beat – in the first battle, at least. After that, Paddy would have to take care of the war himself.

So I figured, with the sweat cold on my skin, my ankle giving me hell's delight, and Lal mumping at my elbow. D'you know, that steadied me – encountering a liver whiter than my own. Well, it don't happen that often. This is what I told him:

"Call your staff together – generals and brigadiers, no colonels. Tej Singh as well. Tell 'em you won't attack Ferozepore, because it's mined, you don't trust the deserters' tale of Littler's weakness, and as Wazir it's beneath your dignity to engage anyone but the *Jangi lat* himself. Also, there's a risk that if you get embroiled with Littler, and Gough arrives early, you may be caught between two fires. Don't let 'em argue. Simply say that Ferozepore don't matter, d'you see – it can be wiped up when you've settled Gough. Lay down the law, high-handed. Very good?"

He nodded, rubbing his face and biting his knuckle – he had the wind up to such a tune that I swear if I'd told him to march on Ceylon, he'd have cried amen.

"Now, your *gorracharra* are deployed already – send them against Gough with their horse artillery, pointing out that they outnumber him two to one. You'll meet him somewhere between here and Woodnee, and if you detach some of your force to entrench at Ferozeshah or Sultan Khan Wallah, you'll reduce the odds, d'you see? Gough will do the rest –"

205

"But Tej Singh?" he bleated. "He has thirty thousand infantry, and the heavy guns –"

"He's to sit down here and watch Littler, in place of your *gorracharra*. Yes, yes, I know – that don't take thirty thousand men. He must divide his force in turn, leaving only enough to watch Ferozepore, while the rest follow you as slowly as Tej can decently arrange – it'll take him time to bring 'em down here from the river, and if he sets about it in the right spirit he can waste the best part of a week, I dare say –"

"But to divide the Khalsa?" goggles he. "It is not good strategy, surely? The generals will not permit –"

"To hell with the generals – you're the Wazir!" cries I. "It's bloody good strategy, you can tell 'em, to send your most mobile troops to meet the *Jangi lat* when he least expects 'em and his own men are so fagged they'll be marching on their chinstraps! Tej Singh will back you up, if you prime him first –"

"But suppose . . . suppose we beat the *Jangi lat* – he has only ten thousand, and as you say, they will be tired –"

"Tired or not, they'll tear your *gorracharra* to pieces if the odds ain't too heavy! And I doubt if Gough's as weak as you think. Good God, man, he's got another twenty thousand somewhere between Ludhiana and Umballa – he ain't going to send 'em on furlough, you know! And the Khalsa will be in three parts, don't you see? Well, none of those three parts is going to be a match for Paddy Gough's boys, let me tell you!"

I believed it, too, and if I wasn't altogether right it was because I lacked experience. I was trusting to the old maxim that one British soldier is worth any two niggers any day. It's a fair rule of thumb, mind you, but I can look back now on my military career and count four exceptions who always gave Atkins a damned good run for his money. Three of them were Zulu, John Gurkha, and Fuzzy-wuzzy. I wasn't to know, then, that the fourth one was the Sikh.

It took me another hour of explanation and argument to convince Lal that my scheme was his only hope of getting his army properly leathered. It was hard sledding, for he was the kind of coward who's too far gone even to clutch at straws – not my kind of funk at all. In the end I gave him Jeendan's recipe to Jawaheer, which you'll recall was to rattle a wench to put him in fighting trim, but whether Lal took it or not I can't say, for I caulked out in an alcove of his pavilion, and didn't wake until noon. By that time Tej Singh had arrived, still fat as butter and quite as reliable, to judge from the furtive enthusiasm with which he greeted me. But while he was every bit as windy as Lal, he was a sight smarter, and once the Flashman Plan had been expounded he hailed it as a masterpiece; let my directions be followed and Gough would have the Khalsa looking like a Frenchman's knapsack in no time, was Tej's view. I guessed that what really commended my scheme to him was that he'd be well away from the firing, but he showed a good grasp of the details, and had some sound notions of his own: one, I remember, was that he would take care to keep his guarding force on the north and west of Ferozepore, so that Littler would be able to slip away and join Gough without hindrance if he wanted to. That, as you'll see, proved to be of prime importance, so I reckon Tej earned himself a Ferozeshah medal for that alone, if everyone had his due.

You must imagine our conference being carried on in lowered voices in Lal's sleeping quarters, and a bonny trio we were. Our gallant Wazir, when he wasn't peeping out to make sure there were no eavesdroppers, was brisking himself up with copious pinches of Peshawar snuff which I suspect contained something a sight more stimulating than powdered tobacco; he seemed to take heart from the confidence of Tej Singh, who paced the apartment like Napoleon at Marengo, heaving his guts before him and tripping over his sabre while describing to me, in a gloating whisper, how the Khalsa would flee in disorder at the first setback; I lay nursing my ankle, trying to forget my own perilous situation and praying that Lal Singh could browbeat his staff into obedience before the effect of the snuff wore off. I wonder if there was ever such a conspiracy in the history of war: two generals intent on scuppering their own army, confabulating *sotto voce* with an agent from the enemy, while their commanders waited impatiently outside for the word that (with luck) would send them marching to ruin? You would think not, but knowing human nature and the military mind, I'd not wager on it.

I stayed hidden when Lal and Tej went out in the afternoon to announce their intentions to the divisional commanders. Lal was brave in silver armour, with a desperate glitter in his eye – half fear, half hashish, I would guess – and they held their conference on horseback, with Ferozepore in view. Tej told me later that the Wazir was in capital form, lining out my plan like a drill sergeant and snarling down any hint of opposition, of which there was less than I'd feared. The fact was, you see, that the strategy looked sound enough, but what impressed them most, apparently, was Lal's refusal to engage any commander except Gough himself. That argued pride and confidence, and they cheered him to the echo, and couldn't wait to get under way. The *gorracharra* were riding east before dusk, and Tej, by his own account, made a great meal of sending orders to mobilise his foot and guns, with gallopers riding in all directions, bugles blowing, and the Commander-in-Chief finally retiring to Lal's tent, having issued orders which with luck would take days to untangle.

The final scene of the comedy took place that night before I rode out. Lal was keen that I should make straight for Gough, to let him know what good boys Lal and Tej were being, offering up the Khalsa for destruction, but I wasn't having that. Gough might be anywhere over the eastern horizon, and I had no intention of hunting him through country which by now was swarming with *gorracharra*; far better, I said, if I rode the couple of miles to Ferozepore, where Littler would see that Gough got the glad news in good time (and Flashy could take a well-earned repose). Tej agreed, and said I should go under a flag of truce, ostensibly carrying the Wazir's final demand to Littler to surrender. Lal boggled at that, but Tej grew excited, pointing out the risk if I tried to sneak into Littler's lines unobserved.

"Suppose he were shot by a sentry?" squeaks he, waving

his podgy hands. "Then the *Jangi lat* would never know of our good will to him, or the plans we have made for the destruction of these Khalsa swine! And our dear friend" – that was me – "would have died in vain! It is not to be thought of!" I found myself liking Tej Singh's style better by the minute.

"But will the colonels not suspect treason, if they see a courier sent to Littler Sahib?" cries Lal. The puggle had worn off by now, and he was lying exhausted on his silken bed, fretting himself witless.

"They will not even know!" cries Tej. "And only think – once our dear *bahadur* has spoken with Littler Sahib, our credit with the Sirkar is assured! Whatever may happen, our friendship will have been made plain!"

That was the great thing with him – to stand well with Simla, whatever happened to the Khalsa. He even proposed that I carry a written message, expressing Lal's undying devotion to the Sirkar; it would be so much more convincing than mere word of mouth. This so horrified Lal that he almost hid under the sheets.

"A written message? Are you mad? What if it went astray? Am I to sign my own death-warrant?" He flung about in a passion. "You write it, then! You announce *your* treason, over *your* signature! Why not, you're Commander-in-Chief, you fat tub of dung –"

"You are Wazir!" retorts Tej. "This is a high political affair, and what am I but a soldier?" He shrugged complacently. "You need say nothing of military matters; a mere expression of friendship will suffice."

Lal said he'd see him damned first, and they snarled and whined, with Lal weeping and tearing the bedclothes. Finally he gave in, and penned the following remarkable note to Nicolson, the political: "I have crossed with the Khalsa. You know my friendship for the British. Tell me what to do."[30] He bilked at signing, though, and after more shrill bickering Tej turned to me.

"It will have to do. Tell Nicolson Sahib it is from the Wazir!"

"From both of us, you greasy bastard!" yelps Lal. "Make

that clear, Flashman *bahadur*! Both of us! And tell them, in God's name, that we and the *bibi sahiba** are their loyal friends, and that we beg them to cut up these *badmashes* and *burchas*† of the Khalsa, and free us all from this evil! Tell them that!"

So it was that in the small hours a *gorracharra* rider with a game leg and a white flag on his lance rode out of the Khalsa lines and down to Ferozepore, leaving behind two Sikh generals, one fat and frightened and t'other having hysterics with a pillow over his face, both conscious of duty well done, I don't doubt. As for me, I went half a mile and sat down under a thorn tree to wait for dawn; for one thing, now that I was so nearly home, I wanted a moment to study how best to wring credit out of my unexpected arrival with such momentous news, and for another, flag of truce or not, I wasn't risking a bullet from a nervous sepoy in the half-light. I was dog-tired, what with lack of sleep, funk, and bodily anguish, but I was a happy man, I can tell you – and happier yet, three hours later, when I'd been admitted by a sentry of the 62nd whose Whitechapel challenge was music to my ears, and hobbled painfully into the presence of Peter Nicolson, who'd seen me off across the Sutlej three months ago.

He didn't know me at first, and then he was on his feet, steadying me as I staggered artistically, bravely gritting my teeth against the agony of my ankle (which was feeling much better, by the way).

"Flashman! What on earth are you doin' here? Good lord, man, you're all in – are you wounded?"

"That don't matter!" gasps I, subsiding on his cot. "Small memento from a Khalsa dungeon, what? See here, Peter, there's no time to lose!" I shoved Lal's note at him, and gave him the marrow of the business in a few brief sentences, insisting that a galloper must ride to Gough at once to let him know that the Philistines were on the move and ready to be smitten hip and thigh. I didn't add "courtesy of H. Flashman", just then; that was a conclusion they could leap to presently.

*Jeendan.
†Ruffians.

He was a smart political, Nicolson: he grasped the thing at once, bawled for his orderly to fetch Colonel Van Cortlandt, pumped my hand in delight, said he could hardly credit it, but it was the finest piece of work he'd ever heard – I'd come through the Khalsa in disguise, been with Lal and Tej, made 'em split their forces, come away with their plans? Good God, he'd never heard the like, etc., etc.

Jallalabad all over again, thinks I contentedly, and while he strode out shouting that a galloper must ride directly to Littler, who was out on a reconnoitre, I heaved up for a *dekko* in the mirror over his washstand. Gad, I looked like the last survivor of Fort Nowhere . . . capital! I slumped back on the cot, and had to be revived with brandy when he and Van Cortlandt arrived, full of questions. I rallied gamely, and described in detail what I'd told Lal and Tej to do; Van Cortlandt, whom I'd heard of as a former mercenary with Runjeet Singh, and a knowing bird, just nodded grimly, while Nicolson slapped his forehead.

"Was ever such a pair of villains! Sellin' their own comrades, the dastards! My stars, it passes belief!"

"No, it don't," says Van Cortlandt. "It fits exactly with our information that the durbar wants the Khalsa destroyed – and with what I know of Lal Singh." He eyed me, frowning. "When did you learn they were ready to sell out? Did they approach you in Lahore?"

This was the moment for my tired boyish grin, with a little gasp as I moved my leg. I could have told 'em the whole horrid tale, and made their hair stand on end – but that ain't the way to do it, you see. Offhand and laconic, that's the ticket, and let their imaginations do the rest. I shook my head, weary-like.

"No, sir, I approached them . . . just a few hours ago, in their camp over there. I'd had word, two nights ago in Lahore, that they were ready to turn traitor –"

"Who told you?" demands Van Cortlandt.

"Perhaps I'd better not say, sir . . . just yet." I was shot if I was giving Gardner credit, when I'd done all the bloody work. "I reckoned I'd better get to Lal, and see what he was up to. But I had a spot o' trouble, getting clear of Lahore

211

. . . fact is, if old Goolab Singh hadn't popped up in a tight corner –"

"Goolab Singh!" cries he incredulously.

"Why, yes – we had to cut our way out, you see, but he ain't as spry as he was . . . and I was rearguard, so to speak, and . . . well, the Khalsa's bulldogs laid hold of me –"

"You said somethin' about a dungeon!" cries Nicolson.

"Did I? Oh, aye . . ." I brushed it aside, and then bit my lip, shifting my foot. "No, no, don't fuss, Peter . . . I doubt if it's broken . . . just held me up a bit . . . ah!" I clenched my teeth, recovered, and spoke urgently to Van Cortlandt. "But, see here, sir . . . what happened in Lahore don't matter – or how I got to Lal! It's what he and Tej are doing *now*, don't you see? Sir Hugh Gough must be warned . . ."

"He will be, never fear!" says Van Cortlandt, looking keen and noble. "Flashman . . ." He hesitated, nodded, and gave me a quick clap on the shoulder. "You lie down, young feller. Nicolson, we must see Littler as soon as he returns. Have two gallopers ready – this is one message that mustn't miscarry! Let's see that map . . . if Gough's approaching Maulah, and the Sikhs have reached Ferozeshah, they should meet about Moodkee . . . in a few hours! Well . . . touch wood! In the meantime, young Flashman, we'll have that leg seen to . . . good lord, he's gone fast asleep!"

There was a pause. "Fellows often do, when they've had a bad time," says Nicolson anxiously. "God knows what he's been through. I say, d'you think the swine . . . tortured him? I mean, he didn't say so, but –"

"He's not the kind who would, from all I've heard," says Van Cortlandt. "Sale told me that after the Piper's Fort business they couldn't get a word out of him . . . about himself, I mean. Only about . . . his men. Heavens . . . he's just a boy!"

"Broadfoot says he's the bravest man he's ever met," says Nicolson reverently.

"There you are, then. Come on, let's find Littler."

You see what I mean? It would be all over camp within the hour, and the Army soon after. Good old Flashy's done it again – and this time, if I says it myself, didn't I deserve

212

their golden opinions, even if I had been passing wind the whole way? I felt quite virtuous, and put on a game show, trying to struggle to my feet and having to be restrained, when they returned presently with Littler, a wiry old piece of teak who looked as though he'd swallowed the poker. He was very trim in spotless overalls, chin thrust out and hands behind his back as he ran a brisk eye over me. More compliments, thinks I – until he spoke, in a cold, level voice.

"Let me understand this. You say that twenty thousand Sikh cavalry are moving to attack the Commander-in-Chief . . . and this is at your prompting? I see." He took a deliberate breath through his thin nose, and I've seen kinder eyes on a cobra. "You, a junior political officer, took it upon yourself to direct the course of the war. You did not think fit, although you knew these two traitors were bent on courting defeat, to send or bring word to the nearest general officer – myself? So that their actions might be directed by someone of less limited military experience?" He paused, his mouth like a rat-trap. "Well, sir?"

I don't know what I thought, only what I said, once I'd recovered from the shock of the icy son-of-a-bitch's sarcasm. It was so unexpected that I could only blurt out: "There wasn't time, sir! Lal Singh was desperate – if I hadn't told him something, God knows what he'd have done!" Nicolson was standing mum; Van Cortlandt was frowning. "I . . . I acted as I thought best, sir!" I could have burst into tears.

"Quite so." It sounded like a left and right with a sabre. "And from your vast political experience, you are confident that the Wazir's . . . desperation . . . was genuine – and that he has indeed acted on your ingenious instructions? He could not have been deceiving you, of course . . . and perhaps making quite other dispositions of his army?"

"With respect, sir," put in Van Cortlandt, "I'm quite sure –"

"Thank you, Colonel Van Cortlandt. I recognise your concern for a fellow political officer. Your certainty, however, is by the way. I am concerned with Mr Flashman's."

"Christ! Yes, I'm sure –"

213

"You will not blaspheme in my presence, sir." The steely voice didn't rise even a fraction. Deliberately he went on: "Well. We must hope that you are right. Must we not? We must resign ourselves to the fact that the fate of the Army rests on the strategic acumen of one self-sufficient subaltern. Distinguished in his way, no doubt." He gave me one last withering glance. "Unfortunately, that distinction has not been gained in command of any formation larger than a troop of cavalry."

I lost my head, and my temper with it. I can't explain it, for I'm the last man to defy authority – it may have been the sneering voice and supercilious eye, or the contrast with the decency of Van Cortlandt and Nicolson, or all the fear and pain and weariness of weeks boiling up, or the sheer injustice, when for once I'd done my best and my duty (not that I'd had any choice, I grant you) and this was the thanks I got! Well, it was the wrong side of enough, and I heaved half off the bed, almost weeping with rage and indignation.

"Damnation!" I bawled. "Very well – sir! What should I have done, then? It ain't too late, you know! Tell me what you'd have done, and I'll ride back to Lal Singh this very minute! He's still cowering in bed, I'll be bound, not two bloody miles away! He'll be glad to change his orders, if he knows they come from you – sir!"

I knew, even in my childish fury, that there wasn't a chance he'd take me at my word, or I'd have confined myself to cussing, you may be sure. Nicolson had me by the arm, begging me to be calm, and Van Cortlandt was muttering excuses on my behalf.

Littler didn't turn a hair. He waited until Nicolson had settled me. Then:

"I doubt if that would be prudent," says he quietly. "No. We can only wait upon events. Whether our messengers find Sir Hugh or not, he will still face the battle which you, Mr Flashman, have made inevitable." He moved forward to look at me, and his face was like flint. "If all goes well, he and his army will, very properly, receive the credit. If, on the other hand, he is defeated, then you, sir" – he inclined his head towards me – "will bear the blame alone. You will

214

certainly be broken, probably imprisoned, possibly even shot." He paused. "Do not misunderstand me, Mr Flashman. The questions I have asked you are only those that will be put to you by the prosecution at your court-martial – a proceeding at which, let me assure you, I shall be the first witness on your behalf, to testify that, in my judgment, you have done your duty with exemplary courage and resource, and in the highest traditions of the service."

Unusual chap, Littler, and not only because he came from Cheshire, which not many people do, in my experience. I can't recall a man who so scared the innards out of me, and yet was so reassuring, all in one go. For he was right, you know. I *had* done the proper thing, and done it well – and much good it'd do me, whatever befell. If Gough was wiped up, they'd need a scapegoat, and who so handy as one of those cocky politicals whom the rest of the Army detested? Contrariwise, if the Khalsa was beat, the last thing John Bull would want to hear was that it had been managed by a dirty deal with two treacherous Sikh generals – where's the glory to Britannia's arms in that? So it would be kept quiet . . . as it has been, to this very day.

You may wonder, then, how I found any reassurance in Littler's tirade. Well, the thought of having that acid little iceberg in my corner, if it came to a court-martial, was decidedly comforting; I've prosecuted myself, and God be thanked I never ran into a defence witness like him. And Broadfoot would stand by me, and Van Cortlandt – and my Afghan reputation must tell in my favour. I got a whiff of that later in the day, when I was nursing my leg and chewing my nails on the verandah after tiffen, and heard Littler's three brigadiers talking behind the chick; Nicolson must have been spreading the tale of my exploits, and they were full of it.

"Sikhs are doin' what Flashman told 'em? Off his own bat? I'll be damned! No end to the cheek o' these politicals."

"Not to Flashman's, anyway. Ask any woman in Simla."

"Oh? In the skirt line, is he? Odd, that . . . wife's a regular stunner. Seen her. Blonde gel, blue eyes."

"She does sound a stunner, is she?"

"Tip-top, altogether."

"I say . . . lady's name. Not in the mess."

"Haven't mentioned her name. Just that she's a stunner. Money, too, I'm told."

"Scamps like Flashman always seem to get both. Noticed that."

"Popular chap, of course."

"Not with Cardigan. Kicked him out o' the Cherrypickers."

"Somethin' in the lad's favour. What for?"

"Don't recall. Feller like that, might be anythin'."

"True. Well, God help him if Gough gets bowled out."

"God will, you'll see. They can't break the man who saved Jallalabad."

"When did Cardigan do that?"

"Didn't. Flashman did. In '4? You were in Tenasserim."

"Was I? Ah, yes, I recollect now. He held some fort or other. Oh, they can't touch him, then."

"Dam' well think not. Public wouldn't stand for it."

"Not if his wife's a stunner."

All of which was heartening, though I didn't care to hear Elspeth bandied about quite so freely. But it was still a long day, waiting in the baking heat of the Ferozepore lines, with the 62nd sweating in their red coats in the entrenchments, and the blue-jacketed sepoy gunners lying in the shade of their pieces, while only two miles away the sun twinkled on the arms of Tej Singh's mighty host. Littler and his staff spent all day in the saddle, riding out south-east to scan the hazy distance: Gough was somewhere out yonder, marching to meet the *gorracharra* that Lal Singh had dispatched against him – if he *had* dispatched them. Suppose he hadn't – suppose he'd ignored my plan, or bungled it? Suppose Littler's fear was well-founded, and Lal had been humbugging me – but, no, that couldn't be, the fellow had been almost out of his wits. He must be advancing to meet Gough . . . but would he mind what I'd said about detaching regiments along the way, so as to even the odds? Suppose . . . oh, suppose any number of things! All I could do was wait,

217

keeping out of Littler's way, limping gamely around the mess, aware of the eyes that glanced and looked away.

It was about four, and the sun was starting to dip, when we heard the first rumble to eastward, and Huthwaite, the gunner colonel, stood stock-still on the verandah, mouth open, listening, and then cries: "Those are big fellows! 48s! Sikh, for certain!"

"How far?" asks someone.

"Can't tell – twenty miles at least, might be thirty . . ."

"That's Moodkee, then!"

"Quiet, can't you?" Huthwaite had his eyes closed. "Those are howitzers![31] That's Gough!"

And it was, white fighting coat and all, with an exhausted army at his heels, ill-fed, ill-watered, and in no kind of order, out-gunned but not, thank God, outnumbered, and going for his enemy in the only style he knew, bull-at-a-gate and damn the consequences. We knew nothing of that, at the time; we could only stand on the verandah, with the moths clustering round the lamps, listening to the distant cannonade which went on hour after hour, long after sunset, when we could even see the flashes reflected on the distant night sky. Not until one of Harriott's light cavalry scouts came back, choked with dust and excitement, did we have any notion of what was happening in that astonishing action, the first in the great Sikh War: Midnight Moodkee.

When I sport my tin on dress occasions, I have clasps for a score of engagements, from "Cabul 42" to "Khedive Sudan 96" – but not for that one, the battle I started. I don't mind that; I wasn't there, praise the Lord, and it wasn't a famous victory for anyone, but I like to think I prevented it from being a catastrophe. Gough's army, which a well-managed Khalsa should have smothered by sheer weight, lived to fight another day because I'd squared the odds for them – and because there are no better horse soldiers in the world than the Light Brigade.

Between them, Hardinge and Gough came damned near to making a hash of it, one by his old-wife caution, t'other by his Donnybrook recklessness. Thanks to Hardinge, we were ill-prepared for war, with regiments held back from the

218

front, no proper supply stations on their line of march (so that Broadfoot and his politicals had to plunder the countryside to improvise them), not even a field hospital ready to move, and Paddy having to drive ahead with his fighting force, forced-marching thirty miles a day, and devil take the transport and auxiliaries straggling behind him all the way to Umballa. Meanwhile Hardinge had decided to stop being Governor-General and become a soldier again – he went careering off to Ludhiana and brought the garrison down to join the march, so that when they reached Moodkee they had about twelve thousand men, pretty fagged out after a day's march – and there were Lal's *gorracharra* waiting for them, ten thousand strong and a couple of thousand infantry.

Now it was Paddy's turn. The Sikhs had stationed their foot and guns in jungle, and Gough, instead of waiting for them to come on, must fly at their throats in case they escaped him – that was all *he* knew. The artillery duelled away, kicking up a deuce of a dust – Hardinge's son told me later that it was like fighting in London fog, and the fact is that no two accounts of the battle agree, because no one could see a damned thing for most of the time. Certainly the *gorracharra* were in such numbers that they threatened to envelop us, but our own cavalry took 'em in flank, both sides, and broke them. The 3rd Lights were riding in among the Sikh guns and infantry, but when Paddy launched a frontal infantry assault they ran into a great storm of grape, and it was touch and go for a while, for when they reached the jungle the Sikh guns were still doing great execution, and there was horrid scrimmaging among the trees. It was dark by now, and fellows were firing on their comrades, some of our sepoy regiments were absolutely blazing into the air, everything was confusion on both sides – and then the Sikhs withdrew, leaving seventeen guns behind them. We lost over 200 dead and three times as many wounded; the Sikhs' losses, I'm told, were greater, but nobody knows.

You might call it a draw in our favour,[32] but it settled a few things. We'd taken the ground and the guns, so the Khalsa could be beaten – at a cost, for they'd fought like

219

tigers among the trees, and took no prisoners. Our sepoys had lost some of their fear of the Sikhs, and our cavalry, British and Indian, had seen the backs of the *gorracharra*. If Gough could follow up quickly enough, and dispose of the rest of Lal's force which was concentrated on Ferozeshah, twelve miles away, *before* Tej's host came to reinforce it, we'd be in a fair way to settling the whole business. But if the Khalsa reunited . . . well, that would be another story.

Some of this was clear as early as next morning, but by then I had other concerns. One of the gallopers whom Littler had sent with news of my arrangement with Lal and Tej, had reached Gough at the height of the battle; it had been an astonishing sight, with twenty thousand horse, foot and guns tearing at each other in the starlight, and the old madman himself raging because he couldn't take part personally in the 3rd Lights' charge on the Sikh flank: "It's damnable, so it is! Here's me, an' there's them, an' I might as well be in me bed! Away ye go, Mickey, an' give 'em one for me – hurroo, boys!"

The galloper had wisely decided that there'd be no talking sense to him for a while, and it wasn't until near midnight, when the fighting was done, that the news had been broken, to Gough and Hardinge, with Broadfoot in tow, as they left the field. The galloper said it was like a strange dream: a huge golden moon shining on the scrubby plain and jungle; the Sikh guns, with their dead crews heaped around them; the mutilated corpses of our Light Dragoons and Indian lancers marking the path of their charge through the heart of the Khalsa position; the great confused masses of men and horses and camels scattered, dead and dying, on the plain; the wailing chorus of the wounded, and the shouts of our people as they sought their fellows among the fallen; the mound of bodies piled up like a cairn where Harry Smith had ridden ahead on his Arab, Jim Crow, planted the Queen's Own's colour at the head of a Khalsa column, and roared to our fellows to come and get it – which they had; Gough and Hardinge standing a little apart, talking quietly in the moonlight, and Paddy finally giving the galloper his reply, and adding the words which brought my heart into my mouth.

"My respects to Sir John Littler, an' tell him he'll be hearin' from me presently – an' he'll oblige me by sendin' that young Flashman to me as soon as he likes! I want a word with that one!"

*　　*　　*

It wasn't a hard word, though; indeed, the first thing he said, when I limped into his presence in the big mess-tent at Moodkee, was: "What's amiss with your leg, boy? Sit ye down, an' Baxu'll get ye a glass of beer. Thirsty ridin', these days!"

First, though, I must be presented to Hardinge, who was with him at dinner, a plain-faced, tight-mouthed sobersides with the empty cuff of his missing left hand tucked into his coat. I disliked him on sight, and it was mutual: he gave me a frosty nod, but Broadfoot was there, with a great grin and a hearty handclasp. That was welcome, I can tell you: the thirty-mile ride from Ferozepore, skirting south in case of *gorracharra* scouts, and with only six N.C. *sowars* for escort, had given me the blue devils and done my game ankle no good at all, and on reaching Moodkee I'd had a most horrid shock. We'd come in at sunset from the south, and so saw nothing of the battlefield, but they were burying the dead in scores, and I'd chanced to glance aside through an open tent-fly, and there, wrapped in a cloak, was the body of old Bob Sale.

It quite undid me. He'd been such a hearty, kind old soul – I could see him mopping the noble tears from his red cheeks at my bedside in Jallalabad, or grinning from his table-head at Florentia's wilder flights, or thumping his knee: "There'll be no retreat from Lahore, what?" Now they were blowing retreat over him, old Fighting Bob; the grapeshot had got him when they stormed the jungle – the Quartermaster-General charging with the infantry! Well, thank God I wouldn't have to break the news to her.

But poor old Bob was soon forgotten in the presence of the G.G. and the army chief, for now I must tell my tale

221

again, to that distinguished audience – Thackwell, the cavalry boss, was there, and Hardinge's son Charlie, and young Gough, Paddy's nephew, but only three faces counted: Hardinge, cold and grave, his finger laid along his cheek; Gough leaning forward, the brown, handsome old face alight with interest, tugging his white moustache; and Broadfoot, all red whiskers and bottle glasses, watching them to see how they took it, like a master while his prize boy construes. It sounded well, and I told it straight, with no false-modest tricks which I knew would be wasted here – bogus message, Goolab Singh, Maka Khan, gridiron, escape, Gardner's intervention (I daren't omit him, with George there), my meeting with Lal and Tej. When I'd done there was a silence, into which George stepped, laying down the law.

"May I say at once, excellency, that I support *all* Mr Flashman's actions unreservedly. They are precisely such as I should have wished him to take."

"Hear, hear," says Gough, and tapped the table. "Good lad."

Hardinge didn't care for it. I guessed that, like Littler, he thought I'd taken a heap too much on myself, but unlike Littler he wasn't prepared to admit that I'd been right.

"Fortunately, no harm appears to have been done," says he coldly. "However, the less said of this the better, I think. You will agree, Major Broadfoot, that any publication of the Sikhs' treachery might have the gravest consequences." Without waiting for George's reply, he went on, to me: "And I would not wish your ordeal at the hands of the enemy to be noised abroad. It was a dreadful thing" – he might have been discussing the weather – "and I congratulate you on your deliverance, but if it were to become known it must have an inflammatory effect, and that could serve no good end." Never mind the inflammatory effect it had had on *my* end; even in the middle of a war he was fretting about our harmonious relations with the Punjab when it was all over, and Flashy's scorched arse mustn't be allowed to mar the prospect. I hadn't liked Henry Hardinge before, but now I loathed him. So I agreed at once, like a good little toady,

222

and Gough, who'd been fidgeting impatiently, got a word in:
"Tell me this, my boy – an' if you're proved wrong I'll not
hold it against ye. This Tej Singh, now . . . ye know the man.
Can we rely on him to do his worst, by his own side?"

"Yes, sir," says I. "I believe so. He'd sit in front of
Ferozepore forever. But his officers may force his hand for
him."

"I think, Sir Hugh," drawls Hardinge, "that it would be
wiser to weigh the facts we know, rather than Mr Flashman's
opinion."

Gough frowned at the tone, but nodded. "No doubt, Sorr
Hinry. But whatever, it must be Ferozeshah. And as soon as
maybe."

I was dismissed after that, but not before Gough had
insisted on drinking my health – Hardinge barely lifted his
glass from the table. The hell with him, I was too fagged to
care, and ready to sleep for a year, but did I get the chance?
I'd barely pulled my boots off, and was soaking my
extremity in cold water, when my tent was invaded by
Broadfoot, bearing a bottle and full of bounce and congratulations, which included himself for being so dam' clever
in sending me to Lahore in the first place. I said Hardinge
didn't seem to think so, and he snorted and said Hardinge
was an ass, and a puffed-up snob who had no use for politicals – but never mind that, I must tell him all about Lahore,
every word, and down he plumped on my *charpoy*,* spectacles a-gleam, to hear it.

Well, you know it all, and by midnight, so did he – bar the
jolly parts with Jeendan and Mangla, which I had too much
delicacy to mention. I made much of my friendship with
little Dalip, spoke in admiring terms of Gardner, and put in
a word for Jassa – d'you know, he'd been aware of that
remarkable rascal's identity all along, but had kept it from
me on principle. When I'd finished, he rubbed his hands
with satisfaction.

"All this will be of the greatest value. What matters, of
course, is that you have gained the confidence of the young

*Native bed.

223

Maharaja . . . and his mother . . ." He glanced sharply at me, and I met his eye with boyish innocence, at which he went pink, and polished his glasses. "Yes, and Goolab Singh, also. Those three will be the vital figures, when all this is over. Yes . . ." He went off into one of his Celtic trances for a moment, and then roused himself.

"Flashy – I'm going to ask you to do a hard thing. You won't like it, but it must be done. D'ye see?"

Oh, Jesus, thinks I, what now? He wants me to go to Burma, or dye my hair green, or kidnap the King of Afghanistan – well, the blazes with it! I've run my mile, and be damned to him. So, of course, I asked him eagerly what it might be, and he glanced at my injured ankle which I'd laid, still pink and puffy, on a wet towel.

"Still painful, I see. But it didn't stop ye riding thirty miles today – and if there's a cavalry charge against the Khalsa tomorrow, you'll be in it if it kills you, won't you?"

"I should dam' well hope so!" cries I, with my heart in my boots at the mere thought, and he shook his head in stern admiration.

"I knew it! No sooner out o' the frying pan than you're itching to be at the fire. Ye were just the same on the Kabul retreat." He clapped me on the shoulder. "Well, I'm sorry, my boy – it's not to be. Tomorrow, *I don't want you to be able to walk a step*, let alone back a horse – d'ye follow?"

I didn't – but I smelled something damned fishy.

"It's this way," says he earnestly. "Last night we fought the sternest action I ever saw. These Sikhs are the starkest, bravest fellows on earth – worth two Ghazis, every man of 'em. I killed four myself," says he solemnly, "and I tell ye, Flashy, they died hard! They did that." He paused, frowning. "Have you ever noticed . . . how *soft* a man's head is?[33] Aye, well . . . what we did last night, we'll be doing again presently. Gough must destroy Lal's half of the Khalsa at Ferozeshah – and unless I'm mistaken it'll be the bloodiest day that ever was seen in India." He wagged a finger. "It may well decide this war –"

"Yes, yes!" cries I, all eagerness, feeling ready to puke.

224

"But what's all this gammon about me not being able to walk –?"

"At all costs," says he impressively, "you must be kept out of the fighting. One reason is that the credit and confidence you've achieved with the folk who'll be ruling the Punjab under our thumb next year – is far too valuable to be risked. I won't allow it. So, when Gough asks for you as a galloper tomorrow – which I know he will – well, he can't have you. But I don't choose to tell him why, because he has no more political sense than the minister's cat, and wouldn't understand. So we must hoodwink him, and the rest of the Army, and your game leg will serve our turn." He laid a hand on my shoulder, owling at me. "It's not a nice thing, but it's for the good o' the service. I know it's asking a deal, from you of all men, that you stand back when the rest of us fall in, but . . . what d'ye say, old fellow?"

You can picture my emotion. That's the beauty of a heroic reputation – but you must know how to live up to it. I assumed the right expression of pained, bewildered indignation, and put a catch into my voice.

"George!" says I, as though he'd struck the Queen. "You're asking me . . . to *shirk*! Oh, yes, you are, though! Well, it won't do! See here, I've done your job in Lahore, and all – don't I deserve the chance to be a soldier again? Besides," cries I, in a fine passion, "I owe those bastards something! And you expect me to hang back?"

He looked manly compassionate. "I said it was a hard thing."

"Hard? Dammit, it's . . . it's the wrong side of enough! No, George, I won't have it! What, to sham sick – humbug dear old Paddy? Of all the cowardly notions!" I paused, red in the face, fearful of coming it too strong in case he relented. I changed tack. "Why am I so confounded precious, anyway? When the war's over, it'll be all one who plays politics in Lahore –"

"I said that was one reason," he cut in. "There's another. I need you back in Lahore *now*! Or as soon as may be. While it's all in the balance, I must have someone near the seat of power – and you're the man. It's the part I designed for you

225

from the first, remember? But your return must be a secret known only to you, me, and Hardinge . . . well, if you sham sick no one will wonder why you're being kept out of harm's way in the meantime." He grinned complacently. "Oh, I ken I'm a devious crater! I need tae be. So you'll go on a crutch the morn – and let your beard grow. When you go north again it'll be as Badoo the Badmash – well, ye can hardly ask admission to Lahore Fort as Mr Flashman, can ye?"

Fortunately, perhaps, I was speechless. I just stared at the red-whiskered brute – and he took silence for consent, when in truth it didn't even signify comprehension. The whole thing was too monstrous for words, and while I sat open-mouthed he laughed and clapped me on the back.

"That puts things in a different light, does it not? You'll be *shirking* your way into the lion's den, you see – so you needn't envy the rest of us our wee fight at Ferozeshah!" He stood up. "I'll speak to Hardinge now, and in a day or two I'll give you full particulars of what you'll be doing when you get to Lahore. Until then – take care of that ankle, eh? Sleep well, Badoo!" He winked heavily, pulling back the tent-fly, and paused. "Here, I say, Harry Smith told me a good one today! Why is a soldier of the Khalsa like a beggar? Can you tell, eh? Give it up?"

"I give up, George." And, by God, I meant it.

"Because he's a Sikh in arms!" cries he. "You twig? A-seekin' alms!" He guffawed. "Not bad, what? Good-night, old chap!"

And he went off chortling. "A Sikh in arms!" They were the last words I ever heard him speak.

You'll have difficulty finding Ferozeshah (or Pheeroo Shah, as we Punjabi purists call it) in the atlas nowadays. It's a scrubby little hamlet about halfway between Ferozepore and Moodkee, but in its way it's a greater place than Delhi or Calcutta or Bombay, for it's where the fate of India was settled – appropriately by treachery, folly, and idiot courage beyond belief. And most of all, by blind luck.

It was where Lal Singh, on my advice, had left half his force when he marched to meet Gough, and it was where his battered advance guard retired after Moodkee. So there he was now, twenty thousand strong with a hundred splendid guns, all nicely entrenched and snug as bugs. And Gough must attack him at once, for who could tell when Tej Singh, loafing before Ferozepore a mere dozen miles away, would be forced by his colonels to do the sensible thing and join Lal, thereby facing Paddy with a Khalsa of over fifty thousand, outnumbering us more than three to one?

So it was bundle and go at Moodkee next day, with the last of the dead being shovelled under, the Native Infantry deploying for a night march, the 29th marching in from the Umballa track, their red coats as yellow as their facings with the rolling dust, and the band thumping out "Royal Windsor", the elephant teams squealing as they hauled up the heavy pieces, camels braying in the lines, fellows shouting and waving papers in every tent opening, the munition carts rolling through, and Gough in his shirt-sleeves at an open-air table with his staff scampering round him. And the discerning eye would also have noted a stalwart figure propped up on a *charpoy* with his leg swathed to the knee in an enormous bandage, cursing the luck which kept him out of the fun.

227

"I say, Cust," cries Abbott, "have you seen? Flashy's got the gout! Has to have beef tea and sal volatile, and *kameela* drenches twice a day!"

"Comes of boozin' with maharanis at Lahore, I dare say," says Cust, "while the rest of us poor politicals have to work for a living."

"When did politicals ever work?" says Hore. "You stay where you are, Flashy, and keep out of the sun, mind! If the goin' gets sticky we'll haul you up to wave your crutch at the Sikhs!"

"Wait till I'm walking and I'll wave more than a crutch!" cries I. "You fellows think you're clever – I'll be ahead of you all yet, you'll see!" At which they all made game of me, and said they'd leave a few Sikh wounded for me to cut up. Cheery stuff, you see. Broadfoot himself had pronounced me *hors de combat*, and I got a deal of sympathy among all the chaff, but Gough insisted that I should be brought along to Ferozeshah anyway, to deal with casualty returns, of which there were likely to be a-plenty. "If he can't ride he can still write," says Paddy. "Besides, if I know the boy he'll be in at the death before all's done." Live in hope, old Paddy, thinks I; I'd expected to be left behind at Moodkee with the wounded, but at least I'd be well out of the way at advance headquarters while the rest of them got on with the serious work.

Broadfoot and his Afghans were out all day, scouting the Sikh position, so I never saw him. I went hot and cold by turns when I thought of the awful prospect he'd unfolded to me the previous night – sneaking back to Lahore in disguise, no doubt to carry treasonable messages to Jeendan, and keep an eye on her and her court of snakes . . . how the devil was it to be done, and why? But sufficient unto the day; I'd find out soon enough.

We marched, after a broiling day of confused preparation, in the freezing small hours, the army in column of route and your humble obedient borne in a *dooli** by minions, which caused much hilarity among the staff-wallopers, who kept stopping by to ask if I needed any gruel or a stone pig to

*Stretcher.

228

warm my toes. I responded with bluff repartee – and noticed that as the march progressed the comedians fell silent; we came within earshot of the Sikh drums soon after dawn, and by nine were deploying within sight of Ferozeshah. I bade my *dooli*-bearers set me down in a little grove not far from the headquarters group, to be out of the heat – with interesting results, as you'll see. For while most of what I tell you of that momentous day is hearsay, one vital incident was played out under my nose alone. This is what happened.

The scouts had reported that the place was heavily entrenched on all sides, in a rough mile square about the village, with the Sikhs' heavy guns among the mounds and ditches that enclosed it. On three sides there were jungly patches which would hinder our attack, but on the eastern side facing us it was flat *maidan*, and Gough, honest man, could see only one way – open up with the guns and sweep straight in, trusting to the bayonets of his twelve thousand to do the trick against twenty thousand Khalsa. During the night Littler had slipped out of Ferozepore with almost his whole seven thousand, leaving Tej guarding an empty town; Paddy's notion may have been to drive the Sikhs out of Ferozeshah and into Littler's path, but I ain't sure.

At all events, I was reclining in my *dooli* in the shade, discussing beef and hardtack and coughing contentedly over my cheroot, admiring the view of our army deployed across my front and feeling patriotic, when there was a commotion fifty yards off, where the HQ staff were at breakfast – Hardinge trying to hog the marmalade again, thinks I, but when I peeped out, here was the man himself striding towards my grove, looking stern, and five yards behind, Paddy Gough with his white coat flapping and bright murder in his eye. Hardinge stops just inside the grove and says: "Well, Sir Hugh?"

"Well, indeed, Sorr Hinry!" cries Paddy, Irish with fury. "I'll tell ye again – you're lookin' at the foinest victory that ever was won in India, bigad, an' –"

"And I tell you, Sir Hugh, it is not to be thought of! Why, you are outnumbered two to one in men, and even more in cannon – and they are in cover, sir!"

229

"And don't I know that, then? I tell ye still, I'll put Ferozeshah in your hand by noon! Dear man, our infantry aren't Portuguese!"

That was a dig at Hardinge, who'd served with the Portugoosers in the Peninsula. His tone was freezing as he replied: "I cannot entertain it. You must wait for Littler to come up."

"An' if I wait that long, sure'n the rabbits'll be runnin' through Ferozeshah! 'Tis the shortest day o' the year, man! And will ye tell me, plain now – who commands this army?"

"You do!" snaps Hardinge.

"And did ye not offer me your services, as a soldier, in whutsoivver capacity, now? Ye did! And I accepted, gratefully! But it seems ye won't take my orders –"

"In the field, sir, I shall obey you implicitly! But as Governor-General I shall, if necessary, exert my civil authority over the Commander-in-Chief. And I will not hazard the army in such a risk as this! Oh, my dear Sir Hugh," he went on, trying to smooth things, but Paddy wasn't at home.

"In short, Sorr Hinry, ye're questionin' my military judgment!"

"As to that, Sir Hugh, I have been a soldier as long as you –"

"I know it! I know also ye haven't smelt powder since Waterloo, an' all the staff college lectures in creation don't make a battlefield general! So, now!"

Hardinge was a staff college man; Paddy, you may suspect, was not.

"This is unseemly, sir!" says Hardinge. "Our opinions differ. As Governor-General, I positively forbid an attack until you are supported by Sir John Littler. That is my last word, sir."

"And this is mine, sorr – but I'll be havin' another one later!" cries Paddy. "If we come adrift through this, with our fellows shootin' each other in the dark, as they did at Moodkee – well, sorr, I won't hold myself responsible unless I am!"

"Thank you, Sir Hugh!"

"Thank you, Sorr Hinry!"

230

And off they stumped, after a conference unique, I believe, in military history.[34] As to which was right, God knows. On the one hand, Hardinge had to think of all India, and the odds scared him. Against that, Paddy was the fighting soldier – daft as a brush, granted, but he knew men and ground and the smell of victory or defeat. Heads or tails, if you ask me.

So Hardinge had his way, and the army set off again, south-west, to meet Littler, crossing the Sikh front with our flank wide as a barn door if they'd care to come out and fall on us. They didn't, thanks to Lal Singh, who refused to budge while his staff tore their hair at the missed chance. Littler hove in view at Shukoor, and our force turned north again, now eighteen thousand strong, and stormed Ferozeshah.

I didn't see the battle, since I was installed in a hut at Misreewallah, more than a mile away, surrounded by clerks and runners and sipping grog while I waited for the butcher's bill. So I shan't elaborate the bare facts – you can read the full horror in the official accounts if you're curious. I *heard* it, though, and saw the results; that was enough for me.

It was shockingly botched, on both sides. Gough had to launch his force in frontal assault on the south and west entrenchments, which were the strongest, just as the sun was westering. Our fellows were caught in a hail of grape and musketry, with mines going off under them, but they stormed in with the bayonet, and drove the Sikhs from their camp and the village beyond. Just on dusk, the Sikhs' magazine exploded, and soon there were fires everywhere, and it was slaughter all the way, but there was such confusion in the dark, with regiments going astray, and Harry Smith, as usual, miles ahead of the rest, that Gough decided to re-form – and the retire was sounded. Our fellows, with Ferozeshah *in their hands*, came out again – and the Sikhs walked back in, resuming the entrenchments we'd taken at such fearful cost. And they wonder why folk go to sea. So we were back where we began, in the freezing night, with the Khalsa sharpshooters hammering our bivouacs and wells.

231

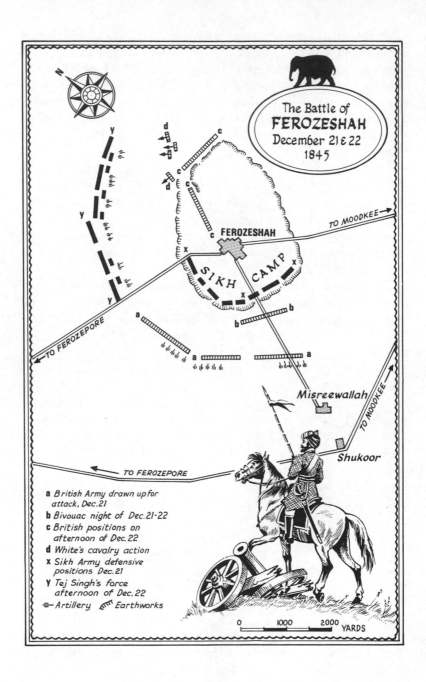

The Battle of
FEROZESHAH
December 21 & 22
1845

TO MOODKEE →

FEROZESHAH

SIKH CAMP

TO FEROZEPORE ←

TO MOODKEE →

Misreewallah

TO FEROZEPORE ←

Shukoor

a British Army drawn up for
   attack, Dec. 21
b Bivouac night of Dec. 21-22
c British positions on
   afternoon of Dec. 22
d White's cavalry action
x Sikh Army defensive
   positions Dec. 21
y Tej Singh's force
   afternoon of Dec. 22
⹀ Artillery 〰 Earthworks

0   1000   2000
              YARDS

232

Oh, aye, and Lumley, the Adjutant-General, went off his rocker and ran about telling everyone we must retire on Ferozepore. Luckily no one minded him.

My memories of that night are a mixture of confused pictures: Ferozeshah, two miles away, like a vision of hell, a sea of flames under red clouds with explosions everywhere; men lurching out of the dark, carrying wounded comrades; the long dark mass of our bivouacs on the open ground, and the unceasing screams and groans of the wounded all night long; bloody hands thrusting bloody papers before me under the storm-lantern – Littler had lost 185 men in only ten minutes, I remember; the crash of our artillery at the Sikh sharpshooters; Hardinge, his hat gone and his coat bloody, calling: "Charles, where are the Ninth – I must visit all my old Peninsulars! See if they have a lady in barracks, what?";[35] a corporal of the 62nd, his trousers soaked in blood, sitting at my hut door with his hussif open, carefully stitching a tear in the white cover of his hat; the sudden blare of bugles and rattle of drums sounding the alarm as a regiment was mustered to make a sortie against a Sikh gun emplacement; a Light Dragoon, face black with powder, and a skinny little *bhisti*,* buckets in their hands, and the Dragoon crying who'd make a dash with them for the well, 'cos Bill must have water and the *chaggles*† were dry; the little German prince who'd played billiards while I romped Mrs Madison, putting in his head to ask ever so politely if Dr Hoffmeister, of whom I'd never heard, was on my lists – he wasn't, but he was dead, anyway; and a hoarse voice singing softly in the dark:

Wrap me up in my tarpaulin jacket, jacket,
An' say a poor buffer lies low, lies low,
An' six stalwart lancers shall carry me, carry me,
With steps that are mournful an' slow.

Then send for six brandies an' soda, soda,
An' set 'em up all in a row, a row . . .

*Water-carrier.
†Canvas water-bags.

233

I hobbled across to headquarters on my unnecessary crutch, to sniff the wind. It was a big bare *basha*,* with fellows curled up asleep on the earth, and at the far end Gough and Hardinge with a map across their knees, and an aide holding a light. By the door Baxu the butler and young Charlie Hardinge were packing a valise; I asked what was to do.

"Off to Moodkee," says Charlie. "Currie must be ready to burn his papers."

"What – is it all up, then?"

"Touch an' go, anyway. I say, Flashy, have you seen the cabbage-walloper – Prince Waldemar? I've to take him out of it, confound him! Blasted civilians," says Charlie, who was one himself, secretarying Papa, "seem to think war's a sightseein' tour!" Baxu handed him a dress sword, and Charlie chuckled.

"I say – mustn't forget that, Baxu!"

"Nay, sahib! Wellesley sahib would be dam-displeased!"

Charlie tucked it under his coat. "Wouldn't mind havin' its owner walk in this minute, though."

"Who's that, then?" I asked.

"Boney. Wellington gave it to the guv'nor after Waterloo. Can't let the Khalsa get hold of Napoleon's side-arm, can we?"

I didn't care for this – when the swells start sending their valuables down the road, God help the rest of us. I asked Abbott, who was smoking by the door, with his arm in a bloody sling, what was afoot.

"We're goin' in again at dawn. Nothin' else for it, with only half a day's fodder for us an' the guns. It's Ferozeshah – or six feet under. Some asses were talkin' about terms, or cuttin' out for Ferozepore, but the G.G. an' Paddy gave 'em the rightabout." He lowered his voice. "Mind you, I don't know if we can stand another gruellin' like today . . . how's the pension parade?"

He meant our casualties. "At a guess . . . maybe one in ten."

*Native house.

234

"Could be worse . . . but there ain't a whole man on the staff," says he. "Oh, I say, did you hear? – Georgie Broadfoot's dead."

I didn't take it in at all. I heard the words, but they meant nothing at first, and I just stood staring at him while he went on: "I'm sorry . . . he was a chum o' yours, wasn't he? I was with him, you see . . . the damnedest thing! I'd been hit . . ." he touched his sling ". . . an' thought I was gone, when old Georgie rides up, shouting: 'Get up, Sandy! Can't go to sleep, you know!' So up I jumped, an' then Georgie tumbled out of his saddle, shot in the leg, but he popped straight up again, an' says to me: 'There you are, you see! Come on!' It was fairly rainin' grape from the south entrenchment, an' a second later, he went down again. So I yelled: 'Come on, George! Sleepyhead yourself!'" He fumbled inside his shirt. "And . . . so he is now, for keeps, the dear old chap. You want these? Here, take 'em."

They were George's spectacles, with one lens broken. I took them, not believing it. Seeing Sale dead had been bad enough – but Broadfoot! The great red giant, always busy, always scheming – nothing could kill him, surely? No, he'd walk in presently, damning someone's eyes – mine, like enough. For no reason I took a look through the remaining glass, and couldn't see a thing; he must have been blind as a bat without them . . . and then it dawned on me that if he was dead, there'd be no one to send me to Lahore again – and no need! Whatever ploy he'd had in mind would have died with him, for even Hardinge wouldn't know the ins and outs of it . . . So I was clear, and relief was flooding through me, making me tremble, and I choked between tears and laughter –

"Here, don't take on!" cries Abbott, catching my wrist. "Never fret, Flashy – George'll be paid for, you'll see! Why, if he ain't, he'll haunt us, the old ruffian, gig-lamps an' all! We're bound to take Ferozeshah!"

And they did, a second time. They went in, Briton and sepoy, in ragged red lines under the lifting mist of dawn, with the horse guns thundering ahead of them and the Khalsa trenches bright with flame. The Sikh gunners fairly battered the advancing regiments and picked off our ammunition wagons, so that our ranks seemed to be moving through pillars of fiery cloud, with the white trails of our Congreves piercing the black smoke. It's the last madness, thinks I, watching awestruck from the rear, for they'd no right to be on their feet, even, let alone marching into that tempest of metal, exhausted, half-starved, frozen stiff, and barely a swallow of water among them, with Hardinge riding ahead, his empty sleeve tucked into his belt, telling his aides he'd seen nothing like it since the Peninsula, and Gough leading the right, spreading the tails of his white coat to be the better seen. Then they had vanished into the smoke, the scarecrow lines and the tattered standards and the twinkling cavalry sabres – and I thanked God I was here and not there as I led the rocketeers in three cheers for our gallant comrades, before being borne back into the shade to a well-earned breakfast of bread and brandy.

Being new to the business, I half-expected to see 'em back shortly, in bloody rout – but beyond our view they were storming the defences again, and going through Ferozeshah like an iron fist, and by noon there wasn't a live Punjabi in the position, and we'd taken seventy guns. Don't ask me how – they say some of the Khalsa infantry cut stick in the night, and the rest were all at sea because Lal Singh and his cronies had fled, with the Akalis howling for his blood – but that don't explain it, not to me. They still weren't outnumbered, and had the defensive advantage, and fought their guns to the finish – so how did we beat 'em? I don't know, I wasn't there – but then, I still don't understand the Alma and Balaclava and Cawnpore, and I was in the thick of them, God help me, and no fault of mine.

I ain't one of your by jingoes, and I won't swear that the British soldier is braver than any other – or even, as Charley Gordon said, that he's brave for a little while longer. But I *will* swear that there's no soldier on earth who believes so strongly in the courage of the men alongside him – and that's worth an extra division any day. Provided you're not standing alongside *me*, that is.

All morning the wounded kept coming back, but fewer by

236

far than yesterday, and now they were jubilant. Twice they'd beaten the Khalsa against the odds, and there wouldn't be a third Ferozeshah, not with Lal's forces in flight for the Sutlej, and our cavalry scouting their retreat. "*Tik hai*, Johnnie!" roars a sergeant of the 29th, limping down with a *naik* of Native Infantry; they had two sound legs between them, and used their muskets as crutches. "'Oo's got a tot o' rum for my Johnnie, then? 'E may 'ave fired wide at Moodkee, but you earned yer chapattis today, didn't yer, ye little black bugger!" And everyone roared and cheered and helped them along, the tow-headed, red-faced ruffian and the sleek brown Bengali, both of them grinning with the same wild light in their eyes. That's victory – it was in all their eyes, even those of a pale young cornet of the 3rd Lights with his arm off at the elbow, raving as they carried him past at the run, and of a private with a *tulwar* gash in his cheek, spitting blood at every word as he told me how Gough was entrenched in the Sikhs' position in case of counter-attack, but there was no fear of that.

"We done for 'em, sir!" cries he, and his yellow facings were as red as his coat with his own gore. "They won't stop runnin' till they gets to La'ore, I reckon! You should 'ear 'em cheer ole Daddy Gough – ain't 'e the boy, though?" He peered at me, holding a grimy cloth to his wound. "'Ere, you orl right, sir? Fair done in you looks, if you'll 'scuse my sayin' so . . ."

It was true – I, who hadn't been near the fight, and had been right as rain, was all at once ready to keel over where I sat. And it wasn't the heat, or the excitement, or the sight of his teeth showing through his cheek (other folks' blood don't bother me), or the screaming from the hospital *basha*, or the stench of stale blood and acrid smoke from the battle, or the dull ache in my ankle – none of that. I believe it was the knowledge that at last it was all over, and I could give way to the numbing fatigue that had been growing through one of the worst weeks of my life. I'd had one night's sleep out of eight, counting from the first which I'd spent gallop-ing Mangla; then there'd been my Khalsa frolic, the Sutlej crossing, the ride from Lal and Tej to Ferozepore, the vigil

237

as we listened to distant Moodkee, uneasy slumber after Broadfoot had given me his bad news, the freezing march to Misreewallah, and finally, the first night of Ferozeshah. Oh, I was luckier than many, but I was beat all to nothing – and now it was past, and I was safe, and could lurch from my stool and fall face-down on the *charpoy*, dead to the world.

Now, when I'm dog-tired with shock, I have nightmares worthy of cheese and lobster, but this one laid it over them all, for I fell slowly through the *charpoy*, into a bath of warm water, and when I rolled over I was staring up at a ceiling painting of Gough and Hardinge and Broadfoot, all figged out like Persian princes, having dinner with Mrs Madison, who tilted her glass and poured oil all over me, which made me so slippery that I couldn't hope to transfer the whole Soochet legacy, coin by coin, from my navel to Queen Ranavalona's as she pinned me down on a red-hot billiard-table. Then she began to pummel and shake me, and I knew she was trying to make me get up because Gough wanted me, and when I said I couldn't, because of my ankle, the late lamented Dr Arnold, wearing a great tartan *puggaree*, came by on an elephant, crying that he would take me, for the Chief needed a Greek translation of *Crotchet Castle* instanter, and if I didn't take it to Tej Singh, Elspeth would commit *suttee*. Then I was following him, floating across a great dusty plain, and the smell of burning was everywhere, and filthy ash was falling like snow, and there were terrible bearded faces of dead men, smeared with blood, and corpses all about us, with ghastly wounds from which their entrails spilled out on earth that was sodden crimson, and there were great cannon lying on their sides or tumbled into pits, and everywhere the charred wreckage of tents and carts and huts, some of them still in flames.

There was a mighty tumult, too, a great cannonading, and the shriek and crash of shot striking home, the rattle of musketry, and bugles blowing. There were voices yelling on all sides, in a great confusion of orders: "By sections, right – walk-march, trot!" and "Battalion, halt! Into line – left turn!" and "Troop Seven – left incline, forward!" But Arnold wouldn't stop, though I shouted to him, and I couldn't see where the troops were, for the horse I was riding was going too fast, and the sun was in my eyes. I raised my left hand to shield them, but the sun's rays burned more fiercely than ever, causing me such pain that I cried out, for it was burning a hole in my palm, and I clutched at Arnold with my other hand – and suddenly he was Mad Charley West, gripping me round the shoulders and yelling to me to hold on, and my left hand was pumping blood from a ragged hole near the thumb, causing excruciating agony, and all hell was loose around me.

That was the moment when I realised that I wasn't dreaming.

An eminent medico has since explained that exhaustion and strain induced a trance-like state when I sank down on the *charpoy*, and that while my nightmares turned to reality, I didn't come to properly until I was wounded in the hand – which is the most immediately painful place in the whole body, and I should know, since I've been hit in most others. In between, Mad Charley had wakened me, helped me to mount (bad ankle and all), and we'd ridden at speed through the carnage of the recent battle to Gough's position beyond Ferozeshah village – and all I'd taken in were those disjointed pictures I've just described. The sawbones had an impressive medical name for it, but I doubt if there's one for the sensation I felt as I gripped my wounded hand to crush the pain away, and took in the scene about me.

Directly before me were two troops of Native horse artillery, firing as fast as they could load, the little brown gunners springing aside to avoid the recoil, the crash of the salvoes staggering my horse by its very violence. To my left was a ragged square of British infantry – the 9th, for I saw the penny badge on their shakos – and beyond them others, sepoy and British, kneeling and standing, with the reserve ranks behind. To my right it was the same, more squares, inclined back at a slight angle, with their colours in the centre, like the pictures of Waterloo. Red squares, with the dust boiling round them, and shot screaming overhead or ploughing through with a clap like thunder; men were falling, sometimes singly, sometimes hurtled aside as a shot tore

239

into the ranks; I saw a great swathe, six files wide, cut by grape at the corner of the 9th's square, and the air filled with red spray. Before me a horse gun suddenly stood up on end, its muzzle split like a stalk of celery, and then it crashed down in a hellish tangle of fallen men and stricken horses. It was as though a gale of iron rain was sweeping the ranks, coming God knew whence, for the dust and smoke enveloped us – and Mad Charley was hauling at my bridle, urging me through it.

There's never a time when pain and fear don't matter, but sometimes shock is so bewildering that you don't think of them. One such time is when you wake up to find that good artillery has got your range and is pounding you to pieces; there's nothing to be done, no time even to hope you won't be hit, and you can't hurl yourself to the ground and lie there squealing – not when you find you're alongside Paddy Gough himself, and he's pulling off his bandana and telling you to wrap it round your fin and pay attention.

"Put your finger on the knot, man! There, now – look ahead and take close note of what ye see!"

He yanked the bandage tight, and pointed, and through tears of anguish and terror I looked beyond the clouds of settling dust.

A bare half-mile away the plain was alive with horsemen. The artillery teams who'd been shelling us, light camel swivels and heavier field pieces, were wheeling away through the advancing ranks of a great tide of cavalry cantering towards us knee to knee. It must have been five hundred yards from wing to wing, with lancer regiments on the flanks, and in the centre the heavy squadrons in tunics of white and red, *tulwars* at the shoulder, the low sun gleaming on polished helms from which stiff plumes stood up like scarlet combs – and only when I remembered those same plumes at Maian Mir did I realise the full horror of what I was seeing. These were Sikh line cavalry, and dazed and barely half-awake as I was, I knew that could mean only one thing, even if it was impossible: we were facing the army of Tej Singh, the cream of the Khalsa thirty thousand strong, who should have been miles away in futile watch on

240

Ferozepore. Now they were here – beyond the approaching storm of horsemen I could see the massed ranks of infantry, regiment on regiment, with the great elephant guns before them. And we were a bare ten thousand, dropping with exhaustion after three battles which had decimated us, and out of food, water, and shot.

Historians say that on that one moment, as the Khalsa's spearhead was rushing at our throat, rested the three centuries of British India. Perhaps. It was surely the moment in which Gough's battered little army stared certain death and destruction in the face, and whatever may have settled our fate later, one man turned the hinge then and there. Without him, we (aye, and perhaps all India) would have been swept away in bloody ruin. I'll wager you've never heard of him, the forgotten brigadier, Mickey White.

It happened in split seconds. Even as I dashed the sweat from my eyes and stared again, the bugles blared along those surging lines of Khalsa horsemen, the *tulwars* rose in a wave of steel and the great forest of lance-points dipped as the canter became a gallop. Gough was roaring to our men to hold their fire, and I heard Huthwaite yelling that the guns were at the last round, and the muskets of the infantry squares came to the present in a ragged fence of bayonets that must be ridden under as that magnificent sea of men and horses engulfed us. I never saw the like in my life, I who watched the great charge against Campbell's Highlanders at Balaclava – but those were only Russians, while these were the fathers of the Guides and Probyn's and the Bengal Lancers, and the only thing to stop them at full tilt was a horse soldier as good as themselves.

He was there, and he chose his time. A few more seconds and the gallop would have been a charge – but now a trumpet sounded on the right, and wheeling out before our squares came the remnant of our own mounted division, the blue tunics and sabres of the 3rd Lights and the black fezzes and lances of the Native Cavalry, with White at their head, launching themselves at the charge against the enemy's flank. They didn't have the numbers, they didn't have the weight, and they were spent, man and beast – but they had

241

the time and the place to perfection, and in a twinkling the Khalsa charge was a struggling confusion of rearing beasts and falling riders and flashing steel as the Lights tore into its heart and the *sowar* lancers raked across its front.[36]

My female and civilian readers may wonder how this could be – that a small force of horsemen could confound one far greater. Well, that's the beauty of the flank attack – think of six hearty chaps racing forward in line, and one artful dodger barges into the end man, from the side. They're thrown out of kilter, tumbling into one another, and though they're six to one, five of 'em can't come at their attacker. At its best a good flank movement can "roll up" the enemy like a window blind, and while White's charge didn't do that, it threw them quite off course, and when that happens to cavalry in formation their momentum's gone, and good loose riders can play the devil with them.

So what happened under our noses was a deuce of a scrimmage, and though White's horse went down, he was here and there like a wild-cat on foot, with the Lights closing round him, the sabres swinging, and Gough up in his stirrups shouting: "You'll do, Mick! That's your sort, my boy! And who," he roars at me, "are those fellows, will ye tell me?"

I shouted that they were Khalsa regulars, not *gorracharra* – Mouton's and Foulkes's regiments, for certain, and Gordon's, too, though I couldn't be sure.

"That's the pick of 'em, then!" snaps he. "Well, White's put a flea in their ear, so he has! Now, take you this glass, and tell me about their infantry! West, note it down!"

So while the cavalry rumpus petered out, with the Khalsa horsemen drawing off, and our own fellows, half of them dismounted, limping back to reform, I surveyed that mass of infantry with a sinking heart, calling them off by name – Allard's, Court's, Avitabile's, Delust's, Alvarine's, and the rest of the divisions. The standards were easy to read, and so were those grim bearded faces, sharp in my glass – I could even make out the silver buckles on the black cross-belts, the aigrets in the turbans, and the buttons on the tunics, white and red and blue and green, just as I'd seen them on Maian Mir. How the devil came they here – had Tej's

242

colonels lost patience and made him march to the sound of the guns? That must be it, and now that White had played our last card, we could only wait for them to advance and swallow us. The victory of Ferozeshah had become a death-trap – and I remembered Gardner's words: "They reckon they can whip John Company." And now John Company could barely stand up in his shot-torn squares, his pouches and magazines empty, his guns silent, his cavalry lame, and only his bayonets left.

Across the plain spurts of flame flickered along the Khalsa batteries like an electric storm, followed by the thunder of the discharge, the howl of shot overhead, and a hideous crashing and screaming as it burst open our squares. They were making sure, the bastards, pounding us to death at leisure before sending in their foot regiments to cut up the remains; again the dust boiled up as the grape and roundshot tore through the entrenchments; we could stand or we could run. John Company chose to stand, God knows why. In my case, he stood as close behind Gough as might be, too scared even to pray – and a bad choice of position it was, too. For as the bombardment reached its height, and the squares vanished in the rolling red clouds, and our army died by inches, with men going down like skittles and the blood running under our hooves, and some heroic ass bawling: "Die hard, Queen's Own!", and Flashy wondering if he dared cut out under the eye of his Chief, and knowing I hadn't the game for it, and even my wound forgotten as the deadly hail swept through us – suddenly Gough wheeled his horse, looking right and left at the wreck of his army, and the old fellow was absolutely weeping! Then he flung away his hat, and I heard him growl:

"Oi nivver wuz bate, an' Oi nivver will be bate! West, Flashman – follow me!"

And he wheeled his charger and went racing out into the plain.

You fall on your bloody sword if you want to, Paddy, thinks I, and would have stood my ground or dived for cover, more like – but Charley was away like a shot, my beast followed suit like the idiot cavalry screw he was, I

243

clutched at the bridle with my shattered hand, near fainted at the pain, and found myself careering in their wake. For a moment I thought the old fellow had gone crazy, and was for charging the Khalsa on his own, but he veered away right, making for the flank square – and as he galloped clear of it and suddenly reined in on his haunches, and rose in his stirrups with his arms wide, I saw what he was at.

All India knew that white coat of Gough's, the famous "fighting coat" that the crazy old son-of-a-bitch had been flaunting at his foes for fifty years, from South Africa and the Peninsula to the Northwest Frontier. Now he was using it to draw the fire from his army to himself (and the two unlucky gallopers whom the selfish old swine had dragged along). It was the maddest-brained trick you ever saw – and, damnation, it worked! I can see him still, holding the tails out and showing his teeth, his white hair streaming in the wind, and the earth exploding round him, for the Sikh gunners took the bait and hammered us with everything they had. And of course, we weren't hit – try turning your batteries on three men at a thousand yards, and see what it gets you.[37]

But you don't reckon mathematical probabilities with a hurricane of shot whistling about your ears. I forced my beast alongside him, and yelled:

"Sir Hugh, you must withdraw! The army cannot spare you, sir!" Which was inspiration, if you like, but wasted on that Irish idiot. He yelled something that I couldn't hear . . . and then the miracle happened. And if you don't believe it, look in the books.

All of a sudden, the firing died away, and across the plain the bugles rang out, and the drums rolled, the great gold banners were raised in the rays of the setting sun, and the Khalsa began to move. It came on in column by regiments, with a line of Jat light infantry leading, green figures with their pieces at the trail – and suddenly Charley West was shouting:

"Look, Sir Hugh! Our cavalry! The guns – my God, they're retiring!"

Not before time, thinks I, 'though it shocked me, I can tell you. For he was right: where we sat, perhaps a furlong ahead

244

of our right flank, we had a clear view of the appalling ruin of our army – the dozen battered squares of red figures, with great gaps in their ranks, the regimental colours stirring in the evening wind, the bodies sprawled on the earthworks, the plain before them littered with dead and dying beasts and men, the whole hideous scene mantled in dust and smoke from the charred wreckage.

And the cavalry, what was left of it, was trotting away southward, across the front of our left-hand squares, which were inclined slightly back from those on the right. They were in column by troops, Native lancers and Irregular Horse, and then the 3rd Lights, with the horse guns following, bouncing along behind the teams.

"They – they can't be runnin'!" cries West. "Sir Hugh – shall I ride to 'em, sir? It must be a mistake, surely!"

Gough was staring after them as though he'd seen a ghost. I guess it was something he'd not seen in half a century – horse and guns leaving the infantry to their fate. But he didn't stare more than a moment.

"After 'em, West! Bring 'em back!" he snapped, and Mad Charley was away, head down and heels in, drumming up the dust, while Gough turned to look again towards the Khalsa.

They were well out on the plain now, in splendid style, infantry in the centre with the horse guns at intervals among them, cavalry on the wings. Gough motioned to me, and we began to trot back towards our position. For the first time I saw Hardinge, with a little knot of officers, just in front of the right-hand squares. He was looking through a glass, and turning his head to call an order. The kneeling squares stood up, the men closing on each other, pieces at the present, the dying sun flickering on the line of bayonets. Gough reined up.

"Here'll do as well as any place," says he, and shaded his eyes to look across the plain. "Man, but there's a fine sight, is it not? Fit to gladden a soldier's heart, so it is. Well, here's to them – and to us." He nodded to me. "Thank you, me son." He threw back the tail of his coat and drew his sabre, loosing the frog to let the scabbard fall to the ground.

245

"I think we're all goin' home," says he.

I glanced over my shoulder. Behind me the plain was open beyond our right flank, with jungle not a mile away. My screw wasn't blown or lame, and I was damned if I'd wait here to be butchered by that juggernaut tramping inexorably towards us; the blare of their heathen music came before them, and behind it the measured thunder of forty thousand feet. From the squares came the hoarse shouts of command; I stole another look at the distant jungle, tightening my sound hand on the bridle . . .

"Dear God!" exclaims Gough, and I started guiltily round. And what I saw was another impossibility, but . . . there it was.

The Khalsa had halted in its tracks. The dust was eddying up before the advance line of Jats, they were turning to look back at the main body, we could hear voices shrilling orders, and the music was dying away in a discordant wail. The great standards seemed to be wavering, the whole vast army was stirring like a swarm, the rattle of a single kettle-drum was taken up, repeated from regiment to regiment, and then it was as though a Venetian blind had opened and closed across the front of the great host – it was the ranks turning about, churning up the dust, and then they were moving away. The Khalsa was in full retreat.

There wasn't a sound from our squares. Then, from somewhere behind me, a man laughed, and a voice called angrily for silence. That's the only noise I remember, but I wasn't paying much heed. I could only watch in stricken bewilderment as twenty thousand of the best native troops in the world turned their backs on an exhausted, helpless enemy . . . and left the victory to us.

Gough sat his horse like a statue, staring after them. A full minute passed before he chucked the reins, turning his mount. As he walked it past me towards the squares, he nodded and says:

"You get that hand seen to, d'ye hear? An' when ye're done with it, I'll be obliged for the return of my neckercher."

So that was Ferozeshah as I saw it – the "Indian Waterloo", the bloodiest battle we ever fought in the Orient, and certainly the queerest – and while other accounts may not tally with mine (or with each other's) on small points, all are agreed on the essentials. We took Ferozeshah, at terrible cost, in two days of fighting, and were at the end of our tether when Tej Singh hove in view with an overwhelming force, and then sheared off when he could have eaten us for dinner.

The great controversy is: why did he do it? Well, you know why, because I've told you – he kept his word to us, and betrayed his army and his country. Yet there are respected historians who won't believe it, to this day – some because they claim the evidence isn't strong enough, others because they just won't have it that victory was won by anything other than sheer British valour. Well, it played its part, by God it did, but the fact is it wouldn't have been enough, without Tej's treachery.

One of the things which confuses the historians is that Tej himself, who could lie truth out of India when he wanted to, told so many different stories afterwards. He assured Henry Lawrence that he didn't push home his attack because he was sure it must fail; having seen the losses we'd taken in capturing Ferozeshah, he decided it was a hopeless position to assail now that we were defending it. He told the same tale to Sandy Abbott. Well, that's all my eye: he knew his strength, and he knew we were at the last gasp, so that won't wash.

Another lie, repeated to Alick Gardner, was that he was off collecting reserves at the time. If that's so, and he wasn't even there, who gave the Khalsa the order to turn about?

247

The truth, I believe, is what he told me many years later. He'd have stayed before Ferozepore till the Sutlej froze, if his colonels hadn't forced him to march to the battle – and once in sight of Ferozeshah he was in a pickle, because he could see that victory was his for the taking. He had to think up some damned fine excuse for not overwhelming us, and Chance provided it, at the last moment, when our guns and cavalry inexplicably withdrew, leaving our infantry as lonely as the policeman at Herne Bay. "Now's your time, Tej!" cries the Khalsa, "give the word and the day is ours!" "Not a bit of it!" says clever Tej. "Those crafty bastards ain't withdrawing at all – they're circling round to take us flank and rear! Back to the Sutlej, boys, I'll show you the way!" And the Khalsa did as they were told.

Well, you can see why. The three days of Moodkee and Ferozeshah had given their rank and file a great respect for us. They didn't realise what poor fettle we were in, or that the withdrawal of our horse and artillery was in fact an appalling mistake. It *looked* as though it might have some sinister purpose to it, as Tej was suggesting, and while they suspected his courage and character (rightly), they also knew he wasn't a bad soldier, and might be right for once. So they obeyed him, and we were saved when we should have been massacred.

You may ask why our cavalry and guns unexpectedly flew off into the blue, giving Tej his excuse for retreating. Well, that was a gift from the gods. I told you that Lumley, the Adjutant-General, had gone barmy during the first day's fighting, and kept saying we must retire on Ferozepore; well, on the second day, all his screws came loose together, he got Ferozepore on the brain entirely, and at the height of the battle he ordered our guns and cavalry away – in Hardinge's name, if you please, so off they went, with the great loony urging them to make haste. So that's how it was – Mickey White, Tej Singh, and Lumley, each doing his little bit in his own way. Odd business, war.[38]

We'd lost 700 dead, and close on 2000 wounded, including your humble obedient who spent the night under a tree, almost freezing to death, and utterly famished, with

248

Hardinge and what was left of his staff. There was no sleep to be had, with my hand throbbing in agony, but I daren't bleat, for Abbott alongside me had three wounds to my one, and was cheerful enough to sicken you. Round about dawn Baxu the butler rolled up with some chapattis and milk, and when we'd wolfed it down and Hardinge had prayed a bit, we all crawled aboard an elephant and lumbered down to Ferozepore, which was to be our seat of government henceforth, while Gough and most of the army camped near Ferozeshah. It was a great procession of wounded and baggage all the way to Ferozepore, and when we reached the entrenchments who should emerge but the guns and cavalry who had abandoned ship at the fatal moment. Hardinge was in a bate to know why, and one of the *binky-nabobs** assured him it had been on urgent orders from Hardinge himself, transmitted by the Adjutant-General.

So now the cry was "Lumley", and presently he appeared, very brisk and with a wild glint in his eye, lashing the air with a fly-whisk and giving sharp little cries; he was dressed in *pyjamys* and a straw boater, and was plainly on his way to the Hatter's for tea. Hardinge demanded why he'd sent off the guns, and Lumley looked fierce and said they had needed fresh magazines, of course, and damned if he'd known where they could get any, bar Ferozepore. He sounded quite indignant.

"Twelve miles away?" cries Hardinge. "What service could they hope to do in time, supposing they had replenished?"

Lumley snapped back, about as much as they'd ha' done at Ferozeshah, with no charges left. He seemed quite pleased with this, and laughed loudly, swatting flies, while Hardinge went purple. "And the cavalry, then?" cries he. "Why did you bid them retire?"

"Escort," says Lumley, picking imaginary mice off his shirt. "Can't have guns goin' about unguarded. Desperate fellows everywhere – Sikhs, don't you know? Swoop, pounce, carry 'em off, I assure you. Besides, cavalry needed a rest. Quite played out."

*Artillery commanders.

249

"And you did this in my name, sir?" cries Hardinge. "Without my authority?"

Lumley said, impatiently, that if he hadn't, no one would have paid him any heed. He grew quite agitated in describing how on the first night he'd told Harry Smith to retreat, and Harry had told him to go to hell. "Usin' foulest language, sir! 'Damn the orders!' – his very words, though I said 'twas in your name, and the battle was lost, and we must buy the Sikhs if we were to come off. He wouldn't listen," says Lumley, looking ready to cry.

Well, everyone except Hardinge could see that the fellow was liable to start plaiting his toes into door-mats, but our pompous G.G. wouldn't let him alone. Why, he demanded, was Lumley improperly dressed in *pyjamys* instead of uniform? Lumley gave a great guffaw and says: "Ah, well, you see, my overalls were so riddled with musket-balls, they dropped off me!"[39]

They sent him home, which made me wonder if he was quite as tap* as he sounded, for at least he got out of it, while the rest of us must soldier on, waiting for Paddy to plan his next bloodbath. I had hopes of keeping clear, with my hand shot through and my supposedly bad leg, but once we'd settled in Ferozepore and taken stock, blowed if I wasn't the fittest junior in view. Munro, Somerset, and Hore of Hardinge's staff were dead, Grant and Becher were wounded, Abbott wouldn't recover for weeks, and the toll among the politicals had been frightful, with Broadfoot and Peter Nicolson dead and Mills and Lake badly wounded. It's a damned dangerous game, campaigning, especially with a sawbones as heartily callous as old Billy M'Gregor. "Man, that's a grand hole in your hand!" cries he, sniffing it. "Nae gangrene or broken bones – ye'll be grippin' a glass or a gun inside the week! Your ankle? Ach, it's fine – ye could play peever† this minute!"

Not what I care to hear from my medical man in war-time; I'd been looking for a ticket to Meerut at least. But with politicals so scarce there was no hope of that, and when

*Mad, usually with sunstroke.
†Hop-scotch.

250

saintly Henry Lawrence turned up to take Broadfoot's place, I was kept hard at it – among other duties, seeing to the provision of fur boots for our elephants against the winter cold. Capital, thinks I, this is the way to serve out the war in comfort.

For one thing now seemed plain: the Khalsa couldn't whip John Company. The bogy had been laid at Ferozeshah, India was safe, and while they were still in strength beyond the river, it remained only to bring them to one final action to break them for good and all. So for the present we sat and watched them, Gough awaiting his chance to strike, and Hardinge turning his mind to great affairs of state and political settlements, with Lawrence, who knew the Punjab better even than Broadfoot, at his elbow.

He was shockingly Christian, Lawrence, but an A1 political for all that. He turned me inside out about Lahore, and wanted me in at the high pow-wows, but Hardinge said I was far too junior, and "over-zealous". The truth was he couldn't abide me, and wanted to forget my existence. Here's why.

We'd had a bloody close call in India, and it was Hardinge's fault. He'd failed to secure the frontier, through pussyfooting and hindering Gough, and the stark truth was that when the grip came, two men had saved the day – Gough and I. I ain't bragging; you know I never do (well, maybe about women and horses, but never about small things). I'd instructed Lal and Tej's treachery, and Paddy had held his ragbag army together, got it to the gate in time, and won his fights. Oh, they'd been costly, and he'd fought head on, and taken some hellish risks, but he'd done the business as few could have done it – Hardinge for one. But that wasn't how Hardinge saw it: he believed he'd stopped Paddy from throwing the army away at Ferozeshah, and from that it was a short step to seeing himself as the Saviour of India. Well, he was Governor-General, after all, and India had been saved. Q.E.D.

Indeed, he seemed to think he'd done it *in spite* of Gough – and inside a week of Ferozeshah he was writing to Peel in London urging that Paddy be given the sack. I saw the letter,

251

accidental-like, when I was rummaging through his excellency's effects in search of cheroots, and it was a beauty: Paddy wasn't fit to be trusted with the war, the army was "unsatisfactory", he'd no head for *bandobast*, he didn't frame orders properly, etc. Well, dash my wig, thinks I, here's gratitude – and the measure of Henry Hardinge. Framing orders, my foot – no doubt "On ye go, Mickey, give 'em one for me!" offended his staff college sensibilities, but he might have remembered another general of his acquaintance whose style wasn't very different: "Stand up, Guards! Now, Maitland, now's your time!" If I'd been a man I'd have scrawled it across his precious letter.

It was plain why he was tattling to Peel, though: shift the blame for the butcher's bill and the near squeak we'd had onto Gough, and who'd think back to the incompetence and fear of offending Lahore and Leadenhall Street that had helped bring on the war in the first place, and damned near lost it? It was artfully done, too, with a tribute to Paddy's energy and courage; you could imagine Peel shuddering at the name of Gough, and thanking God that Hardinge had been on hand.

Don't misunderstand. I ain't championing the old Mick, who was a bloodthirsty savage, and a splendid chap to avoid – but I liked him, because he'd no side, and was jolly, and offended the Quality by commissioning rankers and damn the royal prerogative – aye, and by winning wars with his "Tipperary tactics". Perhaps that was his greatest offence. Oh, I know Hardinge was an honourable man, who never stole a box-car in his life, and that most of what he said of Paddy was true. That ain't the point. That letter would have been shabby if *I'd* written it, dammit; coming from a man of honour it was unpardonable. But it showed how the wind set, and I wasn't surprised, on rooting farther through Hardinge's satchels (most elusive, those cheroots were) to find a note in his day-book: "Politicals of no real use." So there – plainly Flashy would get no credit, either; my work with Lal and Tej would be conveniently forgotten. Well, thank'ee, Sir Henry, and I hope your rabbit dies and you can't sell the hutch.[40]

252

I pondered about informing Paddy anonymously that he was being nobbled, but decided to let it be; mischief's all very well, but you never know where it may end. So I lay low, running errands for Lawrence. He was a gaunt, ill-tempered scarecrow, but he'd known me in Afghanistan and thought I was another heroic ruffian like himself, so we dealt pretty well. He'd seen from Broadfoot's papers that George had been meaning to send me back to Lahore, "but I can't think why, can you? Anyway, I doubt if the G.G. would approve; he thinks you've meddled enough in Punjabi politics. But you'd best let your beard grow, just in case."

So I did, and the weeks went by while we waited for the Khalsa to move, and our own army recovered and grew strong. We celebrated Christmas with the first decorated tree ever I saw,[41] a great fir brought down from the hills and sprinkled with flour to represent snow, our Caledonians boozed in the New Year with raucous mirth and unspeakable song, the reinforcements arrived from Umballa, and we saw the scarlet and blue of British Lancer regiments, the green of the little Gurkha hillmen strutting by with their knives bouncing on their rickety arses, the Tenth Foot with band playing and Colours flying, and everyone pouring out of the tents to sing them in:

    For 'tis my delight
    Of a shining night,
    In the season of the year!

Behind came Native Cavalry and marching sepoy battalions, with Sappers and artillery – Paddy had 15,000 men now, and the young Lancer bucks strutted and haw-hawed and asked when were these Sikh wallahs goin' to show us some sport, hey? God, I love newcomers in at the death, don't I just? There was one quiet Lancer, though, a black-whiskered Scotch nemesis who said never a word, and played the bull fiddle for his recreation. He caught my eye then, and again fifteen years later when he led the march to Peking, the most terrible killing gentleman you ever saw: Hope Grant.

So there we were, cocked and ready to fire, and beyond the river, although we didn't know it, little Dalip's throne was shaking, for it was touch and go whether the Khalsa, raging in defeat and convinced they'd been betrayed, would fight us or march on Lahore to slake their fury on Jeendan and the durbar. They'd have hanged Lal Singh if they could have caught him, but he'd hidden in a hayrick after Ferozeshah, and then in a baker's oven, before sneaking back to Lahore, where Jeendan mocked and abused him when she was sober, and galloped him when she was drunk. Between bouts she was sending messages of encouragement to her half-mutinous army, telling them not to give up, but to march on and conquer; at the same time she shut the city gates against the fugitives from Lal's contingent, who'd deserted in thousands, and even ordered Gardner to recall a Muslim brigade from the front to protect her in case the Khalsa Sikhs came looking for her. Resourceful lass, she was, egging on her army while she turned her capital into an armed camp against them.

Goolab Singh was playing the same game from Kashmir. The Khalsa pleaded with him to bring his hillmen to the war, and even offered to make him Maharaja, but the old fox saw we had the game won, and put them off with promises that he'd join once the campaign was fully launched, while making a great display of sending them supply convoys which he made sure were only quarter loaded and moved at a snail's pace.

Meanwhile Tej Singh was scheming how to lead the Khalsa to final destruction. He had the bulk of them in hand, outnumbering us three to one, and must do something before they lost patience with him. So he threw a bridge of boats over the Sutlej at Sobraon and built a strong position on the south bank in a bend of the river where Paddy daren't attack him without heavy guns, which we still lacked. At the same time, another Sikh army struck over the river farther up, threatening Ludhiana and our lines of communication, so Gough moved north to contain Tej's bridgehead and sent Harry Smith to deal with the Ludhiana incursion. Smith, full of conceit and ginger as usual, stalked the invaders to and

254

fro in the last week of January, and then handed them a fearful thrashing at Aliwal, killing 5000 and taking over fifty guns – and that *did* rattle the Khalsa, for the beaten commander, Runjoor Singh, was a first-class man, and Smith had licked him with a smaller force, and no excuse of treachery this time.

I was in Gough's camp at Sobraon when the news came through, for Hardinge was in the habit of riding the twenty miles from Ferozepore every other day with his new staff of toadies, to have a sniff and a carp at Gough's dispositions,[42] and Lawrence always went along, with your correspondent bringing up the rear. A great roar of cheering ran through the lines, and Paddy fairly danced with joy, and then scudded off to his tent for a pray. Lawrence and other Holy Joes took their cue, and I was about to sidle off to the staff mess when I heard a great groan close by, and there was old Gravedigger Havelock, clasping his bony paws in supplication and looking like Thomas Carlyle with rheumatics – I never seemed to see that man but he was calling on God for something or other: possibly it was the sight of me that did it. He'd prayed over me like a mad monk at Jallalabad, but the last I'd seen of him had been his boots, viewed from under the pool table while I rogered Mrs Madison.

"Amen!" booms he, and left off addressing heaven to wring my hand, glaring joyfully. "It is Flashman! My boy, how long since last I saw you?"

"Sale's billiard-room at Simla," says I, not thinking, and he frowned and said I hadn't been there that evening, surely?

"Neither I was!" says I hastily. "Must have been some other chap. Let's see, when did we last meet? Church somewhere, was it?"

"I have thought of you often since Afghanistan!" cries he, still mangling my fin. "Ah, we smelled the battle afar off, the thunder of the captains, and the shouting!"

"Didn't we just, though? Ah, yes. Well, now . . ."

"But come – will you not join your voice with that of our Chief, in gratitude to Him who hath vouchsafed us this victory?"

255

"Oh, rather! But, I say, you'll have to give me a lead, Graved – skipper, I mean. You always put it so dashed well . . . praying, don't you know?" Which tickled him no end, and in two shakes we were on our hams outside Gough's tent, and it struck me as I looked at them – old Paddy, Havelock, Lawrence, Edwardes, Bagot, and I fancy Hope Grant was there, too – that I'd never seen such a pack of born blood-spillers at their devotions in my life. It's an odd thing about deadly men – they're all addicted either to God or the Devil, and I ain't sure but what the holy ones aren't the more fatal breed of the two.

But mainly I recall that impromptu prayer meeting because it set me thinking of Elspeth again, when Havelock invoked a blessing not only on our fallen comrades, "but on those yet to fall in the coming strife, and on those dear, distant homes which will be darkened with mourning under the wings of Death's angel." Amen, thinks I, but steer him clear of 13a Brook Street, oh Lord, if you don't mind. Listening to Gravedigger, I could absolutely picture the melancholy scene, with the wreath on our knocker, and the blinds drawn, and my father-in-law whining about the cost of crepe . . . and my lovely, golden-haired Elspeth, her blue eyes dim with tears, in her black veil and black gloves and dainty black satin slippers, and long clocked stockings with purple rosettes on her garters and that shiny French corset with the patent laces that you just had to twitch and she came bursting out . . .

"Flashman was much moved, I thought," Havelock said afterwards, and so I was, at the thought of all that voluptuous goodness so far away, and going to waste – at least, I hoped it was, but I had my doubts; heaven knew how many my melting little innocent had thrashed the mattress with in my absence. Brooding on that over supper, and finding no consolation in port and fond musings on my own indiscretions with Jeendan and Mangla and Mrs Madison, I found myself getting quite jealous – and hungry for that blonde beauty on t'other side of the world . . .

Time for a brisk stroll in the cold night air, I decided. We were stopping in Gough's camp by Sobraon, so that he and

256

Hardinge could bicker over the next move, and I sauntered along the lines in the frosty dark, listening to our artillery firing a royal salute in celebration of Smith's victory at Aliwal; barely a mile away I could see the watch-fires of the Khalsa entrenchments in the Sutlej bend, and as the crash of our guns died away, hanged if the enemy didn't reply with a royal salute of their own, and their bands playing . . . you'll never guess what. In some ways it was the eeriest thing in that queer campaign – the silence in our own lines as the gunsmoke drifted overhead, the golden moon low in the purple sky, shining on the rows of tents and the distant twinkling fires, and over the dark ground between, the solemn strains of "God Save the Queen"! I never heard it played so well as by the Khalsa, and for the life of me I don't know to this day whether it was in derision or salute; with Sikhs, you can never tell.

I was thinking about that, and the impossibility of ever knowing what goes on behind Indian eyes, and how I'd misread them all (especially Jeendan's), and reflecting that with any luck I'd soon have seen the last of them, thank heaven – and in that very moment an orderly came running to say, please, sir, Major Lawrence's compliments, and would I wait on the Governor-General at once?

It never occurred to me that my thoughts had been tempting fate, and as I waited in the empty annexe which served as an ante-room to Hardinge's pavilion I felt only mild curiosity as to why he wanted me. Voices sounded in the inner sanctum, but I gave no heed to them at first: Hardinge saying that something was a serious matter, and Lawrence replying that no time must be lost. Then Gough's voice:

"Well, then, a flyin' column! Under cover o' dark, an' goin' like billy-be-damned! Send Hope Grant wi' two squadrons of the 9th, an' he can be in and out before anyone's the wiser."

"No, no, Sir Hugh!" cries Hardinge. "If it is to be done at all, it must be secret. That is insisted upon – if, indeed, we are to believe that fellow. Suppose it is some infernal plot . . . oh, bring him in again, Charles! And find whatever has

257

happened to Flashman! I tell you, it troubles me that he is named in this . . ."

I was listening now, all ears, as young Charlie Hardinge emerged, crying there I was, and bustling me in. Hardinge was saying that it was all most precarious, and no work for a junior man who had proved himself so headstrong . . . He had the grace to break off at sight of me, and sat looking peevish, with Lawrence and Van Cortlandt, whom I hadn't seen since Moodkee, standing behind. Old Paddy, shivering in his cloak in a camp chair, gave me good evening, but no one else spoke, and you could feel the anxiety in the air. Then Charlie was back again, ushering in a figure whose unexpected appearance set my innards cartwheeling in nameless alarm. He sauntered in, no whit abashed by the exalted company, wearing his Afghan rags as though they were ermine, and his ugly face split into a grin as his eye lit on me.

"Why, hollo there, lieutenant!" says Jassa. "How's tricks?"

"Stand there, under the lamp, if you please!" snaps Hardinge. "Flashman, do you know this man?"

Jassa grinned even wider, and just from the glance between Lawrence and Van Cortlandt I guessed they'd already identified him ten times over, but Hardinge, as usual, was proceeding by laborious rote. I said yes, he was Dr Harlan, an agent of Broadfoot's, lately posing as my orderly, and formerly of H.M.'s service in Burma. Jassa looked pleased.

"Say, you remembered that! Thank'ee, sir, that's proud!"

"That will do," says Hardinge. "You may go."

"How's that, sir?" says Jassa. "But hadn't I ought to stay? I mean, if the lieutenant is going to –"

"That will be all!" says Hardinge, down his nose, so Jassa shrugged, muttered as he passed me that it wasn't *his* goddam' pow-wow, and loafed out. Hardinge exclaimed in irritation.

"How came Broadfoot to employ such a person? He's an American!" He said it as though Jassa were a fallen woman.

"Yes, and a slippery one," says Van Cortlandt. "He bore

a bad name in the Punjab in my time. But if he comes from Gardner –"

"That's the point – does he?" Lawrence was brusque. He handed me a plain sealed note. "Harlan brought this, for you, from Colonel Gardner in Lahore. Says it will establish his bona fides. The seal hasn't been touched."

Wondering what the deuce this was about, I broke the seal – and had a sudden premonition of what I would read. Sure enough, there it was, one word: Wisconsin.

"He's from Gardner," says I, and they looked at it in turn. I explained it was a password known only to Gardner and me, and Hardinge sniffed.

"Another American! Are we to rely on a foreign mercenary in the employ of the enemy?"

"On this mercenary – yes," says Van Cortlandt curtly. "He's a sure friend. Without him, Flashman would not have left Lahore alive." That's no way to boost Gardner's stock, thinks I. Hardinge raised his brows and sat back, and Lawrence turned to me.

"Harlan arrived an hour ago. It's bad news out of Lahore. Gardner says the Maharani and her son are in grave peril, from their own army. There's talk of plots – to murder her, to abduct the little Maharaja and place him in the heart of the Khalsa, so that the *panches* can do as they please, in his name. That would mean the end of Tej Singh, and the appointment of some trusted general, who might well give us a long war." He didn't need to add that it might be a disastrous war, for us; the Khalsa were still in overwhelming strength if they had a leader who knew how to use it.

"The boy's the key," says Lawrence. "Who holds him, holds power. The Khalsa knows it, and so does his mother. She wants him out of Lahore, and under our protection. At once. It will be a week at least before we can finish the Khalsa in battle –"

"Ten days, more like," says Gough.

"That is the time the plotters have in which to strike." Lawrence paused, and my mouth went dry as I realised they were all watching me, Gough and Van Cortlandt keenly, Hardinge with gloomy disapproval.

259

"The Maharani wants you to fetch him out, secretly," says Lawrence. "That's her message, given by Gardner to Harlan."

Steady now, thinks I, mustn't puke or burst into tears. Keep a straight face, and remember that the last thing Hardinge wants is to have Flashy stirring the Punjab pot again – that's your hole card, my boy, if this beastly proposal is to be scotched. So I made a lip, thoughtful-like, choked down my supper, and said straight out:

"Very good, sir. I have a free hand, I suppose?"

That did the trick; Hardinge leaped as though he'd been gaffed. "No, sir, you do not! No such thing! You will keep your place, until . . ." He glared, flustered, from Lawrence to Gough. "Sir Hugh, I know not what to think! This scheme fills me with misgivings. What do we know of these . . . these Americans . . . and this Maharani? If this were a plot to discredit us –"

"Not by Gardner!" snaps Van Cortlandt.

"The Maharani has good cause to fear for her child's safety," says Lawrence. "And her own. If anything befell them . . . well, when this war is past, we should find ourselves dealing with a state in anarchy. She and the boy are our only hope of a good political solution."

Gough spoke up. "An' if we don't get one, we must conquer the Punjab. I tell ye, Sir Henry, we have not the means for that."

Hardinge's face was a study. He drummed his fingers and fretted. "I cannot like it. Suppose it were made to appear that we were kidnapping the boy – why, it might be charged that we made war on children –"

"Oh, never that!" cries Lawrence. "We'd be protecting him. But if we do nothing, and he is seized by the Khalsa – murdered, perhaps, and his mother with him . . . well, that would not be seen to our credit, I believe."

I could have kicked him. He'd hit on the best argument to commit Hardinge to this dreadful folly. Credit, that was the thing! What would London think? What would *The Times* say? You could see our Governor-General imagining the outcry if blasted little Dalip got his weasand slit through our

260

neglect. He went pale, and then his face cleared, while he pretended to ponder the thing.

"Certainly the child's safety must weigh heavily with us," says he solemnly. "Humanity and policy both demand it . . . Sir Hugh, what is your thought?"

"Get him out," says Paddy. "Ye cannot do other."

Even then Hardinge must make a show of careful judgment, frowning in silence while my heart sank to my boots. Then he sighed. "So be it, then. We must pray that we are not the dupes of some singular intrigue. But I insist, Lawrence, that either you or Van Cortlandt undertakes it." He shot me a baleful glance. "An older head –"

"By your leave, sir," says Lawrence. "Flashman, be good enough to wait in my tent. I'll join you presently."

So I left obediently – and was round the outside of Hardinge's tent like a frightened stoat, tripping over guy-ropes and slithering in the frosty dark before bearing up in the shadows with an ear cocked under the muslin screen of his window. The man himself was in full cry, and I caught the end of it.

". . . less suitable for such delicate work, I cannot conceive! His conduct with the Sikh leaders was irresponsible to a degree – taking it upon himself to determine policy, a mere junior political officer, flown with self-esteem –"

"Thank God he did," says good old Paddy.

"Very well, Sir Hugh! Fortune favoured us, but his conduct might have brought us to catastrophe! I tell you what, the man's a swaggerer! No," says this splendid and far-sighted statesman, "Flashman shall not go to Lahore!"

"He must!" retorted Lawrence, for whom I was conceiving a poisonous dislike. "Who else can pass as a native, speaking Punjabi, and knows the ins and outs of Lahore Fort? And the little Maharaja worships him, Harlan tells me." He paused. "Besides, the Maharani Jeendan has asked for him by name."

"What's that to the point?" cries Hardinge. "If she wishes her child safe, it is all one whom we send!"

"Perhaps not, sir. She knows Flashman, and . . ." Lawrence hesitated. "The fact is, there is a bazaar rumour

261

that she . . . ah, formed an attachment for him, while he was in Lahore." He coughed and hummed. "As you know, sir, she is a very lovely young woman . . . of an ardent nature, by all accounts . . ."

"Good God!" cries Hardinge. "You don't mean –"

"The young devil!" chuckles Paddy. "Oh, well, decidedly he must go!"

"We'd best not neglect anything that will dispose her well to us," says Van Cortlandt, damn him. "And as Lawrence says, there is no one else."

Eavesdropping fearfully, my mind filled with the horrid prospect of Lahore and its gridirons and ghastly bathrooms and Akali fanatics and murderous swordsmen, I couldn't help recalling that Broadfoot had counted on my manly charms just as these calculating wretches were doing. It's too bad . . . but if you're hell's delight with the fair sex, what would you?

I've no doubt it's what persuaded that pious hypocrite Hardinge, with his mind fixed on political accommodations after the war. By all means let Flashy humour the bitch while he plucked her bloody infant to safety, and wouldn't she be obliged to us, just? He didn't say as much, but you could hear him thinking it as he gave his reluctant consent.

"But hear me, Lawrence – Flashman must understand that he is to proceed in strict accordance to your instructions. He must have no room for independent action of any kind whatsoever – is that clear? This fellow Harlan has brought directions from . . . what is his name, Gardner? – a fine business, when we must rely on such people, let alone this hare-brained political! You must question Harlan closely on how it is to be effected. Above all, no harm must befall the young prince, Flashman must understand that – and the consequences should he fail."

"I doubt if he needs instruction on that head, sir," says Lawrence, pretty cool. "For the rest, I shall give him careful directions."

"Very well. I shall hold you responsible. You have an observation, Sir Hugh?"

262

"Eh? No, no, Sorr Hinry, nothin' of consequence. I was just after thinkin'," chuckles old Paddy, "that I wish I was young again, an' spoke Punjabi."

You never can say you've seen anything for the last time. I'd have laid a million to one that I'd not return to that little stand of white poplars south of the Moochee Gate where I'd sat by the fire with Gardner – yet here I was, only a few weeks later, with the flames crackling under the billy-can resting on the self-same red stone with the crack in it. To our right the road was busy with the wayfarers of daybreak; under the great Moochee arch the gates were swung back, they were dousing the night torches, and the guard was changing: an uncommon heavy one, it seemed to me, for I counted twenty helmets in and about the archway, and since our arrival in the small hours there had been endless cavalry patrols circling the city walls, red lancers with green *puggarees*, and great activity of match-lockmen on the parapets.

"Muslim brigade," says Jassa. "Yes, sir, she's got this old town laced up tighter'n Jemima's stays. Waste o' time, since any plotters'll be on the *inside* – prob'ly in the Fort itself, among her own people. Say, I bet Alick Gardner's sleepin' light, though!"

It was our third morning on the road, for we had taken a wide cast south, crossing the Sutlej at a ghat near Mundole to avoid any enemy river watchers, and keep clear of the Khalsa's main traffic on the upper road through Pettee to Sobraon. We'd ridden in cautious stages, Jassa and I and a trusted Pathan ruffian of Broadfoot's old bodyguard, Ahmed Shah; Gough had wanted to send an N.C. squadron disguised as *gorracharra*, but Lawrence had turned it down flat, insisting that they'd be bound to give themselves away, and anyway, if all went well three would be enough, while if it went ill a brigade would be too few. No one would give any heed to three obvious Afghan horse-copers with a string of beasts – and thus far, no one had.

I shan't weary you with my emotions as we waited, shivering in the frosty dawn, round our fire. I'll say only that in addition to the blue funk I felt at the mere sight of Lahore's frowning gates and brooding towers, I had the liveliest misgivings about the plan whereby we were to spirit young Dalip out of the cobra's nest. It was Gardner's invention, lined out precisely to Jassa, who had repeated it to Lawrence and Van Cortlandt with Flashy palpitating attentively, and since our tartan Pathan wasn't there to be argued with, it was a case of take it or leave it. I know which I'd ha' done, but Lawrence had said it should serve admirably – he wasn't going to be the one sneaking in and out of Lahore Fort in broad daylight, after all.

That seemed to me an unnecessary lunacy: why the devil couldn't Gardner, with all his powers as governor, have contrived to smuggle the brat out to us? Jassa had explained that the city was tight as a tanner by night, and the *panches'* spies had their eye on little Dalip most of the day; the only hour to lift him was his bedtime, to be out and away before curfew, and have all night to make tracks. And we must go into the Fort to do it, for his mother wouldn't rest unless she saw him placed under my protective wing. (They'd all avoided my eye at this; myself, I hadn't liked the sound of it above half.) As to our coming and going at the Fort, Gardner would provide; all we need do was be in the vicinity of Runjeet's Tomb at noon of this, the third day.

So now you see three Kabuli copers herding their beasts through the dust and bustle of the Rushnai Gate, and setting up shop in a crowded square by the Buggywalla Doudy at midday. Ahmed Shah cried our wares, asking exorbitant prices, since the last thing we wanted was to sell our transport, and I held the brutes' heads and spat and looked ugly, praying that no one would recognise Jassa with a patch over his eye, and his hair and five-day beard dyed orange. He had no such fears, but loafed about freely with the other idlers, gossiping; as he said, there's no concealment like open display.

I didn't see the touch made, but presently he ambled off, and I passed the halters to Ahmed and followed across the great square by the marble Barra Deree to the palace gateway where I'd first seen Gardner months before. There were no Palace Guards on the parapet now, only green-jacketed Muslim musketeers with great curling moustachioes, watchful as vultures, who scowled down at the crowds loitering in the square. There must have been several thousand gathered, and enough Sikhs in assorted Khalsa coats among them to set my innards churning; they did nothing but stare up at the walls, muttering among themselves, but you could feel the sullen hostility hanging over the place like a cloud.

"She ain't venturing abroad this weather, I reckon," murmurs Jassa as I joined him in the lee of the gateway. "Yep, there's a sizeable Republican majority right here. Our guide is right behind us, in the *palki*; when I give the nod, we'll tote it through the gate."

I glanced over my shoulder; there was a *palki*, with its curtains drawn, set down by the wall, but no bearers in sight. So that was how we were to get past the gate guard, who were questioning all incomers; even under my *poshteen* I could feel the sweat icy on my skin, and for the twentieth time I fingered the Cooper hidden in my sash – not that six shots would buy much elbow-room if we came adrift.

All of a sudden the mutter of the crowd grew to a babble and then to a roar; they were giving back to make way for a body of marching men advancing across the square from the Hazooree gate on the town side – Sikhs almost to a man, from half the divisions of the Khalsa, some of them with bandaged wounds and powder burns on their coats, but swinging along like Guardsmen behind their golden standard which, to my amazement, was borne by the white-whiskered old *rissaldar-major* I'd seen at Maian Mir, and again at Jeendan's durbar. And he was weeping, so help me, the tears running down to his beard, his eyes fixed ahead – and there behind him was Imam Shah, he of the ivory knives, bare-headed and with his arm in a sling. I was in behind Jassa double-quick, I can tell you.

The crowd were in a frenzy, waving and wailing and yelling: "Khalsa-ji! Khalsa-ji!", showering them with petals as they marched by, but not a man so much as glanced aside; on they went, in column of fours, under the palace archway, with the mob surging behind up to the gate, taking up another cry: "See Delhi! See Delhi, heroes of the Khalsa! *Wa Guru-ji* – to Delhi, to London!"

"Now, who the hell are they?" whispers Jassa. "I guess maybe we got here just in time – I hope! Come on!"

We laid hold on the *palki* and shouldered our way through the mob to the gateway, where a Muslim *subedar** barred our way and stooped to question our passenger. I heard a woman's voice, quick and indistinct, and then he had waved us on, and we carried the *palki* through the gate – and for all my dread at re-entering that fearsome den, I found myself remembering Stumps Harrowell, who'd been the chairman at Rugby when I was a boy, and how we'd run after him, whipping his enormous fat calves, while he could only rage helplessly between the shafts. You should see your tormentor now, Stumps, thinks I; hoist with his own *palki*, if you like.

Our passenger was calling directions to Jassa, who was between the front shafts, and presently we bore up in a little secluded court, and out she jumped, walking quickly to a low doorway which she unlocked, motioning us to follow. She led us up a long, dim passage, several flights of stairs, and more passages – and then I knew where we were: I had been conducted along this very way to Jeendan's rose boudoir, and I knew that pretty little rump stirring under the tight sari . . .

"Mangla!" says I, but she only beckoned us on, to a little ill-furnished room where I'd never been. Only when she had the door closed did she throw off her veil, and I looked again on that lovely Kashmiri face with its slanting gazelle eyes – but there was no insolence in them now, only fear.

"What's amiss?" snaps Jassa, scenting catastrophe.

"You saw those men of the Khalsa – the five hundred?"

*Senior subaltern.

267

Her voice was steady enough, but quick with alarm. "They are a deputation from Tej Singh's army – men of Moodkee and Ferozeshah. They have come to plead with the Rani for arms and food for the army, and for a leader to take Tej's place, so that we may still sweep the *Jangi lat* back to the gates of Delhi!" The way she spat it out, you would have wondered which side she was on; even traitors still have patriotic pride, you see. "But they were not to have audience of the durbar until tomorrow – they have come before their time!"

"Well, what of it?" says I. "She can fob them off – she's done it before!"

"They were not a beaten army then. They had not been led to defeat by Tej and Lal – or learned to mistrust Mai Jeendan herself. Now, when they come to durbar and find themselves ringed in by Muslim muskets, and call to her for aid which she cannot give them – what then? They are hungry men, and desperate." She shrugged. "You say she has wheedled them before – aye, but she is not given to soft words these days. She fears for Dalip and herself, she hates the Khalsa for Jawaheer's sake, and she feeds her rage on wine. She's like to answer their mutinous clamour by blackening their faces for them – and who knows what they may do if she provokes them?"

Red murder, like as not – and then we'd have some usurper displacing Tej Singh and reviving the Khalsa for another slap at us. And here was I, back on the lion's lip, thanks to Gardner's idiot plots . . . should I throw in now, and bolt for India? Or could we still get Dalip out before all hell broke loose . . .?

"When's the durbar?"

"In two hours, perhaps."

"Can Gardner bring the boy to us beforehand . . . now?"

"Run in daylight?" cries Jassa. "We'd never make it!"

Mangla shook her head. "The Maharaja must be seen at the durbar. Who knows, Mai Jeendan may answer them well enough – and if she fails, they may still be quiet, with a thousand Muslims ready to fall on them at a word from Gurdana Khan. Then, when you have seen Mai Jeendan –"

268

"I don't need to see her – or anyone, except her blasted son! Tell Gardner –"

"Why, here's a change!" says she, with a flash of the old Mangla. "You were eager enough once. Well, she wishes to see you, Flashman *bahadur*, and she will have her way –"

"What the devil for?"

"Affairs of state, belike." She gave her insolent slow smile. "Meanwhile, you must wait; you are safe here. I shall tell Gurdana, and bring word when the durbar begins."

And she slipped out, having added bewilderment to my fears. What could Jeendan want with me? I'd thought it rum at the time, her insistence that I should be Dalip's rescuer – to be sure, the kid liked me, but she'd as good as made me a condition of the plan, to Paddy Gough's ribald amusement. Coarse old brute. But it couldn't be *that*, at such a time . . . mind you, with partial females, you never can tell, especially when they're foxed.

But all this was small beer beside the menace of the Khalsa deputies. Could she hocus them again, by playing her charms and beguiling them with sweet words and fair promises?

Well, she didn't even try, as we saw when Mangla returned, after two hours of fretful waiting, to conduct us to that same spyhole from which I'd watched an earlier durbar. This was a different *indaba** altogether; then, there had been tumult and high spirits, laughter even, but now we heard the angry clamour of the deputation and her shrill replies even before we reached the eyrie, when I saw at a glance that this was an ugly business, with the Mother of All Sikhs on her highest horse and damn the consequences.

The five hundred were in uproar in the main body of the great hall before the durbar screen, but keeping their ranks, and it was easy to see why. They were wearing their *tulwars*, but round the walls of the chamber there must have been a full battalion of Muslim riflemen, with their pieces at the high port, primed and ready. Imam Shah was standing forward, addressing the screen, with the old *rissaldar-major*

*Matter, affair.

269

a pace behind; the golden standard lay before the throne on which little Dalip sat in lonely state, the tiny figure brave in crimson, and with the Koh-i-Noor ablaze in his aigret.

Behind the purdah more Muslims lined the walls, and before them stood Gardner, in his tartan fig, the point of his naked sabre resting between his feet. Close by the screen Jeendan was pacing to and fro, pausing from time to time to listen, then resuming her furious sentry-go – for she was in a great rage, and well advanced in liquor, by the look of her. She had a cup in hand, and a flagon on the table, but for once she was modestly clad – as modest, anyway, as a voluptuous doll can be in a tight sari of purple silk, with her red hair unbound to her shoulders, and that Delilah face unveiled.

Imam Shah was in full grievance, shouting hoarsely at the screen. "For three days your faithful Khalsa have lived on grain and raw carrots – they are starving, *kunwari*, and eaten up with cold and want! Only send them the food and munitions you promised and they will sweep the host of the *Jangi lat* to –"

"Sweep them as you swept them at Ferozeshah and Moodkee?" cries Jeendan. "Aye, there was a fine sweeping – my waiting women could have swept as heartily!" She waited, head thrown back, for the effect of this. Imam stood in silent anger, and she went on: "Goolab has sent you supplies enough – why, every wheat-porter in Kashmir makes an endless train from Jumoo to the river, laden –"

She was drowned in a roar of derision from the five hundred, and Imam advanced a yard to bawl his answer. "Aye, in single file, on pain of mutilation by the Golden Hen, who makes a brave show of assistance, but sends not breakfast for a bird! *Chiria-ki-hazri!* That's what we get from Goolab Singh! If he wishes us well, let him come and lead us, in place of that bladder of lard you made our general! Bid him come, *kunwari* – a word from you, and he'll be in the saddle for Sobraon!"

Uproar followed – "Goolab! Goolab! Give us the Dogra for general!" – but still they kept their ranks.

"Goolab is under the heel of the *Malki lat*, and you know

270

it!" snaps Jeendan. "Even so, there are those among you who would make him Maharaja – my loyal Khalsa!" There was silence on the instant. "You send him ambassadors, they tell me . . . aye, in breach of your sacred oath! You whine for food on the one hand, and make treason on the other – you, the Khalsa, the Pure . . ." And she reviled them in fishwife terms, as she had at Maian Mir, until Gardner stepped swifty forward and caught her by the arm. She shook him off, but took the hint – and none too soon, for beyond the screen the five hundred were fingering their hilts, and Imam was black with fury.

"That is a lie, *kunwari*! No man here would serve Goolab as Maharaja – but he can fight, by God! He does not skulk in his tent, like Tej, or flee like your bed-man Lal! He can lead – so let him lead us! To Delhi! To victory!"

She let the shouting die, and spoke in a cold voice, ringing with scorn: "I have said I will not have Goolab Singh – and he will not have *you*! Who's to blame him? Are you worth having, you heroes who strut out to battle with your banners and brave songs – and crawl back whimpering that you are hungry? Can you do nothing but complain –"

"We can fight!" roars a voice, and in a moment they were echoing it, stirring forward in their ranks, shaking their fists, some even weeping openly. They'd come for supplies, and what they were getting was shame and insult. Keep a civil tongue in your head, can't you, I was whispering, for it was plain they'd had their fill of her abuse. "Give us guns! Give us powder and shot!"

"Powder and shot!" cries Jeendan, and for a moment I thought she was going to be out and at them. "Did I not give you both, and to spare? Arms and food and great guns – never was such an army seen in Hindoostan! And what did you make of it? The food you've guzzled, the British have your great guns, and the arms you flung away, doubtless, as you ran cheeping like mice – from what? From a tired old man in a white coat with a handful of red-faced infidels and Bengali sweepers!"

Her voice rose to a shriek as she faced the curtain, fists clenched, face contorted, and foot stamping – and beside me

271

Jassa gasped and Mangla gave a little sob as we saw the ranks of the five hundred start forward, and there was steel glittering amongst them. She'd gone too far, the drunken slut, for Imam Shah was on the dais, the Khalsa coats were surging behind him, shouting with rage, Gardner was turning to snap an order, the Muslim muskets were dropping to the present – and Jeendan was fumbling beneath her skirt, swearing like a harpy, there was a rending of cloth, and in an instant she had whirled her petticoat into a ball and hurled it over the screen. It fell at Imam's feet, draping over his boot – there was no doubting what it was, and in the shocked silence her voice rang out:

"Wear that, you cowards! Wear it, I say! Or I'll go in trousers and fight myself!"

It was as though they'd been stricken by a spell. While you could count ten there wasn't a sound. I see them yet – an Akali, his sword half-out, poised like a gladiator's statue; Imam Shah staring down at the scarlet shift; the old *rissaldar-major*, mouth open, hands raised in dismay; little Dalip like a graven image on his throne; the mass of men still as death, staring at the screen – and then Imam Shah picked up the golden standard, raised it, and shouted in a voice of thunder:

"Dalip Singh Maharaja! We go to die for your kingdom! We go to die for the *Khalsa-ji!*" Then he added, almost in a whisper, though it carried round the hall: "We will go to the sacrifice."

He thrust the standard into the *rissaldar-major*'s hand – and in that moment, unprompted, little Dalip stood up. A second's pause, and the whole five hundred roared: "Maharaja! Maharaja! *Khalsa-ji!*" Then they turned as one man and marched out of the open double doors behind them. Gardner was at the corner of the screen in four quick strides, staring after them, then coming out to take Dalip's hand. Behind the purdah, Jeendan yawned, shook her red hair and stirred her shoulders as though to ease them, took a deep drink, and began to straighten her sari.

Now that is exactly what I saw, and so did Alick Gardner, as his memoirs testify – and neither of us can explain it.

272

Those Khalsa fanatics, stung to madness by her insults, would have rushed the purdah and cut her down, I'm certain, and been slaughtered by the Muslims; God knows what would have followed. But she threw her petticoat at them, and they went out like lambs, prepared to do or die. "Intuition" on her part, Gardner calls it; very well, it did the business. Mind you, young Dalip stood up at exactly the right time.[43]

Jassa was breathing relief, and Mangla was smiling. Below us came a series of thunderous crashes as the Muslims ordered arms and began to file out of the chamber. Little Dalip was behind the purdah, being enfolded in Mama's tipsy embrace, but Gardner had disappeared. Mangla touched my arm, and signing to Jassa to wait, led me up to the rose boudoir – I felt exhausted even looking at it – and through to the passage beyond and a little room which I guessed must be the schoolroom of Dalip and his play-fellows, for there were half a dozen little desks, and a blackboard, and even a globe, and fairy-tale pictures on the walls. There she left me, and a moment later Gardner strode in, breathing fire and wonder.

"You saw that just now? Goddam, but that woman's a bearcat for nerve – a bearcat, sir! Petticoats, by thunder! I wouldn't ha' credited it! Sometimes I think . . ." He paused, eyeing me with a curious frown. ". . . I think she's a mite de-ranged, what with drink and . . . well, no matter. And George Broadfoot's dead? Well, that's hard hearing. You didn't see it? Well, you have one as good in Henry Lawrence, let me tell you that. Maybe even better, as an Agent. Not a better *man*, mind you. No, sir, they don't come better than the Black-coated Infidel."

He was standing, arms akimbo, staring at the floor, and I sensed disturbance – not because he hadn't greeted me, or made reference to my recent adventures, for that was never his style. But there was something on his mind, for all that he tried to cover it with a show of briskness.

"It's past four, and you and Josiah must be clear of the gates before six. You'll go as you came, bearing the *palki*, but this time Dalip will be your freight, dressed as a girl. My

273

subedar will have the palace gate, so you'll be clear there. Once beyond the Rushnai, keep to the *doab*, due south-east, and dawn should see you at Jupindar – it's about forty miles, and not on the map, but you'll see it clear enough. It's a big cluster of black rocks, among low hillocks, the only ones for miles around. There you'll be met –"

"By whom? Our people? Gough wanted to –"

"By sure people." He gave me a hard stare. "All you need do is get that far – and I don't have to tell you that you're carrying the Punjab on your back. Whoever gets that boy, it must not be the Khalsa, *mallum*? He's a good little horseman, by the way, so you can keep up the pace. Dawn, at Jupindar, mind that. Due south-east and you'll fall over it."

For the first time, I felt excitement rather than fear. He had it pat, and it would do. We were going to bring it off.

"What else?" says he. "Ah, yes, one thing . . . Dr Josiah Harlan. I gave him a bad name to you, and he deserved every word. But I allow he's played a straight hand this time, and I incline to revise my opinion. That being the case, you'd better keep a closer eye on him than ever. Well, that's all, I guess . . ." He paused, avoiding my eye. "Once you've paid your respects to the Maharani . . . you can be off."

Now there *was* something up. Gardner uneasy was a sight I'd never thought to see, but he was scratching his grizzled beard and keeping his face averted, and I felt a strange foreboding. He cleared his throat.

"Ah . . . did Mangla say nothing to you? No, well . . . oh, dooce take it!" He looked me full in the face. "Mai Jeendan wants to marry you! There, now!"

Heaven knows why, my first reaction was to look in the mirror on the classroom wall. A fierce-eyed Khyberie ruffian stared back at me, which was no help. Nor was my recollection of what I looked like when civilised. And possibly the Punjab had exhausted my capacity for astonishment, for once the first shock of that amazing proposal had been absorbed, I felt nothing but immense gratification – after all, it's one thing to win a maiden heart, and very fine, but when a man-eater who's sampled the best from Peshawar to

Poona cries "Eureka!" over you, well, it's no wonder if you glance at the mirror. At the same time, it's quite a facer, and my first words, possibly instinctive, were:

"Christ, she ain't pregnant, is she?"

"How the devil should I know?" cries Gardner, astonished. "On my word! Now, sir, I've told you! So there you are!"

"Well, she can't! I'm married, dammit!"

"I know that – but she does not, and it's best she should not . . . for the moment." He glared at me, and took a turn round the room, while I sank on to one of the infants' stools, which gave way beneath me. Gardner swore, yanked me to my feet, and thrust me into the teacher's chair.

"See here, Mr Flashman," says he, "this is how it is. Mai Jeendan is a woman of strange character and damned irregular habits, as you're well aware – but she's no fool. For years now she's had it in mind to marry a British officer, as security for herself and her son's throne. Well, that's sound policy, especially now when Britain's hand is on the Punjab. For months past – this is sober truth – her agents in India have been sending her portraits of eligible men. She's even had young Hardinge's likeness in her boudoir, God help me! As you know, she has your own – well, 'twas the only one she took to Amritsar, and the rest (a score of 'em) have been with the lumber ever since."

Nothing to say to that, of course. I kept a straight face, and he took station in front of me, mighty stern.

"Very well, it's impossible. You have a wife, and even if you hadn't, I dare say you'd not care to pass your days as consort to an Eastern queen. Myself, while I admire her many good qualities," says he with feeling, "I'd not hitch with Jeendan for all the cotton in Dixie, so help me Hannah! But she has a deep fondness for you – and this is no time to blight that affection! Northern India's in the balance, and she's the pivot – steady enough, but not to be disturbed . . . in any way." He stooped suddenly and seized my wrist, staring into my eyes, grim as a frost giant. "So when you see her presently . . . you will not disappoint her hopes. Oh, she'll make no direct proposal – that's not Punjabi royal

275

style. But she'll sound you out – probably offer you employment in Sikh service, for after the war – with a clear hint of
her intentions . . . to all of which you'd best give eager
assent – for all our sakes, especially your own. Hell hath no
fury, you remember." He let go, straightening up. "I guess
you know how to . . ."

"Jolly her along? Oh, aye . . . by God, it's a rum go,
though! What'll happen later, when she finds I ain't a
starter?"

"The war'll be over then, and it won't signify," says he
bleakly. "I dare say she'll get over it. Dirty game, politics
. . . she's a great woman, you know, drunk and all as she is.
You ought to be flattered. By the by, have you any
aristocratic kinfolk?"

"My mother was a Paget."

"Is that high style? Better make her a duchess, then. Mai
Jeendan likes to think that you're a lord – after all, she was
once married to a Maharaja."[44]

As it happened, my lineage, aristocratic and otherwise,
was not discussed in the rose boudoir, mainly because there
wasn't time. When Gardner had spoken of not disappointing
her, I'd supposed (and have no doubt that he meant) that I
must not dash her hopes of becoming Mrs Flashman; accord-
ingly, I bowled in prepared for an exchange of nods and
becks and coy blushes on her part, and ardent protestations
on mine. Only when I stood blinking in the dark, and two
plump arms encircled me from behind, that familiar drunken
chuckle sounded in my ear, and she turned up the lamp to
reveal herself clad only in oil and bangles, did I suspect that
further proof of my devotion was required. "I liked you
better shaven," whispers she (which settled that), and Dalip
or no Dalip, there was nothing for it but to give eager consent, as Gardner had put it. Luckily she was no protractor of
the capital act, as I knew, and I didn't even need to take my
boots off; a quick plunge round the room, horse artillery
style, and she was squealing her soul out, and then it was
back to the wine-cup and exhausted ecstatic sighs, mingled
with tipsy murmurs about the loneliness of widowhood and
what bliss it would be to have a man about the house again

276

. . . fairly incoherent, you understand, but not to be misunderstood, so I responded with rapturous endearments.

"You will abide with me always?" whispers she, nuzzling in, and I said I'd like to see anyone stop me, just. Did I love her truly? Well, to be sure I did. She muttered something about writing to Hardinge, and I thought, by George, that'll spoil his toast and coffee for him, no error, but mostly it was fond drunken babble and clinging kisses, before she turned over and began to snore.

Well, that's that, and you've done your duty, thinks I, as I repaired the sweet disorder in my dress and slid out – with a last backward glance at that jolly rump glistening in the lamplight. I imagined, you see, that I was looking my last on her, and I do like to carry away happy memories – but twenty minutes later, when Jassa and I were fretting impatiently in the schoolroom, and Gardner was damning Mangla's tardiness in bringing young Dalip, in comes a waiting woman to say that the *kunwari* and the Maharaja were awaiting us in her drawing-room. This was a fine apartment close by the boudoir, and there was the Mother of All Sikhs, enthroned in her armchair, as respectable a young matron as ever you saw, and not more than half-soused; how the deuce she'd got into parade order in the time was beyond me.

She was soothing young Dalip, who was standing by in a black fury and a child's sari, with veil and bangles and a silk shawl round his small shoulders.

"Don't look at me!" cries he, turning his face away, and she petted him and kissed away his tears, whispering that he must be a Maharaja, for he was going among the White Queen's soldiers, and must do credit to his house and people.

"And this goes with you, the symbol of your kingship," says she, and held out a silver locket, with the great Koh-i-Noor glittering in a bed of velvet. She closed the case and hung its chain about his neck. "Guard it well, dearest, for it was your father's treasure, and remains your people's honour."

"With my life, mama," sobs he, and hung upon her neck.

277

She wept a little, holding him close, and then stood up and led him to me.

"Flashman sahib will take care of you," says she, "so mind you obey him in all things. Farewell, my little prince, my own darling." She kissed him and put his hand in mine. "God speed you, sahib – until we meet again." She extended a hand, and I kissed it; one warm, glassy look she gave me, with that little curl of her thick lips; she was swaying slightly, and her waiting woman had to step lively to steady her.

Then Gardner was bustling us away, with Jassa carrying Dalip for greater speed, and it was bundle-and-go down to the *palki* in the little court, with Mangla at my elbow insisting that his majesty must eat no oranges, for they gave him the trots, and here was a lotion for the rash on his arm, and a letter for the governess who must be engaged for him in India – "a Kashmiri lady, gentle and well-read, if one can be found, but not some stern English mem-sahib, for he is but a little fellow; I have written of his diet and his lessons." Kidnapping ain't just a matter of lifting the infant, you see, and on my other side Gardner was snarling that the gates would be closing in half an hour. We bundled Dalip into the *palki*, and now he was blubbering that he didn't want to go, and clinging to Mangla, and Gardner was fuming while two of his black robes scouted ahead to see that all was clear, and Jassa and I got between the shafts, and Mangla kissed me quickly on the cheek, leaving a drift of perfume as she hurried away, and Gardner turned to me in the fading light of the little court.

"Due south-east, forty miles, Jupindar rocks," snaps he. "I guess we won't see you in Lahore again, Mr Flashman. If I was you, I'd stay well south of the Sutlej for the next fifty years or so. And that goes double for you, Josiah – you stretched your luck, doctor; come nigh me again and I'm liable to snap it for you! *Jao!*"

"Yes, you an' the Continental Congress!" retorts Jassa. "Go change your sentries, Gardner – that's your sort!"

"*Jao*, I say!" growls Gardner, and the last I remember of him is the brown hawk face with its fierce moustache, twisted in a sour grin under the tartan *puggaree*.

We came down to the Buggywalla Doudy just as the sun was dipping behind the Badshai Musjit mosque, through the bustling noisy crowds all unaware that the two stalwart *palki*-bearers were spiriting their ruler away to the enemy, and him moping fretfully behind the curtains in his little sari and bangles. Ahmed Shah was in a foul humour because he'd had to sell two of our beasts, leaving only five besides our own screws, which meant only one remount for the four of us. We slung the *palki* between two of the led horses, and when I put my head in to see how Dalip did, he whimpered something piteous.

"Oh, Flashman sahib – when can I put off these garments of shame? See, Mangla has put my man's clothes in this bag . . . aye, and cakes and little sweets! She always remembers," says he, and his lip came out. "Why could she not come with us? Now I shall have no song before I sleep!" And he began to weep. "I wish Mangla were here!"

Mangla, you'll note, not Mama. Well, I'd not have turned her away myself. "See here, maharaj'," whispers I, "you'll put on your own clothes directly, and ride with us like a soldier, but now you must stay close and quiet. And when we come to journey's end – see what I have for you!" I was far enough within the *palki* to slip the Cooper from my sash for an instant, and he squeaked and fell back on the cushions, covering his eyes in joy.

We passed under the Rushnai arch even as the *chowkidars* were crying the curfew, and skirted the city walls to the little stand of white poplars, crimson in the last of the sunset. In the gloaming they were beyond eyeshot of the gate, and we lost no time in rousting out little Dalip, for I wanted him in the saddle without delay, so that we could abandon the cumbersome *palki* and put distance between us and Lahore.

He tumbled out eagerly, tearing off his sari and veil and scattering his bangles with childish curses, and was shivering in his vest while Jassa helped him into his little jodhpurs, when there was a clatter of hooves, and out of the deepening dusk came a troop of *gorracharra*, making for the city in

279

haste before the gates closed. There was no time to hide the imp; we must stand pat while they cantered by – and then their officer reined up, staring at the sight of a half-clad infant surrounded by three burly copers and their beasts.

"Where away at this hour, horse-sellers?" cries he.

I answered offhand, hoping to keep him at a distance, for even in the fading light it was ten to one he'd recognise his own monarch if he came any closer.

"Amritsar, captain sahib!" says I. "We take my master's son to his grandmother, who is ill, and calls for him. Hurry, Yakub, or the child will catch cold!" This to Jassa, who was helping Dalip into his coat, and thrusting him up into the saddle. I swung aboard my own screw, with my heart pounding, ignoring the officer, hoping to heaven the inquisitive brute would ride on after his troop, who had vanished into the twilight.

"Wait!" He was sitting forward, staring harder than ever – and with a thrill of horror I realised that Dalip's coat was his ceremonial cloth of gold, packed by that imbecile Mangla, and even in that uncertain light proclaiming its wearer a most unlikely companion for three frontier ruffians. "Your master's son, you say? Let's have a look at him!" He wheeled his horse towards us, his hand dropping to his pistol butt – and the three of us acted as one man.

Jassa vaulted into his saddle and snatched Dalip's bridle even as I slashed my reins across the beast's rump, and Ahmed Shah dug in his heels and charged slap into the advancing Sikh, rolling him from the saddle. Then we were away across the *maidan*, Dalip and Jassa leading, Ahmed and I behind, with the led horses thundering alongside. There was a shout from the dusk, and the crack of a shot, and little Dalip yelled with delight, dragging his bridle from Jassa's grip. "I can ride, fellow! Let me alone! Ai-ee, *shabash, shabash!*"

There had been nothing else for it, with detection certain, and as I pulled out my compass and roared to Jassa to change course to port, I was reckoning that no great harm had been done. We were on fresh horses, while the *gorracharra* had been in the saddle all day; it would take time to mount any kind of pursuit from the city – supposing they thought it worth while, with night coming down; the odds were they'd make inquiry first to see if any child of a wealthy family was missing, for I was sure the officer had taken us for common kidnappers – he'd never have risked a shot at us if he'd known who Dalip was. And if, by some astonishing chance, it was discovered that the Mahajara had taken wing – well, we'd be over the river and far away by then.

I called a halt after the first couple of miles, to tighten girths, take stock, and make certain of my bearing, and then we rode on more slowly. It was pitch dark by now, and while we might have trotted on a road we daren't go above a brisk walk over open country. The moon wouldn't be up for six or seven hours yet, so we must contain ourselves in the sure knowledge that the dark was our friend, and no pursuers could hope to find us while it lasted. Meanwhile we bore on south-east, with Dalip asleep in the crook of my arm – what with distress and elation, he was quite used up, and being lulled by "Tom Bowling" instead of Mangla's song didn't trouble him a bit.

"Is this how soldiers sleep?" yawns he. "Then you must wake me when it is my time to ride guard, and you shall rest . . ."

It was a wearisome trek, and a cold one, hour after hour in the freezing dark, but at least it was without alarm, and by the time we had put twenty miles behind us I was convinced that there would be no pursuit. At about midnight we pulled up to water the horses at a little stream, and stamp some warmth back into our limbs; there was a faint starshine over the *doab* now, and I was remarking to Jassa that we'd be able to raise the pace, when Ahmed Shah called to us.

He was squatting down by a big peepal tree, with his sabre driven into the trunk just above the ground, and his finger on the foible of the blade. I exclaimed, for I knew that trick of old, from Gentleman Jim Skinner on the road above Gandamack. Sure enough, after a moment Ahmed shook his head, looking grim.

"Horsemen, *husoor*. Twenty, perhaps thirty, coming south. They are a scant five *cos* behind us."

281

If I'm a firm believer in headlong flight as a rule, it's probably because I've known such a horrid variety of pursuers in my time – Apaches in the Jornada, Udloko Zulus on the veldt, Cossacks along the Arrow of Arabat, Amazons in the Dahomey forest, Chink hatchetmen through the streets of Singapore . . . no wonder my hair's white. But there are times when you should pause and consider, and this was one. No one was riding the Bari Doab that night for recreation, so it was a fair bet that the inquisitive officer had deduced who our costly-clad infant was, and that every rider from the Lahore garrison was sweeping the land from Kussoor to Amritsar. Still, we had spare mounts, so a sprain or a cast shoe was no matter; our pursuers must be riding blind, since even an Australian bushman couldn't have tracked us, on that ground; seven miles is a long lead with only fifteen to go; and there were friends waiting at the finish. Even so, having your tail ridden is nervous work, and we didn't linger over the next few miles, not pausing to listen, and keeping steadily south-east.

When the moon came up we changed to our remounts; Ahmed's ear to the ground detected nothing, and there was no movement on the plain behind us. It was fairly open country now, with a few scrubby thickets, occasional belts of jungle, and now and then a village. When I reckoned we had only about five miles to go, and still three hours to dawn, we eased to a walk, for Dalip had awoken, demanding food, and after we'd halted for a bite and there was still no sign of pursuers, it seemed sensible to go at a pace that would let him sleep. Of course, he wouldn't, and kept up such a stream of questions and drivel that I came close to fetching him a clip over the head. I didn't, mind you, for it don't pay to offend royalty, however junior: they grow up.

There was still no sign of the Jupindar rocks, and I guessed we'd come a degree or two off course, so I climbed the first tall tree we came to, for a *dekko* about. The moonlight gave a clear sight for miles around, and sure enough, about three miles to our left, the ground rose in a long slope to a summit of tangled rocks – Jupindar, for certain. And I was just preparing to swing down when I took a last look astern, and almost fell out of the tree.

We'd just come through a jungly strip, and behind it the *doab* lay flat as a flagstone to the horizon. Halfway across it, a bare mile away, a line of horsemen were coming at the canter – a full troop, well spread in line. Only regular cavalry ride like that, and only when they're searching.

I was out of that tree like a startled monkey, yelling to Jassa, who was standing guard while young Dalip squatted in the bushes – the little bastard must have had an orange cached somewhere, for he'd done his bit three times since midnight. A precious minute was lost while he got himself to rights, bleating that he wasn't done yet, and Jassa fairly threw him into the saddle; then we were away, drumming across the *doab* for those distant rocks where, unless Gardner had lied, friends were waiting.

There was a mile of scrub and trees before the rocks came into view, at the top of a long incline dotted with sandy hillocks – and there, far off on our flank, the first of the pursuing horsemen were clearing the jungle. A faint halloo sounded on the frosty air, and now it was a straight race for Jupindar before they could head us off.

It was going to be close-run, for with our south-east course having carried us wide, we were having to cut back at an angle, while the pursuing troop had only to make straight forrard. There was nothing in it for distance; the best horsemen would be first to the post – and these were lancers; I could make out the long poles.

Thank God little Dalip could ride. Seven years old, spoiled, garrulous, and loose-bowelled he might be, but he could wear my colours in the National any day. He lay flat to his beast's neck, talking to it when he wasn't squealing with excitement, his long hair flying as he took the jumps over the little dry nullahs that crossed our course. He led me by a length, with Jassa and Ahmed pounding on my quarters; as we breasted the slope for the last mile we were gaining, but there wasn't a sign of life from the rocks loom-

283

ing ahead – God, had Gardner's people failed at the rendezvous? I loosed a warning shot from my Cooper, and in the same moment I saw Dalip's horse stumble. For a moment I thought he was gone, but there must have been a dash of Comanche in him, for he let the bridle go, clutching the mane, the horse made a long stagger and recovered – but it was dead lame and hobbling, and as I swept by I swung him clear by his waistband, heaving him across before me. Out of the tail of my eye I saw the lancers swinging up the slope a bare furlong behind us, Jassa's pistol cracked – and dead ahead, glorious sight, riders were racing down from the Jupindar rocks, two long files at the gallop, riding wide, one circling in behind us, and the other swinging out in a great arc to envelop our pursuers.

I never saw it better done. There were five hundred of 'em if there was one – *gorracharra*, by the look of them, and going like thunderbolts. There were yells of confusion in our rear, and as I steadied my screw and looked back, the lancers were closing on each other in fair disorder, sewn neat as a cat in a bag by those two lines of irregular horsemen, enclosing them front, flanks, and rear. Well met by moonlight, thinks I; you have some capable pals, Gardner. Little Dalip had scrambled to a sitting position before me, clapping and piping cheers at the top of his voice, and Jassa and Ahmed were reining up alongside.

There was a hail from above and ahead of us, and I saw that there was a narrow gorge in the rocks, and at its mouth a little knot of horsemen in mail and with lanced pennons; overhead a standard was fluttering, and to the fore was a burly old stager in spiked helm and steel back-and-breast who raised a hand and roared a greeting.

"*Salaam, maharaj'! Salaam* Flashman *bahadur! Sat-sree-akal!*"

His companions took up the cry, advancing to meet us, but I had eyes only for their leader, grinning all over his ruddy face and white whiskers, sitting his pony at ease for all that he had only one foot in the stirrup; the other, swathed in bandages, rested in a silken sling hanging from his saddle-bow.

284

"Well met again, Afghan-killer!" cries Goolab Singh.

* * *

"Sure people" would meet us, Gardner had said, and like a simpleton I'd taken his word without a thought. He was such a square-shooting white man, you see, and I was so used to thinking of him as a faithful ally and friend – well, he'd saved my hide twice – that I'd clean overlooked that he had other allegiances in the tangled web of Punjabi politics. Well, he'd done me brown – and Hardinge and Lawrence; we'd plucked Dalip Singh out of Lahore just so that he could be dropped into the lap of the whiskered old bandit beaming at me across the fire.

"Think not harshly of Gurdana Khan," says he soothingly. "He has not betrayed thee – or the *Malki lat*; rather has he done thee a service."

"I can see me convincing Sir Henry Hardinge of that!" says I. "Of all the double-dyed Yankee fakers –"

"Nay, nay now! Only consider: Mai Jeendan, rightly fearing for her son's safety, wished to put him under British protection – good! On her behalf, Gurdana Khan set the thing in train with your folk – good! But then, as my friend and agent, he bethought him that the child would be even better in the keeping of . . . myself. Why? Because once the Khalsa heard that their king was in the hands of the British, they would smell treason – aye, they might even cut Mai Jeendan's pretty throat, and set up some new Maharaja who would carry on this plaguey war for years." He wagged his wicked head, looking smug. "But now, when they learn that I, the admired Goolab, hold the child, they will think no evil. Why, they have lately offered me the throne, and the Wazirship, and command of the Khalsa, and I know not what, so well do they respect me! But I have no such ambitions – what, to king it in Lahore, and find a quick grave like Jawaheer, and all those other fortunate occupants of that throne of serpents? Not I, friend! Kashmir will do for me – the British will confirm me there, but never in Lahore –"

285

"You think they will – after this? You've used us, and Gardner's aided and abetted you –"

"And what harm is done? The child is as safe with me as in his mother's bosom – safer, by God, there is less traffic – and when this war is over I shall have the credit of leading him by the hand into the presence of the *Malki lat*!" crows the old villain. "Think of the good will I shall earn! I shall have proved my loyalty to my Maharaja and the British alike!"

And I'd been sneaking about Lahore Fort in peril of my life, conspiring and kidnapping and being hounded by Khalsa lancers, just so that this ancient iniquity could cut a dash in the last act.

"Why the devil did Gardner have to bring us into it at all? Couldn't you have lifted the boy for yourself?"

"Mai Jeendan would never have allowed it. She trusts me not," says he, shrugging, all innocent-like. "Only to Flashman *bahadur* would she yield up her precious ewe lamb – ah, what it is to be young and straight and lusty . . . and British!" He twinkled at me approvingly, shaking with laughter, and refilled my cup with brandy. "Your health, soldier! What, we have stood together, you and I, and heard the cold steel sing! You'll never grudge old Goolab the chance to stand well with your masters!"

That was gammon. For one thing, I'd no choice, and the plain fact was that in Dalip, the only Maharaja acceptable to all parties, he now held the trump card. He'd been trafficking with us for months, while hedging his bets with the Khalsa, and now that the dice had finally fallen in our favour, he was making sure that he could dictate his own terms. And Hardinge could only swallow it and look pleasant – why shouldn't he? With Dalip and Jeendan secure in Lahore, and Goolab confirmed in Kashmir, the northwest frontier would be safe as never before.

"And it will be only for a day or two at most," he went on. "Then I shall take Dalip Maharaja and place him in the Sirkar's arms. Aye, Flashman, the war is done. The Khalsa is bought and sold, and not by Tej Singh only. They think themselves secure in their strong position at Sobraon, where even the *Jangi lat* can hardly assail them, be his guns ever so

286

big – they still dream of sweeping on to Delhi!" He leaned
forward, grinning like a fat tiger. "And even now, plans of
those fine fortifications are on their way to White Coat
Gough – aye, by tomorrow your engineers will know every
trench and tower, every rampart and gun emplacement, in
that fine trap the Khalsa have built for themselves in the
elbow of the river! Their fortress? Their coffin, rather! For
not a man of them shall escape . . . and the Khalsa will be no
more than an evil memory!" He filled his cup again, drank,
and licked his lips, Pickwick in a *puggaree*, nodding benevolently at me. "That is my gift to your government,
bahadur! Is it enough, think you? Will it set the seal on
Kashmir for me?"[45]

There's a point, you know, where treachery is so complete
and unashamed that it becomes statesmanship. Given a shift
of fortune, at Moodkee or Ferozeshah, and this genial, evil
old barbarian would have been heart and soul with the
Khalsa, leading 'em on to Delhi, no doubt. As it was, he was
ensuring their slaughter, and revelling in the prospect, like
the cruel savage that he was. I often wish I could have
introduced him to Otto Bismarck; a fine matched pair they'd
have made.

Well, he had shored up his credit with our side, sure
enough, with little Dalip in his hands for good measure.
That was his affair, and I wished him joy of it; my own
concern was that I'd failed in my own immediate mission,
thanks to him and Gardner, and what was I going to tell
Hardinge?

"Why, that ye had the child safe, but were hard pressed
by Khalsa riders, when in the nick of time came loyal
Goolab to snatch thee and him to safety! Is it not true, after
all? And perforce ye must leave the lad with Goolab, who
would nowise part with him, fearing for his safety with all
these Khalsa bravos loose about the country!" He chuckled
and drank again, wiping his whiskers; you never saw roguery
so pleased with itself. "It will make a brave tale . . . so that
ye tell it right." He fixed me with a meaning eye. "It will
profit us all, Flashman sahib."

I asked, pretty sour, how it could profit me, and he gave

287

me a leery look. "What would ye have that the King of Kashmir can give . . . when he comes into his own? There is rich employment, if you wish it, up yonder. Aye, and a warm welcome from that bonny widow, my good-sister. Think on it, *bahadur*."

Ironic, wasn't it – a queen hoping to wed me, a king offering me golden rewards, when all my worldly ambition was to step from Colaba Causeway to the deck of a homeward-bound Indiaman, and never see their dirty, dangerous country again. I could just thank my stars I'd come this far, to this snug camp under Jupindar rocks, resting and boozing by Goolab's fire, with little Dalip fast asleep in a tent close by (Goolab had fairly grovelled to him, but the lordly mite had been too fagged to do more than accept it coolly and curl up), and the Khalsa lancers disarmed and under guard; they'd taken it without a murmur, once they'd discovered who their captor was. Thus far in safety, and in the meantime all I could do was slope off over the river and report failure to Hardinge – he'd enjoy that.

To my surprise, I slept sound at Jupindar, and it was after noon when I broke the news to Dalip that he would not be coming with me to the Sirkar's army after all, but must stay awhile with his kinsman, Goolab Singh, until it was safe for him to go home to Mama. I'd expected a royal tantrum, but he took it without a blink of those great brown eyes, nodding gravely as he looked about the camp, aswarm with Goolab's followers.

"Aye, I see how it is – they are many, and you are but three," says he. "May I have my pistol now, Flashman *bahadur*?"

That rattled me, I confess. Here he was, not two chamberpots high, lifted in disguise from his mother's palace, fired on and pursued through the dark and cold, left in the hands of a ruffian of whom he could have heard nothing but evil – and all that concerned him was the promised pepperbox. No doubt Sindiawalla princelings were used to alarm and excursion from the cradle, and God knows how much children understand, anyway – but it struck me that whatever faults Dalip Singh developed in later years, funk

288

wouldn't be one of them. Quite awe-inspiring, he was.

We were standing apart from the others, while Goolab drank his morning toddy on a rug outside his tent, watching slantendicular, and Jassa and Ahmed lounged by the horses. I beckoned Ahmed and took out the Cooper, Dalip watching round-eyed as I drew the six loads. I showed him the mechanism, and set the gun in his small fist; he had to grip well up the stock to get his finger near the ring.

"Ahmed Shah will keep these rounds for you, maharaj'," says I, "and load them at your need."

"I can load!" says majesty, struggling manfully with the cylinder. "And I would have the pistol charged – I cannot shoot thieves and *badmashes* with an empty toy!"

I assured him there were no thieves about, and he gave me a forty-year-old look. "And that fat bearded one yonder, the Dogra whom you call my kinsman? Mangla says he would steal the droppings from a goat!"

This boded well for Goolab's guardianship, no error. "Now, see here, maharaj', Raja Goolab is your friend, and will guard you until your return to Lahore, which will be soon. And Ahmed Shah here will bide with you also – he is a soldier of the Sirkar, and my comrade, so you must obey him in all things." Which was stretching it, for I hardly knew Ahmed, but he was a Broadfoot Pathan, and the best I could do. To him I said: "On thy head, Yusufzai," and he nodded and tapped his hilt. Dalip looked at him critically.

"Can he help me to shoot the gun, at need? Well then, so be it. But that great belly yonder is still a thief. I will stay with him, and mind him, but I will not trust him. He may guard me and yet rob me too, because I am little." He was examining the Cooper as he delivered his judgment, sotto voce, on Goolab's character, but then he stuck the pistol in his sash and spoke clear, in his shrill treble.

"A gift for a gift, *bahadur*! Bow your head!"

Wondering, I stooped towards him, and to my amazement he lifted the heavy silver locket from about his neck and threw the chain over my head, and for a moment his little arms locked tight, holding me, and I felt him tremble and his tears suddenly wet on my face. "I will be brave! I will be

289

brave, *bahadur!*" whispers he, sobbing. "But you must keep it for me, till you come again to Lahore!" Then I set him down, and he stood rubbing his eyes angrily, while Goolab came limping, to apologise for intruding on his majesty, but it was time we were all on our various roads.

I asked where he would take the Maharaja, and he said no farther than Pettee, a few miles off, where his fighting men were assembling; he had brought forty thousand down from Jumoo "– in case the *Jangi lat* should need assistance against these rebel dogs of the Khalsa; haply we may cut them up as they flee from Sobraon! Then," and he bowed as far as his belly would let him, "we must see to it that your majesty has a new army, of true men!" Dalip took this with a good grace, whatever he may have been thinking.

It was time to go, and Jassa mounted alongside me – that was the moment when I knew for certain that he hadn't been party to Gardner's little plot. He'd seemed as stunned as I was to find Goolab Singh waiting at Jupindar, but that might have been acting – the fact that he was riding back to Hardinge with me was proof of his innocence. I gave a last salutation to Dalip, standing very small and steady apart from old Goolab, and then Jassa and I rode south from Jupindar rocks – with our tails between our legs, if you like . . . and two million pounds' worth of crystallised carbon round my neck.

He was a canny infant and wise beyond his years, young Dalip – wasn't he just? He knew Goolab wouldn't dare harm his person – but his property was another matter. If the old fox had guessed the Koh-i-Noor was within reach, then that wondrous treasure would surely have found its way to Kashmir. And in his infant innocence, Dalip had passed it to me, for safe-keeping . . .

I brooded on that as we trotted south over the *doab* in the misty afternoon, with Jupindar fading from sight behind us, and the distant green that marked the Sutlej coming into view ahead. By rights I should have been deciding where to cross, and calculating our bearing from Sobraon, where presently all hell would be let loose. But having the most precious object in the world bobbing against your belly concentrates the mind wonderfully; it ain't just the fearful responsibility, either. All kinds of mad fancies flit by – not to be taken seriously, you understand, but food for wild imaginings – like bleaching your hair and striking out for Valparaiso under the name of Butterworth and never looking near England again . . . two million quid, Lord love us! Aye, but how d'you dispose of a diamond the size of a tangerine? Not in Amsterdam . . . probably to some swindling shark who'd set the traps after you . . . I could picture myself going mad in a garret, gibbering at a treasure I was too windy to sell . . . But if you *could*, and disappear . . . Gad, the life you could lead – estates, palaces, luxury by the bucket, gold cigar-boxes and silk drawers, squads of slaves and battalions of willing women, visions of Xanadu and Babylon and unlimited boozing and frolic . . .

No steak and kidney ever again, though – and no Elspeth. No sunny days at Lord's or strolls along the Haymarket, no hunt suppers or skittle pool or English rain or Horse Guards or quarts of home-brewed . . . oh, for Elspeth bare and bouncing and a jug of October and bread and cheese by the bed! All the jewels of Golconda can't buy you that, even supposing you had the nerve to bolt with them – which I knew I had not. No, pinching Koh-i-Noor is like putting t'other side in to bat – you won't do it, but there's no reason why you shouldn't think hard about it.

"Where you aim to cross, lieutenant?" says Jassa, and I realised he'd been gassing since we left Jupindar, full of bile against Gardner, and I'd hardly taken in a blessed word. I asked him, as one who knew the country, where we were.

"About five miles nor'east of Nuggur Ford," says he. "The Sobraon ghat's less than ten miles due east – see, that smoke'll be from the Sikh lines." He pointed to our left front, and on the horizon, above the distant green, you could see it hanging like a dark mist. "We can scout the Nuggur, an' if it ain't clear, we can cast downriver a piece." He paused. "Leastways, *you* can."

Something in his tone made me look round – into the six barrels of his pistol. He'd reined in about ten feet behind me, and there was a hard, fixed grin on his ugly face.

291

"What the hell are you about?" cries I. "Put that damned thing up!"

"No, sir," says he. "Now you sit right still, 'cos I don't wish to harm you. No, don't start to holler an' tear your hair, neither! Just slip off that locket an' chain, an' toss 'em over this way – lively, now!"

For a moment I'd been all at sea – I'd forgotten, you see, that he'd been there when Jeendan had shown the stone to Dalip and put it round his neck, and again when Dalip had passed the locket to me. Then:

"You confounded fool!" I yelped, half-laughing. "You can't steal *this*!"

"Don't bet on it! Now, you do as I say, d'ye hear?"

I was riding Ahmed Shah's screw, with two long horse pistols in the saddle holsters, but I'd no notion of reaching for them. For the thing was wild – hadn't I been turning it over, academic-like, for the past hour?

"Harlan, you're daft!" says I. "Look, man, put up that pepperbox and see reason! This is the Koh-i-Noor – and the Punjab! Why, you'ld not get twenty miles – you'ld be running your head into a noose –"

"Mr Flashman, you can shut up!" says he, and the harsh face with its ghastly orange whiskers looked like a scared ape's. "Now, sir, you pass that item across directly, or –"

"Hold on!", says I, and lifted the tarnished silver case in my hand. "Hear me a moment. I don't know how many carats this thing weighs, or how you think you can turn it into cash – even if you get clear of the Sikhs, let alone the British Army! Good God, man, the mere sight of it and you'll be clapped in irons – you can't hope to sell –"

"You're trying my patience, mister! An' you're forgetting I know this territory, for a thousand miles around, better'n any man alive! I know Jews in every town from Prome to Bokhara who can have that rock in twenty bits quicker'n you can spit!" He threw back his *puggaree* impatiently and raised the pistol, and for all his brag his hand was shaking. "I don't want to shoot you out of the saddle, but I will, by the holy!"

"Will you?" says I. "Gardner said you wouldn't do

murder – but he was right about your being a thief –"
"That he was!" cries he. "An' if you paid heed to him,
you know my story!" He was grinning like a maniac. "I've
followed fortune half a lifetime, an' taken every chance I
found! I ain't about to miss the best one yet! An' you can set
the British *an'* the Punjab in a roar after me – there's a war
to finish, an' more empty trails between Kabul an' Kat-
mandu an' Quetta than anybody's ever thought of – 'cept
me! I'll count to three!"

His knuckle was white on the ring, so I slipped the chain
over my neck, weighed the locket a moment, and tossed it to
him. He snapped it up by the chain, his feverish eyes never
leaving me for a second, and dropped the locket into his
boot. His chest was heaving, and he licked his lips – highway
robbery wasn't his style, I could see.

"Now you climb down, an' keep your hands clear o' those
barkers!" I dismounted, and he side-stepped in and seized
my reins.

"You're not leaving me afoot – and unarmed, for God's
sake!" I cried, and he backed his horse away, covering me
still, and drawing my mount with him.

"You're less'n two hours from the river," says he, grinning more easy now. "You'll make it safe enough. Well,
lieutenant . . . we had our ups an' downs, but no hard feelings my side. Fact, I'm almost sorry to part – you're my sort,
you know." He gave a high-pitched laugh. "That's why I'm
not offering you a partnership in Koh-i-Noor Unlimited!"

"I wouldn't take it. How long have you been planning
this?"

"'Bout twenty minutes. Here – catch hold!" He unslung
the *chaggle* from Ahmed's saddle, and threw it towards me.
"Hot day – have a drink on me!"

He wheeled his horse and was off at the gallop, making
north, with my screw behind, leaving me alone on the *doab*.
I waited until the scrub hid him, and then turned and ran at
full speed in the direction of Nuggur Ford. There was a belt
of jungle that way, and I wanted to be in cover. As I ran, I
kept my hand cupped to my side, feeling the reassuring
bulge of the Koh-i-Noor under my sash. I may day-dream

293

occasional, but when I'm carrying priceless valuables in the company of the likes of Dr Josiah Harlan, I slip 'em out of sight in the first five minutes, you may be sure.

If he'd had the wit to open the locket – well, that would have been another story. But if he'd had that much wit, he'd not have been reduced to running errands for Broadfoot in the first place. The fact is, for all his experience of rascality, Jassa was a 'prentice hand. The Man Who Would Be King . . . but never was.

*   *   *

Only the other day my little great-niece Selina – the pretty one whose loose conduct almost led me to commit murder in Baker Street, but that's another story – remarked to me that she couldn't abide Dickens because his books were full of coincidences. I replied by telling her about the chap who lost a rifle in France and tripped over it in West Africa twenty years later,[46] and added for good measure an account of my own strange experience after I parted from Harlan in the *doab*. That was coincidence, if you like, and damnably mixed luck, too, for while it may have saved my life it also landed me centre stage in the last act of the Punjab war.

Once I reached the jungle belt, chortling at the thought of Jassa stopping presently to gloat over his booty, I went to ground. Even when he found out he'd been diddled, he'd never dare come back to look for me, so I decided to stay put and cross the river when night fell. In my Kabuli attire I could pass for a *gorrachar'* well enough, but the less I was seen the better, so I planned to leave my jungly lair a couple of hours before dusk, slip down to the river, swim across – it wasn't above four hundred yards wide – and lie up on the far shore until daylight.

It began to rain heavily towards evening, so I was glad enough of my shelter, and only when the light began to fade did I venture out, onto a beaten track leading down to the Sutlej. It took me through a little wood, and I was striding boldly along, eager to catch a glimpse of the river, when I rounded a bend in the trees, and there, not twenty yards ahead, was a troop of regular Khalsa cavalry, with their beasts picketed and a fire going. It was too late to turn back, so I walked on, prepared to pass the time of day and pick up the shave, and only when I was almost on them did I notice six or seven bodies hanging from trees within the wood. I bore up in natural alarm – and that was fatal. They were already looking towards me, and now someone yelled an order, and before I knew it I had been seized by grinning *sowars* and hauled into the presence of a burly *daffadar**   standing by the fire, a mess-tin in his hand and his tunic unbuttoned. He eyed me malevolently, brushing crumbs from his beard.

"Another of them!" growls he. "*Gorracharra*, are you? Aye, the faithless rabble! And what tale have you got to tell?"

"Tale, *daffadar* sahib?" says I, bewildered. "Why, none! I –"

"Here's a change! Most of you have sick mothers!" At which all his louts hooted with laughter. "Well, *gorrachar*', where's your horse? Your arms? Your regiment?" He suddenly threw the mess-tin aside and slapped me across the face, back and forth. "Your honour, you cowardly scum!"

It struck the sense out of me for a moment, and I was starting to babble some nonsense about being waylaid by bandits when he hit me again.

"Robbed, were you? And they left you this?" He snatched the silver-hilted Persian knife from my boot. "Liar! You're a deserter! Like those swine there!" He jerked a thumb at the swinging corpses, and I saw that most of them were wearing some remnants of uniform. "Well, you can muster with them again, carrion! Hang him up!"

It was so brutally sudden, so impossible – I wasn't to know that for weeks they'd been hunting down deserters from half the regiments of the Khalsa, stringing them up on sight without charge, let alone trial. They were dragging me towards the trees before I recovered my wits, and there was only one way to stop them.

*Cavalry commander of ten.

"*Daffadar!*" I shouted, "you're under arrest! For assault on a superior officer and attempted murder! I am Katte Khan, captain and aide to the Sirdar Heera Sing Topi, of Court's Division –" it was a name from months ago, the only one I could think of. "You!" I snapped at the goggling *sowar* holding my left arm. "Take your polluting hand away or I'll have you shot! I'll teach you to lay hands on me, you damned Povinda brigands!"

It paralysed them – as the voice of authority always does. They loosed me in a twinkling, and the *daffadar*, open-mouthed, even began to button his tunic. "We are not of the Povinda division –"

"Silence! Where's your officer?"

"In the village," says he, sullenly, and only half-convinced. "If you are what you say –"

"If! Give me the lie, will you?" I dropped my voice from a bellow to a whisper, which always rattles them. "*Daffadar*, I do not explain myself to the sweepings of the gutter! Bring your officer – *jao!*"

Now he was convinced. "I'll take you to him, Captain sahib –"

"You'll bring him!" I roared, and he leaped back a yard and sent one of the *sowars* off at the gallop, while I turned on my heel and waited with my back to them, so that they shouldn't see that I was shaking like a leaf. It had all been so quick – carefree one minute, condemned the next – that there hadn't been time for fear, but now I was fit to faint. What could I say to the officer? I cudgelled my wits – and then there was the sound of hooves, and I turned to see the coincidence riding towards me.

He was a tall, fine-looking young Sikh, his yellow tunic stained with weeks of campaigning. He reined in, demanding of the *daffadar* what the devil was up, swinging out of the saddle and striding towards me – and to my consternation I knew him, and any hope of maintaining my disguise vanished. For it was long odds he'd recognise me, too, and if he did . . . A wild thought suddenly struck me, and before he could speak I had drawn myself up, bowed, and in my best verandah manner asked him to send his men out of

296

earshot. My style must have impressed him, for he waved them away.

"Sardul Singh," says I quietly, and he started. "I'm Flashman. You escorted me from Ferozepore to Lahore six months ago. It's vital that these men should not know I'm a British officer."

He gasped, and stepped closer, peering at me in the gathering dark. "What the devil are you doing here?"

I took a deep breath, and prayed. "I've come from Lahore – from the Maharani. This morning I was with Raja Goolab Singh, who is now at Pettee, with his army. I was on my way to the *Malki lat*, with messages of the highest importance, when by ill chance these fellows took me for a deserter – thank God it's you who –"

"Wait, wait!" says he. "You are from Lahore . . . on an embassy? Then, why this disguise? Why –"

"Envoys don't travel in uniform these days," says I, and pitched my tale as urgent as I knew how. "Look, I should not tell you, but I must – there are secret negotiations in hand! I can't explain, but the whole future of the state depends on them! I must get across the river without delay – matters are at a most delicate stage, and my messages –"

"Where are they?"

"Where? Eh? Oh, Lord above, they're not written. They're here!" I tapped my head, which you'll agree was an appropriate gesture.

"But you have some passport, surely?"

"No, no . . . I can't carry anything that might betray me. This is the most confidential affair, you see. Believe me, Sardul Singh, every moment is precious. I must cross secretly to –"

"A moment," says he, and my heart sank, for while the fine young face wasn't suspicious, it was damned keen. "If you must pass unseen, why have you come so close to our army? Why not by Hurree-ke, or south by Ferozepore?"

"Because Hardinge sahib is with the British army across from Sobraon! I had to come this way!"

"Yet you might have crossed beyond our patrols, and lost little time." He considered me, frowning. "Forgive me, but

297

you might be a spy. There have been many, scouting our lines."

"I give you my word of honour, I'm no spy. What I say is true . . . and if you hold me here, you may be dooming your army to death – and mine – and your country to ruin."

By God, I was doing it purple, but my only hope was that, being a well-educated aristocrat, he must know the desperate intrigue and dealing that were woven into this war – and if he believed me, he'd be a damned bold subaltern to hamper a diplomatic courier on such a vital errand. Alas, though, subalterns' minds travel a fixed road, and his was no exception: faced with a momentous decision, my dashing escort of the Lahore road had turned into a Slave of Duty – and Safety.

"This is beyond me!" He shook his handsome head. "It may be as you say . . . but I cannot let you go! I have not the authority. My colonel will have to decide –"

I made a last desperate cast. "That would be fatal! If word of the negotiations gets out, they're bound to fail!"

"There is no fear of that – my colonel is a safe man. And he will know what to do." Relief was in his voice at the thought of passing the parcel to higher authority. "Yes, that will be best – I'll go to him myself, as soon as our watch is ended! You can stay here, so that if he decides to release you, it can be done without trouble, and you will have lost little time."

I tried again, urging the necessity for speed, imploring him to trust me, but it was no go. The colonel must pronounce, and so while he trotted back to his squadron post in the village, I must wait under guard of the glowering *daffadar* and his mates, resigned to capture. Of all the infernal luck, at the last fence! For it mattered not a bean whether his colonel believed my cock-and-bull story or not – he'd never speed me on my way without going higher still, and God alone knew where that might end. They'd hardly dare mistreat me, in view of the tale I'd told; even if they disbelieved it, they'd not be mad enough to shoot me as a spy, at this stage of the war, surely . . . mind you, some of those Akali fanatics were bloodthirsty enough for anything . . .

298

On such jolly reflections I settled down to wait in that dripping little camp – for it was raining heavily again – and either the colonel had gone absent without leave or Sardul spent an unconscionable time gnawing his nails in indecision, for it must have been well into the small hours before he returned. By that time, worn out with wet and despair, I had sunk into a doze, and when I came to, with Sardul shaking my shoulder, I didn't know where I was for a moment.

"All is well!" cries he, and for a blessed second I thought he was going to speed me on my way. "I have spoken with the colonel sahib, and told him . . . of your diplomatic duty." He dropped his voice, glancing round in the firelight. "The colonel sahib thinks it best that he should not see you himself." Another reckless muttonhead ripe for Staff College, plainly. "He says this is a high political matter . . . so I am to take you to Tej Singh. Come, I have a horse for you!"

If he'd told me they were going to send me on shooting leave to Ooti I'd have been less astonished, but his next words provided the explanation.

"The colonel sahib says that since Tej Singh is commander-in-chief, he will surely know of these secret negotiations, and can decide what should be done. And since he is in the camp below Sobraon, he will be able to send you to the *Malki lat* with all speed. Indeed, you will be there sooner than if I released you now."

That was what I'd talked myself into . . . Sobraon, the very heart of the doomed Khalsa. Yet what else could I have done? When you've just been within an ace of being hanged out of hand, you're liable to say the first thing that comes to mind, and I'd had to tell Sardul *something*. Still, it could have been worse. At least with Tej I'd be safe, and he'd see me back to Hardinge fast enough . . . flag of truce, a quick trot across no man's land, and home in time for breakfast. Aye, provided the dogs of war didn't come howling out of the kennel in the meantime . . . what had Goolab said? "A day or two at most" before Gough stormed the Khalsa lines in the last great battle . . .

"Well, let's be off, hey?" cries I, jumping up. "The sooner the better, you know! How far is it – can we be there

299

before first light?" He said it was only a few miles along the river bank, but since that way was heavy with military traffic, we would be best to take a detour round their positions (and prevent wicked Flashy from spying out the land, you understand). Still, we should be there soon after dawn.

We set off in the rainy dark, the whole troop of us – he was taking no chances on my slipping my cable, and my bridle was tied firmly to the *daffadar's* pommel. It was black as sin, and no hope of a moon in this weather, so we went at little better than a walk, and before long I had lost all sense of time and direction. It was my second night in the saddle, I was weary and sore and sodden and fearful, and every few moments I nodded off only to wake with a start, clutching at the mane to save myself from falling. How far we came before the teeming downpour ceased and the sky began to lighten, I can't tell, but presently we could see the *doab* about us, with wraiths of vapour hanging heavy over the scrub. Ahead a few lights were showing dimly, and Sardul reined up: "Sobraon."

But it was only the village of that name, which lies a mile or two north of the river, and when we reached it we must turn sharp right to come down to the Khalsa's reserve positions on the northern bank, beyond which the bridge of boats spanned the Sutlej to the main Sikh fortifications on the southern side, hemmed in by Gough's army. As we wheeled and approached the rear of the reserve lines, fires were flickering and massive shadows looming in the mist ahead, and now we could see the entrenchments on either flank, with heavy gun emplacements commanding the river, which was still out of sight to our front. As we trotted through a sea of churned mud to the lines, trumpets were blaring the stand-to, the Sikh drums were beginning to rattle, troops were swarming in the trenches, and from all about us came the clamour and bustle of an army stirring, like a giant rousing from sleep.

I didn't know, nor did they, as drum and trumpet called them, that the Khalsa was answering its last reveille. But even as we entered the rearmost line, from somewhere far beyond the grey blanket mantling the northern shore ahead of us, came another sound, stunning in its suddenness: the thunder of gunfire echoing along the Sutlej valley in a continuous roar of explosions, shaking the ground underfoot, reverberating through the mists of morning. Beyond our view, on the southern shore, an old Irishman in a white coat was beating his shillelagh on the Khalsa's door, and with a sinking heart I realised that I had come a bare hour too late. The battle of Sobraon had begun.

The best way to view a clash of armies is from a hot-air balloon, for not only can you see what's doing, you're safely out of the line of fire. I've done it once, in Paraguay, and there's nothing to beat it, provided some jealous swine of a husband doesn't take a cleaver to the cable. The next best place is an eminence, like the Sapoune at Balaclava or the bluffs above Little Bighorn, and if I can speak with authority about both those engagements it's not so much because I was lashing about in the thick of them, as that I had the opportunity of overlooking the ground beforehand.

Sobraon was like that. The northern bank of the Sutlej at that point is higher than the southern, giving a sweeping view of the whole battlefield, and miles beyond. I wasn't to see it for another hour or so, for when the cannonade began Sardul called a halt, and left me in the care of his troop while he dashed off to see what was up. We waited in the clammy dawn, while the Sikh support troops stood to inspection in the trenches and gun emplacements about us, and the gunners stripped the aprons from their heavy pieces, piling the cartridges and rolling the big 48-pound shot on to the stretchers, all ready to load. They were cool hands, those artillerymen, manning their positions quiet and orderly, the brown bearded faces staring ahead towards the battle of barrages hidden beyond the river mist.

Sardul came spurring back, spattering the mud, wild with excitement. Gough's batteries were hammering the fortifications on the southern shore, but doing little harm, and the Sikh gunners were giving him shot for shot. "Presently he will attack, and be thrown back!" cries Sardul exultantly. "The position is secure, and we may go down in safety to

302

Tej Singh. Come, *bahadur*, it is a splendid sight! A hundred and fifty great guns thunder against each other – but your *Jangi lat* has blundered! His range is too long, and he wastes his powder! Come and see!"

I believed him. Knowing Paddy, I could guess he was banging away just to please Hardinge, but couldn't wait for the moment when he would turn his bayonets loose. That must be soon, by the sound of it; even if he'd brought the whole magazine from Umballa, he couldn't keep up such a barrage for long.

"Never in all India has there been such a fight of heavy guns!" cries Sardul. "Their smoke is like a city burning! Oh, what a day to see! What a day!"

He was like a boy at a fair as he led the way down through the silent gun positions, and presently we came to a little flat promontory, where a group of Sikh staff officers were mounted, very brave in their dress coats. They spared us not so much as a glance, for at that moment the mist lifted from the river like a raised curtain, and an astonishing sight was unfolded before us.

Twenty feet below the bluff the oily flood of the Sutlej was swirling by in full spate, the bubbling brown surface strewn with ramage which was piling up against the great bridge of boats, four hundred yards long and anchored by massive chains, that spanned the river to the southern shore. There, in a half-moon a full mile in extent, the Khalsa lines lay in three huge concentric semi-circles of ramparts, ditches, and bastions; there were thirty thousand fighting Sikhs in there, the cream of the Punjab, with their backs to the river and seventy big guns crashing out their reply to our artillery positions a thousand yards away. Over the whole Sikh stronghold hung an enormous pall of black gunsmoke, and above the widespread distant arc of our guns a similar pall was hanging, thinner and dispersing more quickly than theirs, for while their batteries were concentrated within that mile-wide fortress, our sixty pieces were scattered in a curved line twice as long – and Sardul was right, their range was too great. I could see our mortar shells bursting high over the Sikh positions, and the heavy shot throwing up

303

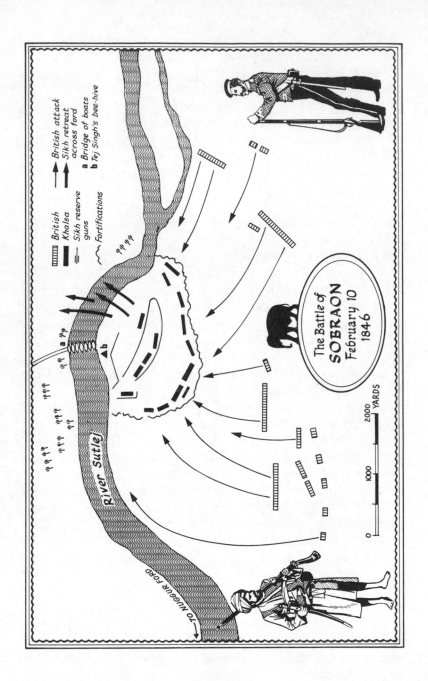

British
Khalsa
Sikh reserve guns
Fortifications

British attack
Sikh retreat across ford
a Bridge of boats
b Tej Singh's bee-hive

River Sutlej

TO NUGGUR FORD

The Battle of
SOBRAON
February 10
1846

0   1000   2000
YARDS

304

fountains of red earth, but causing little damage; far to the right we had a rocket battery in action, the long white trails criss-crossing the black clouds, and some fires were burning at that end of the Sikh lines, but all along the forward fortifications the Khalsa gunners were blazing away in style – Paddy wasn't going to win the shooting-match, that was certain.

Even amidst the din of the cannonade we could hear them cheering in the entrenchments across the river, and the blare of their military bands, with drums throbbing and cymbals clashing, and then the salvoes from the British guns died away, and the smoke cleared over our distant positions; the trumpets in the Sikh camp were sounding the cease-fire, and presently the last wraiths dispersed above their positions also, and Sam Khalsa and John Company looked each other in the eye across a half-mile of scrubby plain and patchy jungle, like two boxers when their seconds and supporters have left off yelling abuse, and each scrapes his feet and flexes his arms for the onset.

With the enemy snug behind his ramparts, it was for Gough to make the first move, and he did it in classic style, with a straight left. Sardul caught at my arm, pointing, and sure enough, far off on our right front, steel was glinting through the last of the mist; he had a little spy-glass clapped to his eye, but now he passed it to me and my heart raced as I saw the white cap-covers and red coats spring into close vision in the glass circle, the fixed bayonets gleaming in the first sunlight, the officers and drummers to the fore, the colour stirring in the breeze – I could even make out the embroidered "X", but it can only have been in imagination that I heard the fifes sounding:

> The gamekeeper was watching us,
> For him we did not care,
> For we can wrestle and fight, my boys,
> And jump o'er anywhere . . .

as the Tenth Lincoln came on in line, their pieces at the port, with the horse guns bounding past their flank, and alongside them the shakos and white belts of the Native Infantry, and then another British colour, but I couldn't make out which, and again our guns began to crash as Paddy poured his last rounds of covering fire over their heads and the dust billowed up on the Khalsa's right front.

The Sikh batteries exploded in a torrent of flame, and I saw our line stagger and recover and come on again before the clouds of smoke and dust hid them from sight. On the extreme right a great body of horse emerged from the entrenchments, swinging wide to charge our rocket batteries whose missiles were weaving in above the advancing infantry and exploding on the breastworks. The Sikh horse rounded our flank and went for the rocket stand like Irishmen on holiday, but the battery commander must have seen his danger and given the word to raise the frames, for he let them come to point-blank range before loosing the whole barrage at ground level, whizzing in to burst among the horsemen, and the charge dissolved in a cloud of white smoke and orange flame.

The staff men beside us were suddenly shouting and pointing: while Gough's left wing was closing through the smoke on the Sikhs' right front, out on the plain, beyond the scrub and jungle, there was a stirring in the heat haze; tiny figures, red, blue, and green, were coming into view, long extended lines of them, with the horse guns in the intervals between. I swung the glass on them, and here were the yellow facings of the 29th, there the buff of the 31st, everywhere the red coats and cross-belts of the Native Infantry . . . the red and blue of the Queen's Own . . . on the flank the dark figures of the 9th Lancers and the blue coats and *puggarees* of the Bengali horsemen . . . the crimson-streaked plumes of the 3rd Lights . . . the little goblin figures of the Gurkhas, trotting to keep up, and even as I watched there was a flash of silver rippling along their front as the great leaf-bladed knives came out. The whole of our army was on the move towards the centre and left of the Khalsa's position – twenty thousand British and Native foot, horse, and guns coming in against odds of three to two, and the Sikhs' heavy metal was ranging on them, kicking up the dust-plumes all along the great arc of our advance.

306

Now all the forward entrenchments were exploding, sweeping the ground with a hail of grape and canister, blotting out the scene in a thick haze of dust and smoke. I caught my breath in horror, for it was Ferozeshah all over again, with that raving old spud-walloper risking everything on the sabre and the bayonet, hand to hand – but then the Sikhs had been groggy from Moodkee, in positions hastily dug and manned, while now they were entrenched in a miniature Torres Vedras, with ditch-and-dyke works twenty feet high, enfiladed by murderous camel-swivels and packed with *tulwar*-swinging lunatics fairly itching to die for the Guru. You can't do it, Paddy, thinks I, it won't answer this time, you'll break your great thick Irish head against this fortress of shot and steel, and have your army torn to ribbons, and lose the war, and never see Tipperary again, you benighted old bog-trotter, you –

"Come!" calls Sardul, and I tore my eyes away from that billowing mirk beyond which our army was advancing to certain death, and followed him down the muddy slope to the bridge of boats. They were big barges, lashed thwart to thwart and paved with heavy timbers which made a road as straight and solid as dry ground – hollo, says I, there's a white sapper in the woodpile, damn him, for no Punjabi ever put this together. We drummed across with the troop at our heels and came into the rear of the Khalsa position – their last line of defence where the general staff directed operations, aides hurried to and fro between the tents and hutments, carts of wounded rumbled through to the bridge, and all was activity and uproar – but it was a disciplined bedlam, I noticed, in spite of the deafening crash of guns and musketry rolling back from the lines.

There was a knot of senior men grouped round a great scale model of the fortifications – I caught only a glimpse of it, but it must have been twenty feet across, with every trench and parapet and gun just so – and a splendid old white-bearded *sirdar* with a mail vest over his silk tunic was prodding it with a long wand and bellowing orders above the din, while his listeners despatched messengers into the sulphurous reek which blotted out everything beyond fifty

307

yards, and made the air nigh unbreathable. This was clearly the high command – but no sign of Tej Singh, general and guiding spirit of the Khalsa, God help it, until I heard his voice piercing the uproar, at full screech.

"Three hundred and thirty-three long grains of rice?" he was shouting, "Then get them, idiot! Am I a storekeeper? Fetch a sack from the kitchen – run, you pervert son of a shameless mother!"

Close by the bridgehead was a curious structure like a huge beehive, about ten feet high and built of stone blocks. Before it, in full fig of gold coat, turbaned helmet, and jewelled sword-belt, stood Tej himself – he wasn't above ten yards from the staff conference, but they might have been in Bombay for all the heed each paid to the other. Before him cringed a couple of attendants, a *chico* held a coloured brolly over his head, and at a table near the beehive's entrance an ancient wallah in an enormous *puggaree* was studying charts through a magnifying glass, and making notes. Watching the scene with some amusement was an undoubted European in kepi, shirt-sleeves, and a goatee beard.

That is what I saw, through the drifting smoke and confusion; the following, above the thunder of the great battle in which India was being lost and won, is what I heard – and it's stark truth:

Ancient wallah: The inner circumference is too small! According to the stars, it must be thirteen and a half times the girth of your excellency's belly.

Tej: My belly? What in God's name has my belly to do with it?

A.W.: It is your excellency's shelter, and must be built in relation to your proportions, or the influence of your planets will not sustain it. I must know your circumference, taken precisely about the navel.

European (producing foot-rule): A metre and a half, at least. Here, this is marked in English inches.

Tej: I am to measure my belly, at such a time?

European: What else have you to do? The *sirdars* have the defence in hand, and my fortifications will not be overrun if they are properly manned. By the way, three hundred and

308

thirty-three long grains of rice make about three and a quarter English yards.

A.W. (agitated): The measurement must be exact!

European: A grain of rice may be exact in the stars, astrologer, but not on earth. Anyway, three yards of stone will stop any missile the British are likely to throw at us.

A.W.: Not if the circumference is too small! It must be enlarged –

European (shrugging): Or the general must lose weight.

Tej (enraged): Damn you, Hurbon . . . And who in Satan's name are you, and what do you want?

For by this time Sardul Singh was before him, saluting and then whispering urgently. Tej gave a start, and turned an uncomprehending stare at me, as though I'd been a ghost. Then he recovered, beckoned me urgently, and dived into the beehive.[47] I followed and found myself in a tiny circular chamber, stuffy and stinking from a single oil lamp. Tej wrenched the door to, and the sound of battle died to a distant murmur. He fairly clutched at me, his chops wobbling.

"Is it you, my dear friend? Ah, thank God! Is this thing true? Is there a secret negotiation?"

I told him there wasn't, that it was a lie I'd told Sardul on the spur of the moment, and he let out a great wail of dismay.

"Then what am I to do? I cannot control these madmen! You saw them out yonder – they pretend that I do not exist, and take my command away, the mutinous swine! Sham Singh directs the defence, and your army will be dashed to pieces! I did not seek this engagement! Why, oh why, did Gough sahib force it upon me!" He began to rave and curse, beating his fat fists on the stone. "If the *Jangi lat* is beaten, what will become of me! I am lost! I am lost!" And he subsided on the floor, a quaking blubber in his gold coat, weeping and railing against Gough and Sham Singh and Jeendan and Lal Singh, and anyone else he could call to mind.

I didn't interrupt him. It may have been the sudden quiet of that little refuge, but for the first time in hours I found myself able to think, and was deep in fearful calculation. For here I was, by the strangest turn of fate, prisoner in the heart of the enemy's camp, at the supreme moment of imperial crisis, while all yet hung in the balance – and a small voice in my coward soul was telling me what had to be done. Only to think of the risk set me shaking . . . anyway, it all depended on one thing. I waited until Tej's lamentation reached a high pitch, slid quietly out of the beehive, closed the door, and looked about me, my heart racing.

Everywhere was choking confusion, with visibility a poor twenty yards, but round the command group was a cheering press of Sikhs, dancing and waving *tulwars* – so our first attack had failed, although the pounding of gunfire was as deafening as ever. A horse artillery team came clattering from the bridge; a wounded officer, his blue coat sodden with blood, was being carried past by servants; the European, Hurbon,[48] was mounting a pony and riding off into the smoke; the old astrologer was still muttering over his charts – but the one thing for which I'd been hoping had come to pass: Sardul Singh and his troop, having done their duty by delivering me, were gone. And with all attention directed towards the death-struggle just up the road, no one was paying the least heed to the big Kabuli *badmash* scratching himself furtively outside the Commander-in-Chief's funkhole.

It was my heaven-sent chance to act on the inspiration which had come to me while Tej blubbered at my feet. I braced myself, breathed a silent prayer, took a dozen flying strides, gathering speed as I went, and with one last almighty bound hurled myself from the bank and plunged into the boiling flood of the Sutlej.

According to the *Morning Post*, or the *Keswick Reminder*, I forget which (or it may even have been the *Lincoln, Rutland and Stamford Mercury*) I was pursued by "a horde of furious foes, whose discharges rent the waters about my head," but the truth is that no one saw my "spirited dash for freedom" except a couple of dhobi-wallahs slapping laundry in the shallows (cool hands, those, to be doing the wash while the battle raged), which just shows that you should never trust what you read in the papers. Why, they even credited me with "breaking free from my bonds" and cut-

310

ting down a couple of "swarthy foemen" in the course of my escape "from the jaws of the Seekh Khalsa"; well, I never said so. The facts are as I've stated, and while I may have embroidered 'em a little for Henry Lawrence's benefit, the lurid press accounts were pure gammon. But it's a journalistic law, you see, that heroes can never do anything ordinary; when Flashy, the Hector of Afghanistan, beats a reluctant retreat, there must be an army howling at his heels, or the public cancel their subscriptions.

You, knowing the truth of my inglorious evasion, may cry out in disgust at my desertion in the hour of need; well, good luck to you. I shan't even remark that 'twould have served no purpose to stay, or pretend that if there had been a bomb handy I'd have paused to heave it at the Khalsa's high command before lighting out – someone would have been sure to notice. I was intent only on flight, and the Sutlej called to me; as I ploughed frantically away from the bank I was prepared to drift all the way to Ferozepore if need be, rejoicing in the knowledge that the flood was carrying me beyond the reach of foe and friend alike. And so it might have done, if the river hadn't been swollen seven feet above its normal level, developing currents that bore me almost diagonally to the northern bank; struggle as I might I couldn't stay in midstream, for there was a terrific undertow that kept sucking me down, and it was all I could do to stay afloat. I'm a good swimmer, but a river in spate is a fearsome thing, and I was half-drowned when I found myself in the northern shallows, and struggled, spewing and gasping, on to the muddy shore.

I lay for a couple of minutes, taking breath, and when I peeped out from among the reeds, there before me on the far side was the extreme flank of the Khalsa fortifications, with the bridge of boats a bare half-mile upstream. Which meant that on the bluff directly above me were the Sikh reserve batteries we'd passed through on the way in – and if an idle gunner chanced to look over the edge, there was I, like a fish on a slab.

I burrowed through the reeds, cursing my luck, and crawled into the lee of the bluff, which was about thirty feet

311

high. Above me, just below the overhanging lip, was what looked like a sandy ledge. If I could clamber up to it I should be hidden both from above and below, so I began to climb the almost perpendicular bank, gouging holds in the wet clay. It was heavy going, but my one fear was that at any moment a dusky head would pop over and challenge me. Nearing the top, I could hear them chattering in the emplacements, which fortunately were about twenty yards back from the edge; I scrambled the last few feet with my heart in my mouth, gained the ledge, and was overjoyed to find that it extended back a good yard beneath the overhang; in two shakes I was prone beneath the lip, safe hidden but with a clear view for a mile upriver and across the Khalsa position on the southern shore. And there before my eyes was the great Battle of Sobraon.

Any soldier will tell you that, in the heat of a fight, sights and sounds imprint themselves on your memory and stay vivid for fifty years . . . but you lose all sense of time. I can still *see* George Paget's cheroot clamped in his teeth as he leaned from the saddle to haul me to my feet in the Balaclava battery; I can *hear* Custer's odd little cough as he rocked back on his heels with the blood trickling over his lip – but how long those actions lasted, God alone knows. Balaclava was twenty minutes, they tell me, and Greasy Grass about fifteen – well, I was through both, start to finish, and I'd have put them at an hour at least. At Sobraon, where admittedly I was more spectator than actor, it was t'other way round. From the moment Sardul and I rode down to the bridge, to the time I reached my ledge, I'd have reckoned half an hour at most; in fact it was between two hours and three, and in that space, while Tej was bickering about the size of his hideyhole, and I was swallowing the Sutlej by the gallon, Sobraon was being lost and won. This is how it was.

The attack by our left wing, which I'd witnessed, had been beaten back with heavy loss. Our advance on the other flank and centre had been intended as a feint, but when Paddy saw our left come adrift he changed the feint into a pukka assault, through a murderous hail of fire; somehow our men

312

survived it and stormed the Sikh defences along almost the whole curved front of two and a half miles, and for nigh on an hour it was a hideous hacking-match over the ditches and ramparts. Our people were repulsed time and again, but still they forged ahead, British and Indian bayonets and Gurkha knives against the *tulwars*, with shocking slaughter; no manoeuvring or scientific soldiering, but hand-to-hand butchery – that was fighting as Paddy Gough understood it, and weren't the Sikhs ready to oblige him?

They fought like madmen – and perhaps that was their undoing, for whenever an attack was beaten back they leaped down into the ditches to mutilate our wounded. Well, you don't do that to Atkins and Sepoy and Gurkha if you know what's good for you; our people stormed back at 'em in a killing rage, and when the scaling-ladders wouldn't reach they climbed on each other's shoulders and on the piled dead, and fairly pitchforked the Sikhs out of their first line entrenchments, almost without firing a shot. Good bayonet fighters will beat swordsmen and spearmen every time, and they ran the Sikhs back over two furlongs of rough ground to the second line, where the Khalsa gunners made a stand – and then Paddy showed that he was a bit of a general as well as a hooligan.

From my eyrie to the Sikhs' second line was a bare half-mile, and I could see their gunners plain as day, for the wind was streaming their smoke away downriver. They were working their field pieces and camel-swivels and musketry until they must have been red-hot; the line looked as though it was on fire, so constant was the roar of the discharges, sweeping the ground and almost blotting out in a dust-storm the outer entrenchments from which our infantry and horse-guns were trying to advance. Between the Sikhs' second line and the river the Khalsa horse and foot were re-forming in their thousands, preparing to counter-attack if the chance arose. Gough made sure it never did.

Directly across from me there was a sudden colossal explosion in the flank entrenchments of the second line; bodies were flying like dolls, a field-gun went cartwheeling end over end, and a huge pillar of dust arose, like a genie

313

from a bottle. As it cleared I saw that our sappers had driven a great cleft in the ramparts, and through it who should come trotting but old Joe Thackwell, as easy as though he were in the Row, with a single file of 3rd Lights at his heels, wheeling into line as they cleared the gap. Behind them were the blue *puggarees* and white pants of the Bengali Irregulars, and before the Sikhs knew what was up Joe was rising in his stirrups, waving his sabre, and the 3rd Lights were sweeping down the *rear* of the gun positions, brushing aside the supporting infantry, sabring and riding down everything in their path. In a moment the rear of the second line was a turmoil of men and horses, with the sabres rising and falling in the sunlight, and into it the Bengalis drove like a thunderbolt. Farther down the line our infantry were pouring over the ramparts, a wave of red coats and bayonets, and all in a moment the whole line had caved in, and the Khalsa battalions were falling back to the third line of entrenchments a bare two hundred yards from the river. They weren't running, though; they retired like guardsmen, pouring volley after volley into our advance, while the Bengalis and Dragoons harried them front and flank, and our horse-guns came careering through the outer lines to unlimber and turn their fire on the doomed Sikh army.

For it was done at last. Solid as a rock it looked as it stood in the elbow of the river, squares formed, squadrons ordered, standards raised, and the ground before it heaped with its dead – but it was hemmed in by an enemy who had overcome odds of three to two by sheer refusal to be stopped . . . and it had lost its guns. Now, as the horse artillery and field pieces cut great lanes in its ranks, it could reply only with musketry and steel to the charges of our horse and the steady advance of our infantry; it swayed and fell back, almost step by step, contesting every inch – and I looked to see the standards come down in token of surrender. But they didn't. The Khalsa, the Pure, was dying on its feet, with its *sirdars* and generals scrambling up on the broken entrenchments, willing it to stand firm. I even made out the tall figure of the old war-horse I'd seen directing the high command; he was up on a shattered gun carriage, his white robes

314

gleaming in the sunlight, shield on arm and *tulwar* raised, like some spirit of the Khalsa, and then the smoke enveloped him, and when it cleared, he was gone.[49]

Then they broke. It was like a dyke bursting, with first a trickle of men making for the river, and then the main body giving back, and suddenly that magnificent host that I'd gaped at on Maian Mir had dissolved into a mass of fugitives pouring back to the bridge of boats, spilling into the river on either side of it, or trying to escape along the banks. In a few moments the whole length of the bridge was jammed with struggling men and horses and even gun-teams, vainly trying to win across; the sheer weight of them and the force of the stream caused the great line of barges to bend downriver like a gigantic bow drawn to the limit. It swayed to and fro, half-submerged, with the brown water boiling over it like a weir, and then it snapped, the two ends surged apart, and the milling thousands were pitched into the flood.

In an instant the whole width of the river beneath me was alive with men and beasts and wreckage, sweeping past. It was like a lumber-jam when great areas of the water cannot be seen for the whirling mass of logs, but here the logs were men and horses and a great tangle of gear bound together by the force of the current. Upturned barges, black with men clinging to them, were dashed against each other, rolling over and over to be lost in the spray or flung onto the mudbanks; for the first time above the din of the firing I could hear human sounds, the shrieks of wounded and drowning men. Some may have lived through that first appalling maelstrom when the bridge gave way, but not many, for even as they were carried downstream our horse artillery were tearing along the southern shore, unlimbering, and wheeling their pieces to rake the river from bank to bank with grape and canister, churning it into a foaming slaughterhouse. The Yankees talk of "shooting fish in a barrel"; that was the fate of the Khalsa, floundering and helpless, in the Sutlej. Farther up, beyond the bridge, the carnage was even worse, for there the water was shallower, and as the great close-packed mass of fugitives struggled neck-deep to cross the ford they were caught in a murderous

315

cross-fire of musketry and artillery. Even those who managed to reach the north bank were caught in the deadly hail of grape as they struggled ashore, and only a few, I'm told, managed to scramble away to safety.

Below me, bodies both still and struggling were being borne past or swept ashore by a brown tide hideously streaked with red, while the shot lashed the water around them; close to the shore, where the current bore in most strongly, the Sutlej was running blood.

Directly across from my position, I could see the red coats of our infantry, British and Indian, lining the banks, firing as fast as they could load; among them were horse-guns and captured camel-swivels pouring their fire into the stricken wreck of an army. Shots were slapping into the bank below me, and I huddled back into my refuge, flat on my face and instinctively clawing the soil as though to burrow into it. How long it lasted, I can't say; ten minutes, perhaps, and then that hellish cannonade began to slacken, a bugle on the far side was blowing the cease-fire, and gradually the guns fell silent, and the only sound in my half-deafened ears was the river rushing past.

I lay for a good half-hour, too shaken to drag myself from the bosom of Mother Earth, and then I inched my way forward on the ledge and looked down. Below me, as far as I could see on either hand, the shore was thick with corpses, some on the bank itself, others washing to and fro in the crimson shallows, more drifting by on the current. Out in the stream, the low mud-banks were covered with them. Here and there a few were stirring, but I don't recall hearing a single cry; that was the uncanny part of it, for on every other battle-field I've seen there's been a ceaseless chorus of screams and wails above the groaning hum of the wounded and dying. Here, there was nothing but the swish of the stream through the reeds. I lay, staring down in the noon sunlight, too used up to move, and by and by there were no more bodies drifting down from the upper ford and the shattered bridgeheads and the smoking lines of Sobraon. Then the vultures came, but you won't care to hear of that, and I didn't care to watch; I closed my stinging eyes and

316

rested my head on my arms, listening to the distant thump of explosions from the other shore as the fires burning in the Sikh lines reached the abandoned magazines. The hutments at the bridgehead were burning, too, and the smoke was hanging low over the river.

If you wonder why I continued to lie there, it was part exhaustion, but mostly caution. I knew there must be some survivors on my side of the water, doubtless full of spleen and resentment, and I'd no wish to meet them. There was no sound from the reserve positions behind me, and I imagined the Sikh gunners had taken their leave, but I wasn't stirring until I was sure of a clear coast and friends at hand. I doubted if our lot would cross the river today; John Company would be dog-tired, binding his wounds, taking off his boots, and thanking God that was the end of it.

For it was over now, no question. In most wars, you see, killing is only the means to a political end, but in the Sutlej campaign it was an end in itself. The war had been fought to destroy the Khalsa, root and branch, and the result was lying in uncounted thousands on the banks below Sobraon. The Sikh rulers and leaders had engineered it, John Company had executed it . . . and the Khalsa had gone to the sacrifice. Well, *salaam Khalsa-ji. Sat-sree-akal.* High time, mind you.

"For that little boy. And for their salt." Gardner's words came back to me as I lay on that sandy ledge, letting the pictures of memory have their way, as they will on the edge of sleep . . . the bearded faces of those splendid battalions, in review at Maian Mir, and swinging down to the war through the Moochee Gate . . . Imam Shah staring down at the petticoat draped across his boot . . . Maka Khan grim and straight while the *panches* roared behind him . . . "To Delhi! To London!" . . . that raging Akali, arm outflung in denunciation . . . Sardul Singh shouting with excitement as we rode to the river . . . the old *rissaldar-major*, tears streaming down his face . . .

. . . and a red and gold houri wantoning it in her durbar, teasing them in her cups, cajoling them, winning them, so that she could betray them to this butchery . . . standing half-naked above the bleeding rags of her brother's body,

317

sword in hand . . . "I will throw the snake in your bosom!"
Well, she'd done all of that. Jawaheer was paid for.

And if you ask me what she'd have thought if she could
have gazed into some magic crystal that day, and seen the
result of her handiwork along the banks of the Sutlej . . .
well, I reckon she'd have smiled, drunk another slow
draught, stretched, and called in Rai and the Python.

They say ten thousand Khalsa died in the Sutlej. Well, I didn't mind, and I still don't. They started it, and hell mend them, as old Colin Campbell used to say. And if you tell me that every man's death diminishes me, I'll retort that it diminishes him a hell of a sight more, and if he's a Khalsa Sikh, serve him right.

Knowing me, you won't marvel at my callousness, but you may wonder why Paddy Gough, as kindly an old stick as ever patted a toddler's head, hammered 'em so mercilessly when they were beat and running. Well, he had good reasons, one being that you don't let up on a courageous adversary until he hollers "Uncle!", which the Sikhs ain't inclined to do – and I wouldn't trust 'em if they did. Nor do you feel much charity towards an enemy who never takes prisoners, and absolutely enjoys chopping up wounded, as happened at Sobraon and Ferozeshah both. Even if Gough had wanted to stop the slaughter, I doubt if anyone would have heeded him.[50]

But the best reason for murdering the Khalsa was that if enough of the brutes had escaped, the whole beastly business would have been to do again, with consequent loss of British and Sepoy lives. That's something the moralists overlook (or more likely don't give a dam' about) when they cry: "Pity the beaten foe!" What they're saying, in effect, is: "Kill our fellows tomorrow rather than the enemy today." But they don't care to have it put to them like that; they want their wars won clean and comfortable, with a clear conscience. (Their consciences being much more precious than their own soldiers' lives, you understand.) Well, that's fine, if you're sitting in the Liberal Club with a bellyful of port on top of your dinner, but if you rang the bell and it was answered not by a steward with a napkin but an Akali with a *tulwar*, you might change your mind. Distance always lends enlightenment to the view, I've noticed.

Being uncomfortable close, myself, my one concern when I'd slept the night away was to slide out in safety and rejoin the army. The difficulty was that when I crawled out of my refuge and stood up, I tumbled straight down again and almost rolled over the ledge. I had another go, with the same result, and realised that my head ached, I felt shockingly ill and dizzy, I was sweating like an Aden collier, and some infernal Sutlej bug was performing a polka in my lower bowels. Dysentery, in fact, which can be anything from fatal to a damned nuisance, but even at best leaves you weak as a rat, which is inconvenient when the nearest certain help is twenty miles away. For while I could hear our bugles playing Charlie, Charlie across the river, I wasn't fit to holler above a whimper, let alone swim.

By moving mostly on hands and knees I made a cautious scout of the emplacements on the bank behind me; luckily they were empty, the Sikh reserve having decamped, taking their guns with them. But that was small consolation, and I was considering the wild notion of crawling down to the corpse-littered bank, finding a piece of timber, and floating down to Ferozepore *ghat*, when out of the dawn mist came the prettiest sight I'd seen that year – the blue tunics and red *puggarees* of a troop of Native Cavalry, with a pink little cornet at their head. I waved and yelped feebly, and when I'd convinced him that I wasn't a fugitive *gorrachar'* and received the inevitable, heart-warming response ("Not Flashman – Flashman of Afghanistan, surely? Well, bless me!") we got along famously.

They were 8th Lights from Grey's division which had been watching the river at Attaree, and had been ordered across the previous night as soon as Gough knew he had the battle won. More of our troops were invading over the Ferozepore ghat and Nuggur Ford, for Paddy was in a sweat to secure the northern bank and tidy up the remnants of the Khalsa before they could get up to mischief. Ten thousand had got away from Sobraon, with all their reserve guns, and there

320

were rumoured to be another twenty thousand up Amritsar way, as well as the hill garrisons – far more than we had in the field ourselves.

"But they ain't worth a button now!" cries my pink lad. "The shave is that their *sirdars* have hooked it, and they're quite without supplies or ammunition. And the hidin' they got yesterday will have knocked all the puff out of 'em, I dare say," he added regretfully. "I say, were you in the thick of it? Lor', don't I just wish I'd had your luck! Of all the beastly sells, to be ploddin' up an' down on river patrol, and not so much as a smell of a Sikh the whole time! What I'd give for a cut at the rascals!"

Between his babble and having to totter into the bushes every half-mile while the troop tactfully looked the other way, I was in poor trim by the time we reached Nuggur Ford, where they slung me a hammock in a makeshift hospital *basha*, and a native medical orderly filled me with jalap. I gave my little fire-eater a note to be forwarded to Lawrence, wherever he was, describing my whereabouts and condition, and after a couple of days in that mouldering hovel, watching the lizards scuttle along the musty beams and wishing I were dead, received the following reply:

> Political Department,
> Camp, Kussoor.
> February 13, 1846.

> My dear Flashman – I rejoice that you are safe, and trust that when this reaches you, your indisposition will have mended sufficiently to enable you to join me here without delay. The matter is urgent. Yrs & c,
> II. M. Lawrence.

It gave me qualms, I can tell you; "urgent matters" were the last thing I needed just then. But it was reassuring, too, for there was no reference to my Dalip fiasco, and I guessed that Goolab had lost no time in advising Lawrence and Hardinge that he was looking after the lad like a mother hen. Still, I hadn't covered myself with glory, and knowing Hardinge's dislike of me it was surprising to find myself in

321

such demand; I'd have thought he'd be happy to keep me at arm's length until the peace settlement was concluded. I knew too much about the whole Punjabi mischief for anyone's comfort, and now that they'd be patching it all up to mutual satisfaction and profit, with lofty humbug couched in fair terms, neither side would want to be reminded of all the intrigue and knavery that had been consummated at Moodkee and Ferozeshah and Sobraon; things would be easier all round if the prime agent in the whole foul business wasn't leering coyly at the back of the durbar tent when they signed the peace.

And it wasn't just that I'd be a spectre at the diplomatic feast. I suspected that Hardinge's aversion to me was rooted in a feeling that I spoiled the picture he had in mind of the whole Sikh War. My face didn't fit; it was a blot on the landscape, all the more disfiguring because he knew it belonged there. I believe he dreamed of some noble canvas, for exhibition in the great historic gallery of public approval – a true enough picture, mind you, of British heroism and faith unto death in the face of impossible odds; aye, and of gallantry by that stubborn enemy who died on the Sutlej. Well, you know what I think of heroism and gallantry, but I recognise 'em as only a born coward can. But they would be there, rightly, on the noble canvas, with Hardinge stern and forbearing, planting a magisterial boot on a dead Sikh and raising a penitent, awe-struck Dalip by the hand, while Gough (off to one side) addressed heaven with upraised sword before a background of cannon-smoke and resolute Britons bayoneting gnashing niggers and Mars and Mother India floating overhead in suitable draperies. Dam' fine.

Well, you can't mar a spectacle like that with a *Punch* cartoon border of Flashy rogering dusky damsels and spying and conniving dirty deals with Lal and Tej, can you now?

However, Lawrence's summons had to be obeyed, so I struggled from my bed of pain, removed my beard, obtained a clean set of civilian linens, hastened down to Ferozepore by river barge, and tooled up to Kussoor looking pale and interesting, with a cushion on my saddle.

While I'd been laid up with the dolorous skitters, Gough

and Hardinge had been prosecuting the peace with vigour. Paddy had the whole army north of the Sutlej within three days of Sobraon, and Lawrence had been in touch with Goolab, who now figured it was safe to accept openly the Wazirship which the Khalsa had been pressing on him, and come forward to negotiate on their behalf. There were still upward of thirty thousand of them under arms, you remember, and Hardinge was on fire to come to terms before the brutes could work up a new head of steam. For it was a ticklish position, politically: we simply hadn't the men and means, as Paddy had pointed out, to conquer the Punjab; what was needed was a treaty that would give us effective control, dissolve the last remnants of the Khalsa, and keep Goolab, Jeendan, and the rest of the noble scavengers content. So Hardinge, with a speed and zeal which would have been useful months ago, had his terms cut and dried and ready to shove down Goolab's throat a mere five days after the war ended.

Kussoor lies a bare thirty miles from Lahore, and Hardinge had installed himself and his retinue in tents near the old town, with the army encamped on the plain around. As I trotted through the lines I could feel that air of contented elation that comes at the end of a campaign: the men are tired, and would like to sleep for a year, but they don't want to miss the warm feeling of survival and comradeship, so they lie blinking in the sun, or rouse themselves to skylark and play leapfrog. I remember the Lancers at baseball, and a young gunner sitting on a limber, licking his pencil and writing to the dictation of a farrier-sergeant with his arm in a sling: ". . . an' tell Sammy 'is Dad 'as got a Sikh sword wot 'e shall 'ave if 'e's bin good, an' a silk shawl for 'is Mum – stay, make that 'is dear Mum an' my best gel . . ." Sepoys were at drill, groups of fellows in vests and overalls were boiling their billies on the section fires, the long tent-lines and ruined mosques drowsed in the heat, the bugles sounded in the distance, the reek of native cooking wafted down from the host of camp-followers, fifty thousand of them, camped beyond the artillery park, somewhere a colour sergeant was waking the echoes, and a red-haired ruffian with a black eye

323

was tied to a gun-wheel for field punishment, exchanging genial abuse with his mates. I stopped for a word with Bob Napier the sapper,[51] who had his easel up and was painting a Bengali *sowar* sweating patiently in full fig of blue coat, red sash, and white breeches, but took care to avoid Grave-digger Havelock, who sat reading outside his tent (the Book of Job, most likely). It was all calm and lazy; after sixty days of fire and fury, in which they'd held the gates of India, the Army of the Sutlej was at peace.

They'd earned it. There were 1400 fewer of them than there had been, and 5000 wounded in the Ferozepore bar-racks; against that, they'd killed 16,000 Punjabis and broken the best army east of Suez. There was a great outcry at home, by the way, over our losses; having seen the savagery of two of the four battles, and knowing the quality of the enemy, I'd say we were lucky the butcher's bill was so small – with Paddy in charge it was nothing short of a miracle.

If there was an unbuttoned air about the troops, head-quarters resembled Horse Guards during a fire alarm. Hardinge had just issued a proclamation to say that the war was over, it had all been the Sikhs' fault, we desired no extension of territory and were fairly bursting with pacific forbearance, but if the local rulers didn't co-operate to rescue the state from anarchy, H.M.G. would have to make "other arrangements", so there. In consequence, messen-gers scurried, clerks sweated, armies of bearers ran about with everything from refreshments to furniture, and bouquets of new young aides lounged about looking bored. No doubt I'm uncharitable, but I've noticed that as soon as the last shot's fired, platoons of these exquisites arrive as by magic, vaguely employed, haw-hawing *fortissimo*, pinching the gin to make "cock-tails", and stinking of pomade. There was a group outside Lawrence's tent, all guffaws and fly-whisks.

"I say, you, feller," says one. "Can't go in there. Major ain't receivin' civilians today."

"Oh, please, sir," says I, uncovering, "it's most awfully important, you know."

"If you're sellin' spirits," says he, "go an' see the – what

324

d'ye call him, Tommy? Oh, yaas, the *khansamah* – the butler to you, Snooks."

"Who shall I say sent me?" says I, humbly. "Major Lawrence's door-keepers?"

"Mind your manners, my man!" cries he. "Who the devil are you, anyway?"

"Flashman," says I, and enjoyed seeing them gape. "No, no, don't get up – you might land on your arse. And speaking of butlers, why don't you go and help Baxu polish the spoons?"

I felt better after that, and better still when Lawrence, at first sight of me, dismissed his office-wallahs and shook hands as though he meant it. He was leaner and more harassed than ever, in his shirt-sleeves at a table littered with papers and maps, but he listened intently to the recital of my adventures (in which I made no mention whatever of Jassa), and dismissed my failure to deliver Dalip as of no account. "Not your fault," snaps he, in his curt style. "Goolab writes that the boy is well – that's all that matters. Anyway, that's past. My concern is the future – and what I have to tell you is under the rose. Clear?" He fixed me with that gimlet eye, pushed out his lantern jaw, and pitched in.

"Sir Henry Hardinge doesn't like you, Flashman. He thinks you're a whippersnapper, too independent, and careless of authority. Your conduct in the war – with which I'm well pleased, let me tell you – doesn't please *him*. 'Broadfoot antics', you understand. I may tell you that when he learned that Goolab had got the boy, he spoke of court-martialling you. Even wondered if you had acted in collusion with Gardner. That's the curse of Indian politics, they make you suspect everyone. Anyway, I soon disabused him." For an instant I'll swear the dour horse face was triumphant, then he was glowering again. "At all events, he doesn't care for you, or regard you as reliable."

My own sentiments about Hardinge exactly, but I held my peace.

"Now, Goolab Singh comes here tomorrow, to learn the treaty terms – and I'm sending you to meet him and conduct him into camp. That's why I summoned you. You have the

325

old fox's confidence, if anyone does, and I wish that to be seen and known. Especially by Sir Henry. He mayn't like it, but I want him to understand that you are necessary. Is that clear?"

I said it was, but why?

"Because when this treaty is settled – I can't tell you the terms; they're secret until Goolab hears them – it is likely that a British presence will be required at Lahore, with a Resident, to keep the durbar on a tight rein. I'll be that Resident – and I want you as my chief assistant."

Coming from the great Henry, I guess it was as high a compliment as Wellington's handshake, or one of Elspeth's ecstatic moans. But it was so unexpected, and ridiculous, that I almost laughed aloud.

"That's why I'm putting you forward now. Goolab will be the *éminence grise*, and if he is seen to respect and trust you, it will help me to win the G.G. over to your appointment." He gave a sour grin. "They don't call us politicals for nothing. I'll have to persuade Currie, too, and the rest of the Calcutta wallahs. But I'll manage it."

When I think of the number of eminent men – and women – who have taken me at face value, and formed a high opinion of my character and abilities, it makes me tremble for my country's future. I mean, if they can't spot *me* as a wrong 'un, who can they spot? Still, it's pleasant to be well thought of, and has made my fortune, at the expense of some hellish perils – and minor difficulties such as conveying tactfully to Henry Lawrence that I wouldn't have touched his disgusting proposal with a long pole. My prime reason being that I was sick to loathing of India, and the service, the Sikhs, and bloody carnage and deadly danger, and being terrified and bullied and harried and *used*, when all I wanted was the fleshpots of home, and bulling Elspeth and civilised women, and never to stir out of England again. I daren't tell him that, but fortunately there was a way out.

"That's most kind of you, sir," says I. "I'm honoured, 'deed I am. But I'm afraid I have to decline."

"What's that you say?" He was bristling in an instant; ready to fight with his own shadow if it contradicted him, was H.M.L.

326

"I can't stay in the Punjab, sir. And now that the war's over, I intend to go home."

"Do you indeed? And may I ask why?" He was fairly boiling.

"It's not easy to explain, sir. I'd take it as a favour . . . if you'd just allow me to decline – with regret, I assure you – "

"I'll do no such thing! Can't stay in the Punjab, indeed!" He calmed abruptly, eyeing me. "Is this because of Hardinge?"

"No, sir, not at all. I'm simply applying to be sent home."

He sat back, tapping a finger. "You've never shirked – so there must be a good reason for this . . . this nonsense! Come, man – what is it? Out with it!"

"Very well, sir – since you press me." I figured it was time to explode my mine. "The fact is, you ain't the only one who wants me at Lahore. There is a lady there . . . who has intentions – honourable, of course – and . . . well, it won't do, you see. She's – "

"Good God!" I'm probably the only man who ever made Henry Lawrence take the name of the Lord in vain. "Not the Maharani?"

"Yes, sir. She's made it perfectly plain, I'm afraid. And I'm married, you know." For some reason, God knows what, I added: "Mrs Flashman wouldn't like it a bit."

He didn't say anything for about three minutes – d'you know, I'm sure the blighter was absolutely wondering what advantage there might be to having the Queen Mother of the Punjab panting for his assistant. They're all alike, these blasted politicals. Finally, he shook his head, and said he took my point, but while it ruled out Lahore, there was no reason why I should not be employed elsewhere –

"No, sir," says I, firmly. "I'm going home. If necessary, I'll sell out." Perhaps it was that I hadn't got over my illness, but I was sick and tired and ready for a stand-up fight if he wanted one. I think he sensed it, for he became quite reasonable, and said he would see to it. He wasn't a bad chap, you know, and quite half-human, as he showed towards the end of our conversation.

327

"I can see that you might furnish me with material for another romantic novel," says he, looking whimsical. "Tell me: is the lady as personable as they say?"

He wasn't the only one to ask me that kind of question. It has been my fate to make the acquaintance of several mysterious beauties who excited the randy interest of my superiors – I recall Elgin going quite pink with curiosity about the Empress of China, and the gleam in the eyes of Colin Campbell and Hugh Rose when they cross-examined me about the Rani of Jhansi. Lincoln and Palmerston, too. I told Lawrence she was a little stunner, but given to alcoholic excess, and on no account to be trusted – political information, you see, but no lascivious details. He said he'd be interested to meet her, and I advised him that Gardner was his man.[52]

"You'll conduct Goolab Singh, at least," says he, which I didn't mind, since it was sure to infuriate Hardinge, and the next afternoon found me trotting out along the Lahore road, in uniform again, to meet the elephant train bringing the Khalsa emissaries down from Loolianee. Lawrence had told me that they were to be shown no ceremony, and I should wait about half a mile out and let them come to me, for form's sake. But they halted a good mile from the town, and I could see the mahouts picketing the beasts and tents being raised for the *sirdars*, while a small body of *gorracharra* mounted guard about them; I continued to sit my pony, waiting, and presently I saw a solitary horseman cantering down towards me, and it was Goolab himself. He gave a wave and a great bellow of "*Salaam*, soldier!" as he drew rein alongside, grinning all over his rogue's red face, and taking my hand. To my surprise he was wearing no armour or finery, only a simple robe and turban.

"It is not for the envoy of a beaten foe to come in state and pride!" says he. "I am but a poor suppliant, seeking mercy from the *Malki lat*, and so I dress the part. And a single soldier comes to meet me – albeit a distinguished one. Ah, well, these are hard times."

I asked him where Dalip was. "In good hands. A wilful child, who shows me no respect; he has been too much

328

among women, so doubtless they will be his downfall some day. Presently I shall bring him – leading him by the hand, remember?" He chuckled and looked sly. "But only when the treaty is agreed beyond peradventure; until then I keep the bird in my hand."

We were moving at a walk towards the Kussoor lines, for he seemed in no hurry; indeed, for a man bound on a delicate embassy he was uncommon carefree, joking and making small talk, with an air of great contentment. Only when I mentioned that I'd be going home in a day or two, did he rein up in astonishment.

"But why? When fortune awaits you here? No – not that royal slut in Lahore Fort! Gurdana has told me of that; you would not be such a fool! As well mate with a krait. But in Kashmir, with me!" He was grinning and frowning together. "Did you doubt me, when I promised you a golden future yonder? Regiments to command, a general's rank, lordships and revenues – Gurdana has accepted already! Aye, he leaves Lahore, to come to me! And why should not you? Is the Bloody Lance of Afghanistan less of a soldier than Gurdana, or that dog-dirt Harlan, who lorded it under Runjeet, or Avitabile and the rest?" He struck me on the shoulder. "And we have stood up together, you and I – and who stands with Goolab has a friend!"

If that was how he remembered our scuffle in the Lahore alleys, let him – but wasn't there a movement to recruit Flashy these days, just? Reputation and credit, there's no currency to touch them. Lawrence, Goolab . . . even a queen setting her cap at me. Aye, but they ain't home. I thanked him, explaining politely that I wasn't a soldier of fortune, and he shook his head, threw up his great shoulders, and let it go. I asked him if he was so sure of getting Kashmir, and he said it was in the treaty. It was my turn to stare.

"But the terms are secret – you don't know 'em yet!"

"Do I not? Oh, not from Lawence Sahib, or any of your people." He rumbled with laughter. "Is this the Punjab, and shall I not know what passes? A treaty of sixteen articles, whereby the durbar will give up to Britain the Sutlej

329

banks, and the Jullundur Doab, and keep only a *kutch-**
Khalsa of a mere 20,000 bayonets and 12,000 horse, and pay
a mighty indemnity of a million and a half sterling . . ." He
burst out laughing at my amazement. "You need not tell
Lawrence Sahib and the *Malki lat* that I know it all – let
them sleep at nights! But if you should, it is no matter – they
will keep the bargain, because it is all they need – a rich
province of the Punjab, to punish us and show the world the
folly of challenging the Sirkar; a tiny, feeble Khalsa – oh,
aye, to be commanded by that lion among warriors, Tej
Singh, with Lal as Wazir; and a submissive durbar to do your
bidding, with Dalip and his mother obedient puppets –
handsomely subsidised, to be sure. So the Punjab remains .
free – but its mistress is the White Queen."

I didn't doubt his information – in a land of spies there are
no secrets. And it was the best of bargains for us: control
without conquest. One thing, though, I couldn't see.

"How on earth is the Lahore durbar to pay a fine of a
million and a half? They're bankrupt, ain't they?"

"Assuredly. So, having no money, they will pay in kind –
by ceding Kashmir and the hill country to the British."

"And we'll give you Kashmir, for services rendered?"

He sighed. "No . . . you will *sell* me Kashmir, for half a
million. Your countrymen don't overlook opportunities for
profit. And they say the Jews are sharp! The price is *not*
mentioned in the treaty – nor is another item which is to be
surrendered as a token of Punjabi good faith and loyalty."

"What's that?"

"You have heard of our Mountain of Light – Koh-i-Noor,
the great diamond of Golconda? Well, that too is to be taken
from us, as a trophy for your Queen."

"Ye don't say? Her Majesty's share of the loot, eh? Well,
well!"

"Let her have it," says Goolab magnanimously. "To the
strong, the prize. And to the patient, gold-bought slave . . .
Kashmir."

Hardinge evidently hadn't been warned that I was infest-

*Inferior.

330

ing headquarters again, for he started visibly when I ushered Goolab into the big durbar tent, and darted an indignant glance at Lawrence. There was a fine gallery, including Mackeson, who had narrowly lost the Agent's post to Lawrence after Broadfoot's death; Currie, the government secretary; and any number of "Calcutta wallahs", as Lawrence had called them. As I presented "His Highness, the Raja Goolab Singh", I could almost read Hardinge's mind: conspiracy, he was thinking, the little bugger's been wangling a 99-year lease on the Khyber Pass. He was all frost and dignity to Goolab, who truckled like a good 'un, leaning on a stick and making much of his gouty foot in the hope of being asked to sit, which he wasn't; Hardinge returned his greeting with a formal statement conveying (but without saying so, for he was a dab hand at diplomatic chat) that the terms which he would shortly hear had been designed to cut the Punjab down to size, and they could think themselves lucky to get off so lightly. He then turned the old chief over to Currie and Lawrence, who would explain the treaty, and they took him off. Hardinge gave me another cold glare, and for a moment I thought he was going to address me, but he changed his mind; from the way the Calcutta toadies sniffed and eyed me askance I could see that the word was out that Flashy was a Bad Penny, so I lit a cheroot, hoping to be rebuked; I wasn't, so I tooled out to take the air.

Lawrence had told me that morning that I should go down to Umballa the following day (and so home, thank God!), so when I left the durbar I made a few calls, to collect letters and any trinkets that my comrades might want transported – quicker and safer than the Army post, you see. There was general lamentation at my departure (for as Thomas Hughes has told you, I had a gift of popularity), and dear old Paddy Gough absolutely called me into his command tent and insisted on my having a glass with him.

"The best men always get kilt, or married, or retire!" says he, pledging me. "Ye've done the last two, Flashman, my son – here's wishin' you never do the first! Which reminds me – did ye give that neckercher back after Ferozeshah? Ye did nott, ye light-fingered young divil! Would ye believe it, Smith – a staff galloper that plunders his own gineral's effects in the presence o' the inimy? He did, though! Ye nivver saw the like o' that in the Peninsula, I'll be bound!"

This was to Harry Smith, looking more like Wellington than usual. "Never trust a political," says he. "Health, Flashman." And as they drank, d'ye know, I felt quite moved, for Paddy had been having some conference or other, and his marquee was full of leading men – Joe Thackwell, and Gilbert with his arm in a sling from Sobraon, and the Gravedigger, and younger fellows like Edwardes, and Johnny Nicholson, and Rake Hodson, and Hope Grant. Well, 'tisn't every day you have your health drunk by chaps like those.[53]

Their talk was all of Sobraon, of course: the Gravedigger had had his *fifth* horse of the campaign shot out from under him, and Thackwell said they'd have to start charging him for remounts; Harry Smith said it was the fourth worst scrap he'd ever been in, the first three being Waterloo, Badajoz, and New Orleans, in that order, which set them arguing; old M'Gregor, the poultice-walloper, enthralled me with a charming dissertation on the different effects on the frame of a musket ball and a grapeshot, with a tasteful description of knee-wounds;[54] and I made them laugh with my account of Tej Singh's funkhole, and a modestly doctored version of my escape across the Sutlej.

"An' I thought it was just Sikhs we were shootin' at!" cries Hodson. "Oh, Flashy, if only we'd known!"

And in the midst of all the noise and laughter who should come mincing in but the little squirt of an aide with whom I'd bandied words outside Lawrence's tent the day before. In that company you'd have thought he'd have slipped in quietly, but he was fresh from Eton or Addiscombe or one of those shops, for he marched straight up to Paddy's table, took off his hat, and in a shrill voice asked permission to deliver a message from the Governor-General. No compliments, or anything of the sort, but Paddy, at ease with his glass, and supposing it was for him, told him to fire away. The squirt turned to me with a malicious glint in his eye.

"Mr Flashman!" squeaks he, and as he spoke the chatter died away altogether. "Sir Henry Hardinge understands that you are leaving the Army of the Sutlej tomorrow. He instructs me to tell you that your services are no longer required on his personal staff, and that you are to consider yourself withdrawn from all military and political duties forthwith. I am also to remind you that smoking in the durbar tent is strictly prohibited."

There wasn't a sound for a moment, except M'Gregor's wheezing. Then someone said "Good God!" And I, dumbfounded by that deliberate insult, uttered in the presence of the flower of the Army, somehow found the wit to reply quietly.

"My compliments to the Governor-General," says I, "and my thanks for his courtesy. That's all. You can go."

He couldn't, though. While everyone, after a stunned pause, was talking to his neighbour loudly as though nothing had happened, the Gravedigger was looming over the squirt like an avenging angel.

"Boy!" thunders he, and I'll swear the lad quivered. "Are you lost to propriety? Are you unaware that a personal communication is delivered in private? Outside, sir, this instant! And when you have purged your insolence, you may return, to offer your apology to this officer, and to the Commander-in-Chief! Now – go!"

"I was told –" pipes the oaf.

"Do you defy me?" roars Havelock. "Go!"

And he went, leaving me with my cheeks burning, and black rage inside me. To be spoken to, in that company, by a niddering green from the nursery, and not a thing to be done about it. But it couldn't have happened before better men; in a moment they were laughing and prosing away, and Gough gave me a grin and a shake of the head. Harry Smith got to his feet, and as he passed out he clapped my arm and whispered: "Hardinge never intended that, you know." And Johnny Nicholson and Hodson rallied round, and M'Gregor told a joke about amputations.

Looking back, I don't blame Hardinge, altogether. With all his faults, he knew what was fitting, and I don't doubt

333

that, in his irritation at seeing me to the fore with Goolab, he had muttered something like: "That damned pup is everywhere! Leaving tomorrow, is he? Not before time! Tell him he's suspended from duty, before he does any more mischief! And smoking, too, as though he were in a pot-house!" And Charlie, or someone, passed it on, and the squirt was given the message, and thought to hand me a set-down. He knew no better. Aye, but Hardinge should have seen that the thing was done decently – dammit, he could have sent for me himself, and coupled rebuke with a word of thanks for my services, whether he meant it or not. But he hadn't, and his creature had made me look a fool. Well, perhaps two could play at that game.

In the meantime, old Goolab Singh was closeted in talk with Currie and Lawrence, and no doubt holding up his paws in horror as each successive clause of the treaty was put to him.[55] I'm sure he never let on that he knew it all before-hand, but had a jolly time shaking his grizzled beard and protesting that the durbar would never agree to such harsh terms. The negotiations went on all afternoon and evening – leastways, Goolab did, for Currie gave up after a few hours, and left him, and Lawrence lay down on his *charpoy* and pretended sleep. It was all gammon, for Goolab was bound to agree in the end, but he kept at it for appearance's sake, and didn't run out of wind till the small hours. I was on hand, indulging my 'satiable curiosity, when Lawrence saw him off, but didn't speak to him. He limped away from the tent, climbed stiffly aboard his pony, and trotted off towards the *sirdars'* camp, and that was the last I ever saw of him, a burly old buffer on horseback, looking like Ali Baba off to gather firewood in the moonlight.[56]

"All right and tight, and ready to be signed when we come to Lahore," says Lawrence. "Prosy old beggar. Well pleased, though, if I'm a judge. He should be – you don't have a kingdom dropped into your lap every day. He'll bring the little Maharaja to Hardinge in a day or two." He yawned and stretched, looking at the night sky. "But by then you'll be hasting home, you fortunate fellow. Stay a moment and we'll have a rum-shrub to set you on your way."

This was condescension, for he wasn't sociable as a rule. I took a turn along the tent-lines as I waited, admiring the moon shadows drifting across the empty *doab*, and looking along the grey, straight ribbon of the Lahore road which, God willing, I'd never take again. Not long ago it had shaken to the tramp of a hundred thousand men, and the rumble of great guns . . . *"Khalsa-ji!* To Delhi, to London!" . . . and the march had ended in the burning ruins of Ferozeshah and the waters under Sobraon. The whirlwind had come raging out of the Five Rivers country, and now it was gone without a whisper . . . and as Lawrence put it, I was hasting home.

Hardinge had his peace, and his hand on the reins of the Punjab. Goolab had his Kashmir, Britain her frontier beyond the Sutlej where the hills began, and the northern door of India was fast against the Moslem tide. Little Dalip would have his throne, and his delectable mother the trappings of power and luxurious ease with all the booze and bed-men she desired (with one grateful exception). Tej Singh and Lal Singh could enjoy the fruits of their treachery, and old Paddy had still "nivver bin bate". Alick Gardner would have his fine estate in the high hills beyond Jumoo, dreaming no doubt of far Wisconsin, and Broadfoot and Sale and Nicolson their lines in the *Gazette*. Maka Khan and Imam Shah had their graves by Sobraon *ghat* (although I didn't know that, then). Mangla was still the richest slave-girl in Lahore, and like to be richer . . . I could feel a twinge at the thought of her – and still do, whenever I see black gauze. And Jassa had got an open road out of town, which is usually the best his kind can ever hope for.

All in all . . . not a bad little war, would you say? Everyone had got what they wanted, more or less . . . perhaps, in their own mad way, even the Khalsa. Twenty thousand dead, Sikh, Indian, and British . . . a lot of good men, as Gardner said. But . . . peace for the rest, and plenty for the few. Which reminds me, I never did discover what happened to the Soochet legacy.

No one could foresee, then, that it would all be to do over, that in three short years the Sikhs would be in arms again,

335

Paddy's white coat would come out of the closet reeking of camphor, and the bayonets and *tulwars* would cross once more at Chillianwalla and Gujerat. And afterwards, the Union Flag would fly over the Punjab at last, Broadfoot could rest easy, and the twice-beaten but never-conquered Khalsa would be reborn in the regiments which stood fast in the Mutiny and have held the Raj's northern border all through my time. For the White Queen . . . and for their salt. The little boy who'd exulted over my pepperbox and ridden laughing to Jupindar rocks would live out a wastrel life in exile, and Mai Jeendan, the dancing queen and Mother of all Sikhs, her appetite undiminished and her beauty undimmed, would pass away, of all places, in England.*

But all that happened another day, when I was up the Mississippi with the bailiffs after me. My Punjab story ends here, and I can't croak, for like all the others I too had my heart's desire – a whole skin and a clear run home. I wouldn't have minded a share of the credit, but I didn't care that much. Most of my campaigns have ended with undeserved roses all the way to Buckingham Palace, so I can even smile at the irony that when, for once, I'd done good service (funking, squealing, and reluctant, I admit) and come close to lying in the ground for it, all I received was the cold shoulder, to be meekly endured . . . well, more or less.

Lawrence and I walked over to the big marquee which served as mess and dining-room; everyone seemed to be there, for Hardinge had waited up for news of the treaty talk with Goolab, and he and the Calcutta gang were enjoying a congratulatory prose before turning in. Lawrence gave me a quick glance as we entered, as much as to say would I rather we went to his quarters, but I steered ahead; Gough and Smith and the best of the Army were there, too, and I chaffed with Hodson and Edwardes while Lawrence called up the shrub. I downed a glass to settle myself, and then took an amble over to where Hardinge was sitting, with Currie and the other diplomatics.

*See Appendix II.

"Good evening, sir," says I, toady-like, "or good morning, rather. I'm off today, you know."

"Ah, yes," says he, stuffy offhand. "Indeed. Well, good-bye, Flashman, and a safe journey to you." He didn't offer his hand, but turned away to talk to Currie.

"Well, thank'ee, your excellency," says I. "That's handsome of you. May I offer my congratulations on a successful issue from our recent . . . ah, troubles, and so forth?"

He shot me a look, his brow darkening, suspecting insolence but not sure. "Thank you," snaps he, and showed me his shoulder.

"Treaty all settled, too, I believe," says I genially, but loud enough to cause heads to turn. Paddy had stopped talking to Gilbert and Mackeson, Havelock was frowning under his beetle-brows, and Nicholson and Hope Grant and a dozen others were watching me curiously. Hardinge himself came round impatiently, affronted at my familiarity, and Lawrence was at my elbow, twitching my sleeve to come away.

"Good *bandobast* all round," says I, "but one of the clauses will need a little arrangement, I fancy. Well, 'tain't a clause, exactly . . . more of an understanding, don't you know –"

"Are you intoxicated, sir? I advise you to go to your quarters directly!"

"Stone cold sober, excellency, I assure you. The Leith police dismisseth us. British constitution. No, you see, one of the treaty clauses – or rather the understanding I mentioned – can't take effect without my assistance. So before I take my leave –"

"Major Lawrence, be good enough to conduct this officer –"

"No, sir, hear me out, do! It's the great diamond, you see – the Koh-i-Noor, which the Sikhs are to hand over. Well, they can't do that if they haven't got it, can they? So perhaps you'd best give it 'em back first – then they can present it to you all official-like, with proper ceremony . . . Here, catch!"

[*The ninth packet of the Flashman Papers ends here, with typical abruptness. A few weeks later the Koh-i-*

337

Noor was again in the possession of the Lahore durbar, and was shown round at the treaty ceremony, but it was not finally surrendered until the annexation of the Punjab in 1849 after the Second Sikh War. The diamond was then presented to Queen Victoria by Hardinge's successor, Lord Dalhousie. Doubtless on Flashman's advice, she did not wear it in her crown at the 1887 Jubilee. See Appendix III.]

APPENDIX I:

The Sutlej Crisis

The origins of the First Sikh War are not to be summed up in a few paragraphs. Flashman has given a reasonably fair account of the developing crisis, from close range, and perhaps all that can usefully be done is to stand farther back and try to balance some of the factors which seem specially important.

It is easy to say that with a powerful, arrogant Khalsa bent on invasion, war was inevitable; no one in the Punjab could restrain them (or wanted to), so what could the British do but prepare to meet the storm? Something, according to Cunningham, a most respected historian, who believed that, while the Khalsa took the initiative, the British were "mainly to blame" for the war. His conclusion has been eagerly seized on in some quarters, but his argument boils down to the suggestion that Britain, "an intelligent power" faced with "a half barbarous military dominion," should have acted with more wisdom and foresight. It is rather lofty, even for 1849, and perhaps "equally" or "partially" would be fairer than "mainly". At the same time, George Bruce is certainly right when he accuses Hardinge of mental paralysis, and of making no rational move to prevent war; he points to the massive failure of communication. Still, considering the state of the Lahore durbar, and the motives at work among its principals, perhaps Britain should not be shouldered with too much of the responsibility.

Granted that Broadfoot was not the ideal man for the sensitive post of North-west Agent. Like many Britons, he obviously felt that the sooner Britain was running the Punjab, the better – but then, considering what had been happening north of the Sutlej for years, can he be blamed for that? There is a tendency to cast him as the villain of the piece, and certainly he was belligerently ready to make the worst of the situation, but so were many on the other side. Jeendan and her associates wanted the Khalsa destroyed, and the Khalsa was ready to rush to destruction – it would have taken an Agent of massive forbearance, and a Governor-General of genius, which Hardinge certainly was not, to settle matters peacefully. The impression one gets of the British peace lobby, as personified by Hardinge, is that they wished the Punjab would go away – or rather that it would settle down into the strong, disciplined stability it had known under Runjeet Singh. But Hardinge had no idea of how that was to be achieved.

On the Sikh side, one can understand their apprehension. Below the Sutlej, they were well aware, was a giant who had shown an alarming tendency to conquest – Sind was a recent, appalling example. The Sikh who did not take seriously the possibility that Britain was bent on swallowing the Punjab, would have been a fool; if he was objective, he would see the logic of it. That the Company had neither the power nor the inclination for farther expansion (for the moment, anyway) would not be evident in Lahore. And the Khalsa? Bellicose, and itching for a slap at the reigning champion as they were, they had some reason to suspect that if they didn't start the fight, Britain would.

These are very general observations, and to every one of them can be added the qualification "Yes, but . . ." One may scan Broadfoot's correspondence, or the provocations offered from the Sikh side, in detail, but weighing all such things as evenly as one can, it seems that the war happened because it was actively desired by the Khalsa, with Jeendan and others egging them on for deplorable reasons, while on the British side there were some, including Hardinge, who lacked foresight and flexibility, and others who were ready, with varying degrees of eagerness, to let it happen. It should be remembered, too, that the fighting men on either side underestimated each other; for all their fears, the British, with far greater experience, had a deep conviction of invincibility, and while it was rudely shaken in the field, it was justified in the end. The Khalsa seem to have had no

340

doubts at all, and even with the treachery of their leaders stacked against them, they kept their confidence until the last moments of Sobraon.

Even then, after the peace, with the Punjab a British protectorate, the spirit of the Khalsa remained: they would come again. The fuel was there, in the British presence at Lahore which began by protecting the position of the Punjab's nominal rulers and ended by assuming power; in the intrigues of Jeendan and Lal Singh who found the new order of things less rewarding than they had expected (both were eventually exiled); but most of all, perhaps, in the abiding belief of the Sikh soldiery that what they had nearly done once could be done at the second attempt. The result was the Second Sikh War of 1848–9, which ended in complete British victory – Gough, hesitant for once, fought a costly action at Chillianwalla, and was about to be replaced, but before his successor arrived he had won the decisive victory at Gujerat. The Punjab was annexed, Dalip Singh was deposed, and as Gardner had foretold, Britain inherited something infinitely more valuable than the Punjab or the Koh-i-Noor – those magnificent regiments whose valour and loyalty became a byword for a hundred years, from the Great Mutiny to Meiktila and the Rangoon road.

APPENDIX II:

Jeendan and Mangla

There is no way of verifying all Flashman's recollections of Maharani Jeendan (Jindan, Chunda) and her court; one can say only that they are entirely consistent with the accounts of reputable contemporary writers. "A strange blend of the prostitute, the tigress, and Machiavelli's Prince," Henry Lawrence called her, and he was right on all three counts. Strikingly beautiful, brave, wanton, and dissipated, a brilliant and unscrupulous politician and a quite shameless exhibitionist, she would have been a darling of the modern tabloid press, who could have invented nothing more sensational than the story of her rise to power, and her exploitation of it.

She was born apparently about 1818, the daughter of Runjeet Singh's kennel-keeper, and for the lurid details of her early life we are indebted to Carmichael Smyth; he had much of his information from Gardner, who knew her well and greatly admired her, and who has left an account of his own. Jeendan's father was a sort of unlicensed jester to Runjeet, and pestered the Maharaja with his daughter, then only a child, suggesting jokingly that she would make a suitable queen. Gardner's version has Runjeet taking her into his harem, "where the little beauty used to gambol and frolic and tease . . . and managed to captivate him in a way that smote the real wives with jealousy." She was sent to a guardian in Amritsar when she was thirteen, and went through a series of lovers before being brought back to Lahore "to enliven the night scenes of the palace." In 1835 she went through a form of marriage with Runjeet, but continued to take other lovers, with the Maharaja's knowledge and even (according to Smyth) his encouragement – "to give a detail . . . of scenes acted in the presence of the old Chief himself and at his instigation, would be an outrage on common decency." Not surprisingly, when Dalip was born in 1837, there were doubts about his paternity, but Runjeet was happy to acknowledge him.

After the old Maharaja's death, little is heard of Jeendan until Dalip's accession in 1843 (he was eight, not seven, when Flashman knew him). Thereafter, as Queen Mother and co-regent with her brother, she was occupied with intrigue, pacifying the Khalsa, and what Broadfoot, agog for scandal, called her misconduct and notorious immorality. The Agent said he felt more like a parish constable outside a brothel than a government representative, compared her to Messalina, and was in no doubt that drink and debauchery had turned her mind ("What do you think . . . of four young fellows changed as they cease to give satisfaction passing every night with the Rani?"). No doubt he was ready to retail all the salacious gossip he could get, with the implication that such a corrupt regime called out for British intervention, but even allowing for exaggeration there is no doubt that, as Khushwant Singh puts it, the durbar "abandoned itself to the delights of the flesh." And even before her brother's murder Jeendan and her confederates were conspiring to betray the country for their safety and profit; Jawaheer's death was what finally determined her to launch the Khalsa to destruction – "thus did the Rani . . . plan to avenge herself on the murderers."

How she did it Flashman recounts fairly and in greater detail than is to be found elsewhere. It was a delicate, dangerous operation which she managed with considerable skill, and unlike many later war criminals, she got away with it, for a time at least. After the war she continued as Regent until the end of 1846, when under a new treaty the British Resident at Lahore (Lawrence) was given full authority, and Jeendan was pensioned off. She did not take it meekly, and had to be removed from court – "dragged out by the hair," in her own words – and kept under guard. Suspected of conspiracy, she was deported from the Punjab – and suddenly, with discontent against the British rising, she was a national heroine, and the darling of the Khalsa again. But there was to be no happy return, and when the Second Sikh War ended and Dalip had gone into English exile, she followed him. She was only in her mid-forties when she died, in 1863, and her son took her ashes back to India.

Mangla (or Mungela) was perhaps a more important influence on the Lahore durbar than Flashman realised. The child of white-slavers, she was born about 1815, and sold by her parents when she was ten. She worked in a brothel at Kangra and was bought by (or ran away with) a *munshi*, as his concubine, before setting up as a prostitute on her own account in Lahore. She prospered, and became the mistress of one Gulloo Mooskee, a personal attendant of Runjeet Singh's. He passed her on to his nephew, a lover of Jeendan's. This was in 1835, and the two young women began a partnership in intrigue which was to last for many years. Mangla became a member of Runjeet's harem, and played a leading role in convincing him that he was the father of Dalip Singh. In the next ten years she made herself indispensable to Jeendan as adviser and go-between, became the lover of Jawaheer Singh, and after his death obtained control of the treasury, adding to her already considerable fortune. Less beautiful than her friend and mistress, Mangla had "a pair of fine hazel eyes of which she could make a most effective use, and an easy, winning carriage and address."

(See Carmichael Smyth, Gardner, Khushwant Singh, Bruce.)

344

APPENDIX III:

The Koh-i-Noor

The Koh-i-Noor has the longest and most exotic history of any existing jewel and, until the discovery of the Cullinan diamond in 1905, was the largest and most precious stone in the world. It is believed to have been mined from Golconda, Hyderabad, in or before the 12th century, and subsequently passed through the hands of the Sultan Ala-ed-din, the Mogul Emperors, the Persian conqueror Nadir Shah (who is said to have named it "Mountain of Light" in 1730), the rulers of the Punjab, and Queen Victoria, before coming to rest among the British Crown Jewels in the present century. Death, torture, imprisonment, ruin, and exile befell so many of its Eastern owners that its ill-luck (for male wearers) became proverbial; in its time it was hidden, unsuccessfully, in the turban of a defeated monarch, and in the mud wall of another's prison cell, and for a time it lay forgotten in the pocket, and later the stud-box, of John Lawrence, Henry's brother.

Despite its fame, the Koh-i-Noor has never been considered an especially fine stone. Originally it was almost 800 carats (the Cullinan was 3106 carats, about 22 oz) but was later recut more than once to increase its brilliance. In 1852 a Dutch cutter began work in the presence of Prince Albert and the Duke of Wellington, and recut it to 108 carats; the result was a stone about 1½ by 1¼ in, much improved but still considered too shallow.

Only female members of the British Royal Family have worn the Koh-i-Noor. Queen Victoria wore it as a brooch at the Crystal Palace Exhibition of 1851, and in Paris, and it has been in the crowns of Queen Alexandra, Queen Mary, and Queen Elizabeth (the Queen Mother), who wore it at the coronation of her husband, George VI. It is now in her platinum crown in the Tower.

345

The last male to wear the Koh-i-Noor, little Maharaja Dalip Singh, had his share of misfortune. Deposed and exiled, he saw the great diamond again when it was shown to him by Queen Victoria on his arrival in England, and expressed pleasure that she should wear it. He was sixteen at the time, and unusually handsome, and the Queen (no doubt unaware that one of his relatives was referring to her as "Mrs Fagin") was much taken with him; unfortunately his good looks were not Jeendan's only legacy, for he became a noted libertine, to the Queen's distress, and died, "poor, portly, and promiscuous," in 1893. He is buried in the grounds of his home, Elveden Hall, Suffolk.

(See *The Queen's Jewels,* by Leslie Field, 1987; Weintraub.)

Notes

1. "A very extraordinary and interesting sight," as the Queen recorded in her journal on May 11, 1887.   [p. 13]
2. Whether at Flashman's prompting or not, the Queen engaged two Indian attendants in the following month, one of whom was the pushing and acquisitive Abdul Karim, known as "Munshi" (teacher); he became almost as great a royal favourite as the celebrated ghillie, John Brown, had been, and was even more unpopular at Court. "Munshi" not only tutored the Queen in Hindustani, which she began to learn in August 1887, but was given access to her correspondence, blotted her signature, and even buttered her toast at tea-time. He claimed to be the son of an eminent physician (one rumour said a Surgeon-General of the Indian Army) but investigation showed that his father was a prison pharmacist at Agra. There was, as Flashman says, a very Indian flavour to the Queen's Jubilee celebrations of 1887. During her reign, the population of the rest of the Empire had increased from 4,000,000 to 16,000,000, while that of the sub-continent had risen from 96,000,000 to a staggering 254,000,000. The Indian festivities began on February 16, and ranged from illuminations and banquets to the opening of new libraries, schools, hospitals, and colleges all over the country; in Gwalior, all arrears of land-tax (£1,000,000 in all) were remitted. In Britain itself the celebrations did not reach their climax until June 21, when the Queen, at the head of a procession led by the Indian Princes, attended a service in Westminster Abbey; there were loyal demonstrations everywhere (except in Cork and Dublin, where there were riotous demonstrations), and much rejoicing in the United States, where the Mayor of New York presided over a great Festival of Thanksgiving. (See *The Life and Times of Queen Victoria*, vol. ii (1888), by Robert Wilson, which has a detailed account of the Jubilee; *Victoria*, by Stanley Weintraub (1987).)   [p. 15]
3. Flashman's memory is slightly at fault here. He was not, as he says, "retired on half-pay" at this time; in fact, he had been in Singapore inspecting Australian horses for the East India Company army, and it was during this visit that his wife, Elspeth, was kidnapped by Borneo pirates, and the adventure began which culminated in the Flashmans' rescue from Madagascar in June, 1845. In the circumstances, his failure to remember his exact military status is understandable. As to his allowing himself to be bullied into going to India, he may not have

347

been quite as reluctant as he suggests; the Governor of Mauritius certainly had no power to compel him, and it may well have been that the Punjab crisis (which had not yet assumed serious proportions) seemed a less daunting prospect than returning to face his ill-willers in England. [p. 21]

4. "Elphy Bey" was Major-General William Elphinstone, commander of the British force which was wiped out on the retreat from Kabul in 1842, in which Flashman ingloriously won his first laurels. A fine soldier who distinguished himself at Waterloo, Elphinstone was hopelessly inept in Afghanistan; crippled by gout, worn out, and according to one historian, prematurely senile, he was incapable of opposing either his political advisers or the Afghans, but in fairness he was less to blame than those who appointed him to a post for which he was unfitted. Flashman gives a perceptive but characteristically uncharitable sketch of him in the first volume of the Flashman Papers. (See also J. W. Fortescue's *History of the British Army*, vol. xii (1927); Subedar Sita Ram's *From Sepoy to Subedar* (1873), and Patrick Macrory's *Signal Catastrophe* (1966).) [p. 22]

5. "John Company" – the Honourable East India Company, described by Macaulay as "the strangest of all governments . . . for the strangest of all empires," was Britain's presence in India, with its own armed forces, civil service, and judiciary, until after the Indian Mutiny of 1857, when it was replaced by direct rule of the Crown. Flashman's definition of its boundaries in 1845 is roughly correct, and although at this period it controlled less than half of the sub-continent, his expression "lord of the land" is well chosen: the Company was easily the strongest force in Asia, and at its height had a revenue greater than Britain's and governed almost one-fifth of the world's population. (See *The East India Company*, by Brian Gardner (1971).)

Flashman, writing in the early years of the present century, occasionally uses the word *Sirkar* when referring to the British power; the word in this sense means "government," but it was probably not applied exclusively to British authority as early as 1845. [p. 23]

6. The origins and development of the Sutlej crisis are controversial, and it is difficult even today to give an account that will satisfy everyone; nevertheless, Flashman's summary seems an eminently fair one. His racy little narrative of the power struggle at Lahore after the death of Runjeet Singh is accurate so far as it goes; indeed, it spares readers some of the gorier details (no doubt only because Flashman was unaware of them). His view of the gathering storm, the precarious position of the Lahore durbar, the menace of the Khalsa, and the misgivings of the British authorities about the loyalty of their native troops, and their ability to deal with an invasion, are reflected in the journals and letters of his contemporaries. Other points and personalities he mentions will be dealt with more fully in subsequent Notes. (See Appendix I, and G. Carmichael Smyth, *History of the Reigning Family of Lahore* (1847); W. Broadfoot, *The Career of Major George Broadfoot* (1888); Charles, Viscount Hardinge,

348

Viscount Hardinge (1891); W. L. M'Gregor, *History of the Sikhs*, vol. ii (1846); Khushwant Singh, *History of the Sikhs*, vol. 2 (1966); J. D. Cunningham, *History of the Sikhs* (1849); George Bruce, *Six Battles for India* (1969); Fortescue; Vincent Smith, *Oxford History of India* (1920).)   [p. 26]

7. Sir Hugh Gough (1779–1869) was that not unusual combination: a stern and ruthless soldier, but a kindly and likeable man. He was also entirely "Irish" – reckless, good-humoured, careless of convention and authority, and possessed of great charm; as a general, he was unpredictable and unorthodox, preferring to engage his enemy hand-to-hand and trust to the superiority of the British bayonet and sabre rather than indulge in the sophistications of manoeuvre. He attracted numerous critics, who drew attention to his shortcomings as a military organiser and tactician but could not deny his saving grace as a commander – he kept on winning. By 1845 he had a combat record unequalled by any soldier living, Wellington included, having been commissioned at 13, fought against the Dutch in South Africa and Surinam, pursued brigands in Trinidad, served throughout the Peninsular War (in which he received various wounds and a knighthood), commanded a British expedition to China, stormed Canton, forced the surrender of Nanking, and beaten the Mahrattas in India. At the time of the Sutlej crisis he was 66 years old, but sprightly in body and spirit, handsome, erect, with long receding white hair and fine moustaches and side-whiskers. The best-known portrait shows him in his famous white "fighting coat", pointing with an outstretched arm: it is said to illustrate one of the many critical moments in his career when, at Sobraon, he shouted: "What? Withdraw? Indeed I will not! Tell Sir Robert Dick to move on, in the name of God!" (See R. S. Rait, *Life and Campaigns of Hugh, 1st Viscount Gough* (1903); Byron Farwell, *Eminent Victorian Soldiers* (1985) and other works cited in these Notes.)

Sir Robert ("Fighting Bob") Sale was another highly combative general, celebrated for leading from the front, and once, when his men were mutinous, inviting them to shoot him. He fought in Burma, and in the Afghan War, where he was second-in-command of the army, and earned distinction as the defender of Jallalabad (See also Note 9.)   [p. 26]

8. War with the Gurkhas in 1815 brought the British to Simla, and the first European house was built there in the 1820s by one Captain Kennedy, the local superintendent, whose hospitality may have laid the foundations of its popularity as a resort. Emily Eden was the sister of Lord Auckland, Governor-General 1835–41. (See the excellently-illustrated *Simla: a British Hill Station*, by Pat Barr and Ray Desmond (1978).)   [p. 27]

9. Adapting Raleigh's famous judgment on Henry VIII, one may say that "if all the patterns and pictures of the *mem-sahibs* of British India were lost to the world, they might be painted to the life from Lady Sale." Born Florentia Wynch, she was 21 when she married the

349

dashing young Captain Robert Sale, by whom she had twelve children, one of whom, as Mrs Alexandrina Sturt, shared with her mother the horrors of the march from Kabul. Lady Sale was then 54, but although she was twice wounded and had her clothing shot through by *jezzail* bullets, she worked tirelessly for the sick and wounded, and for the women and children who took part in that fearful journey over the snowbound Afghan passes. Throughout the march, and during the months which she suffered in Afghan captivity, she kept the diary which is the classic account of the Kabul retreat in which all but a handful died out of 14,000. It is one of the great military journals, and a remarkable personal memoir of an indomitable woman, who recorded battle, massacre, earthquake, hardship, escape, and everyday detail with a sharp and often caustic eye. Her reaction, when soldiers were reluctant to take up their muskets to form an advance guard was: "You had better give me one, and I will lead the party." Other typical observations are: "I had, fortunately, only *one* ball *in* my arm," and the brisk entry for July 24, when she was a prisoner: "At two p.m. Mrs Sturt presented me with a grand-daughter – another female captive." During the march her son-in-law, Captain Sturt, had died beside her in the snow. Her heroism on the march was rewarded by an annual pension of £500 from Queen Victoria, and when she died, in her sixty-sixth year, her tombstone was given the appropriate inscription: "Under this stone reposes all that could die of Lady Sale."

Flashman writes of her with considerable affection; no doubt her forthright and unconventional style appealed to him. Her habit of putting a foot on the table to ease her gout (not rheumatism) is also recorded by one of Simla's medical officers, Henry Oldfield. (See her *Journal of the Disasters in Affghanistan* (1843), ed. Patrick Macrory (1969); Barr and Desmond; *DNB*.)   [p. 28]

10. Eugene Sue's *The Wandering Jew* was published in 1845, and may conceivably have been available in Simla that September, but Flashman's memory has probably confused it with the author's equally popular *Mysteries of Paris* which appeared in 1842–3. Dumas's *The Three Musketeers* was first published in 1844; Flashman may well have borrowed it from one of the French officers who rescued him from Madagascar in June, 1845.   [p. 29]

11. George Broadfoot, a large, red-haired, heavily-bespectacled and pugnacious Orcadian, was one of the early paladins of the North-west Frontier. He had distinguished himself in the Afghan War as a ferocious fighter, engineer, and military organiser, and it was in large part due to him that Jallalabad was successfully defended after the disastrous Kabul retreat. He was awarded a C.B. and a special mention in despatches, and went on to serve in Burma before being appointed North-west Agent in 1845. He and Flashman served together on the Kabul road, and Broadfoot's brother William had been killed in the residency siege of November, 1841, in which Flashman took a reluctant part. The reference to Broadfoot's "Scotch burr" is interesting,

since although he was born in Kirkwall he had lived in London and India from the age of ten.

Captain (later Sir) Henry Havelock, known to Flashman as "the Gravedigger", no doubt because of his grim appearance and religious zeal, was to become famous in the Indian Mutiny, where he relieved and was besieged in Lucknow. Flashman knew him there, and also during the Afghan campaign.

The "cabbage-eating nobleman" with the lisp was certainly *Prince Waldemar of Prussia*, who visited Simla in 1845 and subsequently accompanied the British army in the field. He travelled under the name of Count Ravensburg, but his hosts seem to have addressed him by his real title.   [p. 30]

12. The rate of pay for an East India Company sepoy at this time was 7 rupees a month. The Khalsa was paying 14, and 45 rupees for cavalrymen.   [p. 31]

13. Sind, the territory lying between the Punjab and the sea, was annexed in 1843 by Lord Ellenborough, Sir Henry Hardinge's predecessor as Governor-General; this gave Britain control of the Indus, and an important buffer against possible Moslem invasion from the north-west (see map). It was a cynical piece of work, in which Ellenborough goaded the Sind Amirs by forcing an unacceptable treaty on them; when this provoked an attack by the Baluchi warriors, Sir Charles Napier promptly conquered the country, winning the battles of Miani and Hyderabad. Public reaction to the annexation was reflected by the House of Commons, which postponed for a year the normal vote of thanks to the successful general, and by *Punch*, which gleefully accepted a contribution from a Miss Catherine Winkworth, aged 17, suggesting that Napier's despatch to Ellenborough must have read: "Peccavi, I have Scinde" (sinned). (See under Foreign Affairs, *Punch,* May 18, 1844.) The annexation did not pass unnoticed in Lahore, and no doubt convinced many Sikhs that it would be their turn next.   [p. 31]

14. Young as he was, Flashman should have known that Afghanistan was not an exception, and that political officers, who were usually Army, normally fought along with the rest. It is true that no post in battle was more dangerous than general's aide, and he may well have been right to assume that it would be especially perilous when the general was Hugh Gough.

Alexander Burnes had been Flashman's political chief at Kabul, where *Sir William McNaghten* was head of the Political Mission; he saw both of them murdered by the Afghans. (See *Flashman.*) [p. 36]

15. The details which Flashman gives of the Soochet legacy case are substantially correct. Raja Soochet had sent his fortune, amounting to 14 lakhs of rupees (about £140,000), to Ferozepore shortly before his death in March 1844; it was buried there in three huge copper vessels and dug up by Captain Saunders Abbott. Dispute as to the ownership then arose, with the Lahore durbar claiming its return, and the British government holding that it was the property of Soochet's heirs. (See Broadfoot, pp. 229–32, 329.)   [p. 43]

16. The famous Shalamar or Shalimar gardens and pleasure grounds were laid out in the seventeenth century by Shah Jehan, creator of the Taj Mahal. Originally there were seven gardens, representing the seven divisions of Paradise, but now only three remain, covering about 80 acres. The Lahore Shalamar is not to be confused with the gardens of the same name in Kashmir. [p. 53]

17. When Flashman talks of the Khalsa he means simply the Punjabi army, but the term has much deeper significance. The Sikhs ("disciples"), founded by Nanak in the fifteenth century as a peaceful religious sect, were transformed two hundred years later by their tenth and last Guru, Gobind Singh, into a military power to resist Muslim persecution. Gobind founded the Khalsa, the Pure, a baptised brotherhood which has been likened to the Templars and the Praetorian Guard, and rapidly became the leading order of Sikhism and the embodiment of Sikh nationhood. Among Gobind's institutions were the abolition of caste, the adoption of the surnames Singh and Kaur (lion and lioness), and the famous five k's (bangle, shorts, comb, dagger, and uncut hair). It was a fighting order, soon numbering 80,000, and under Runjeet Singh it reached the height of its power. Contact with the British seems to have inspired him to build an army on European lines, with the assistance of French, Italian, British, American, German, and Russian instructors. The result was a superb force, quite as disciplined and formidable as Flashman describes it, well trained and equipped, and (a point not to be overlooked in examining the origins of the Sikh War) bent on conquest. Once Runjeet's iron hand was gone, the Khalsa was the real power in the Punjab, whose rulers could only hope to conciliate it. The *panches* which controlled it were elected by the men in accordance with village tradition.

   At Runjeet's death, the numerical strength of the Khalsa was estimated at 29,000, with 192 guns. By 1845 this had risen to 45,000 regular infantry, 4000 regular cavalry, and 22,000 irregular horse (*gorracharra*), with 276 guns. That this figure rose further during the year seems certain; Flashman and his contemporaries mention both 80,000 and 100,000, but how many of these would be effectives it is impossible to say. He also uses the terms Khalsa, Sikhs, and Punjabis loosely when referring to the Punjab army; it should be remarked that the Khalsa as he knew it was not composed exclusively of Sikhs. (For a breakdown of the Khalsa's strength in 1845, see Carmichael Smyth, *Reigning Family*, appendix; for notes on the foreign mercenaries employed by Runjeet Singh, see Gardner's *Memoirs*. Also works already cited in Note 6.) [p. 54]

18. The Akalis were the commandos of the Khalsa, a strict sect known variously as the Timeless Ones, the Children of God the Immortal, and the Crocodiles; a footnote to George Broadfoot's biography typically describes them as "devoted to misrule and plunder". [p. 56]

19. Since Flashman refers later in the manuscript to a Cooper pepperbox, it is probable that the pistol he drew on Dalip Singh was a Cooper

also. They were manufactured from about 1840 by J. R. Cooper, a British gunsmith, and fired six rounds. (See *The Revolver, 1818–65*, by A. W. F. Taylerson, R. A. N. Andrews, and J. Frith (1968).) [p. 63]

20. There is a mystery here: the "tough, shrewd-looking heavyweight" who called on Flashman with Bhai Ram Singh hardly sounds like the "good, kind, and polite old Fakir Azizudeen" who had been Runjeet Singh's foreign minister, and was still to the fore at this time, although he died of natural causes a few weeks later. Both the physical description and the style are inconsistent; indeed, the only way in which Bhai Ram's companion resembles Azizudeen is in his uncompromising honesty. Either Flashman's visitor was another courtier altogether, and he has simply got the name wrong, or his descriptive memory is playing him false for once. [p. 69]

21. Flashman has caught the spirit but slightly misquoted the letter of Robert Herrick's "Upon Julia's Clothes":

> Next, when I cast mine eyes and see
> That brave vibration each way free;
> O how that glittering taketh me!

He quotes Herrick again (p. 277), but it is doubtful if he had any special affection for the poet, or would even have recognised his name. The Flashman Papers abound in erratic literary allusions – the present volume contains echoes of Donne, Shakespeare, Macaulay, Coleridge, Voltaire, Dickens, Scott, Congreve, Byron, Pope, Lewis Carroll, Norse mythology, and obscure corners of the Old Testament – but it would be rash to conclude that Flashman had any close acquaintance with the authors; more probably the allusions were picked up second hand from conversations and casual reading, with two exceptions. He knew Macaulay personally, and had certainly read his *Lays*, and he seems to have had a genuine liking for Thomas Love Peacock, whose caustic humour and strictures on Whiggery, political economy, and academics probably appealed to him. For the rest, we may judge that Flashman's frequent references to *Punch*, Pierce Egan's *Tom and Jerry*, and sensational fiction like *Varney the Vampire*, more fairly reflect his literary taste; we know from an earlier volume that the word Trollope meant only one thing to him, and it was not the author. [p. 88]

22. Alexander Haughton Campbell Gardner, "Gurdana Khan" (1785–1877), is an extraordinary figure even for an age and region which saw such adventurers as "Sekundar" Burnes, Count Ignatieff, Yakub Beg, Pottinger, Connolly, Avitabile, and John Nicholson. He was born on the shore of Lake Superior, in what is now Wisconsin, the son of a Scottish surgeon and his Anglo-Spanish wife; Dr Gardner had served on the American side in the War of Independence, and knew both Washington and Lafayette. Young Alexander spent some years in Ireland, where he seems to have learned military gunnery, possibly in the British Army, went to Egypt, and travelled by caravan from

353

Jericho to Russia, where his brother was a government engineer. Thence he went to Central Asia, where for several years his life was one of continual warfare, raid, ambush, escape and exploration among the wild tribes; he fought as a mercenary, and for a time appears to have been little more than a wandering bandit – "Food we obtained by levying contributions from everyone we could master," he writes in his *Memoirs*, "but we did not slaughter except in self-defence." He seems to have had to defend himself with fatal frequency, both as soldier and freebooter, as well as escaping from slave-traders, being attacked by a wolf-pack, leading an expedition against Peshawar under the sacred banner of the Khalifa ("all burning with religious zeal and the desire to work their will in the rich city") and spending nine months in an underground dungeon. He rose to command a hill region with his own private fort under the rebel Habibullah Khan, who was opposing the Afghan monarch, Dost Mohammed, and it was on a foray to kidnap a princess from Dost Mohammed's harem (with her treasure) that he met his first wife – an incident described in his best laconic style:

> In the course of the running fight to our stronghold I was enabled to see the beautiful face of a young girl who accompanied the princess. I rode for a considerable time beside her, pretending that my respect for the elder lady made me choose that side of her camel . . . On the following morning Habibulla Khan richly rewarded his followers, but I refused my share of the gold and begged for this girl to be given to me in marriage . . .

She was, and for two years they lived happily, until Gardner returned from an action in which he had lost 51 men out of 90, to find that his fort had been attacked, and his wife had stabbed herself rather than be taken prisoner; their baby son had also been murdered. Although he continued in Afghanistan for some years, and was reconciled with Dost Mohammed, he eventually took service in the Punjab with Runjeet Singh, training the Khalsa in gunnery, fought in various actions, and was in Lahore in the six years of bloodshed and intrigue following Runjeet's death. He was guard commander to the infant Dalip Singh and Rani Jeendan at the time of his meeting with Flashman, but he was strongly pro-British (his friends included Henry Lawrence) and believed that India's future would be best served by ever closer communion with the United Kingdom. In his letter "from John Bull of India to John Bull of England," he envisaged the development of India as a great industrial nation, with Indians playing their part in the highest posts in civil and military life, and being represented in both Houses at Westminster. Physically, Gardner was as Flashman describes him – six feet tall, fierce, lean, and of iron constitution. As a result of one of his numerous wounds he was unable to swallow solid food, and could drink only with the help of an iron collar, but even in his eightieth year he was said to be as active as a man of fifty, lively and humorous, and speaking an English which was "quaint, graphic, and wonderfully good considering his fifty years among Asiatics." The photograph in his *Memoirs* shows a splendid old war-horse, beak-nosed and with bristling whiskers, seated sword in hand and clad in a full suit of tartan, even to his plumed turban. He bought the cloth from a Highland regiment in India, but which tartan it is cannot be told from the monochrome picture, and thereby hangs a small mystery.

Flashman says it was the tartan of the 79th (Cameron) Highlanders, and describes it as red or crimson – which is slightly puzzling, since the 79th's kilt is largely dark blue, being a hybrid of the MacDonald and a crimson element from the Lochiel Cameron. It may be that Flashman, who knew his military tartans, regarded it as "red" only by contrast with those of the four other Highland regiments, which are predominantly dark blue-green. The only other explanation is that he was entirely mistaken, and Gardner was wearing not the 79th tartan but the red and resplendent Lochiel Cameron – in which case the Colonel must have been a sight to behold.

(See *Memoirs of Alexander Gardner*, ed. Hugh W. Pearse (1890).)
[p. 98]

23. It is quite possible that Kipling based Daniel Dravot, the hero of *The Man Who Would Be King*, on Dr Harlan. He would surely have heard of the American, and there is a strong echo, in Dravot's fictional Kafiristan adventure (published in 1895), of Harlan's aspirations first to the throne of Afghanistan, and later successfully to the kingship of Ghor, as described in Gardner's *Memoirs* (published in 1890); whether Harlan's story was true is beside the point. Like many passages in his astonishing career, it lacks corroboration; on the other hand it was accepted, along with the rest, by such authorities as Major Pearse, who was Gardner's editor, and the celebrated Dr Wolff.

Josiah Harlan (1799–1871) was born in Newlin Township, Pennsylvania, the son of a merchant whose family came from County Durham. He studied medicine, sailed as a supercargo to China, and after being jilted by his American fiancée, returned to the East, serving as surgeon with the British Army in Burma. He then wandered to Afghanistan, where he embarked on that career as diplomat, spy, mercenary soldier, and double (sometimes treble) agent which so enraged Colonel Gardner. The details are confused, but it seems that Harlan, after trying to take Dost Mohammed's throne, and capturing a fortress, fell into the hands of Runjeet Singh. The Sikh maharaja, recognising a rascal of genius when he saw one, sent him as envoy to Dost Mohammed; Harlan, travelling disguised as a dervish, was also working to subvert Dost's throne on behalf of Shah Sujah, the exiled Afghan king; not content with this, he ingratiated himself with Dost and became his agent in the Punjab – in effect, serving three masters against each other. Although, as one contemporary remarks with masterly understatement, Harlan's life was now somewhat complicated, he satisfied at least two of his employers: Shah Sujah made him a Companion of the Imperial Stirrup, and

Runjeet gave him the government of three provinces which he administered until, it is said, the maharaja discovered that he was running a coining plant on the pretence of studying chemistry. Even then, Runjeet continued to use him as an agent, and it was Harlan who successfully suborned the Governor of Peshawar to betray the province to the Sikhs. He then took service with Dost Mohammed (whom he had just betrayed), and was sent with an expedition against the Prince of Kunduz; it was in this campaign that the patriotic doctor "surmounted the Indian Caucasus, and unfurled my country's banner to the breeze under a salute of 26 guns . . . the star-spangled banner waved gracefully among the icy peaks." What this accomplished is unclear, but soon afterwards Harlan managed to obtain the throne of Ghor from its hereditary prince. This was in 1838; a year later he was acting as Dost's negotiator with the British invaders at Kabul; Dost subsequently fled, and Harlan was last seen having breakfast with "Sekundar" Burnes, the British political agent.

Thus far Harlan's story rests largely on a biographical sketch by the missionary Dr Joseph Wolff; they met briefly during Harlan's governorship of Gujerat, but Wolff (who of course never had the advantage of reading the present packet of the Flashman Papers) confesses that he knows nothing of the American after 1839. In fact, Harlan returned to the U.S. in 1841, married in 1849, raised Harlan's Light Horse for the Union in the Civil War, was invalided out, and ended his days practising medicine in San Francisco; obviously he must have revisited the Punjab in the 1840s, when Flashman knew him. Of his appearance and character other contemporaries tell us little; Dr Wolff describes "a fine tall gentleman" given to whistling "Yankee Doodle," and found him affable and engaging. Gardner mentions meeting him at Gujerat in the 1830s, but speaks no ill of him at that time.

His biographer, *Dr Joseph Wolff*, D.D., LL.D (1795–1862), was a scholar, traveller, and linguist whose adventures were even more eccentric than Harlan's. Known as "the Christian Dervish", and "the Protestant Xavier," he was born in Germany, the son of a Jewish rabbi, and during his "extraordinary nomadic career" converted to Christianity, was expelled from Rome for questioning Papal infallibility, scoured the Middle and Far East in search of the Lost Tribes of Israel, preached Christianity in Jerusalem, was shipwrecked in Cephalonia, captured by Central Asian slave-traders (who priced him at only £2.50, much to his annoyance), and walked 600 miles through Afghanistan "in a state of nudity," according to the Dictionary of National Biography. He made a daring return to Afghanistan in search of the missing British agents Stoddart and Connolly, and narrowly escaped death at the hands of their executioner. At other times Dr Wolff preached to the U.S. Congress, was a deacon in New Jersey, an Anglican priest in Ireland, and finally became vicar of a parish in Somerset. As Flashman has remarked, there were some odd fellows about in the earlies. (See Gardner; *The Travels and*

Adventures of Dr Wolff (1860); Dictionary of American Biography; D.N.B.) [p. 102]
24. Flashman's is by far the fullest of the many descriptions of the murder of Jawaheer Singh on the 6th of Assin (September 21), 1845. He differs from other versions only in minor details: obviously he was unaware that two of the Wazir's attendants were also killed, and that for a time Dalip Singh was a prisoner of the troops. But his description of the Rani's reaction, while more graphic in detail, is borne out by other writers, who testify to her hysteria and threats of vengeance. (It has been suggested that she was a party to her brother's death, but this seems most improbable, although on one occasion she had contemplated his arrest.) That Jawaheer knew of his peril is certain; he had, as Flashman says, attempted to buy his security on the previous evening, but on the fatal day he seems to have believed that he would escape with his life. In fact, he was foredoomed, not only because of Peshora Singh's death, but (according to Cunningham) because the Khalsa believed he would "bring in the British." (See Cunningham, Carmichael Smyth, Khushwant Singh, Gardner, and others.)

At first glance, Flashman's comparison of Jeendan to Clytemnestra would seem to refer to the Hon. J. Collier's celebrated painting of Agamemnon's queen, but this cannot be the case. Flashman wrote the present memoir before 1902 – so much is clear from his noting on p. 20 that it was written *before* his Borneo adventure, which he set down in or soon after that year. Since Collier's painting was not exhibited until the Royal Academy of 1914, Flashman must be referring to some earlier, as yet unidentified, painting of Clytemnestra.
[p. 120]
25. Confirmation of the details of this deplorable episode is to be found in Carmichael Smyth. [p. 122]
26. Flashman's detailed eye-witness account of this durbar cannot be confirmed in all its particulars, but its substance is to be found in other authorities, including such contemporaries as Broadfoot and Carmichael Smyth. Jeendan plainly knew how to manage her troops, whether by overawing them with royal dignity, or captivating them by appearing unveiled and dressed as a dancing-girl. Carmichael Smyth describes her initial refusal to listen to their entreaties after Jawaheer's death, her dictation of terms at the Summum Boorj, her insistence on Lal Singh as Wazir rather than Goolab, and her dispersal of the Khalsa on the understanding that she would soon launch it across the Sutlej. Broadfoot's account, quoting Nicolson, speaks for itself:

> Court's brigade was in favour of making Raja Gulab Singh minister; the other brigades seemed disposed to support the Rani, who behaved at this crisis with great courage. Sometimes as many as two thousand of these reckless and insubordinate soldiers would attend the Darbar at one time. 'The Ranee, against the remonstrances of the chiefs, receives them unveiled, with which they are so charmed that even Court's brigade agreed

357

to confirm her in the government if she would move to their
camp and let them see her unveiled whenever they thought proper.' These strange disorderly ruffians, even when under the
direct influence of her great beauty and personal attractions,
reproved her for her unconcealed misconduct with Raja Lal
Singh, and recommended her, as she seemed to dislike solitude,
to marry; they told her she might select whom she pleased out of
three classes, namely, chiefs, akalis, or wise men. She adopted a
bold tone with the troops, and not only reproached them, but
abused them in the grossest language, whilst they listened with
pretended humility. [p. 137]

27. Flashman is consistently vague about dates, and does nothing to clear
up the longstanding mystery of when exactly the Sikhs invaded across
the Sutlej. December 11 is the favourite date, but estimates by both
British and Indian historians vary from the 8th to the 15th. Sir Henry
Hardinge formally declared war on the 13th, and as Khushwant
Singh points out, this almost certainly followed the crossing of the first
Sikh units; the whole operation must have taken some days. Nicolson,
at Ferozepore, says the invasion began on the 11th; Abbott, however,
is definite that Broadfoot received word of it on the morning of
the 10th. [p. 172]

28. If Flashman were not so positive, one might be tempted to regard this
reference to "Drink, puppy, drink" as another misplaced musical
memory; elsewhere in the Papers he occasionally errs in "remembering" tunes (e.g. "The Galloping Major", "Old Folks at Home")
before they have been written. At first sight, "Drink, puppy, drink"
and "The Tarpaulin Jacket", which he quotes on p. 233, look like
similar cases of faulty recollection; both were written by Flashman's
fellow-officer George Whyte-Melville (1821–78), none of whose writ-
ings appear to have been published before his first retirement from
the Army in 1849. So how can Flashman have known them in 1845,
and be so sure of "Drink, puppy, drink" that he refers to it no fewer
than three times in his memoirs of that year?

There is a plausible explanation. Although no reference to Whyte-
Melville has yet appeared in The Flashman Papers, it is quite possible
that they met as early as their first year in the Army, when Flashman
was stationed at Glasgow and Whyte-Melville was a subaltern in the
93rd (later Argyll and Sutherland) Highlanders. In such a small
society it would be strange if two young men with so much in common
did not come together: they were the sons of landed gentlemen who
had married into the aristocracy, were both outstanding horsemen,
keen sportsmen, and popular convivialists, and may even have discovered a bond of suffering from their schooldays (Flashman at
Arnold's Rugby, Whyte-Melville at Eton under the notorious Keate).
And when it is remembered that Whyte-Melville's considerable literary talent was of that precocious, carefree kind which may be called
amateur in the true sense (in later life he gave all his royalties to
establishing reading-rooms for stable boys, and similar charities), it

358

seems quite probable that such songs as "Drink, puppy, drink" were being sung in messes and clubs long before their genial author had even thought of looking for a publisher.

An interesting discovery, from Flashman's dungeon ordeal, is that in roasting Tom Brown so memorably before the schoolroom fire at Rugby (see *Tom Brown's Schooldays*), he was simply passing on a lesson learned from the deplorable Dawson, to whom he also refers in *Flashman in the Great Game*.   [p. 178]

29. How many Sikhs crossed the Sutlej it is impossible to say, far less how many were in the field on both sides of the river. Flashman's eventual figure of 50,000 may not be far out, but it can be regarded as a maximum; Cunningham's estimate is 35,000–40,000, plus another force of unspecified size advancing on Ludhiana. Against this Gough had about 30,000 at most, but only 22,000 of these were on or near the frontier, and they were widely dispersed. The Khalsa, according to Cunningham, had a superiority of almost two to one in artillery.
                                                                      [p. 199]

30. Lal Singh did send this note to Peter Nicolson, word for word except that where Flashman gives "Khalsa" Lal wrote "Sikh army." He also informed Nicolson of Jeendan's friendship, with the hope that the British would "cut up" the invaders. Nicolson's reply was that Lal should not attack Ferozepore, but delay and march to meet the British – thus confirming what Flashman had already told the Wazir. These proofs of treachery by the Khalsa's own leaders were not published immediately, as a result of Nicolson's death, but Dr M'Gregor, writing within a year of the event, obviously knew the truth: having pointed out that a leader like Runjeet Singh would have caused as much havoc as possible by burning and sacking on a wide front, he adds: "We are almost tempted to believe that the Sikh leaders wished to keep their troops together, in order that the British might have a full and fair opportunity of destroying them!" In 1849 Cunningham was stating bluntly that the object of the Sikh leaders was "to get their own troops dispersed by the [British]." He knew of Lal's correspondence with Nicolson, but not the details. In the light of what these two respected historians wrote at the time, it is remarkable to find William Broadfoot, forty years later, disputing the charge of treachery against Lal and Tej. Nor was he alone; at least one other British historian discounted it. If, in the light of the evidence available, any doubt remained, Flashman has surely dispelled it. (See Cunningham, Khushwant Singh, M'Gregor, Broadfoot, and Herbert Compton, "Mudki and Firozshah", in *Battles of the Nineteenth Century* (1896).)   [p. 209]

31. Flashman's memory is almost certainly at fault. Lieut.-Col. Huthwaite may well have been able to tell which guns were being used, but the British howitzers did not arrive at Mudki until the following day. (See Fortescue.)   [p. 218]

32. A fair judgment, and Flashman had cause to be pleased with his strategy, for although the British force was only slightly larger than

the Sikh, it had an advantage of four or five to one in infantry, which was decisive. "Unsatisfactory and unduly costly" is Fortescue's verdict, and he is rightly critical of Gough for attacking head-on an enemy stationed in jungle. But considering that the British force had covered sixty miles in two days before going into action, it could have been worse. [p. 219]

33. This remarkable observation, so characteristic of Broadfoot, was originally made by him after a skirmish in Afghanistan from which he emerged perspiring heavily and with a blood-stained sabre, having killed three men and been wounded himself. (See Broadfoot.) [p. 224]

34. This is the only existing account of the extraordinary exchange between Hardinge and Gough before Ferozeshah, although the gist of their conversation was communicated to intimates soon afterwards. Charles Hardinge, in his father's biography, was an eye-witness from a distance, but apparently out of earshot. Unique or not, the dispute arose from Hardinge's decision to place himself under the *military* command of Gough, while retaining overall authority as Governor-General. In theory it was a risky arrangement, but understandable; it would have been foolish not to use Hardinge's military experience. He had been twice wounded in the Peninsular War, losing a hand, served as deputy quartermaster-general of the Portuguese army, and been attached to Prussian headquarters in the Waterloo campaign, in which he was again badly wounded. He was active in politics, serving as Wellington's Secretary for War, before being sent to India as Governor-General. (See Hardinge, and Note 40.) [p. 231]

35. This military pleasantry was still going the rounds in the Second World War. Only the 9th Foot (Royal Norfolk) could take a lady into barracks, the "lady" being the figure of Britannia on their cap badge. [p. 233]

36. Historians disagree about the behaviour of the Sikh cavalry. One describes their advance as hesitant, Fortescue says they were stationary, but an eye-witness called it "the most splendid sight of the campaign, their horses caracoling and bounding, and the bright sunlight flashed from steel armour and spears . . . they came on at a rapid pace to within four hundred yards of the British line." Gough's biographer hardly mentions it. Obviously it depends on the point of view, but Flashman is probably right in thinking that White's intervention was decisive. [p. 242]

37. This incident is true. Gough "with my gallant aide" (C. R. Sackville West; he had obviously forgotten Flashman) deliberately rode ahead to draw the Khalsa's fire, and succeeded. He has been criticised for needlessly endangering himself; on the other hand, it has been argued that the effect on his troops' morale was considerable. Gough himself probably never gave a thought either to danger or morale; he seems to have acted emotionally, on the spur of the moment. [p. 244]

38. Flashman's account of the two days of Ferozeshah is so full and accurate that little need be added to it. For both sides, it was a battle

360

of missed opportunities: the British should have had it won on the first day, but they ran out of daylight (thanks to Hardinge, according to Gough supporters) and in the confusion of the night fighting they lost the advantage they had gained. The Sikhs should have overwhelmed Gough's force on the second afternoon, but Tej's treachery robbed them of victory; a point Flashman does not mention is that Tej seems to have waited until he was sure Lal Singh's defending force had been thoroughly routed (some had deserted in the night, including Lal himself, whose personal headquarters had been attacked and looted by the furious Akalis).

It has been suggested that on the first night of the battle the British commanders had decided to surrender: one Sikh historian says it quite flatly, quoting the diary of Robert Cust, a young political officer who was not even at Ferozeshah. In fact, it is plain from the papers of both Gough and Hardinge that surrender was never contemplated. Hardinge says clearly that he was approached by some officers "with timid counsels of retreat" which he flatly rejected. Gough too was approached by officers ("some of rank and in important situations") who urged retreat, two of them claiming that they spoke for Hardinge. Gough did not believe them, stated his intention of fighting on, and consulted Hardinge, who repudiated the officers' statement, and agreed with Gough "that retreat was not to be considered for a moment." Plainly there were some in favour of retreat (apart from the unfortunate Lumley); just as plainly, Gough and Hardinge gave them short shrift.

Flashman has dealt fully with Tej Singh, subscribing to the general view that it was his treachery alone that turned the tide. That Tej was a traitor seems obvious, but it is just possible that the reasons he gave for not attacking Gough's exhausted force had some justification; he probably did not know, for example, that the British artillery was out of ammunition, and hesitated to attack their fortified position. It is also possible that some of his commanders agreed with him, for what seemed to them sound military reasons. At any rate, it is difficult to believe that the Sikh army were turned back against the united will of their regimental commanders, simply by Tej's word alone.

Napoleon's sword, which had been presented to Hardinge by Wellington, was sent back from Ferozeshah, and Dr Hoffmeister, one of Prince Waldemar's suite, was killed on the first day. (See Rait, Hardinge, Fortescue, Compton, *Autobiography of Sir Harry Smith*, ed. by G. C. Moore Smith, vol. ii (1901); Cunningham, Broadfoot, M'Gregor, and *History of the Bengal European Regiment*, by P. R. Innes (1885).) [p. 248]

39. This was, in fact, the excuse given to Hardinge by Lumley for appearing in informal dress. (See Hardinge.) [p. 250]

40. Flashman's attitudes to his military superiors vary from affection (Colin Campbell, Gough, Scarlett) to poisonous hatred (Cardigan), with degrees of respect (Ulysses Grant, Hugh Rose, Hope Grant), contempt (Raglan, Elphinstone), and amused anxiety (Custer) in

361

between, and most of them are understandable. Why he so disliked Hardinge is less obvious, for the Governor-General seems to have been an amiable man enough, and not unpopular; his portrait gives no hint of the pomposity and coldness that Flashman found in him. It is quite likely that their instant mutual antipathy was our hero's fault; enjoying the euphoria of having done good service for once, he probably let his natural impudence show, and was less inclined than usual to toady (as witness his uncharacteristic outburst to Littler). The bouncy young political no doubt brought out the worst in Hardinge, and Flashman, a ready hater, has repaid with interest in a portrait which probably does the Governor-General less than justice, especially where Gough is concerned. Hardinge was surely sincere in writing to Peel that Gough was "not the officer who ought to be entrusted with the conduct of the war," and can hardly be blamed for seeking the appointment of a less mercurial C-in-C. Disaster had been avoided by a miracle, and the Governor-General might well be nervous of a general who was once heard to say, when his guns ran out of ammunition, "Thank God, then I'll be at them with the bayonet!" At the same time, Hardinge failed to recognise that many of Gough's difficulties had been created by Hardinge himself, and it may well be, as Gough's biographer suggests, that the Governor-General had a tendency "to attribute to himself all vigorous action" and to take all credit for success. Whether he was right to override Gough at Ferozeshah we cannot know; he may have averted a catastrophe or prevented Gough winning a victory at less cost in lives. It was a curious and difficult situation for both men, and it says much for them that they remained on good terms and co-operated efficiently throughout the campaign. Gough never knew of the letter to Peel, and while Flashman (smarting at the suggestion that politicals were of little use) would emphatically disagree, this was probably tact on Hardinge's part. (See Rait.) [p. 252]

41. Christmas trees were reintroduced into England by Prince Albert after his marriage to Queen Victoria in 1840. [p. 253]

42. Gough and Hardinge were repeating, at Sobraon, their quarrel at Ferozeshah: Gough wanted to make a frontal attack, but Hardinge insisted that he must wait for heavy artillery from Umballa (Gough had, in fact, asked for these guns weeks before, and been refused by Hardinge). The Governor-General proposed that an attack be made by crossing the river and falling on the Sikhs' reserve position, but this was vetoed by Gough. [p. 255]

43. This scene is described in detail by Gardner. He gives the strength of the Rani's guard as four battalions. [p. 273]

44. "The Rani used to wonder why a matrimonial alliance was not . . . formed for her with some officer . . . who would then manage State affairs with her. She used to send for portraits of all the officers, and in one especially she took great interest, and said that he must be a lord. This fortunate individual's name has not transpired, and, much to the Maharani's mortification, the affair went no further. She con-

362

sidered that such a marriage would have secured the future of herself and her son." (See Gardner, *Memoirs*, p. 273.) [p. 276]
45. Plans of the Khalsa fortifications certainly reached the British, but they apparently added little to their knowledge. [p. 287]
46. This certainly refers to the curious case of Captain Battreau who, as a young private soldier in the French Army, carried a Chassepot rifle, serial number 187017, in the Franco-German War of 1870; in 1891, during a skirmish in the Dahomey jungle, Battreau, now an officer in the Foreign Legion, disarmed an enemy and discovered that the weapon he had captured was the same Chassepot he had handed in at the end of the 1870 campaign. The story was verified by P. C. Wren, himself an ex-Legionnaire, who included it in his book, *Flawed Blades* (1932). Flashman died in 1915, and his own Legion service preceded Battreau's by many years, so it seems probable that he read the story in a French newspaper in 1891. [p. 294]
47. The private shelter which Tej Singh had built for himself at Sobraon was as Flashman describes it. It was constructed according to the specifications laid down by a Brahmin astrologer: the inner circumference was thirteen and a half times Tej's waist measurement, and the wall itself had a thickness of 333 long grains of rice laid end to end. Tej spent more time supervising its building than he did on his duties as commander-in-chief, retiring within it frequently to pray. Assistance in measurement was lent by a European engineer (probably Hurbon) with a foot-rule. (See Carmichael-Smyth.) [p. 309]
48. Colonel Hurbon, a Spaniard, was the only European officer who served against the British in the Sikh war. He is said to have designed the fortifications at Sobraon, which the historian Cunningham, who was also an engineer, dismissed as unscientific. Perhaps they were, since superior numbers did not suffice to hold them. Gardner describes him simply as "a fine soldier" and remarks on his bravery. [p. 310]
49. Almost certainly this was Sham Singh Attariwala, a veteran of more than forty years' service, who led the Khalsa's last stand at Sobraon. (See Khushwant Singh, M'Gregor.) [p. 315]
50. Sobraon was the decisive battle of the Sikh War – perhaps one of the decisive battles of history, for it secured Britain in India for another century, with all that that implied for the future of Asia. Gough described it as the Indian Waterloo (an appellation which Flashman attaches to Ferozeshah) and there are few controversies about it: for once, treachery played little part in what was a straight contest between the Khalsa and the Company. Luck was against the Sikhs insofar as the unusual rise of the Sutlej denied them any possibility of retreat and fighting another day; hemmed in, they could only fight it out, which they did with a discipline and courage which excited unanimous admiration from their enemy, Gough in particular. "Policy precluded me publicly recording my sentiments on the splendid gallantry . . . or the acts of heroism displayed . . . by the Sikh army," he wrote. "I could have wept to have witnessed the fearful

363

slaughter of so devoted a body of men." Thackwell, who led the British cavalry, said simply: "They never ran." Hardinge wrote: "Few escaped; none, it may be said, surrendered." There is a difference of opinion among historians on one point – the collapse of the bridge of boats. Many believe that it was destroyed deliberately by Tej Singh, who fled during the battle and supposedly had one of the middle barges removed; on the other hand Charles Hardinge actually saw it collapse, and his account, like Flashman's, suggests that it was unbroken until the weight of the fugitives caused it to carry away: "I saw the bridge at that moment overcrowded with guns, horses, and soldiers of all arms, swaying to and fro, till at last with a crash it disappeared . . . The river seemed alive with a struggling mass of men."

The Sikh losses were about 10,000, against 320 dead and more than 2000 wounded on the British side, but it has to be remembered that most of the Khalsa died in the river, and for a time the battle had been on a knife-edge. After the repulse of his first attack, Gough launched an assault on the right and centre, and his recorded comment, as he watched Gilbert's men storming the ramparts, was: "Good God, they'll be annihilated!" (See Hardinge, Innes, Rait, Khushwant Singh, and others.) [p. 319]

51. Later Field-Marshal Lord Napier of Magdala (1810–90), famous for perhaps the most successful campaign in British imperial history, the march on Magdala, Abyssinia (1868), in which Flashman is believed to have taken part. Napier was a brilliant soldier, organiser, and engineer, but his great devotion was to art, and he was still taking lessons at the age of 78. [p. 324]

52. Sir Henry Lawrence (1810–57) is best known for his defence of Lucknow in the Indian Mutiny, in which he was killed, but he previously had a distinguished career in the army and the political service, serving in Burma and in the Afghan and Sikh wars. Tall, gaunt, hot-tempered and impatient of contradiction, he also had a romantic side, and was the author of a love story, *Adventurer in the Punjaub*, which, according to Dr M'Gregor, was also a mine of information about the country and its politics. And he succeeded in seeing the Maharani Jeendan in Lahore after the war, when Gardner persuaded her to show her head and shoulders over a garden wall, "to the gratification of the officers [Lawrence and Robert Napier]." (See M'Gregor, Gardner, *D.N.B.*) [p. 328]

53. As in previous volumes of the Papers, one is reminded of how small was the group of officers who shaped the course of empire in Africa and the Far East; the same names cross Flashman's path again and again – Napier, Havelock, Broadfoot, Lawrence; Herbert Edwardes, who was Lawrence's assistant and won great fame in the Mutiny; wild John Nicholson, who was literally worshipped as a divinity by a frontier sect, the Nickleseynites; Hope Grant, the monosyllabic, 'cello-playing Scot who led the march to Peking and was rated by Flashman the most dangerous fighting man alive; "Rake" Hodson, the violent

ruffian who commanded the famous Guides and founded Hodson's Horse; and others whom he knew elsewhere, but not in the Punjab – Frederick ("Bobs") Roberts; Garnet Wolseley, the original "model of a modern major-general"; "Chinese" Gordon of Khartoum, and one-armed Sam Browne whose belt has made him the most famous of them all. A distinguished company who tended to go one of two ways: knighthood (or peerage) and general rank, or a grave in the outposts.
[p. 332]

54. Dr W. L. M'Gregor, who served throughout the Sikh War, is one of its major historians, and an enthusiast on military medicine. Anyone wishing to study the war is recommended to him, and to Captain J. D. Cunningham, who also served in the campaign, and was in political intelligence. They do not always agree with each other, but their knowledge of the Punjab and its personalities makes them invaluable sources. [p. 332]

55. The terms of the first Treaty of Lahore, March 9, 1846, are to be found in Cunningham, M'Gregor, and Hardinge. They are as Goolab Singh predicted, with additional clauses giving Britain passage for troops through the Punjab, a pledge not to interfere in Punjabi internal affairs, and a prohibition on the enlistment of European or American mercenaries in the Punjab without British consent. Supplementary articles provided for the stationing of a British force at Lahore for one year – this was at the request of the Lahore durbar, who rightly conceived themselves to be in need of protection.
[p. 334]

56. Goolab Singh, the "Golden Hen" and stormy petrel of Kashmir, was every bit as deplorable, and quite as personally engaging, as Flashman portrays him. He was born about 1788, and to describe his career of intrigue, murder, warfare, and knavery would take a long chapter; it suffices to say that as a leading light of the Dogra Hindus who opposed the Sikhs in the power struggle following Runjeet Singh's death, he not only survived but ended with a kingdom of his own, Kashmir. He did it by shameless duplicity, conspiring with the British while pretending sympathy for the Punjab cause, and no one was ever more expert at playing both ends against the middle. His character was admirably summed up by his friend and agent, Colonel Gardner, who described it as repulsive, ambitious, avaricious, and capable of the most inhuman systematic cruelty simply to invest his name with terror; at the same time he was charming, genial, opium-addicted, given to telling long stories, and hail-fellow with the poorest of his subjects. A fine soldier and sturdy fighter, he was also a wise and careful ruler, and perhaps the most revealing thing about him is that while Gardner published his character study in Goolab's lifetime, they remained the best of friends. (See Gardner, Carmichael Smyth, and others.) [p. 334]

365

A NOTE ON THE TYPE

The text of this book was set in a type face called
Times Roman, designed by Stanley Morison (1889–1967)
for *The Times* (London) and first introduced by that
newspaper in 1932.
Among typographers and designers of the twentieth
century, Stanley Morison was a strong forming influence—
as a typographical advisor to The Monotype Corporation,
as a director of two distinguished English publishing
houses, and as a writer of sensibility, erudition, and
keen practical sense.

Composed in Great Britain
Printed and bound by The Haddon Craftsmen, Inc.,
Scranton, Pennsylvania

Title page and binding design by
George J. McKeon